"I AM THE EXORI— AND THE EXORI CAN DO THINGS NO MAN CAN DO."

Before Ascendant Su's apprehensive stare, Colin plunged the blade deeply into his own palm, dragging the blade viciously from one side to the other, laying the flesh open to the bone. Blood poured, a thick torrent, down his wrist and arm.

"Could I have cured you, Ascendant? Watch."

The Presence rose full in him, and he felt a distant warmth in his hand. Slowly, impossibly, the edges of that horrible wound began to close, knitting together once again. Colin lifted his hand high and closed it into a fist. He felt himself laughing in triumph, and he was frightened.

"You see!" Colin heard himself shout. "Can you still deny me?"

"THE BONES OF GOD is easily the best and most important novel of Stephen Leigh's burgeoning career."

Mike Resnick, author of
Tales of the Velvet Comet

THE
BONES
OF GOD

Stephen Leigh

AVON
PUBLISHERS OF BARD, CAMELOT, DISCUS AND FLARE BOOKS

AVON BOOKS
A division of
The Hearst Corporation
1790 Broadway
New York, New York 10019

Copyright © 1986 by Stephen Leigh
Published by arrangement with the author
Library of Congress Catalog Card Number: 86-90769
ISBN: 0-380-89961-2

First Avon Printing: November 1986

AVON TRADEMARK REG. U.S. PAT. OFF. AND IN OTHER COUNTRIES, MARCA REGISTRADA, HECHO EN U.S.A.

Printed in the U.S.A.

K–R   10 9 8 7 6 5 4 3 2 1

This one is for Denise—

she made certain that all the characters
spoke with their own true voices

THE YEARS BEFORE

2058—Simon ben Zakkai is born in Syria.

2091—Third All-Faith Conference is held in Rome under the guidance of ben Zakkai. He once again espouses his proposal to bond together the great monotheistic religions of Christianity, Judaism, and Islam.

2092—Simon ben Zakkai assassinated by Sino-American agents.

2098—Fourth All-Faith Conference is held and the Church of Zakkai is formally organized.

2192—After nearly a century of unprecedented growth, the Zakkaist church begins "God's War" against most secular governments.

2310—For all intents and purposes the Zakkaist church has established the first global government, a theocracy. The years from, roughly, 2315 to 2476 are often referred to as the Pax Zakkai.

2312—First contact with the Stekoni.

2345—With the use of Stekoni farship technology, the first interstellar human colony, Zion, is founded.

2353—The first bans on the use of Stekoni technology are announced by the Ascendants. Monitoring of the sanity of Veil pilots is begun to stifle the rumors concerning the Stekoni Voice, which the aliens claim is a god.

2372—Birth of the Obdurate movement. Its goal: to splinter the Church into its former componets.

2378—The first human MulSendero cleric is ordained by the Stekoni clergy. She is quickly jailed by the Ascendants.

2380—The founding of Nexus, a mining colony outside the direct control of the Holdings, as the Zakkaist empire is now being called.

2456—The birth of James Badgett (also known as Colin Fairwood). The birth of Hallan Gelt.

2459—The birth of Huan Su.

2472—The Galicht guild is established in the Fringes in opposition to the Zakkaist-controlled freight lines.

2476—With a bloody riot in London and Berlin, the Obdurate Rebellion begins.

2478—The purge of New York. Fairwood and Gelt flee the insurrection in farships. Colin's ship is damaged. His flight will take the subjective time of five years for him, while sixty-three years will elapse for the inhabitants of the Holdings.

2480—End of the Obdurate Rebellion with the massacre of its leaders in Santa Fe.

2493—Birth of Joseph Culper.

2509—Hallan Gelt returns from a Veildream with the Geltian Scriptures. He begins preaching of MolitorAb and the imminent arrival of the Sartius Exori, the "Black Beginning."

2513—Hallan Gelt dies at the hands of the Zakkaist church in New York.

2541—Colin's farship is rescued by a Galicht craft in the Fringes. Later that year, he joins the Galicht himself, as Gelt had done.

2557—Colin loses a smuggling cache of flamestones and meets FirstBred Pale.

Lo, I will send you Elijah the Prophet,
Before the day of the Lord comes, the great and terrible day.
OLD TESTAMENT, Malachi 3:23

Before the method of utilizing the so-called Veils was invented by the Stekoni race, their religion was like that of many other cultures: nature-based, full of gods with names such as Storm-Bringer and BrightFang. Yet that religion, it is important to note, was still vital and revered. Within a decade of the discovery of the Veils, that religion fell. Completely. Utterly. The faith of MolitorAb swept through the Stekoni culture, demolishing all the old ways. The new god's prophets were the Mad Ones, those who had begun to believe in the reality of the hallucinations induced by Veil travel. The MulSendero religion, that of the Many Paths, spread like a plague. Within twenty years, all of the Stekoni were devout MulSenderians bowing to MolitorAb.

The old gods had only scorn and ridicule as the legacy of the centuries of their worship by the Stekoni. Think of that: centuries gone in but a handful of years.

In many ways, that quick and catholic embrace of a new faith illustrates best the vast differences between Stekoni and Human.

—From a lecture by Huan Su, Ascendant
of the Church of Zakkai, Tokyo, Old
Earth, March 2, 2548

THE BONES OF GOD

MAY 15, 2478

Hell screamed behind them, a nightmare of fire and death.

Panting, terrified, James Badgett and Hallan Gelt found themselves near the moon-shadowed grouping of Zakkaist farships in Central Park. Behind them, all of Manhattan near the Cathedral of Prophet Simon seemed to be burning. The night wind carried the smell of blood and terror and the faint, thin shouting of the rioters. They had been lucky, these two—the initial assault from the cathedral had beaten past them, and they had been able to flee down a side street and away. Breathing so harshly that they were certain some guardsman would hear them, they crouched near the front landing leg of one of the craft.

The attention of those around the farships was on the conflagration and the distant sounds of the continuing fight. They had not noticed the two young men.

James couldn't slow his breathing. There was a shrieking in him that pounded at his chest, aching to tear from his throat. His face and neck were being consumed by a scarlet agony. He dug his nails into the palms of his hands to stop himself from gouging at his cheeks with desperate fingers. Finally, unable to stand the pain, he reached out to touch his cheek. Hallan's hand caught his wrist.

"Don't, Jim," Hallan said. His eyes were bright and wide in the moonlight, touched with red from the fires. "Don't touch it."

Jim forced down the scream. His voice shook with the effort of whispering. "What do I look like, Hal? You have to tell me. Please."

Watching Hal's face, Jim could see him hesitate between lie and truth. They had been friends since childhood. Together, they'd been caught up in the fervor of the Obdurate movement within the church. Together, they'd been appalled to see demonstrations in London and Berlin turn into running battles between Obdurates and police. Together, they'd been in the forefront of the Concerned Citizen's March on the cathedral.

1

Together, still obsessed by the idealistic dreams of young adult-hood, they'd felt the horror of the church's anger, neither entirely understanding the harshness of the church's reactions.

It had all gone wrong so quickly. Inside Jim the core of discontent hardened into hatred. "Tell me, Hal," he insisted. He clutched at the silver sphere cut with deep jagged lines that hung from a chain around his neck—the symbol of the Obdurates. Touching it gave him no solace.

Hal glanced at Jim, then quickly looked away. There was a catch in his voice, and Jim knew his friend well enough to realize that Hallan was crying. "It isn't good, Jim. Ahh, man, I can't believe ... We should have known, Jim. London and Berlin should have told us. Maybe you should stay here—they'll get you a doctor. They'll fix you up."

"The fucking Zakkaists? Hal, you saw what happened. They aren't looking for more arrests; they've decided they want bodies." Jim swallowed hard. He looked up at the gleaming curve of the farship. "Look, no one's going to be on these ships but the pilots—everyone else is too busy gawking. You take one, I'll take another. We'll Veilshift a few times, then bring them back down somewhere after things have quieted a little. The desert, maybe, or even one of the Fringe worlds..."

Hal was shaking his head. "You can't do it. Jim, you're in shock. A few hours and the pain's really going to hit. You can't see your face, Jim. The burns are *bad*. You need to get treatment."

"I can do it. I swear to God. Turn yourself in if you want to. I'm not going to let the bastards make a martyr of *me.*"

In the end, Hal agreed. Jim made as if to move away, but Hal stopped him, hand on Jim's arm. His pale eyes stared. "Jim," he said. "I pray that God goes with you. See you again soon, huh?" He made an attempt at a smile.

Jim could feel dead skin pulling as he tried to smile in return. "Yeah," he said. "I'll be praying for you too. We need all the help we can get."

Jim watched as Hal ran across to the nearest farship and slipped through the open hatch. When he was gone from view, Jim rose and swung himself into the ship above. They were both armed—the march organizers had suggested that such might be needed, though both of them had scoffed. Jim had taken an old gun he'd once seen hidden in his father's bureau; he didn't know if it was loaded or if it would fire. He held its strange weight in his hand as he stumbled down the corridor to the pilot's deck.

Afterward, the events that followed were never quite clear, lost as they were in a fog of pain. He found the pilot and somehow bluffed the woman into taking the farship up. Jim never found out whether it was naval defense action or a ploy on the pilot's part that caused the farship to tumble. He was suddenly aware of the gun in his hand and of his finger moving on the trigger as he shouted in alarm. He heard the pilot groan, watched her sag in her seat, and suddenly smoke was filling the cabin.

The automatics quickly doused the fire, and there was the glorious realization that he was free. It was true that the pilot was dead and that he had no idea how to control a farship, but (with the optimism of youth) he thought he had all the time in the world to figure it out.

He would veilshift, cross the quanta to some other place, and escape the pursuit that might come. Then he would return and continue the fight that the Church had begun.

It took a month. A month spent in a haze of painkillers and antibiotics he'd found in the medical locker, a month with a rising stench in the ship that even stowing the pilot's body in the back cargo bay would not eliminate. On system drive, the craft continued to accelerate away from Old Earth on a pitifully slow course to nowhere. Still, using the Veils, he could be in another star system within days. He made the calculations, checked them far too often through the on-board computer, logged in the coordinates. He activated the vanes and waited for them to pulse and tear the farship from reality.

Nothing happened.

Eventually the ship would reach near light speed. Even so, it was a damned long way to the stars.

DENIAL

2557

CHAPTER ONE

When they hear our revelations, the unbelievers almost devour you with their eyes. "He is surely possessed," they say.
                                    KORAN, The Pen 68:51

The difficulty with our messianic tradition is that there's, oh, a dozen people a year who claim to fulfill the loose prophetic qualifications. The proper response to such claimants is simply to wait. They'll make fools of themselves soon enough.

The true Sartius Exori—our Black Beginning—will announce himself all too clearly.

Unfortunately.

—Attributed to Jasper Keller,
Primus of the MulSendero

July 6, Old Earth calendar. Celebrated as the day of Hallan Gelt's death. On most of the Fringe worlds, alive with the religious fervor Gelt had inspired, that meant a day of impassioned faith. Nexus was no different from any other world—there, too, crowds formed around street-corner speakers, and the MulSendero churches were full. Even in the taverns, the mood of the day influenced conversations.

"What do you think, Fairwood? My guess is that Gelt made up the entire Scripture from nothing, pulled it out of a veildream."

"I *knew* him, once."

The words silenced Mari. She stared at Colin Fairwood. He was not pleasant to look upon. Some accident had torn and shredded his face; for whatever reasons, Colin had never bothered to have his features restored with cosmetic surgery. The reconstruction of his head showed far too plainly—a knitting of plastalloy muscles and tendons over a skeletal framework that shone like porcelain, a lacework of veins and arteries pulsing over it. Colin's face was a mask of horror: part flesh, the rest was open under a layer of transparent skinbase.

A human patchwork. Colin might once have been handsome— no longer.

Mari had done most of the talking tonight, which was usual. Colin sat quietly at the inn table, half listening. They were both Galicht free-traders; Colin had run across Mari a dozen times over the years. He sometimes thought that he liked her. Once she'd even let him take her to bed—in darkness, in thrashing silence. The sex hadn't been good, but at least there had been a sort of affection between them. In return, he'd told her some of his past, of how he'd come to be far older than his appearance.

She might even have believed him.

"I knew him," Colin repeated in a more contemplative tone. Muscles bunched and relaxed around his jaw. He leaned his head back against the tavern wall and gazed at the smoky reaches of the ceiling. A burst of high-pitched laughter caused him to roll his head to one side and look at the isolette near the door—a few Stekoni had gathered there, the aliens who had given mankind the farships. "Hallan Gelt hated the Zakkaist church," he continued. "Like most Galicht, he'd've been happy to run arms for any secessionist movement within the Holdings—just to hurt the Church."

"Then you agree with me—Gelt invented his Divine Visitations." Mari's sleeves were wet with spilled beer and there was a drunken heartiness to her voice.

"Didn't say that, did I?" Eyes the color and hardness of flint, Colin stared at the isolette and the stick-thin aliens. "He was a religious man, an idealist. I don't know what Hallan saw in the Veils, but I think he probably believed it—he wouldn't have had the imagination to lie about it."

"You think he actually saw MolitorAb, talked with the Stekoni god? Hell, come *on,* Fairwood..."

Plastalloy ligaments rippled as Colin scowled. "Mari, be very careful how you say things. I respond badly to being called a liar." There was a brooding violence in his words.

Mari grimaced, looking not at Colin but at her beer. "Hey, if you're a MulSendero, I'm sorry I don't believe in your god, not that I've ever seen you go to church. Fairwood, I thought we were going to have a quiet night out, then maybe..."

"You can disagree all you want, Mari. Just remember that I was old before you ever joined Galicht-guild. Gelt and I were the same age."

"And Gelt died nearly fifty years ago—he'd be at least a hundred if he were still alive. You're awfully damned young for a centurian, Fairwood," she said in a scoffing tone. "Yes, I know that story you told me, but it can be a little hard to believe. You can understand that, can't you?" Her voice was sullen.

Colin stared at her, his jaw clenched. Mari met his look, but he noticed that she didn't let her gaze drift from his eyes down to the disfigured cheeks and neck. He found himself simultaneously acknowledging her chastisement of him and being coldly amused by her avoidance of his deformities. He leaned back in his chair once more. "It doesn't matter," he said to the ceiling, looking up at the pitted local metal. "Gelt made himself into a damn prophet and turned a lot of people into fanatics. It's a poor world that doesn't have its own messiah now. Eventually it will all pass."

"Doesn't look like it's going away to me," Mari said. The sullen petulance was still in her voice. "Lots of people listen to the MulSendero, especially among the Galicht. As you said, each world's got its savior: Nexus has Naley, Far Shore has Mitchell, and so on."

Colin didn't answer. He closed his eyes. After a moment, Mari sighed and started talking about what she'd seen in a veildream on her last trip to Old Earth.

Colin was lost in his own thoughts. He felt uneasy; he wished he were back on the *Anger*, his farship, and away from Nexus. He knew he could tell Mari nothing, none of the uncertainties that haunted him. If he spoke to her of what *he'd* seen in his passages between the Veils, she'd think he'd gone mad. The thought decided him. He would go to the Galicht-house tonight and take whatever cargo was offered—anything that would get him off this rock and away. It had not been a good few months.

His last shipment had been bioelectronics intended for Bifrost. Colin had been on Kethrid Four, and the Galicht Master there had called him into his office—he had a client who wished to move a small cache of flamestones. Highly profitable, but highly illegal. The customer was willing to pay for alterations to the *Anger* to facilitate the transfer. Colin had agreed: it was a rare Galicht who never ran contraband.

The departure from Kethrid Four had not been auspicious. The Veils, the energy lines on which the farships fed like sailing ships on the wind, had shifted. There was no direct or easy route to Bifrost open, and the best path Colin could devise took him near Old Earth. He'd taken that way despite intuitive fear, and the dreams he'd had during the Veil passage were again full of the same ghosts—Hallan Gelt calling Colin's name, his *true* name, and the thunderous Voice that the Stekoni named MolitorAb.

He'd come down-quantum to find a Holdings cruiser nearby. There was no time to shift into the Veils again. He had been forced to match vectors with the cruiser and let a party board.

The group had numbered the captain, two marines, and a priest. The priest seemed piously gleeful, the officer merely bored. He was middle-aged, this captain, his hair beginning to turn gray and recede, too old for his rank. An incompetent, Colin decided, stuck out on routine patrols until all ambition had been burnt out of him. The priest, however, was young, and her drive pulsed from every part of her, from the spotless robe to the polish of the Zakkaist triangle on the heavy chain around her neck. She viewed her role as one step in an upward climb; the captain had found a comfortable niche.

Routine. He won't want trouble. Don't give him any and he'll leave you alone. Colin forced the remnants of the Veildream away and smiled for them.

"You're one ugly son of a bitch." That was the first thing the captain said. He motioned to the marines to begin searching the ship. Colin checked his temper, pretending not to care that the *Anger* was being probed. "Is that some new Galicht fashion?"

"An accident," Colin said.

"Why didn't you let them finish the job?"

"I ran out of money." It was easier to lie. "And if I don't get that crap in the cargo pod to Bifrost this month, I won't be able to afford the organics I need to keep this heap running."

The captain touched an ear and cocked his head in an attitude of nonchalance. "You're Colin Fairwood, Galicht Senior, owner of the *Anger?*"

Colin nodded.

"You've two unpaid violations on my com, Fairwood."

"Your information's outdated, then. I paid the fines on Kethrid Four." *He won't want trouble.* "You know how slow communications can be, and the Veils are lousy coming in this way. Call your base, Captain. Old Earth should have the records by now." Colin's tone was a careful blend of assertion and subservience. The captain locked gazes with him for an instant, then glanced around the small cabin: a control module with the Veil attenuators, a small and battered holocube viewer, a bed-netting—except when he had visitors,

Colin lived in freefall. It was an austere, cluttered, and disordered environment.

"You're doing a good job pretending that you don't care about being searched, Galicht."

"There's nothing to find, Captain."

The man shrugged. "Fairwood, I almost tend to believe you." *Yes, he doesn't want trouble.* "Do you swear that those fines were paid?"

They hadn't been. He truly didn't have the money. "By the one true God."

"Then you're logged as saying so. I hope for your sake that it's the truth, or the next fleet officer you run into won't be as lenient with you." He waved to the marines, who came back from their desultory examination. They grinned. The captain seemed to sigh, thinking of the food or rest or entertainment awaiting him on the cruiser. He looked around the cabin once more, shaking his head. "You Galicht are crazy," he said. "You could make good money and have a career with the navy or the shipping companies anywhere in the Holdings. Yet you stick with your dirty, patched-up, wretched little ships. Subsistence living. I don't understand you." He turned to go, gesturing to the others.

But the priest hadn't moved. "You swore by the one true God," she said. The captain glanced at her and the sourness in his eyes told Colin that the two had argued before. "Do you mean 'God' or 'MolitorAb,' Galicht?"

"One's as good as the other."

"Not by the Torah, the Koran, or the Bible. Not by the decrees of the Ascendants."

"Mother Crowell," the captain said, "we hardly need a theological discussion now. The Galicht Fairwood has been cleared to proceed."

"Captain Pierson," she answered, "the Church has her own duties. One of those is to see that God is properly addressed, not fouled by the alien term so fashionable now." She turned back to Colin. She was smiling, a predatory look on her fair face. She wanted disagreement, anticipated it. Colin knew that she was one of those who would have quite happily carried out her proper duty and killed Hallan Gelt however the Ascendants ordered it done. She gave Colin a quick view of white and even teeth. "Galicht Fairwood?"

"Mother, what's to stop me from simply saying 'I call Him God' and avoiding this discussion entirely?"

She smiled again, and Colin saw pleasure in her dark eyes. *She loves verbal sparring; she'll be hard to shunt aside.*

"A man who wanted to avoid confrontations and questions would have had his face completely restored, no matter what the cost," she said. Unlike many, she did not turn away from him; in fact, she seemed to enjoy her contemplation of his face. She waited patiently for his reply, uncaring of the impatient glances Captain Pierson threw at her.

Colin knew he would have to tread carefully. A word to the proper ears from an Ascendant and cargoes could become scarce, even out in the Fringes. The Church must be dealt with politely, no matter how it grated. "A man who avoided theology might also be loath to admit that he wonders about the divine origin of the three holy books and Simon ben Zakkai's fusing of the monotheistic religions."

"That is something the old Obdurates might have said."

Careful. "Let me finish, Mother. That same man would also be skeptical of the claims for Gelt's veildreams."

She laughed and clapped her thin hands. "An agnostic in this day and age? You *do* surprise me, Galicht Fairwood. I thought it was impossible to ride the Veils and remain so unconvinced."

"Not all pilots are mad." *I am not mad.*

"They seem to easily turn so. I know how carefully Captain Pierson must screen his pilots, how often they need to be psych-tested, and how prone they are to neuroses."

"That's the curse the Stekoni gave us along with the ability to travel, Mother. We should perhaps be grateful. Without the Stekoni, there would only be one world for the Church to rule."

"You have sympathy for the Stekoni?"

Colin shrugged. "They gave us the farships, and they shared their mysticism, which came with the ships—they're not to be blamed for anyone's belief. I know of no Stekoni who professes to be Zakkaist, but that doesn't stop the Church's attempts to convert *them,* does it?"

The priest did not like that. Colin could see the spite in her face. Her smile had vanished and her hands were thrust into the pockets of her robe. In the cabin, she was like a shadowed apparition. "Tell me, Galicht Fairwood, do *you* see things in the Veils?"

Yes, a thousand terrible things, Mother. I see a dead man calling out for me with a bright, bright sword in his hands, and he wants to give that weapon to me. Mother, I think I may have already gone mad. "There are always hallucinations in the Veils, Mother," he said. "During the passage, a pilot's mind can't avoid them."

"Do you attribute these sights to MolitorAb, the Great Consciousness of the Stekoni?"

"I see where some could."

"Do you believe that Hallan Gelt—a Galicht and once an Obdurate—spoke with MolitorAb and was granted a vision of the future? Do you believe that this Sartius Exori of the MulSendero will come as a new messiah?"

"Gelt may have conversed with his veildreams, Mother. I've known it to happen." *I do it every time. Go away, Gelt, I say. Go away.* "I personally have no belief one way or the other. We'll learn the truth in time."

"Pah!" She spat her disgust, her face suddenly becoming lined. "You play badly with words, Galicht. Hallan Gelt began a greater heresy than that he had with the Obdurates. You can't tell me that the Galicht don't believe the foolishness of their brother."

Ligaments and muscles rippled down Colin's neck. *Don't get angry; that's what she wants, for some reason.* "Galicht-guild is just an organization of individuals, Mother. Independents. We've no unified policies at all, religious or otherwise. Just because Gelt happened to be a Galicht . . . that's just an accident, a title we share accidentally."

"Yet the title defines the man. For example, we have Captain Pierson here." She waved her hand at him; he seemed puzzled. "If I assured him that there was, ah, a smuggling compartment built into the cargo pod of your ship, he would be forced—by his title—to search for it."

Silence. Colin tried to appear quizzical and undisturbed, but his mind panicked. By God, the woman *knew.* He could see that in her eyes, in her posture. It was not simply a bluff. There was too much haughty confidence about her. He wondered how she'd learned of it—who had leaked the information and told the authorities which veillines Colin would most likely take. Now he understood the unlucky presence of the cruiser. All he could do was play out the game, discover what it was that she wanted from him. Colin didn't like the grudging eagerness of Pierson's face. If the man learned that the flamestones were hidden aboard . . . "What of the title 'Priest,' Mother? What does that compel one to do?"

"One becomes concerned with blasphemy wherever one finds it. You see that the laws of the Ascendants, which are the laws of God, are upheld. The Ascendants place us on all farships both for the religious needs of the crew and for the glory of the Church. Smuggling, to use my last example, is counter to the laws. I certainly couldn't allow it to continue if I found it."

"What if this smuggler repented, decided that he'd seen the errors of his ways? All the chapters of the Koran begin with the salutation: 'In the name of Allah, the Compassionate, the Merciful.'"

It was all up to her, Colin realized. If the priest wanted him, there was no escape. He couldn't fight the cruiser any more than he could deal with Pierson and his two marines. The prisons of Old Earth were infamous—he had no desire to find the truth of the tales. Colin swore to himself that if he got out of this, he would find and strangle the one who had spoken to the Church of his trip and his cargo.

"It's very easy to say 'I repent' and mean nothing, Galicht."

"Mother, I don't think that a smuggler would dare lie so easily. After all, words sometimes travel faster than farships. This smuggler could not hope to pass an inspection at his destination. I think that he would be forced to dispose of his contraband in space, between the Veils." *That will work if she believes that I have drugs or firearms.*

She nodded, and Colin nearly sighed. "An intelligent move. A priest could simply notify all worlds along the current Veil paths and alert port officials." She smiled again, and the hands came out of her pockets. Colin nodded. *Don't know how she knew, but she's one of the forgiving ones. She's going to give you the second chance that you don't deserve and let you go.*

The priest nodded back to him. "I'd continue our discussion, Galicht Fairwood, but the captain has given you his permission to leave. Perhaps we'll see one another again."

"Perhaps, Mother Crowell."

She reached into the pocket of her robe once more, producing a small booklet. She held it out to Colin. "You might find this intriguing. It defines the Church's position on the veildreams. I'd suggest you glance through it before your next transfer through the Veils." There was a strange emphasis to her words, and her eyes seemed to mock him as she turned and nodded to the captain. Colin escorted them from the *Anger* to their shuttle, then returned to his cabin.

He picked up the booklet and riffled the pages. A sheet of paper fell from it—the page bore a set of coordinates, nothing else. Colin knew without checking that the area designated by those numbers would be on the most direct path to Bifrost. Nor did he doubt that he was intended to drop the flamestones there. Colin knew who would pick them up.

"Damn!" He slammed a hand against a bulkhead. Muscles twitched in his open face. "The bitch played me for a fool."

A grating voice pulled Colin from the memory. The inn snapped into focus around him. The patrons were staring at a man who stood, hands on hips, in the center of the room. He bellowed from beneath dark and shaggy hair.

"All of you, listen! The worst sin is that of indifference! I declare myself with the voice of MolitorAb! I tell you: THE VOICE OF THE VEILS MOVES MY TONGUE! HEAR HER WORDS!" He glowered under tangled locks, his gaze sweeping the room. Madness touched the man. Colin could see it in his eyes; the wide, unblinking stare of a Veil-touched Galicht. This one was not alone in his delusion though. A ragged group had followed him into the establishment, all of them as unkempt as their leader. The disciples swayed behind him, hands locked together, chanting a strange ululation.

"LOOK AT ME, FOOLS! You gaze upon the Sartius Exori, the Black Beginning, he who holds the future! MolitorAb has said this to me!" His hands were spread wide and weren't particularly clean. Every word he spoke was a shout. His followers howled at the name of the Stekoni god.

Mari leaned toward Colin to whisper, "That's Roland Naley. Used to be Galicht; now he's the newest messiah. Nexus is crawling with idiots like him. He's got a big following though."

Naley must have sensed Mari's words, for he turned to their table as his disciples moaned in atonal chorus behind him. "Don't SCOFF at me!" he roared. "You Galicht, more than the rest, should be at my feet. You have the opportunity to be with MolitorAb often, yet you have failed to listen to the Voice!"

Mari shook her head. Colin could see the laughter in her even as she tried to hold it back. Others in the room were smiling as well, amused by the scene, probably happy that Naley had not fixed his attentions on them. The Stekoni gawked from their isolette, silent.

"I'm sorry," Mari said to Colin. "Naley's just..." With that, helpless laughter burst from her.

Naley strode toward them.

He was tall and burly as well as shaggy. His eyes were his best feature, dark under thick brows, large and compelling—it was easy to see how, in the god-obsessed atmosphere of the Fringes, he had come to find believers. His stare was intense and unblinking, maniacal.

"Woman, you ride the Veils. How have you not seen MolitorAb? Are you blind to God because you see too much of this world? Then you should pluck out your eyes and grind them underfoot so they do not deceive you."

Mari's laughter died. She recoiled, her spine straight against the back of her chair. "Get away from me, Naley."

"I'm not Naley. Not any more. I am the Sartius Exori—listen to what the Veils tell you!"

"Naley, I've listened. Like all Galicht, I've heard some strange things, but I've never once heard of you."

Naley's face convulsed. His hand became a fist and he struck the table in front of Mari and Colin. Glasses jumped, clattering. Colin began to push his chair back from the table, the loss of his flamestones forgotten.

"MolitorAb isn't a human God," Mari was saying. "She *can't* be our God."

"You're infected by the Church's filth! You listen to false words. MolitorAb encompasses all the old gods—they are but shades and images of the Truth!"

"Look, I don't care what you believe. Leave me alone, would you?"

"Listen to me, Galicht!"

"I'm too fucking tired of your voice to listen, Naley," Mari answered.

The self-proclaimed prophet's face reddened. With one swift, unexpected movement, he cuffed Mari backhanded. She was knocked from her chair, gasping in surprise and pain.

Colin surged to his feet, shoving the table aside as he rose. Naley backed away a step, grinning and showing jagged teeth. "Easy, Galicht, or you'll face MolitorAb's fury."

"You ass..." Adrenalin flooded through Colin. He realized that this was exactly what he wanted: a physical confrontation. He wanted to fight and be fought, to lose the feeling of impotence and frustration that had followed him since the encounter with Mother Crowell, to forget for a minute the haunting veildreams.

To lose himself in blood.

With an inarticulate cry of rage, he rushed Naley.

Fists drew back, poised.

Held.

Something in the man's eyes captured Colin. Naley's gaze had gone distant even as Colin had begun to strike. There had been a mad fury in Naley, and now . . . Now it fled, leaving the man slack-jawed. Naley's fist wavered, opened like an ugly flower, and fell.

Colin would have struck, grabbing the sudden opportunity, but found that he couldn't.

"I didn't realize . . ." Naley muttered. His voice held a growling, tired softness.

"Realize *what?*" Colin flung back. "What the hell's the matter with you?"

Naley's arrogance flickered back to life for an instant. "You don't know, do you, ugly man?" He laughed briefly, his amusement choked with phlegm. "You don't even acknowledge MolitorAb yet, do you?"

"It's mystical crap."

"That's what you say. It's not at all what you believe."

Colin shook his head. The fury was still inside him, raging. He wanted to drive his fist into Naley's face, wanted to rejoice in pain, in catharsis. "You're good at telling others what they think, Naley. You're good at hitting people who haven't done anything to you."

"And you're the brave hero leaping to their defense?" Naley's gaze smoldered, the glint of madness returning. "You fight because you can't stand the taste of your thoughts."

Colin could feel the stares of those in the room. The Stekoni were chattering among themselves. Behind him he could hear Mari getting to her feet. Colin's eyes narrowed as he braced himself for Naley's inevitable attack.

But Naley did nothing. Nothing.

The man shook his head and gesticulated abruptly to his disciples. "You make me unhappy, ugly man," Naley said in a voice that only Colin could hear. "You tell me that I'm not what I thought I was. I'm sorry for you, and I'll pray for you."

With that, he turned and walked from the inn. His followers, obviously confused, lagged behind him.

Colin stood in the middle of the floor, feeling unsatisfied, his hands still fisted at his waist. He inhaled deeply and traced the line of a muscle down his neck with a forefinger. The skinbase felt cold under his fingertip. "You all right, Mari?" he asked as the last of Naley's group left.

"I'm fine. Next time let me fight my own damn battles, huh?"

He couldn't read her voice, couldn't tell if she were joking or irritated. He turned to her; looking at her face didn't ease the confusion. "What the hell was all that about?" she asked, unsmiling. One cheek was an angry red, and blood trickled from a nostril.

Colin shrugged.

"Damned if I know," he said.

CHAPTER TWO

*If anyone tells you at that time, "Look, the Messiah is here,"
or, "He is there," do not believe it.*

NEW TESTAMENT, Matthew 24:23

*Then the Voice spoke again, saying, "He shall be called Sartius
Exori, for he is the Darkness before the Day. He will herald peace,
but he is not peace. He is the hammer that breaks the stones, and
from those stones My city shall be built."*

GELTIAN SCRIPTURE, 8:31

Noise. Darkness.

The two defined Nexus. Colin was engulfed in both as he emerged
from the inn a few hours later.

Darkness: a twilight pall shrouded the streets, which were tunneled avenues lit with the pale fungal glow of phoslamps. Noise:
the clamor of the city-world slammed against him from the rock
walls of Nexus, a wordlet carved from the living stone of a mis-
shapen, sunless glob of iron, riddled with the wandering shafts of
miners. The McCarthy Field Generators, buried far below, lent their
own basso growling as they enhanced the scant gravity of Nexus.

People shouted their way around Colin, calling to neighbors,
complaining, laughing. Vendors called their wares from open stands;
near him, a MulSendero preacher proclaimed the words of Gelt to
a circle of followers. Groundcars rumbled slowly past, nudging
through the thick flow of pedestrians. On Nexus, you were never
far enough from other people—Colin was jostled, assaulted by the
city-world and its inhabitants.

He'd been drinking too much. The alcohol hadn't helped: his
head reeled and his legs were unsteady. Mari had left not long after
the confrontation with Naley. She'd made it obvious that she didn't
care for his company on the way home. Colin had used her rejection
as an excuse to drink; from that point on, he hadn't let his glass

get empty. Now, bewildered by the chaos of Nexus, he found shelter in the lee of a building and leaned against a wall. "Jesus, don't you people ever sleep?" he muttered.

"Begging pardon, but this one would think that Nexus simply proclaims its vitality."

A pervasive scent of bitter oil accompanied the words, making Colin's nose wrinkle. The smell, the blurred sibilance of the words, and the stilted grammar told Colin that the speaker was a Stekoni. Colin turned, eyes half open. "You always make excuses for things that annoy you?"

The Stekoni looked no different than any other Colin had seen: she was a head shorter than Colin; gaunt, a wide, lipless mouth set with protuberant, flat-surfaced teeth; large ovals of golden eyes set too closely together over a triple slit of a nose. Around her waist were the openings of her young-pouches—none seemed occupied. Her body and face were furred in a soft pattern of browns that Colin knew to indicate status among the race but which meant nothing to him. The fur was slick with the Stekoni's glandular secretions; the lower body and genitalia were swathed in a white cloth stained with that oil.

She stared at Colin's face, at the latticework of muscles underneath the skinbase. Her eyes widened impossibly. Colin smirked. "Like it?" he asked. He was just drunk enough for the remark to seem funny to him. He laughed, then had to close his eyes as the noisy street whirled around him.

Hesitantly, the alien smiled with her molar-rich mouth, looking as if she would prefer to melt back into the crowds. The smile seemed more learned than natural. "This one's name would be FirstBred Pale," she said, ignoring Colin's question. "This one saw the confrontation of the Galicht-pilot and Mad One Naley."

The creature's breath was warm and full of that oily tang. A group of people passing by scowled and moved away. The smell made Colin briefly nauseous. He stepped back one deliberate pace, keeping his back to the wall.

"What about it?" He didn't give his name as politeness demanded. That confused the Stekoni.

"No offense is meant, please. This is a matter of import to this one and her studies. She would ask what frightened the Mad One, what made him turn from you. This one has watched the Nexian Pretender for several days. He is most appallingly—ahh—*aggressive*. He has hurt many, even among his followers, and he has even killed. He does not like mockery or opposition, yet he retreated from you."

"You a priest, FirstBred Pale? Is that what your pattern means?"

Pale blinked—a slow motion of underlids—and what might have been a sadness flickered in her eyes. "No, Galicht-sir. This one is not that far in the graces of MolitorAb, though she will admit..." Long-fingered hands plucked at her loincloth, smearing oil. "This one talks far too much. You must give pardon, Galicht-sir. FirstBred Pale is a watcher. She waits for the Sartius Exori."

That made Colin laugh again. Above them, someone screamed down a curse. "If your Naley's an example of the applicants for the position, you'll have a long wait."

"This is not what the prophet Gelt has said."

"It isn't, huh? What makes you think that old Hallan knew what the hell he was talking about?" The alcohol made him more belligerent than he intended. Colin scowled at the realization, then saw that Pale had mistaken the expression for more animosity. He leaned his head back against the wall, closed his eyes, and tried to smile. "Hey, it's been a long night for me, FirstBred Pale. I've had enough god-talk for an evening. Unless you have a new topic, I'm going to go collapse into one of the Galicht-house beds."

Pale stepped from Colin's direct path. No Stekoni had ever offered much resistance to a human; it was not their way. The ancestors of the Stekoni had possessed no natural defenses against predators but their inborn cunning. Herbivorous, they had no hunting skills and very little aggressiveness toward other species. Stekoni did not war among themselves, did not fight; their politeness was legendary. Yet Pale so obviously wanted to speak that Colin paused. He rubbed at his eyes. "What?" he demanded brusquely.

"Where will you be tomorrow, Galicht-sir?"

"On my ship. Somewhere past the Veils with a new cargo and gone from this hole."

"There is no offense meant, Galicht-sir, but this one does not think that will occur."

Colin shook his head. His drunkenness threatened to make him laugh again. "Not to be unnecessarily melodramatic," he said very slowly, "but who's going to stop me?"

Pale blinked again. Her mouth opened, closed. "This one would not, she assures you. There is no threat intended, not in the slightest. It is simply that outgoing cargoes are scarce, and this one has heard that a certain Galicht is not in favor at the moment because of a lost cargo that was not on his manifest. Also, the Veil paths are very poor at the moment unless one is going inward to the Holdings. Given that..." The Stekoni wriggled—it might have been a shrug.

Colin put his hands on his hips, though he was careful not to move away from the wall. The creature's odor plus his alcoholic fuzziness made him shake his head. The street danced around him. He could not decide if he was supposed to be angry. "You seem to know a lot, FirstBred Pale."

"This one has made a study of humanity. It is her work. So she is supposed to know such things."

"Yeah. Well, this time you're wrong. I'm leaving Nexus tomorrow. I don't care much what the cargo is—there'll be something going somewhere."

The Stekoni paused, her mouth slightly open. A thick tongue moved from side to side. "This one hopes that you will understand if she says that her perception differs."

Suddenly, desperately, Colin wanted only to go to sleep. All desire to talk had fled, and the worldroar of Nexus threatened to devour him. "Good-bye, FirstBred Pale," he said abruptly. He pushed away from the wall, stumbling slightly as he shouldered past the Stekoni.

From behind him, she persisted. "This one had hoped..."

"No."

"Still, this one—"

Colin whirled around, reaching a hand out to steady himself. He nearly struck a passerby in the process. Someone shouted at him; he ignored it. "This one is awfully bold for a Stekoni," he said. He glared at Pale, seeing the creature's eyes widen again. "You're making me angry. When I get angry, I get violent. Better watch out, Pale, or I might treat you the way I treated Naley. Huh?"

That moved Pale back. "Galicht-sir," she began. In her fear, Pale's accent became strong and guttural and the smell worsened, yet Pale did not flee as Colin had expected. "This one begs pardon."

"Shut up. Leave me alone."

That ended it. Pale nodded—a peculiar twisting motion of the stalk-thin neck. The Stekoni backstepped into the eternal Nexian crowd and was gone.

Colin held his head. A pounding had begun in his temples that made the street waver before him. The bright colors of the crowds hurt his eyes, the din swelled inside his head. He lurched into the moving press of humanity.

When he reached the Galicht-house, it was all he could do to find his bed and collapse into it.

CHAPTER THREE

And the Lord thy God will put all these curses upon thine ene-
mies, and on them that hate thee, that persecuted thee.
                              OLD TESTAMENT, Deuteronomy XXX, 7

MolitorAb laughed and the heavens shook. The Voice said, "There
is a rot in those that would deny Me. Like a tree gone dead inside,
they may as easily fall of their own disease as to the axe."
                              GELTIAN SCRIPTURE, 7:6–7

The windows looked out to the vine-wrapped rubble of Manhattan. That bleak landscape was supposed to inspire a contemplation of man's fragility.

For Ascendant Huan Su, who could remember when the fires
burned there, the scene caused his stomach to churn. Those times—
the days when interchurch rivalries had spawned violence—came
back to him all too often in his nightmares.

Such was the cost of age. The Obdurates had gone to a bloody,
fiery death in a long series of riots, but the church molded by the
prophet Simon ben Zakkai had survived. The Church remained.
Huan Su remained. He could count the years in the aching of his
joints, in the searing gut-pain that made his nights miserable.

You're just a husk, a shriveled body barely retaining its grasp
of the soul. Your time is nearly over.

He shook the thought away. Today there was to be a full meeting
of the Ascendants, the private conclave. It was too important to
miss. To this he needed to give his full attention. *Let God worry*
about your health. If He wants you, you won't be able to deny Him.
Be content.

Two days earlier the doctor had shaken his head as he departed
Su's apartments in the Tokyo Cathedral. Su had smiled at the man's
somberness. "I've known you a long time, David. Please don't look

23

so distressed. I've felt the death inside me for a year or more now.
There's nothing you can do."

David had looked sour. "Don't say that, Huan. Not yet. There
are tests I still want to take, and with new techniques—"

"Accept the inevitable. Don't worry, my friend—I am not bothered by the thought of dying. I don't look for the end of this life.
I'll probably fight it when it comes. But it *does* come." Su had
smiled then.

"You're giving me the speech I was rehearsing for you."

"I'm a leader of the Church, David. Why should I be afraid to
meet my God at last?"

To that, David could say nothing.

Su turned from the windows reaching from floor to distant ceiling. Behind him, he could hear a soft click as Carl entered the
room. Carl was Su's aide, a young priest whose sense of history
more than anything else had attracted Su. The priest went to the
cabinet and brought out the brocaded surplice that Su would wear
that day. Carl held it out and Su turned to slip his arms into the
garment. "Thank you, Carl," he said. "I think these vestments
become heavier each year." He gave a soft chuckle and was puzzled
when Carl didn't return it. "Carl—" he began, glancing over his
shoulder.

Su could see the stiletto then, a tapering, razor-thin blade. Carl
had raised the weapon to strike, but had not.

Conflicting emotions warred on his face.

Su flung himself to one side as the blade whipped down. The
weapon caught in the heavy cloth of the surplice and was wrenched
from Carl's grasp. Su hit the floor, his breath going out of him, but
he heard the stiletto clatter against a wall. The Ascendant struggled
to his knees gasping and lunged for his desk. He slammed a fist
against a contact there.

His side ached as he pulled himself to a standing position. Carl
had retrieved the stiletto. Su hobbled around his desk, putting its
bulk between Carl and himself. "It's over," he said. "Please don't
make it worse, Carl."

Already there were footsteps in the corridor. The doors were
flung open, crashing back against their stops. Two guards rushed
into the room, weapons drawn. When they saw Carl, the ugly snouts
of their guns swung about. *"Don't!"* Su shouted; then, to Carl:
"Please. Drop the knife."

The young man's face was drawn up in a fierce mask. He looked as if he might weep. His fist clenched the stiletto, white-knuckled, and then he released the blade. It fell noiselessly to the carpet.

Su let out a breath he hadn't known he'd been holding. He dropped into the chair behind the desk, suddenly weak and nauseous, aware of a new aching in his left side. His stomach knotted and he nearly doubled over, clutching at the edge of the desk. He waved back the guards as they moved to take Carl's arms. "No. Leave him alone for a moment."

Su closed his eyes for a second, then opened them. "Carl, why?"

He felt very old.

Carl's hands waved helplessly. He glanced from Su to the guards and back. "You won't understand, Ascendant."

"I think I might, maybe more than most. Tell me this—was it just you, or did you do it for another?"

"I did it for the Church."

"Could you think of no better alternative than killing, my friend?"

Carl grimaced. The guards tensed as the man's eyes narrowed, but Carl made no move. "Don't claim me as a friend, Ascendant. And don't preach to me of 'other ways.' God is aware of the blood on *your* hands. How many Obdurates did you kill when the Church asked you to?"

So that's what they used—that old, sad guilt. The memories summoned by Carl's accusation brought pain. Su's temples pulsed with it and for a moment he could not speak. "That was another time," he said at last, though he knew the defense to be a sham. He had never been able to accept that excuse either.

"This is another time as well."

Su could only shake his head. He did not want to say any more in front of the guards—there would be too much gossip already. Su nodded and the guards moved toward Carl.

"You've a pious facade, Ascendant," Carl spat out. "Once I even admired you for it—now I see that your weakness can only hurt the Church." As the guards grasped him, his hands went into his pockets.

"Carl, I can't believe this bitterness I hear from you." The guilt that he sometimes thought dispelled returned in a rush. *You can't ever hide from what you've done. You can beg forgiveness, but it never truly comes in this lifetime. This is your fault, old fool. Your fault, not Carl's.* "Tell me why this happened. Help me to understand."

"Ascendant, you'll never know how much I regret my failure here," Carl replied. With a sudden motion, he shrugged off the guards' hold. His hand went from pocket to mouth—he bit and swallowed.

As Su watched in horror, Carl screamed. His body shivered, his lips drew back from gritted teeth, and tendons stood out in his neck.

He collapsed, held between the guards.

Su rushed to the man and lowered Carl to the carpet. He motioned the guards back—hesitantly they obeyed. Leaning close to Carl's face, he whispered what he did not want the guards to hear.

"Which one was it, Carl? Which of the Ascendants?"

There was no answer.

Su felt for the carotid artery. The pulse was a ragged, faint beating that failed under his fingertips. Su bent his head, whispered a soft prayer, then looked up again.

"Get a doctor here. Immediately," he ordered. The guards fled.

"Ahh, Carl. Carl." He sighed.

Su picked up the stiletto.

He put it under his robe.

The steel chilled his skin as Su took the slideway to the hall where the other Ascendants waited. He wanted time; there was none. His heart still raced from the exertion and he could still see the final agony on Carl's face. *Culper. It had to be Culper. No one else would have dared anything so bold. No one else could have suborned Carl. And that person used Carl, expecting that the boy would fail. There are a hundred better and more certain ways than a knife. Why?*

Perhaps that was the message intended, Su realized: You are alone. You can trust no one. Such a feeling would hamper Su's effectiveness in this meeting—it already had, for his mind was not on the Church's concerns any longer. Su did not doubt his intuition that Culper was somewhere behind it.

He means to force something through the council this morning.

Su liked New York least of the Great Cathedrals—it was, after all, the province of Ascendant Joseph Culper. Su preferred the ornamental geegaws found in every nook of Jerusalem; the heavy Gothic spirituality of Paris; and best, the quiet, garden-strewn isolation of his own Tokyo. Law required that the monthly conclaves be rotated. He always hated coming to New York. The sight of the Obdurate ruins depressed him, and he found the cathedral itself too large, too starkly modern.

It would be worse now. New York would always bring back thoughts of Carl and betrayal.

Su entered the cavernous hall. On the far wall were glowing, twisting holograms of the symbols of the monotheistic faiths: the cross of Christianity, the scimitar of Allah, the star of David—all circumscribed by Simon ben Zakkai's triangle. The twenty-three Ascendants were seated in a similar pattern, tiered in a triangle around three empty chairs. The others were already present—Su was the last to enter. He could feel their gazes on him; he knew that by now most were aware of the attempt on his life. Certainly Ascendant Culper, as the current curator of justice, would have been quickly informed.

Stepping from the slideway, Su nearly stumbled. The ache in his side had become dull and persistent, and there was a catch in his hip as he walked, twisting him slightly sidewise. He could manage no better than a hobble as he moved to his seat. The Ascendants watched, appraising, gauging his weakness.

Predators.

Across the polished tiles he moved, bowing to the vacant chairs representing the three aspects of God, and climbed the short set of chairs.

Su was wheezing before he sat. His hip was a knotted agony that eclipsed the eternal burning in his gut. He kneaded his stomach with one hand and forced himself to smile and nod to the gathering.

His hand touched the stiletto. That made it easier.

Ascendant Joseph Culper, to Su's left, nodded back. Su thought he could read disappointment on the man's face.

The proceedings opened with prayer, then plunged into a litany of current temporal matters: an economic depression on Zion, a proposal to increase aid to the new world Slowfall, a document from the bishop of the outlying world Chebar citing continuing troubles with the Buntaro sect of the MulSendero, a report on ecclesiastical work in the Fringes. Petitions were advanced and rulings made in the name of God and the Ascendants.

Su listened to it all, his eyes closed. He tried to find Culper's hand in any of it. He could see only Carl. Su began to wonder if his guess was wrong, that perhaps Carl had acted on his own.

He heard Culper's voice. He opened his eyes.

Joseph Culper was charismatic. Even Su would admit that. He had risen quickly from the ranks, becoming curator of justice before he was thirty and continuing to hold that title even when elevated to the rank of Ascendant. Almost sixty years old now, Culper's appearance was impressive. His hair was a stern iron gray flecked with residual black, his physique strong, his voice resonant and deep. The face was rough-hewn, the planes too abrupt to be classic, yet he compelled trust. Culper was gifted with a presence, and he knew quite well how to use that gift. In the decade since he had been named Ascendant, he had come to wield an influence far surpassing that of those with more seniority. The Ascendants' conclaves had once been dominated by the ascetic, monkish Su—that was no longer the case.

Beside Culper, Su's wizened, frail appearance paled.

Su told himself that he was not jealous. He knew that to be partially a lie.

"I'm weary," Culper said. The others fell silent. "I'm weary because we must sit here and deal with matters best left in the hands of our subordinates. By seeing too much, we blind ourselves to the true threat to the Church."

There were a few sighs from the Ascendants—it was an old subject for Culper—but Su saw most of them nodding agreement. *Here it is then.* He felt the hilt of the stiletto, warm from the touch of his fingers.

"I know that some of you would rather not listen to this again," Culper continued. "I promise you that this time we face a challenge comparable to the Obdurates. When humankind is given the freedom to ignore the true faith, when we let false ideals and false gods exist unmolested, we invite our own destruction. We slap the face of god.

"The facts are simple, Ascendants. Today, in the Fringes and perhaps even within the Holdings, those of the MulSendero are praying to Hallan Gelt as a prophet on the day of his death. A prophet of a false and base god!"

His voice thundered. It rang.

Su coughed. His words were soft and plain. "Let's not be so dramatically pessimistic, Ascendant Culper. God teaches us to have patience and hope. Don't you believe that those of the Many Paths may yet be guided to God?"

Culper stared at Su. For a long moment, he did not look away. *Yes, Culper's the one. Carl's blood is ultimately on his hands.* Then the moment was gone as Culper glanced around the room. "No," he said flatly. "We delude ourselves if we think we can convert them. Does even *one* of the Stekoni profess to believe in God?"

"You're proposing genocide?" Su mocked him with unsubtle sarcasm.

"'Those that deny the revelations of their Lord shall suffer the torment of a hideous scourge.' That is what the Koran says," Culper replied. "But no, Ascendant Su, I am not proposing that. I would mention, however, that this conclave once *did* pass such a measure against the Obdurates—*you* would remember that, Ascendant, having been among those who carried out our predecessors' wishes."

How many Obdurates did you kill when the Church asked you to? Carl's words. Su could not answer. He felt very old and uncertain, and he knew that this was exactly what Culper had intended.

"It had been forty-four years since the death of Gelt," Culper said. "Before Gelt and his veildreams, the MulSendero religion was merely a minor nuisance, a heresy limited to the Stekoni and a few deluded humans. But all of you have seen the awful growth of this malignancy. Each year more pledge themselves to the false MolitorAb. Certain of them—the Buntaro—even resort to terrorism against the Church. They riot in the Holdings, they dispute our work in the Fringes. The MulSendero wish to see God's Church broken and the work of Prophet Zakkai undone. They would let loose chaos among the worlds."

Then his voice dropped in volume and pitch. "The MulSendero have a weakness, set in their own belief system—the Geltian prophecies. My proposal is simple. We must make certain that the heretics find their messiah, their Sartius Exori, and that they make their claim official. Their scripture says it: 'MolitorAb's arms will enfold him and protect him.' We will let them choose the Sartius Exori; we will *guide* their choice."

Culper paused. He gazed at the symbols of the Church, at the Ascendants.

"Then we will kill him," he said.

The uproar surpassed anything Su had seen in the assembly. All the Ascendants burst into speech, some rising from their seats to shout. Nearby Ascendants exchanged passionate words, their arms waving. Su watched the pandemonium, forcing himself to think and judge the reaction. His appraisal frightened him. If it came to a vote now, Culper might succeed. Blood would again stain the Church. *How many did you kill?* Su watched Culper, and the smile on the man's face frightened Su. He grasped the stiletto, but the weapon gave him no more comfort.

The tumult was slow in subsiding, but at last Culper raised his hands and cleared his throat.

"I can well appreciate your reactions. I've wrestled with the same feelings myself. I've prayed to God that I be shown his will in this and I remain convinced of the rightness of this course. I know that many of you object for good reasons. All I can do is point to precedent—when confronted by the Obdurate heresy three-quarters of a century ago, the Church ordered the dissidents executed. Remember that point: I will return to it later.

"At least some of us think of a messianic martyr *before* the time of Simon ben Zakkai and what happened after he was crucified. I say that the analogy fails: Christ claimed no divine protection. The Sartius Exori does. Christ predicted his own death. Compare that to Geltian scripture: 'While he so wills, he will live despite those that conspire against him.'

"Others will say, 'What if the assassination fails? We would simply add to the false messiah's reputation.' Ascendants, I have no answer to that objection—it is entirely correct. We could not afford a failure when we make our final move. We must be very certain of any plan."

Su's gut knotted. He forced his mind into calmness, remembering the peace of the Tokyo gardens and trying to push away the vision of Carl's body curled in that room. *Don't let that death intrude here, not now. You need a clear head.* "I can only assume that you've chosen your—ahh—*victim,* Ascendant," Su said.

Culper had expected more of a frontal assault; Su could see that. Culper hesitated, looking for meaning behind the question. "I do have a candidate," he said finally. "Some of you might know Mother Anna Crowell, an aide on my staff. She must take credit for this—her intuition and God's hand."

"God *spoke* to you on this?" Su did not bother to disguise his contempt: *Let the man take offense.*

Culper shook his head. "I say that simply because the events behind the choice comprise such extreme coincidences that I can well believe God guided the events. Mother Crowell was aboard a patrol vessel—it is part of my routine that staff members within the curator of justice's department serve occasional duty in the real world. Mother Crowell had earlier received notification that a Galicht craft might arrive in her sector carrying flamestones stolen from a bishopric on Kethrid Four. Mother Crowell made arrangements to recover the gems. But this Galicht pilot impressed Mother Crowell and she acted on her own initiative, a brilliant improvisation."

The hall was silent. Su waited.

"The Galicht's name is Colin Fairwood. His face is ravaged by some old injury. As you might know, the curator's office keeps files on all Galicht: Mother Crowell had of course checked these and found rumors concerning Fairwood. The Galicht say that he is time-dilated, a relativistic accident following the failure of a farship's

Veil drive. Fairwood has said little concerning the journey—where he had come from, *when* we had left. We know only that his farship was found in 2541 within the Fringes, and Fairwood was rescued. Mother Crowell, Ascendants, has a brilliant mind, a good imagination, a flair. The rescuers of Fairwood had noted that the farship was of an outmoded design and that the direction of travel indicated that Fairwood may have come from somewhere in the Holdings. Mother Crowell found the inspiration to go one step further. She knew of a tale dating back to the Purge of New York—two farships were stolen during the first night of rioting."

Su knew that tale as well. He knew what Culper would say next, and the realization struck him like a blow.

"Hallan Gelt stole one of the ships. The other was lost and assumed destroyed. Gelt claimed that a friend of his, James Badgett, had been the hijacker of that second craft. Ascendants, it is curious but true that 'Colin' was the first name of James Badgett's paternal grandfather. 'Fairwood' was the family name of his maternal grandparents. Not a bad deception, actually—I am still amazed that Mother Crowell could ferret it out."

Culper cast a sidelong glance at Su, and there was triumph in his eyes. "I've examined all the prophetic passages of Gelt. Colin Fairwood, Gelt's Obdurate companion James Badgett, fits them as well as anyone."

Outrage welled up in Su, a fury born of Carl's death and his own guilt, his own sins. He almost shouted. "You'd murder the man for that?"

"I mentioned an earlier precedent, Ascendant Su. The Church ordered death for the Obdurate heretics. You remember that ruling, no?"

Burning, bitter: you can never be forgiven. "I repeat—you'd kill the man for that? The Obdurates were a plague long ago destroyed. Let us forget them."

"Ascendant, I admire your conviction." Culper turned to face the others. "Ignore the MulSendero and they will become the next Obdurates. This old enemy will lead them."

"Only if *we* elevate him. You said that yourself," Su persisted.

"Better a known enemy than the alternative."

Su felt despair. The other Ascendants were simply watching, and that deepened his sadness. He had hoped that a few, at least, would give open support to him. Surely McGinnis or Behlow or Hahn—one of them would feel the same horror that Su felt. But no one rose to speak and Su knew that Culper had arranged this too well. Carl's ghost roamed through Su's head, slowing reactions. He couldn't think, couldn't find the right words.

"You invent danger," he declared. "You're sacrificing your soul to eradicate a phantom."

"No one can deny the riots, the deaths. The Buntaro openly declare war on us; the MulSendero leaders might publicly decry the violence, but they laugh at the disruption of Church rule."

"I deny that we require such a drastic solution."

"Ascendant, none of us is safe until Gelt's ghost is laid to rest. One of us could be the next victim."

The two locked gazes. *Joseph Culper, you have blackened your soul today.* That thought did little to allay Su's pain. There was nothing to be gained by more argument. Su could see it in all their faces, arrayed against him. *A bitter day to see a friend's hand raised against you, to see the Church do this.* "I move that we vote on the matter."

Culper nodded; others seconded the motion.

"I vote nay," Su declared. "I hope that others here have the courage to vote with their hearts as well. Ascendants, I know better than any of you what it is you do here—this would feed your guilt for the rest of your lives."

The vote was closer than Su expected. Nine of the Ascendants sided with him.

The remaining twelve went with Culper.

Afterward, Su limped toward the group around Culper.

His hand was under his robe. His fingers brushed the cold hilt of the knife. He was not yet sure what he would do with it.

Conversation trailed off as Su approached. Culper glanced at him, smiling a false welcome, but he made no move toward Su, who had to walk the length of the room. Su was exhausted by the effort. He had to wait before he could speak.

"You . . . would murder . . . this Fairwood?"

"With my own hands, Ascendant. A small evil for a greater good." His voice was smug. Culper threw back his shoulders as if to accentuate the difference in their height.

"I was so certain of myself once," Su replied. A decision came to him then and his hand tightened around the hilt. "I think I have an appropriate gift for you, Joseph."

Su brandished the stiletto. His hand trembled; it looked alien in his weak grasp. Before any of them could react, Su reversed the blade clumsily, presenting it to Culper hilt foremost.

When Culper would not reach out to take it, Su let it fall. The clatter of the stiletto's impact brought all gazes to him.

Culper's stare was venomous. That pleased Su.

"You should remember, Joseph, just how close I was to you," Su whispered. "Then you should thank God I don't deal with a threat to the Church as you would."

In halting dignity, Su made his way from the hall.

CHAPTER FOUR

Because they have opposed his revelations, He will frustrate their works.

KORAN, Mohammed 47:9

Do you expect that I shall take your hand and lead you? I want not the sheep but the wolf, who sees his opportunity and grasps it.

GELTIAN SCRIPTURE, 5:15

Colin woke to a twin pounding: one in his head; another, softer one passing by the thin shielding of his bed. He closed his eyes and groaned. Rubbing his temples only increased the pain.

"Open," he growled. Yellowed plastic petalled open over him and slid under the bed. He narrowed his eyes against the room's harsh light. Most of the other beds in the large dormitory were empty; the wall clock told him that it was late. One other person was in the room, a woman reading in her bed, light from a viewer spilling green over her face and shoulders.

"Is Mari around, Sarah?"

The woman shrugged without looking up. "Haven't seen her."

"Where's the master?"

"Where you'd expect her to be." Her gaze flicked from the screen to Colin and back.

"Thanks. You've been very helpful," he said, with no inflection.

Her answer was almost gay. "Anytime, Fairwood. Anytime."

Colin grimaced, his thoughts dark against the pulsing in his head. He levered himself from the bed, feeling the distant thrumming of the McCarthy generators. Foam slid away to the sides of the bed, air chilled his skin. He dressed.

The door to Master Kym's office gave back an image of Colin. He scratched at his cheek and watched the reflection do the same. Under the skinbase, he could see striated muscles stretching, arteries pumping. "You look good this morning," he told himself softly as

34

he knocked. A muffled voice called out from behind the mirror:
"Just a moment." Then the mirror Colin shivered and dissolved.
Master Kym stared at Colin from behind her desk. "Come in,
Fairwood," she said. "Mari said that you'd be in late."

There was no friendliness in her voice.

Master Kym looked as if age and responsibility had leached
substance from her. She was hard and thin and small, her face
framed by dry white hair, the mouth snagged in lines. Her hands,
folded on the desk, were skeletal. "What did you want?" she said.

Colin stood before her uneasily. "Cargo," he said. "Anything
going anywhere."

Her eyes narrowed under sagging lids. "I don't have anything
for you at the moment."

"You're sure?" Colin glanced pointedly at the terminal on her
desk. "Maybe something new's come in since last night."

His suspicions were confirmed when Kym made no move even
to check the terminal. The loss of the flamestones *was* going to
haunt him. Colin cursed his impulse to take the gems in the first
place, cursed the damned priest Crowell for forcing him to get rid
of them, cursed his headache for making him surly and slow.

He seemed to remember that a Stekoni had told him that this
would happen.

"I'm sorry, Fairwood. There's nothing for you." Pleasure glinted
in her eyes.

"Damn it, you haven't checked."

Her hands knotted and her mouth drew into a thin line. "I'm
master here, Fairwood. So I'd advise you to listen to me now like
a good boy. If you ever want to get off this rock, you'll remember
this: when I tell you that there's no cargo for you, there's no need
for me to check twice. I run the Galicht on Nexus, not you." Kym
exhaled sharply and snapped her gaze away from him. "Now get
the hell out of here."

"It's because of the flamestones."

"You don't listen, do you?"

"I'm listening to what you're not saying. There's no cargo because I botched the smuggling run to Bifrost. Pressure's been put
on you to punish me for it. That much is obvious. Who was it, the
Holding ambassador on Nexus? The Zakkaist bishopric here? Or
just the one who stole the gems in the first place?"

"Garbage!" Kym glared at Colin. A thick-jointed forefinger
stabbed toward him. "You've a paranoia complex, Fairwood. I don't
much care that you fouled up some smuggling scheme—that's not

Galicht business; it's between you and your contacts. *My* business is Nexus and moving freight from here to somewhere else. It's also my business to assign those cargoes—*you* don't have one because I've none to give to you."

"You're lying."

"Fairwood—"

"Master Kym, I know your problem. I even sympathize. Someone's told you that they'd be pleased if Colin Fairwood sat for awhile and contemplated the empty hull that's going to cost him a fortune in berth rental. All that means to you is that I'm going to be in here every single day bothering you and wasting your time. Master Kym..." Colin sighed and continued in a softer tone. "I'll take anything that comes close to paying my expenses—I'll trust to God or MolitorAb to get me something that'll pay a profit at my next stop. Just get me off Nexus. Please."

"Deadhead it," she answered. "Run empty."

Colin spread his hands. "Master, I don't have savings and the *Anger*'s already mortgaged as far as she'll go."

"Then you're stuck, Galicht." She looked pleased.

Colin slammed a fist down on her desk. *"No!"*

"Get out!" Master Kym roared back, rising to her feet. "Get out now or you'll *rot* here before I find cargo for you. I'll stick you so far down the list that the *Anger*'ll rust before she moves. Do you understand?"

Colin could feel muscles leaping in his jaw, and he knew that Kym could easily see the tension there. He relaxed his jaw with an effort. "I understand," he said. "I understand very well."

"Good." She sat again, folding her hands on the desk.

"Where can I find Mari?"

"She's gone. Inward to Zion."

Colin was too stunned to be angry. "You gave her cargo? I was here three days before she—" He stopped the retort with an effort, before the words became too furious to halt. Master Kym did not look up at him.

On some worlds there were doors to slam. Colin could only stalk ineffectively through a haze of dissolving mirrors. Accompanied by shards of himself, he left the room.

Outside, the pulsing throb of the McCarthys was joined by the worldroar. Colin plunged into bright crowds, hands in pockets. Under the cold glow of the lamps, he made his way into the warren of narrow lanes that was Nexus. The conversations of thousands bounced at him from the walls, and the undercurrent of the worldlet growled under his feet.

I would like a drink. Several drinks. Colin rounded a corner and broached a crowd of youths shouting to each other. Immediately, he was enveloped by a familiar, faintly acrid scent that wrinkled his nose.

"Galicht Fairwood?"

Fingers of shadow stroked a wide face: the Stekoni stepped from the darkness between two buildings. Colin thought it might be the same one that had accosted him the night before—he seemed to recall that sandy fur pattern, but the name would not come to him. "What?" he said.

The Stekoni quivered and took a step backward. "Begging pardon, Galicht Fairwood. This one means no offense. This one would have you remember our conversation last night." The alien hobbled back and forth on thin legs as if anxious; the long mouth looked as if she were trying to smile, though the effort was closer to a leer.

"What of it?"

"This one had mentioned that there would be no cargo for Galicht Fairwood. Did you not find that this one spoke the truth? There was truly no cargo for you, yes? This one can see your anger— one should not be angered when MolitorAb insists on a path."

The mention of MolitorAb brought back memories of veildreams and Hallan Gelt. "Look—"

"This one's name, as this one is sure you know, is FirstBred Pale." Her voice was a soft remonstrance.

"Then, FirstBred Pale, let me tell you that I don't care about your skill as a seer *or* your religious fulfillment. Please stop bothering me."

Translucent underlids fluttered over golden eyes as Pale leered again. "Asking forgiveness once more, Galicht Fairwood, but this one would make the assumption that you would welcome a cargo."

"Was that hard for you to figure out?" Colin asked snidely. "You claim to be a student of humanity, FirstBred Pale; I seem to recall that much. I'd think you'd realize that Galicht controls most of the commerce going out from Nexus. If there are no cargoes at the guild house, then I don't have a hell of a choice. If Master Kym wishes me to sit here until the next century, then I'd better find a soft chair. Now, can we call the lesson finished?"

The leer widened and four-fingered hands touched one of the young-pouches near the stained loincloth. The Stekoni's movements stirred the air and brought the creature's smell to Colin. He grimaced and glanced away.

"Galicht does not control the passage of travelers, nor are Galicht pilots forbidden to seek such. This one has a passenger for you, Galicht Fairwood."

Colin backed away, his hands up. "No, Pale. No. The only reason that someone would want to ship out on my little farship is that they're in trouble. I don't need any more of that than I already have."

"How long can this Galicht-sir afford to stay on Nexus?" she persisted. "This one understands the feelings against Galicht Fairwood might be very strong. He might be Nexus-trapped for some time. No money, no Veil travel, no chance to commune with MolitorAb."

"I don't talk to MolitorAb in the veildreams." Colin's answer was too sharp, too quick. The Stekoni cocked her head and watched him strangely.

"Would it do harm to speak with this passenger, Galicht Fairwood?" she asked at last. "Just to speak?"

"Is the passenger *you*, FirstBred Pale?"

Her head bobbed from side to side. "No, Galicht Fairwood. A human young-bearer. A female."

Colin pondered the offer. The day had not begun well; to spend the rest of it trying to find solace at the bottom of a bottle would solve nothing. Master Kym would give him a cargo or not—he could not affect that decision. If the Stekoni's offer held even a glimmering of a solution, he should know more about it.

You can always say no. All you'll lose is time, and you've a surplus of that commodity.

"Fine, FirstBred Pale," he said. "I'll see the woman. Take me to her."

The Stekoni blinked heavily: once, then again. The hands slid along the loincloth and plucked at a knot on the side. "MolitorAb does guide you," she said. "You have made a wise decision. This one is certain you will not regret it."

"I doubt that, Pale," Colin replied. "Somehow I doubt that very much."

CHAPTER FIVE

A good man produces goodness from the good in his heart; an evil man produces evil out of his store of evil. Each man speaks from his heart's abundance.

NEW TESTAMENT, Luke 6:45

Evil? Good? What are these words, what do they mean? They are simply empty shells. To MolitorAb, they mean no more than "man" or "woman." For the Voice is both: evil and good, one and many, father and mother, son and daughter. What is not All cannot be called God. Thus it does not matter what you do as long as it serves MolitorAb.

THE WORDS OF THE SARTIUS EXORI, Pain 5:7

The room was a niche chiseled into the walls of Nexus in an area known as the Barrens. A thousand holes pocked the cliffs here, served by a latticework of treacherous stone stairs and makeshift ladders. Refuse was piled below the cliffs; here and there Colin could see someone pawing through the garbage. He followed Pale to a dwelling halfway up the rampart of cold stone and looking out at the backside of the city. The worldroar echoed loudest here, and the curtain set at the entrance of this cave-within-a-cave did little to abate the noise.

Kiri Oharu sat in the loud dimness. To Colin, she seemed weary, her skin darkened under pit-black eyes, her face drawn tightly over oriental cheekbones. Her hair was long and straight and the same utter black as the eyes. It fell over her face as she slid a tray toward Pale and Colin. Cups were set around a steaming pot there.

"Tea?" she asked.

She had hardly glanced at Colin since he had entered the room. Her gaze was always averted.

"This one thanks you." Pale reached out and poured herself a cup. The fragrant steam mingled with the Stekoni's odor.

"It's little enough to offer," Kiri replied. She rose and moved to the back of the room to turn off the portable stove. Colin noticed that she limped, her face grimacing with each step. Kiri came back and sat on the floor in front of them, gingerly folding her legs underneath her. "This is your Galicht friend, FirstBred Pale?"

Colin began to speak, but then Kiri looked at him. He saw her mouth twist as she stared at the patchwork on his face. Slowly, her features began to relax, and she nodded with a small smile. "I try to imagine how you must have once looked," she said. Her voice was mild and soft. "You must have endured great pain, Galicht-sir. What did that to you?"

Her candor surprised him. He shrugged before he answered. "An accident. And yes, it was very painful." *Now, like all the rest, she'll ask the inevitable question: "And why didn't you have the surgery completed?" They never say it quite so bluntly, but they all want to know.* The answer—one of several stock replies—was already on his lips.

"I admire you," she said. "Not everyone would care to be reminded of such an experience every day." Her fatigue-marked eyes held his.

Colin was stunned into momentary silence. "My name is Colin Fairwood," he said at last. "'Galicht-sir' is too formal. Try 'Colin.'"

With the ritualistic politeness that Colin had seen in the Stekoni, she bowed to him. "You honor me, Colin. Tea?"

"Thank you." She poured and offered him a cup. He could see the weariness in every motion, as if only her will kept her moving. Her hands trembled slightly, shivering the coppery liquid. She poured for herself and sat back again. As she leaned back, a small golden chain swung at her throat and Colin caught a glimpse of a sphere cut with lines—once he had worn a similar symbol. *That explains it. She's Buntaro. She's in trouble.* The Buntaro had borrowed the sign of the broken sphere from the Obdurate movement—he'd seen it before in the Fringes. Colin wondered about Kiri's limp, wondered about her fatigue. He felt her gaze on him and looked up to see that she smiled, as if she knew his thoughts.

"You own a farship, Colin," she said quietly. "FirstBred Pale tells me that you're having difficulty finding a cargo. She says that you might consider taking passengers so that you can leave Nexus."

"I might," Colin replied. "It depends on where that passenger might be going and how much she'd be willing to pay. It also might depend on how dangerous it is for me to carry her." He sipped his tea and placed the cup carefully back on the tray. "If she were Buntaro and wanted to travel to a Holdings world, I might be accused of aiding anti-Church factions. The Zakkaists could jail me, or worse."

The Stekoni glanced from Kiri to Colin, obviously distressed at the conversation, but Kiri still smiled gently. "You're observant, Colin. I didn't think that many people knew our symbology."

"I'm Galicht. We see all sorts of oddities and hear a lot of gossip. Where'd you hurt your leg?"

Her smile became hard and defensive. Her almond eyes tightened. "It was just an accident, Colin. The same as you, neh?"

"Is that 'accident' going to cause me problems when some customs official looks at your papers? The Zakkaists don't seem to care for MulSendero much at all—and they like the Buntaro even less."

"Why do we have to be going into the Holdings, Colin? I could be going to another Fringe world."

"There's a dozen better ways for you to do that."

Pale had listened with increasing agitation. Now she rose and went to the curtain, lifting it and peering out. Colin watched as Pale glanced about and then let the fabric slide back into place. "Please," Pale began, and she shivered. "This one would not like this conversation to be overheard."

"Why, Pale?" Colin demanded. "Because you know that she's Buntaro? I thought that the Stekoni hated violence. Do you know what this woman's probably done? Bombed a cathedral here or there, incited a riot or two, maybe gunned down some poor priest in the streets. She's a Buntaro, and whoever is against MolitorAb should be eradicated. Isn't that correct, Kiri?"

She had remained calm during the outburst. Her reply matched her demeanor. "You overdramatize, Colin, and you know it. The Buntaro only want what the rest of the MulSendero want—the right to worship as we wish without interference. Anywhere."

"And you'll go to whatever lengths you must to get those rights."

For a second, it seemed that she was going to argue. Then she nodded. "Basically, I suppose that's correct."

"Galicht Fairwood," Pale interjected, "you are right in assuming that no Stekoni would do as the Buntaro. This one has argued your very points with Kiri Oharu. Yet at least she believes in the True Faith. This one has disagreement with her methods although not her basic tenets. You believe in MolitorAb as well, do you not?"

That only increased Colin's irritation. "Do you think I'm a Veil-mad idiot like Naley?"

"Colin," Kiri said, "I don't care that you don't like me, my politics, or my religion. Our arrangement will simply be one of mutual convenience. Will you take us as passengers?"

"Us?"

"Yes. FirstBred Pale and me."

That decided Colin. He rose. "No. You can find another way."

Kiri watched him. Something about the woman intrigued him— the way she seemed unaffected by his appearance, her studied calmness, the quiet intensity with which she drove herself when it was obvious that she needed rest. "Is it simply because I'm Buntaro, Colin?" she said.

His answer was reflex. "No." He didn't elaborate. He couldn't. He didn't know why he'd answered that way—he knew only that her question gigged him and caught on the doubts that had shadowed him these past months. He felt his life was being distorted, twisted to fit some whim, and he did not enjoy the sensation.

Gelt. Gelt and the Voice.

"Why, then, Colin? You don't have to answer, but I'd like to know."

"You'll bring me trouble. It's not that hard to understand. You might not want to do so, but you won't be able to help it."

"How do you know this?" Kiri's voice was suddenly eager, as if she had glimpsed something beyond his words.

"I know it, that's all."

"If FirstBred Pale is right about you, Colin, then you can't avoid trouble."

Quick rage coursed through Colin. Ligaments pulled at skinbase: he turned to glare at the Stekoni. "What have you told her?" he demanded. "What have you been saying about me?"

Pale stuttered, backing against the wall with her hands out in supplication. "Galicht Fairwood, this one—"

Colin didn't wait for the answer. With a guttural curse, he flung aside the curtain and left the cave. He could hear Kiri shouting after him as he made his way down the crumbling rock staircase. "Colin! I'll pay twice the rate! Please!"

He made no answer.

In the room, Kiri stared at Pale accusingly. The Stekoni still kept her spine to the wall. "If this one is right, he will be back. He must be, Kiri Oharu."

Kiri continued to look at her for a long moment, then rose to her feet with a grimace. Limping, she went after Colin.

"Fairwood, what in God's name did you stick under old Kym's ass?"

"What are you talking about, Sarah?"

There were several more pilots in the dormitory of the Galichthouse. Most had glanced up when Colin entered. Sarah was playing cards with several of the other Galicht, all of whom had looked quickly away. "Pair of eights," Sarah said to the group. "Fairwood, go look at the new cargo roster. Your name's at the bottom."

"Damn!" Colin rubbed at his temples. His head was beginning to ache again. *You did it to yourself. If Kym has her way, you'll sit here for an eternity.* "Hell, didn't you say anything to her?"

"Hell," another of the pilots said, mockingly using Colin's tone of voice. "We all want our chance, Fairwood. I'm not going to scream to Kym about your bad luck, not when Nexus is this slow. Three fours, people—and thank you all for betting so generously."

Colin stood there as the pilot scooped in the pile of coins in the center of the table. He longed to vent his anger and knew that he couldn't. He felt trapped, locked into a decision that he didn't want to make. *Are you doing this to me, Gelt?* The thought came unbidden, and he shivered, thrusting it away. *Only the veilmad think such things.*

He turned away from the game and strode over to his bed. He took his bag from the overhead compartment and stuffed his clothing into it. As he passed the table again, he said, "Tell Kym that I've found another way—and I'll be staying on the *Anger* until I leave."

None of them looked up. Sarah was dealing a new hand. When no one said anything, Colin left.

He was only half surprised to find Kiri waiting outside the Galichthouse. She looked at him, then at the bag in his hand. "You have a ride," he said. "For twice the normal rate, right?"

She nodded. When he started to walk away, she fell in alongside him. "You're angry," she said. "Your face is even more telling than most people's. I can see the flush, see how tense your muscles are."

"Good for you."

"If you're so furious, why didn't you confront the master? You were only in the house for five minutes."

Colin took a deep breath. He halted abruptly, letting people jostle and curse their way around them. "What good would it do?"

"You can't get anything without fighting for it."

"Is that official Buntaro policy? I don't happen to believe that."

She said nothing, waiting while the eternal crowds of the city-world pushed around them. The cacophony of Nexus rose and fell, battering at them from the walls and distant roof like a live thing. After a time, Colin began to walk again and Kiri matched steps beside him. "I believed it once," he said. "I fought the Zakkaists for awhile, until I was removed from the scene—it doesn't really matter how. When I came back, I saw that nothing I had tried to correct had been accomplished. The Church was still powerful and arrogant, still ignorant of the teachings of its founders. I think that I stopped wanting to fight then."

"Changes can take a long time, Colin. And you didn't stop caring—your words tell me that. What has passivity gained? Gelt was killed by the Church for preaching of MolitorAb. The Church controls the rich worlds while the Fringes get the leftovers, the marginal places. In the Holdings, you can't hold office unless you're Zakkaist, can't own property, can't be a legal heir, can't speak or say or do anything that might run counter to Church doctrine. You can't openly worship any other God. We won't change all that by allowing it to go on unmolested."

"You won't change it with bombs and guns. Assassination removes a person; it doesn't alter attitudes or affect the laws of the Ascendants. You just make them even more intolerant."

"You let your rage feed on your soul, Colin. You care, you bleed, and you won't let it show. You're holding yourself back and pretending that you're not hurting."

"Is psychology your profession or just a hobby?"

"You see, you joke about it. Look at the people around us, Colin. Don't you see how God-touched we all are? You remember yesterday, all the preaching and praying and open faith in the streets? It was like that everywhere in the Fringes. There haven't been many times like this through history, maybe not since Simon ben Zakkai was preaching, fusing the old faiths. Something will happen soon. It must."

"Ahh, the Buntaro passion. Is that what allows you to blow things up so gleefully?"

"Why do you try so hard to make me dislike you, Colin?"

"It shouldn't be hard for you. You've seen my face."

"And as I said, I find that admirable. It takes courage on your part."

"God, woman..."

He realized then that Kiri had led them through the labyrinth of streets. Colin had not cared—he had only wanted to walk, to move, to put distance between himself and the Galicht-house. Now he saw that they were in the Barrens once more. He could see the cliff dwellings rising behind the nearest buildings. The crowds had thinned slightly; the streets were narrower and even more twisting, the houses shabby. Beggars stretched out open hands to them, indigents slept in the avenues or lay along the maze of stairs leading upward. Kiri had walked past him. Now she looked over her shoulder, her eyes questioning. Colin hefted his bag in his hand and walked after her as she limped up the crumbling steps.

She held the blanket aside for him as they reached her room. "Come in, Colin."

"Why?"

She blinked. "Would you rather go back to the Galicht-house?"

He went inside.

Pale was gone, though her scent still lingered. Kiri went to the back of the room and rummaged in a small trunk. "Would you like more tea?"

"Fine."

She brought back the cups, handed him his, and sat on the floor facing him. Colin studied her face as she pursed her lips to blow steam from her tea and sipped. "Why did you say that about my face?" he asked.

She glanced at him over the rim of the cup. "Because it was true. I thought you might like to know it. I doubt that most people think about it in that way."

"You're either lying or very unusual."

She didn't respond to that. She set her cup on the wooden slats that were the floor of the cave and moved closer to him. On her knees, she reached out and softly traced the lines where flesh met skinbase. Colin started to turn his face away, then forced himself to allow her slow examination. When she had finished, she sat back on her haunches again. "How did it happen?"

"How doesn't matter much. But the Church was responsible—the Zakkaists."

"Colin..." She covered one of his hands with hers, lacing fingers with him. "You and I are more alike than you want to pretend. I can feel your hurt."

"No, you can't," he said. He realized how curt that sounded and tried to soften the gruffness with explanation. "What happened to me isn't understandable unless you've been through it. Sometime I might tell you that story. Not now." Her hand was still caught in his, and a warmth seemed to spread from it. He wanted to be closer to her and at the same time wanted to snatch his hand away from her embrace. Colin was not used to affection; he felt clumsy with it, never knowing how to react—it was too rare. He didn't know what Kiri wanted of him and didn't know how to ask, didn't know what to do. "Most people just don't *want* to understand," he said. "They think that they already do."

She said nothing. Her jet eyes stared at him and did not look away. Colin averted his gaze. He did not understand what happened next.

Kiri reached out and drew his head to hers. He stiffened against her touch for an instant and he felt her begin to let him go. Then he willed himself to relax. Her head tilted; her lips parted slightly. Her eyes watched him as their lips touched. The kiss was tentative and very gentle; they drew back, their gazes questioning, searching. Kiri leaned forward again and this time she was hungrier, demanding.

"Why?" he asked when they broke apart. He knew that to question her was somehow wrong, but she only smiled.

"Some things you should learn not to ask," she said. Her arms went around him and she pulled him to her. Colin responded, his rising excitement a dark heat. Her hands traced his spine, circled his waist, and brushed between his legs. He felt himself responding, his own hands stroking the shallow curve of her breasts. He fumbled with her clothing and she laughed under his mouth. "Here," she said. She touched her throat and her blouse parted. She stood away from him and unbuckled her pants, letting them fall and stepping out of them. She seemed shy as she stood before him naked. Her body was thinner than Colin had thought, with boyish hips and small breasts. A mottled bruise purpled one thigh and he now knew why she limped; a long, discolored scar furrowed its way from just below her right breast to her left hip, puckering the skin. Her chin lifted a little, almost in defiance, as he looked at her. Colin reached out and took her hands, pulling him down to her. He kissed her, caressed her, and felt her response. Her neck arched back and a long, throaty sigh escaped her. "You're overdressed," she whispered.

She helped him to struggle from his clothing, then rolled onto the floor, bringing him on top of her. She held him, guiding him into her fluid warmth, and hugged him with her arms and legs. He began to move with her.

And, inexplicably, the excitement left him. Suddenly. He could not explain it. It was simply gone as if it had never been there. She felt it as well, for she held him tighter and put her lips to his ear. "Ssshh, Colin. Don't worry. Here, lay back. Close your eyes and stop thinking." She rolled on top of him, moved lower.

After a few minutes, Colin gently pushed her aside. "Kiri, forget it," he said gruffly. "Thank you for trying."

"You give up too easily."

"I know myself."

"You're certain?"

He nodded. "Yes." She knelt beside him, brushing her hair back with one hand. There was tension between them now—he could feel it growing and he cursed himself. "It's not you," he said.

"I know. Want to talk?"

"No." His answer was emphatic. He wanted only to be away from here, away from the situation and the embarrassment. "I should go to my ship."

"You don't need to. You can stay with me for the night—you make the rules. We can talk, we can cuddle, we can try again, or just sleep. Whatever you want."

"I can't. I have to get the berthing papers for the *Anger,* register the flight with Port Authority, check the Veil reports." He knew that he was making too many excuses: he could not look her in the eyes. *You're such a lousy liar, Colin. Why do you try?*

As if she had sensed his thoughts, she stroked his chest. "Why are you running away from me, Colin?"

The question struck his guilt and sparked anger. He scowled, brushing her hand away and sitting up. "I guess I might wonder why you bothered with this. Do you want to make sure that you still have the ride, or is it just for the novelty? You didn't have to, you know—the only payment I demand of you is cash." He said the words knowing that they were a mistake, a foolish attempt to placate his fury with himself.

She was calm, almost sad. "Colin, why can't you believe that someone would be willing to give you affection simply because they think that they might like you?"

"You don't know me at all. We didn't meet until today."

"Sometimes you know just that quickly. I think both of us are lonely people—affection is too rare for each of us."

"You don't have to make excuses, Buntaro. You still have your pilot."

He could see tears forming in the corners of her eyes. Kiri shook her head and padded silently to the back of the room. Taking a robe from a hook on the wall, she sat, knees to her chest. He could feel her gaze on him as he dressed and went to the entrance. The world-roar of Nexus howled at him as he lifted the curtain. He glanced back at her, caught in shrouded twilight. There were a hundred things for him to say and he could speak none of them.

He said nothing therefore. He left.

Jasper Keller liked holding the originals of the Geltian scripture. Written on cheap paper in ordinary Galicht logbooks, still they never failed to impress him. Hallan Gelt's handwriting was small and spiky, half printing and half cursive; quirky, like the man. Most amazing to Keller was the absence of cross-outs or errors despite the historical evidence that the text had been written in only a few days. The words simply flowed, unbroken. To Keller, that was in itself one of the most compelling reasons to believe the Scripture to be divinely inspired. He glanced down at the page opened in front of him.

They will speak against you, saying that you act only from the darkness of hatred. Tell them that night and day are but phantoms. One can move from twilight to dawn simply by standing still. Thus can hatred become love.

MolitorAb, speaking to the Sartius Exori to come, if one believed the scholarly interpretation. Keller had experienced veildreams him-self, but the breadth of Gelt's vision awed him. He closed the book and his eyes, trying to remember the sound of the Voice.

Jasper Keller was Primus of the MulSendero faith—head of the human faithful, at least until such time as the Sartius Exori revealed himself. Keller sat at his desk in the cathedral on Secundus. The planet was a Stekoni world, the gravity too light for Keller's taste, the air overlaid with a brassy smell that mixed unpleasantly with the odor of the Stekoni themselves. Keller could taste the contam-ination even in his offices where the air was heavily filtered. Out-side, he could not breathe it long without becoming ill. The nasal inserts helped. Even so, his sinuses seemed to be eternally dripping.

A small penance to bear, I know, MolitorAb. But one I would gladly forgo.

Someone knocked. Keller opened his eyes and sniffed. "A mo-ment," he said. He picked up Gelt's logbook, placed it back with the others, and reactivated the shields of the Repositorium. A brief flicker of purplish light sterilized the papers once more. Keller smoothed his orange robes and ran a knobby hand through gray-speckled hair.

"Come in," he said.

A Stekoni bowed her way to him, her fur marbled with the brown and yellow pattern of the priest caste, the loincloth wrapped in the style of the Third Darkness family. A fledgling peered with sleepy eyes from one of the young-pouches. The priest began, "This one begs your pardon, Primus Keller, but a message has arrived which this one felt would interest you." She remained in the bow, head down.

"Thank you, GoldenShell Third Darkness. Please, not so formal here, remember? What's this message?"

The priest straightened. "Excuse this one, Primus. You must think this one a stupid male who has no idea how to properly behave. Here is the message." She handed Keller an infocap. He broke open the seal and scanned the scroll of thin paper that unrolled from the capsule. "You read this?" he said.

"Yes."

"And what are your thoughts?"

The priest seemed upset at Keller's abruptness, so unlike the polite circuitousness of the Stekoni. She squinted, pushing the head of her fledgling down into the young-pouch as if she didn't want it to hear. "FirstBred Pale is eager—all Pales are: that's their weakness. They speak too quickly, and a Pale is liable to exaggerate in her enthusiasm. Still..." She paused, and Keller glanced up from the scroll.

"Still?" he prompted. "You know that this one values your opinions, GoldenShell Third Darkness. The thoughts of any Third Darkness must be given reflection and savored. Please..."

The Stekoni seemed mollified and Keller hid the smile that tugged at his lips. *We all have our vanities, the Stekoni no less than humans.* GoldenShell bowed slightly to Keller.

"This one is pleased that you honor her so, Primus Keller. As to this matter, it can only be good that the Nexian Pretender has dispersed his following and that FirstBred Pale witnessed the altercation between Mad One Naley and this Galicht Colin Fairwood immediately prior to that dispersion. Whether the two have any direct connection or not is unclear and speculative, despite FirstBred Pale's assumptions. Certainly the incident in the tavern was unspectacular, even ordinary. Remember too that FirstBred Pale was equally impressed by Roland Naley at *his* first appearance."

"You're saying that we can only wait."

She seemed to smile. Her hands patted the fledgling's head.

"This one believes that FirstBred Pale's intuitions are to be taken with suitable caution but not to be entirely discounted."

Keller nodded. He moved across the room to where the Scriptures were displayed. Running a hand along the shelves of the Repositorium, he could feel the prickling of the shield on his skin. "At least Roland Naley has renounced his claim. That certainly doesn't displease me. His leaning was too Buntarist."

"The Buntaro believe in the teachings of MolitorAb, Primus. They are part of our fold, no matter what their politics."

Keller turned to look at the Stekoni, whose large eyes, built to see in a dimmer light than those of humankind, stared back at him. Keller was always surprised that the Stekoni were so placid about the Buntaro. It made no sense in a creature whose first impulse on confronting violence was to respond with flight. Seeing Golden-Shell's calmness, he wondered as he often had before how much of the Stekoni psychology humanity had simply failed to comprehend. *Surely we would not have so gladly given the Stekoni our technology and our help had we been the ones to come to them instead of the other way around. We would have been suspicious and threatening. And in moments of weakness—forgive me, MolitorAb—I also wonder if that means that we fail to understand You, who came first to them.*

"I know, one cannot understand the infinite, and You are part of all the old gods," he whispered to himself.

"Primus Keller?"

"Nothing. Nothing, my friend. What do we know of this Colin Fairwood?"

"Very little, Primus Keller. FirstBred Pale had told us that the man is a Galicht as was Hallan Gelt and that he has a terrible facial disfigurement, which Fairwood claims was the work of the Zakkaists. Like other Galicht, he has run contraband and been in trouble with Holdings and Fringe officials. Most strange is that Fairwood was rescued from a crippled farship in '41, before he became Galicht. He has since claimed to be time-dilated, though to what extent we cannot know. He also claims to have known Gelt."

"Given the time dilation, I suppose that's possible—or even without, if he is old enough."

"He is not."

Keller nodded. "What of his religion?"

GoldenShell gave the shiver that was a Stekoni shrug. "That is not known. He is certainly neither Zakkaist nor any of the proscribed human religions, but that does not make him MulSendero. This one has been unable to discover what Colin Fairwood's theological leanings might be."

"So for the time being, he's simply another of the Pretenders."

"Less than that, Primus Keller, if this one may be permitted to disagree. He has no following. He does not proclaim himself as Sartius Exori, does not even profess to our faith. He is simply FirstBred Pale's infatuation. This one brought the report to your attention only because of the Nexian Pretender's abdication. Otherwise, this one would have said nothing."

Keller smiled. He had hated Naley and his wrathful screamings, his brawling and his dirtiness. Keller had prayed to MolitorAb that Naley not be the One. *He was not a leader I would have cared to follow, though I would have done so had You said that I must, MolitorAb. Thank You for Your wisdom in humbling Mad One Naley.* "We must continue to be patient, GoldenShell Third Darkness."

"The Stekoni have always been patient, Primus. When one deals with aggressiveness by waiting for the correct situation to arise, one learns much about that art." She stroked her fledgling; it crooned nonsense syllables to her.

Primus Keller gazed appraisingly at the alien. "Yes, I suppose you do," he said.

CHAPTER SIX

Write down, therefore, whatever you see in visions—what you see now and will see in time to come.

NEW TESTAMENT, Revelation 1:19

The Testament of Aaron *relates that "after vanquishing the Pretender of Nexus, the Sartius Exori began to preach, gaining a thousand disciples among the populace. From his power came a hundred signs and healings, and there was a great lament when he departed." (Aaron 1:24–26) The MulSendero interpretation of this passage is that the author of the testament was using apocalyptic numerical symbology, a "thousand" signifying a multitude. Surely, taking into account the low Nexian population at the time, a thousand was more likely to be a hundred. Close examination of the remaining Nexian literature of the time indicates that the author of* Aaron *was even more biased than the MulSendero scholars believe. I am of the opinion that the Sartius Exori's preaching took place privately before small, sympathetic congregations. The total number of converts was probably no more than twenty or thirty at that time.*

MYTH AND FACT IN MULSENDERO GOSPEL,
Hassim al' Kimar, Ph.D.

A Veil passage is a journey through a dream state. It is individualistic and existential. A hundred papers have been written theorizing why the human and Stekoni minds react as they do to the disturbing stimuli of the non-Einsteinian continuum. Galicht pilots have always read such treatises for their amusement value. Like all who travel the Veils frequently, they know that the passage will mark you or not, will leave you sane or not, will be pleasant or not. All that is simply up to the whim of MolitorAb or Allah or Jahweh or Christ or Fate. Explanations do not matter: the neural pathways are disrupted by nonrelativistic particles, thus loosing a flood of hallucinatory free associations; (or conversely) the mind simply cannot cope without the bondage of time-locked logic and thus becomes briefly insane; (or) There Is Another World Beyond This One.

Whatever.

If you want to travel between the suns with any speed, you must use the Veils. There is no other way without time distortion. Colin knew that too well.

Nexus was gone behind them, its scant gravity well forgotten. FirstBred Pale and Kiri Oharu shared the cabin with Colin, the Stekoni in a jury-rigged isolette in one corner. They had hardly spoken on the way out. Colin hadn't looked up from his module when they came aboard but had spoken over his shoulder. "Chebar's where you want to go—is that still correct?"

"Yes," Kiri had said. He would not look at her. Pale put a sympathetic hand on her shoulder. Kiri smiled at her and limped back to her webbing.

What followed were two days of stiff politeness and avoidance. The situation pleased no one. Colin was glad when he could key the coordinates into the computer and extend the Veil attenuators from the craft. He had begun to dread these insertions into the Veils, into the world where Gelt and the Voice lurked—*maybe this one will at least be quiet and peaceful. Please, MolitorAb.* He took the sticky tangle of probes and touched them to his forehead. A klaxon sounded. Colin fixed his eyes on the controls. With an effort, he let down the barriers to his mind. Somewhere in the heart of the *Anger*, machinery responded.

The ship shuddered.

Melted.

Colin fell away into a storm.

Lightning tore at him, winds shrieked past. Cold, wet clouds rushed through him and he was...somewhere. There was a deck firm beneath his feet and his face was a burning agony. "No," he moaned in pain and denial. He reached up to touch the shreds of flesh separating from bone, the skin and muscles there charred like overcooked steak. Warm fluid slicked his fingers—he could not believe he was still alive, still able to see and talk and hear. *The priest did it. The priest with sorrow in his eyes and steel in his hands. The priest who had cried out in his own anguish as he did this thing to you.*

It was starting again. Sobbing, Colin began to scream.

"Vector 3.8," a voice said. A wall sped toward them. His breath coming ragged and fast, his heart pounding in his chest, his eyes half-blind with tears, Colin forced himself to leave the dream. *You're on the* Anger. *Fly her.* The ship bucked under him, turned away from the wall. He sighed and let himself fall.

He fell into a darkness that was not darkness but shadows twisting and writhing. The tendrils merged and flowed, becoming a face: Hallan Gelt. "Go away! Leave me alone!" Colin shouted, but he was being pulled toward the face faster and faster. It was huge. Red scarves of blood flowed down the mountains of Gelt's cheeks, a stale and fetid odor welled from the drooling, open mouth, and thick vomit dripped ponderously from the chin. "The Church did this to me, Colin, as they did to you. Why do you deny our kinship, my friend? Colin who was James, you are the one. Open yourself to MolitorAb."

"*No!* It's not me. Choose someone else."

"You," the mouth whispered.

"I deny you, Hallan." Colin stared in fascination at the bloody froth on Gelt's lips—moving closer, ever closer. Colin spoke faster, the words tumbling over themselves. "You could have made up the tales, Hallan. You could have gone veilmad."

"You're not mad, Colin/James."

"I'm *not!*"

"You only argue with yourself."

"How can I believe you when I know how much you hated the Zakkaists? You were just a man, Hallan. No prophet, no seer."

Gelt laughed then, blood and spittle spattering Colin. Gelt's mouth gaped, larger and larger, and Colin fell into the black maw.

"Vector 5.3." The words rumbled in the darkness. Glowing blue threads began to snarl around him. Colin shook himself, thought, and the farship coalesced underneath him once more, twisting between the lines of blue.

"Well done," she said. Kiri's hands came around him. She was naked, the scar somehow gone from her body. The warmth of her fired his lust. Her neck arched back for him as he reached for her. He kissed her hard. Sighing, he drew back for a moment. Her eyes were closed. He ran a fingertip along the line of her eyebrows and she opened her eyes. She looked at him.

She screamed.

Furious, Colin flung her away from him. She slapped at him. "Vector 9.7," she howled. Fires arced from her fingertips, enveloping him, burning. "You have nothing!" she shrilled. "Why can't you take what is offered to you?"

"It's madness! It's false!" he yelled back. The *Anger* came back around him. He could hear the wailing of a Voice, a lament in all audible registers, and he felt the ship vibrate in response to that sound. Colin willed the craft to go the other way, to where the Voice was not.

Stars slammed into place around him. The veildream slid away, fading.

Colin opened his eyes. He was covered in sweat. He breathed.

In the monitor in front of him, the small disk of a sun burned. A fleck of light pulsed nearby, where no light should have been.

Whenever Ascendant Joseph Culper walked into the subbasement level of the security wing of New York Cathedral, he was reminded of the time when Hallan Gelt had resided there. Culper had been a brash novitiate then, his vows newly taken and his guidance entrusted to the harsh disciplines of the late Ascendant Caliri, then prelate of New York and already curator of justice. Culper had come to the security wing at the order of Caliri. He had entered Gelt's cell to be confronted by the sight of the prelate, his sleeves rolled up past his elbows and his cassock stained with sweat above the swell of his paunch. Caliri was striking Gelt, seated before him: open-handed, back and forth. *Slap! Slap!* The sound of the blows was rhythmic. Gelt's features were almost unrecognizable, the eyes nearly swollen shut, his cheeks gashed from Caliri's rings, the lips torn and bloody. Gelt's head wobbled.

Culper had stopped in the doorway, horrified. Caliri had turned to him, and his hands were stained to the wrist with Gelt's blood. "I want you to see this, Joseph," he had said to Culper. "I want you to see how the Church's work must sometimes be done, as distasteful as it must seem. Hallan Gelt holds a billion souls in his corrupt hands, Joseph. If we let him do as he wishes, he will stain all those souls in God's eyes. If we jail him, his presence will steal from behind those bars like a demon, infecting all who come in contact with it. Hallan Gelt is a disease, a virus that must be stamped out. He is now even more lost than he was as an Obdurate." Caliri had paused, looking at the battered man somehow still sitting upright in the chair. Gelt's lips had moved, but he'd said nothing. "It would be easier and more pleasing to simply do as we are allowed by Church law, Joseph. We could commit his soul to the judgement of God and execute him quickly. But we must take the larger view. One day you might be curator of justice. You might need to make the same kind of decision I've made. If I could have Gelt renounce his tales of MolitorAb, have him admit his sins in espousing the

MulSendero heresy, think of the good that would have been done. Think of the souls brought back into the fold of the Church to be cleansed. Joseph," the heavy voice continued as Culper stared, "don't be appalled by my methods. Don't think me barbaric. The crude ways, the old ways, still work best. In this, terror is God's ally."

Culper had nodded, speechless, not truly comprehending, still dazed by the violence he had just seen. Caliri shook his jowled head at him. "I know that this is hopeless, Joseph, yet I must still make the attempt, must still bear the guilt for my acts. A small sin can pay for a larger good. In the judgement of God, I will be atoned. No, Gelt will not repent—I know that in my heart. But we must try. We must try."

We must try. Caliri had been correct. Gelt had remained stubborn despite all Caliri's promptings. In the end, the Church had decided that an "accidental" death at the hands of another inmate would be best, avoiding the necessity of a trial and Gelt's appearance as a martyr.

Gelt had been killed. Culper had watched it.

The subbasement always stank of fear to him, despite the fact that the area was meticulously cleansed by the maintenance staff. Scrubbed, disinfected, polished: the maze of corridors should have exuded an aroma of sterility.

No. There was always a stench, as if the pheromones of hysteria had sunk deep into the concrete.

The guard outside opened cell door 5 for Culper, the locks grating. A young priest glanced up from her book, her mouth still moving with the words of the Prophet Simon. "'...for He will welcome the worst of sinners into His arms if that sinner comes with repentance in his heart. Even the foulest...' Good evening, Ascendant."

"Good evening, Mother Crowell," he replied. "Anna, has our Mr. Ott shown any signs of *his* repentance?"

Crowell half smiled, sadly. "I'm afraid not, Ascendant."

Culper looked at the prisoner. Ott lay on a tongue of concrete extruded from the wall. His hands were manacled to a ring set above his head, his feet to another ring. Only a rattan mattress separated him from the cold cement. Ott stared back at Culper in defiance— dark Mediterranean eyes, a hawkish nose, the bony face covered with the dark stubble of a new beard. "You've been reading Simon to him, Anna?"

"Every day, Ascendant, and we pray for his soul nightly." Her smile became rueful. "In truth, I pray alone, I'm afraid. Our guest won't join me—he still insists that his God is MolitorAb."

"His God is death and destruction and the devil, Mother Crowell." Culper spoke more to the prisoner than to the priest. "That is what the Buntaro worship."

"Spare me the lecture, Ascendant," Ott said. His voice was raspy and weak. "I get them at regular intervals from this priest of yours."

"You should be grateful. You're well attended by her. I'm told that your treatment has been fair, and yet you refuse us the two small things that we desire. One temporal request, one spiritual request. Tell us who your compatriots are here on Old Earth, and join us in the peace of God—the *true* God. In time, once your debt to those you've wronged has been paid, you will go free—a man cleansed in body and soul. That's a good vision, isn't it? You would walk among the faithful in a world full of God's mercy."

"I'd rather cut off my ears than listen to that drivel, Ascendant. Your words are all sugar-coated crap."

Culper shook his head sadly. He sighed dramatically. "Mother Crowell, would you please leave us?"

Crowell bowed and gathered up her books. She knocked on the door for the guard. Culper waited, hands clasped behind his back, until the solid metal door had clanged shut again. Then he moved across the room to stand beside Ott, gazing down at the man. "You truly grieve me, Ott. You could save lives with your cooperation. You could do so much good, yet you consistently refuse. We've treated you well; why don't you reciprocate?"

Silence.

Culper reached out with one strong hand. His fingertips traced the manacled wrist of Ott, moved along the pinioned hand until he had Ott's forefinger in his fist. He jerked Ott's finger toward the back of the man's hand. He smiled at Ott's sudden intake of breath, at the frightened widening of his eyes. "Yes," he murmured, his voice a gentle whisper. "That is painful, isn't it? That's just the *smallest* of what could await you if you don't repent, Ott. There can be no torment here on Earth that can match what you'll find in the afterlife, but I assure you that I can give you a hell here that, in your folly, will make you scream for a release into that eternal punishment."

Ott started to speak, but Culper put more pressure on the strained finger. Ott arched his back, trying to ease the tension on the joint. He writhed, beads of sweat beginning to stand out on his forehead, his jaws clenched against the pain. "It would be so easy, Ott. All you need do is talk. Ease the burden of your conscience. Spill out that poison you hold. There's nothing difficult about that, nothing awful." More pressure, and a whimper forced its way from Ott's throat, a low keening of agony. Culper let the finger up slightly, and Ott gasped in relief. "Will you talk?" Culper asked.

The man's eyes glared hatred. Culper shrugged. He suddenly wrenched back the finger with all his strength. There was a sharp *crack* like a dead twig being snapped, and the finger dangled at a grotesque angle. Ott screamed; his body quivered. Culper could smell urine; there was a dampness between Ott's legs. Culper walked calmly toward the door as Ott began to sob, his eyes squeezed shut. "I'll be back, Ott. Every once in a while. If you haven't already spoken to Mother Crowell, I'll ask you these same questions again, with the same kind of inducement. Think about that."

"You're a monster! You enjoy this!" Ott cried.

Culper smiled beatifically. "No, I don't. I hate it. I abhor it as any good churchgoer would. Can't you tell? It's simply that I must bow to necessity. So must you, Ott. So must you. If I were you, I'd pray for guidance. Pray to *God*, Ott."

Culper rapped on the door. As it swung open, he nodded to Mother Crowell, waiting outside in the corridor. "You might notify the doctor on call that our Mr. Ott has suffered a slight accident. Talk to him as well, Anna. I sense that he's starting to see the error in his thinking." He nodded as Mother Crowell bowed. As she went inside the cell, he gestured to the guard to close and lock the door again.

He took the elevator to the ground level of the cathedral. Culper was pleased; pleased to be leaving the subbasement and its foul atmosphere, pleased that Ott had proven to be so easily manipulated. Gelt had never broken, but Ott would.

Culper thought about the ugly snapping of bone, of the rictus of pain that had twisted Ott's features.

He smiled. He promised himself that he would pray to God tonight to forgive him the small pleasure that moment had brought.

Colin knew too quickly what that flickering of light outside the *Anger* signified—the intersystem drive of a Holdings naval cruiser. The hailing frequency clicked open even as Colin shook his head to dispel the mists of veildreams.

"This is Commander Eric Blaine of the cruiser *Bright Faith*. Prepare to be boarded, *Anger*. Shut down all system drives immediately. Is that understood, Galicht Fairwood?"

Colin slammed a fist on the arm of his chair. "This is getting too familiar." He glared at Kiri, who gazed at him placidly. "I thought you said there'd be no problems," he said.

"I'd ask you how your veildreams were, Colin, but I can see by your reactions that you were disturbed by them. I'm sorry."

Colin began to retort, then turned away with a curse. *Talk about it later, if you must. You're not veilmad. You're not.* Colin touched the contact for the com. *"Anger* here, *Bright Faith.* Shutting down all drive systems as requested."

"That's it, Galicht. Be a good little boy."

"Uh-huh." Colin let his hand drop from the panel. "Shit," he breathed.

"This one wonders what we can do," Pale said from the isolette. The Stekoni looked impossibly terrified, her overlarge eyes wider than normal, the mouth open to show the huge molars.

"We can't do a thing, Pale. Nothing. We'll let them board and poke around all they want, and we'll pray that your friend here has papers that will pass inspection."

Kiri pulled an identidisk from her breast pocket. "This would have cost you a month's wages," she said quietly. "They're supposed to be excellent. I can't find any fault with them."

"You're not going to be the one looking at them."

"Why are you so agitated?" she asked Colin. "They can't touch you. All they can do is arrest me."

"Right. What utopia are you living in?"

He could nearly see the small reflection of himself in her eyes. Colin put his attention elsewhere.

"Who did you see in the Veils, Colin?" she persisted.

"Nobody. Nothing at all," he shot back at her. He knew that his voice was too loud, too irritable.

She could see his fears. She gazed at the openness of his face. She said nothing. For Colin, it was enough.

The boarders were a sallow-faced lieutenant and two marines— no clergy, though all of them wore the prominent triangle of Zakkai on their collars. When they looked at Colin, he could see expressions of disgust. Colin heard the whisper of one of the marines to his companion: "God, if he can't get it fixed, he could at least have the decency to wear a mask." When Colin glared, the marine simply grinned back at him and hefted his weapon significantly.

"Jesus, it stinks in here," the lieutenant said. "Can't you tell that your isolette's leaking?" He flipped through Colin's papers, threw them back at Colin.

"Sorry, Lieutenant"—Colin glanced at the name tag on the uniform—"Espara. I didn't notice."

"That surgery foul up your sense of smell too?" Espara snickered at his own joke; the marines laughed.

"Not that I know of."

Espara gave Colin a strange look that told him the lieutenant was hoping for an excuse to make trouble. *Say the wrong thing and he'll loose the two trained dogs on you.* Espara held out his hand to Kiri, who gave the lieutenant her identidisk. "Why did you stop me, Lieutenant?" Colin asked as gently as he could. He didn't want Espara's full attention on the identidisk, not in the man's current mood. "Is it policy now to stop all Galicht going into the Holdings?"

Espara flicked a glance at Colin. "Commander Blaine always checks when someone's paid two violations several months late— you never know what a desperate pilot might be tempted to haul. Some of them would even haul a lousy Stekoni."

Espara shoved the identidisk back at Kiri. The way the lieutenant turned his attention to Pale, across the cabin, made Colin shiver with a sudden chill. *By MolitorAb, he's a frigging bigot with an axe to grind against the Stekoni. Now what?* Espara stalked across the cabin to the isolette, the two smiling marines strolling behind the officer. Espara wrinkled his nose in an exaggerated fashion as he stood, hands on hips, before the isolette. He reached through the barrier of static-charged air, palm up. "Let's see 'em," he said gruffly.

Pale's hands flitted to her waist, touching the young-pouches in a reflexive Stekoni gesture. "This one will get them, Lieutenant Espara. A moment—"

"This one probably doesn't have them." Espara stepped fully through the barrier, roughly grasping the fur at Pale's shoulder. He shoved her back against her webbing, and Pale squawked in surprise. Espara held out his hand, which now shone with oil. "Jesus, you're worse than most," he said. "Search her good," he waved to the guards.

"Hey, she said she'd get the papers," Colin protested.

Espara whirled around and what Colin saw in the man's eyes made his stomach knot. "Shut up," the lieutenant said, his voice low and menacing.

Kiri was nearer to the officer. As Espara began to turn back to Pale, she grasped at his arm. "Leave her alone," she hissed. "Pale has your damn documents—just give her a chance."

Espara snarled. His arm moved in a quick arc, pinning Kiri's hand and twisting. Kiri cried out at the sudden pain and Espara flung her aside. She fell hard against the control panel near Colin, gashing her head on a corner of the equipment. Sprawling on the deck, she held her hand to her temple, blood flowing between her fingers. Pale, in the rough grasp of the marines, howled shrilly, and one of the men cuffed her.

Colin moved without thinking. He lunged for a side panel in the wall of the ship, punched at the contact, and took what was inside. *"Enough!"* he shouted.

Everyone turned to the Galicht. Colin was holding a battered weapon, and the flanged barrel pointed directly at Espara's stomach. "Off my ship, Lieutenant," he said. "Now."

Espara shook his head, hatred smoldering in his gaze. "Do you have any idea of what you're doing, Galicht? You can't threaten me like this."

"I just did."

"Fairwood, when I make my report to Commander Blaine, he'll impound this piece of junk, maybe even turn you into a little cloud of gas particles. You can still get out of this mistake by putting that thing down and letting me finish my job here."

From the corner of his eye, Colin could see Kiri. She was staring at Colin, blood trickling down the side of her face, her emotions hidden as always. She watched, impassive. Colin hesitated, wondering what impulse had caused him to act so rashly. *You could have stayed out of it. They'd have roughed up Pale, maybe at worst given her a broken arm or so. Nothing permanent. You could have let it happen and been safe.*

Now it was too late.

"You've done all that you need to do," he said. "Get back to your cruiser." Espara didn't move. *"Now!"* Colin barked.

Espara shrugged and nodded to the marines. They let go of Pale and moved behind the officer. For a moment, Colin thought that Espara was going to charge at him, calling his bluff and forcing Colin to make a crucial decision. He could see Espara hesitating, weighing the odds. Then the man jerked his head toward the lock and their shuttle. "Let's go," he said to his men. "We'll let the commander deal with him." As he passed near Colin, he paused. "You're an ugly, stupid fool," he said. "But I doubt that you have much longer to worry about it."

Colin was shaking after they left. The cabin was fetid with the smell of Pale's fear. "This one thanks you," Pale said to Colin.

"For what, Pale? I just gave you very good odds of meeting MolitorAb a little prematurely."

Kiri had gotten to her feet. She leaned against the control module. "You did what you needed to do. Most people just let the Zakkaists do as they please."

"Sometimes that's the best way. And you keep talking about the Zakkaists as if they're evil. They're not—most of them aren't any better or worse than any of us. I was stupid. Stupid."

"We'll protest at Chebar Port, Colin. You know that what they were doing was beyond even Holdings law."

"That's fine, *if* we get the chance." Colin ran a thumb along the skinbase of his neck—warm, slick—and stared at the monitor where the distant bulk of the *Bright Faith* blotted out the stars. "No chance," he said as if to himself. "Our drive's shut down—not that it makes any difference. Damn, this commander should have done *some*thing by now."

Yet there was no sign of a response from the cruiser for several more minutes. Colin waited with mounting frustration and apprehension. Kiri placidly tended to her cut and then sat on the deck in a lotus position. Pale paced the borders of her isolette, chattering to herself in one of the Stekoni dialects.

Finally the voice came. "Fairwood?"

"Here."

"This is Commander Blaine. You're cleared to dock at Chebar Port."

"Commander—" Colin began wonderingly.

"That's all, Fairwood." Blaine's voice was harsh edged, as if the words he spoke choked him. "Be satisfied with that, Galicht— I could have turned your farship into garbage."

"Thank you, commander." Colin leaned back in his chair. Pale and Kiri stared at him, but he said nothing to them then; nor did he speak until the *Anger* was docked two days later. Then he had just one thing to say to them.

"Get off my ship," he said. Very slowly and distinctly.

CHAPTER SEVEN

Had it been Allah's will, He could have made them all of one religion. But Allah brings whom He will into His mercy; the wrong-doers have none to befriend or help them.

KORAN, Counsel 42:8

And the Galicht Master said to him, "Are you the One?" For truly the Master was uncertain. "I am," the Sartius Exori replied. Thus on Chebar was the task begun.

THE TESTAMENT OF AARON, 2:4

Chebar was one of the first worlds settled after Stekoni technology had unlocked the stars for humanity. As with most of the settled worlds of the Holdings or Fringes, Chebar had vast expanses of empty land. A few cities dotted the continents, and there most of the population could be found.

In two centuries, a city can begin to show age. Christos, the capital of Chebar, was a rude cross between frontier town, river town, and sophisticated urban center. Her income was dependent on offworld trade—through Chebar Port—and the custom of those exploiting the riches of the interior. Christos had much in common with similar towns throughout history: most of the inhabitants knew each other perhaps too well, there was a rough edge to the city's urbanity, and gossip traveled very quickly.

Colin had been glad to see the last of Pale and Kiri. He told himself that he was well rid of them, that this strange episode in his life was over. The customs inspection of the *Anger* had been rigorously thorough, almost harsh, though within the limits of the Holdings law. Colin had made no move to protest the unfriendly and brusque treatment. He had simply absorbed the insults in silence, swallowing any irritation he might have felt. If he heard whispered comments, he said nothing. The people swarming over his ship seemed far too eager to have Colin make an offensive move.

It took him six hours to move from the berthing slips through the various gauntlets between the port authority and the streets.

The Galicht house was a forbidding structure in the decaying center of Christos. The town had expanded to the west, leaving this original sector of the city to wallow in a slow disintegration. The house seemed to be an old warehouse converted to its new purpose; its high windows now bricked up, its mortar flaking like snow between blocks of dull native sandstone, it stood squarish and dull. Colin went into a dim foyer stuffed with shabby furniture. Someone was sitting on one of the chairs, a leg draped over the frayed cloth of the armrest. Colin could see nothing of the person's head: it was wreathed in coiling blue-white streaks of lightning—a neural damper. Colin smelled the sharpness of ozone, heard tiny, high cracklings.

"Hey," he called out. "Who's master here? Still Hobsworth?"

A form within the globe of lightning turned. The stormy sphere died with the motion of an arm, and a slack-mouthed narrow face regarded Colin from within a cage of snarled golden wires. Slowly, the mouth closed and gray eyes blinked. There was the sound of an indrawn breath. "Fairwood?"

"Still addicted, I see, Master Hobsworth."

"There's little else to do here, Fairwood. You're too used to the Fringes." Hobsworth got to his feet groaning and came toward Colin. He was tall, stick thin, and walked with a self-conscious slouch. An undergrowth of stubble forested pocked cheeks. "The Galicht get only the dregs here, my boy. Why the hell do you think you pilots avoid the fucking place? All you're going to get from me is crap that the big freighters don't want to bother with." Hobsworth canted his head to one side, looking at Colin with narrowed eyes, then letting his gaze drop. "You took a hell of a chance out there, Fairwood. One would almost think that you knew what you were doing, though, the way it turned out."

"So you've heard already."

"Long before you got out of the port authority. I understand that a lot of the MulSendero are talking about it too. I can't understand why you're still alive, m'boy. Almost makes me half believe some of what I've heard in the last few weeks."

"What have you heard?"

Hobsworth wouldn't look Colin in the eyes. One hand, splotched with dark liver spots, toyed with the wires around his head. "You can't tell me that you don't know."

Colin shook his head warily. "That's exactly what I'm telling you. Why don't you enlighten me?"

"Hey, I remember last time you were here—you used to talk about knowing Gelt, didn't you?"

"I knew him." Colin nodded. "So did you—you've been around long enough. What about it?"

"And he's come to you in veildreams?"

Colin made a disgusted noise, scowling. "Look, Master Hobsworth, I swear I'm not veilmad. You can't help what you see in the Veils. I *don't* claim that I've really talked to Gelt, if that's what you're implying. I'm perfectly competent—"

"No one's saying that you're not, Fairwood." Hobsworth looked to his left, apparently to examine the raveled nap of his chair. "I'm just saying some of what I've heard. Me, I'm Zakkaist—that's easiest here. But half the Galicht that come through are MulSendero, so I hear them talking. Most of them are just plain god-crazy..."

"Hobsworth—"

"Yeah. I know." He stuck a finger through the gold netting around his head and scratched at his stubble. "It's a little hard for me to say this, Fairwood, not knowing how you feel about it and not believing it myself. But I can't help hearing the whispers. That's part of my job here. A couple Galicht came through a week ago from Nexus, and they said that people are beginning to talk about you as one of the Pretenders. I've even heard the title used: Sartius Exori."

Even delivered in Hobsworth's apologetic drawl, the words stunned Colin. *"What!"* he shouted. He felt heat rise in his face, knew that under the skinbase, ligaments stretched taut. For a second, his mind reeled and images of the veildreams that had haunted him for the past year came back to him: Gelt and that thunderous, quiet Voice. Colin forcibly had to hold back a quick surge of panic. When he could see again, Hobsworth had backed away from him, fear showing in his pinched eyes.

You have nothing. Why can't you take what is offered to you? That vision of his dreams hammered at his sanity. *Colin, you're not veilmad. You've done nothing—it's all happening around you and you can't control it. Circumstances.* "I've made no such claim, Master Hobsworth." Colin couldn't keep his voice from trembling, a symptom of the emotions that raced through him. "I don't claim to be a prophet."

"I am familiar enough with MulSendero gospel to know that

your denial doesn't matter, Fairwood. 'With the words of his own mouth, he will deny himself.' That's what it says, doesn't it?" Still backing away, Hobsworth came up against a chair, and he nearly fell. "I don't want trouble here, Fairwood. That's why I mention this. You can do whatever the hell you want to do—just don't connect Galicht-guild Chebar or me with it. Understand?" Then, as if the man feared he might have spoken too harshly: "Please?"

"Hobsworth..." Colin began to speak, then shook his head. "If someone's talking about me, he's doing so without my knowledge. I—"

"You overthrew Roland Naley on Nexus, didn't you?"

"I *spoke* to him. That's all. I don't know anything about the rest, about what Naley may have done or said."

"You just threw naval personnel off your ship while they were conducting a legal search, and you somehow managed to walk away from it. Fairwood, by rights you should be dead or in jail."

"What they were doing was beyond Holdings law and they knew it, Master. I got angry. Any Galicht..."

Hobsworth raised a hand. "Most Galicht would have protested to me or to the port authority—they'd have filed some formal complaint. They wouldn't have taken any more chance than that." Hobsworth sat in the chair, peering at the dimness beyond Colin's shoulder through the filaments out of the neural damper still encircling his head. "So tell me again how you haven't done anything."

Colin didn't reply. *Hallan, why can't you just leave me alone? What did I do to you that you must haunt me?* Finally, he exhaled loudly. "You've a lousy bunch of evidence, Master Hobsworth. You're listening to rumors and tall tales, that's all. Look, find me something to fill my hold and I'll be gone and no problem to you. Can you do that?"

Hobsworth managed to look impossibly relieved. He nodded, the wires of the neural damper glinting. "It might take a day or two, but yes, I can. Where do you want to go, Fairwood?"

"Wherever you send me. It doesn't matter."

The man nodded again. "Fairwood, I'm sorry about this."

"So am I, Master Hobsworth. Especially since what I say doesn't seem to matter a great deal to anyone."

Hobsworth's hand moved to a small box looped through his belt. Sparks began to drift along the wire paths of the damper, obscuring the man's face. Colin could see the worried features relaxing into an empty smile; then they were gone behind a screen of flickering light.

* * *

It was a mistake to leave the Galicht-house. Colin soon wished he had ignored the impulse. But two days of watching Hobsworth immerse himself in brainfire had quickly become tedious. Thus far, the streets had proved to be no better entertainment.

First it was the people. They stared. Colin was used to rudeness, to people stopping dead in their tracks to watch him pass. Nor was Chebar a provincial backwater where the thousands of differing customs that sprang up from world to world were unknown. Still, this was a Holdings land, ruled by the Church, and that gave the society a cloistered homogeneity, a sense of isolation. Colin was Galicht: his bright clothing, his loose walk, his free manner all shouted 'stranger.' By themselves, these traits would have garnered him attention. Add to them the mutilation of his face, and he inevitably became the focus of intense interest.

The expressions on the faces of the people around him conveyed everything from fascination to horror. Colin ignored the scrutiny with the ease of long habit, pretending not to notice and noticing far too much.

The city Christos showed its true heritage once Colin was away from the bedraggled, tired area near the Galicht-house. The streets became wider and cleaner, the people better dressed and often so preoccupied that they failed even to see him as anything other than another neutral obstacle to be avoided in the walkways. The buildings were low, in the land-wasteful style of architecture that was universal on new worlds. Spearing upward from the ground-hugging clutter, the tall spires of the Zakkaist churches beckoned. Colin could see three of them within a few blocks of where he stood, and he knew that at least as many others dotted the city like upraised fingers, each tipped with the achingly white pyramid of Zakkai. The towers caught the brick-red glare of Chebar's sun and flung the bloody light back into the streets.

The design of the city drew one's attention to the churches. Perhaps it was deliberate. In any case, it caused Colin to reflect that it had been a long time since he had prostrated himself before the altars. *More than seven decades for most people; for me, maybe fifteen years. A lifetime ago. In another world. I'm not the same person at all—I'm no longer James Badgett, Obdurate, raging against the Church's bonds.*

The sight of the steeples tugged at a part of him he'd believed was gone, the source of a vague, uneasy summons he'd not thought he'd ever feel again. He would have said that such an impulse had been burnt away with his flesh in the purge. He'd never felt it in the Fringes, where the Zakkaist spires mingled with the slant-roofed needles of the MulSendero chapels. Nor could Colin recall this yearning from earlier visits to the Holdings. Never before.

What do you want of me, Lord?

Colin began walking toward the nearest church with no idea of what he would do when he got there. He didn't think he could pull open those heavy doors and kneel as he once had—he didn't know what he believed any more. His faith had been lost in the confusion of his life, in the veildreams and the compelling, sonorous Voice of MolitorAb.

My Lord, are You MolitorAb, as the MulSendero claim? Is Gelt with You?

He began to hear the tumult before he was within a block of the church. Sirens screeched distress, while voices made harsh by amplification screamed orders. Colin soon found himself in the press of people whose curiosity carried them toward the source of the disturbance. He moved with the growing crowd in part because it was easier, in part because they too had the church as their goal.

A police van shrieked by overhead, the siren fading as the vehicle canted at an angle and slid behind the roof of a building to the right. Lost in the surging crowd, Colin turned toward the steeple, rounded a corner, and was stopped by a police barricade.

Jostled and hemmed in, he gawked with the rest of them. The noise rivaled the roar of Nexus: sirens, shouting confusion—the racket assaulted the crowd. In the center of a square tiled with a checkerboard pattern of red and white stood the church. Official vehicles swarmed around it, and no one moved on the wide, sweeping steps or through the exterior gardens who was not wearing a uniform. The police at the barricades were trying to shove back the mass of onlookers, but those who turned to obey were simply trapped by the weight of the people behind. Rumors flashed through the crowd, sparks on dry tinder: a fire in the basement, a terrible accident that had killed the bishop, terrorists holding a congregation hostage.

A thin haze of smoke coiled up from the belfry of the steeple. There was a sudden flash; the sound of an explosion soon followed. Colin shaded his eyes, gasping with the crowd. He squinted into the glare and the pink wash of sky. The smoke had begun roiling, coalescing, forming into a mass that defied the wind. Another flash shot through the cloud, soundlessly this time, and words began to scroll along its smoky flank, slowly dissolving.

MOLITORAB IS GOD.

ALL THE OLD GODS ARE BUT SHADES OF HER.

BEWARE, FOR THE TIME IS COMING.

The letters flickered green against the ash-gray cloud, moving down slowly. As the last word faded, the images began: holographic, lasting several seconds at first, but coming ever faster and faster. A woman's voice began to speak over the scenes—a soft, husky voice that was filled with a searing anger that belied the calm delivery. A voice Colin knew.

Kiri's.

She spoke as the cloud became a view of Christos as seen from above, at an angle that accentuated the steeples prodding the sky. "Chebar is faithful," she said. "The people of our world are religious, certain that they know God. Yet even here there are those that would worship MolitorAb. Where can *we* go to pray among this wealth of churches? Nowhere—the Ascendants forbid it."

A lightning bolt lanced the scene, destroying it with a dazzling brilliance that left dancing afterimages. When Colin could see again, the cloud had given way to a sequence of hurtling images almost too obvious in content: Ascendant Huan Su, against the backdrop of the lush perfection of Tokyo Cathedral, smiling; the gaunt faces of the children of Slowfall's parched desserts where crop failures had meant death by starvation, a holy feast at some nameless church, the tables laden with food until they seemed to groan under the weight; a prisoner whose haunted face was pressed against the stained bars of his cell; a crowd packing the nave of Jerusalem mosque at Prophet Simon's feast; a Stekoni's terrified posture before the stern pose of some uniformed official.

The contrast between the alternating scenes was trite and cliché, but the crowd watched in rapt silence. The scenes came ever faster, building to a crescendo. They flickered past so quickly the mind barely had time to register them before they were gone. Now the people had begun shouting around Colin, fists raised in the air, their words lost in the general roar.

Then Colin was shouting with them.

He had seen his own face in that flurry of stills, mingled with the pictures of pain and hate.

Kiri's voice had begun to speak again; he was not certain when he had begun to hear it again. *"He comes! The Sartius Exori comes to change all! Be ready when he casts down the old ways!"*

"NO!" he was screaming back at her. "NO!" He did not see the visual assault any more—there was only that one awful instant when he saw himself as if in a cosmic mirror. That moment, impaled on his thoughts. "NO!" he screamed again, his voice raw.

The word was lost, buried under the voices surrounding him.

But as if in answer, there came a deafening roar. The steeple leaned slowly, hesitating for an eternity before sagging inward. Then the building began to collapse in on itself in a fury of stone and dust, roaring as if alive. The crowd answered with a wail of its own. The choking pall of destruction surged over them, stinging Colin and the front ranks of the onlookers with fragments of sharp-edged stone. Colin flung up his hands to protect his face. Coughing, blinded by the stinging dust, he was pushed by the crowd as everyone simultaneously tried to move backward and away. He nearly lost his balance; someone near him was not as lucky—Colin heard a shout and a thin wailing that was suddenly cut off.

The crowd howled—in outrage, in pain, in strange exhilaration. Colin fought against the bodies in his path, wanting only to be away from here, to be elsewhere. Anywhere. He was cursed, and blows struck his shoulders and chest. He ignored all of it.

He saw only one thing.

His face in the Buntaro cloud. His face scowling down at the masses just before the church collapsed into rubble.

His face.

His.

Stolen from him.

That evening, in the Galicht-house, Colin watched the local newscasts. The incident was, inevitably, headlined. Nine people had been killed during the incident, five of them in the crowd. The prelate of the church—St. Alicia's, he learned—had refused to leave despite the fact that someone had contacted the rectory with a warning some ten minutes before the explosion. Two of the police had been too near the steeple. The remaining body had yet to be identified. Colin watched it all, trying to ignore Hobsworth's mumbling. The master was still lost in the haze of the neural damper.

When the newscast replayed a portion of the incident showing the Buntaro propaganda cloud, Colin leaned forward to peer into the holotank. The recorded images lacked the intensity of the afternoon's experience—they came across distilled and dry. The scene rushed past, and then there was a commotion that was too distant and small.

Colin leaned back, frowning.

Nowhere in the holocaust of the propaganda cloud had he seen his face. Nowhere had there been that moment of awful recognition as Kiri's voice began to speak a second time. Colin thought that perhaps he'd missed it; he hurriedly switched channels in time to see the events replayed from a slightly different angle.

There was no patchwork face in this cloud either. No horror of skinbase and plastalloy.

No Colin.

He switched off the holo. In the silence and darkness, he sank back into his chair. He was frightened now. His hands shook and he clenched the arms of his chair tightly.

Hallan, what have you done to me?

What have you done?

CHAPTER EIGHT

Then he strictly ordered his disciples not to tell anyone that he was the Messiah.

NEW TESTAMENT, Matthew 16:20

Take a hundred witnesses to any event and have them write down their description of what they saw. I guarantee that you'll have a hundred different stories. You may even find that some of the accounts vary so radically you will wonder whether any two are talking about the same thing. That's human nature: the police will be the first to tell you that "eyewitness accounts" are riddled with terrible lapses and mistakes, if not simply deliberate lies.

Now add the distance of five years to our hypothetical event. By now, the constant retelling of the tale and faulty memories have shaved off all the rough edges—our witnesses will have refined the event. They now think of it as "their" story. The memory/tale may resemble the reality only in general outline. Make this happening an episode that is vitally important to its observers, an incident that has a direct impact on their lives and sense of history—an assassination, say, or a crime of huge proportions; a disaster, rather than a simple accident—and now you've added a huge incentive to improve upon the truth.

What this means is that you can't trust what anyone says about an incident. In fact, you can't trust yourself. Admit it, you've done the same thing, haven't you?

Now let me tell you about Colin Fairwood.

—From a lecture by Roland Naley,
Nexus, OE March 13, 2578

There are moments when a person realizes that he has come to that place where the roads of fate visibly diverge. There always seem to be at least three choices at these unmarked crossroads: you can act forcefully; you can take the easiest route that still involves

some action on your part; or you can dither and procrastinate—
which will lead you into the brambles of the third path.

Sitting in the dim lounge of the Galicht-house, Colin could see
the rutted paths as if he stood before them. His stare was fixed on
Hobsworth, at the snarling, sharp stars crawling along the wires
netting his head. Master Hobsworth had always taken that last path,
Colin knew. Hobsworth let the world move him—the underbrush
had seemed too heavy anywhere else.

It's what you've done for the past several years. Colin accused
himself and knew the indictment to be true. He could rationalize
that he was not entirely to blame: the flight from Old Earth and
New York had been shorter for him than for the society from which
he fled, but it had been six long years of pain and loneliness.

And madness. He'd almost lost himself in that time. The wounds
of his face had nearly killed his body, and the despair had almost
driven him to open the locks and let in that quick, waiting death
outside. He'd survived only at the cost of altering his soul. James
Badgett had died on that trip: Colin Fairwood was the chrysalis that
had emerged.

Change. He'd come from the ship aching to be revenged, to
rejoin the Obdurate fight. He'd given the false name and the false
tale that he had thought he would need—he'd had so much time
to make it all up, to be certain that it sounded halfway reasonable.
They had nodded, his rescuers, and taken him back to a changed
universe, one in which Colin's revenge and its motives made no
sense at all.

Change. The Obdurates were gone, forgotten. Hallan Gelt was
old and dead. Gelt had become the Prophet of MolitorAb, which
had only been a distant, unreal name for James Badgett, an alien
god.

Change. Colin had become what he thought he needed to become: quiet, self-sufficient, lonely. He'd insisted that the reconstruction of his face be left visible, a reminder to himself of what
the Zakkaists had done. It was a private battle scar, a souvenir of
the dead James Badgett. Something to carry so that Badgett would
never be entirely lost.

And now Hallan returned to him in his veildreams. The
MulSendero had become the new Obdurates for the Church, and
his friend's dead hands were weaving a net to trap him. Colin sat
in its folds and did nothing.

The third path. The easiest.

Hobsworth's brainfire sounded like cackling laughter in the background.

Sit. Be still, it mocked him. *Be Colin Fairwood the Silent. The Man Living In The Past. Sit and let God find you if He wants to—whatever His name may be, whatever gender you might use to refer to Him/Her. And remember that once, as an Obdurate, you felt that a person had to prove his faith, to act on it.*

And what damn good did it do? Colin railed at that voice. *It destroyed my face; it took away the world I knew and gave me back something totally unfamiliar, with everything changed. All the faces were new and my passions were tales from the history books. I'd lost my family, lost Hallan, lost my ideals—all in one second that took six years.*

So you feel sorry for yourself. So you think that you know better than the God you believe in.

No! It's just that I don't know at all. Anything.

Then you have to find out. Maybe that's why you lived when you should have died on that broken farship. Maybe that is why MolitorAb saved you. Maybe that is your task.

"No," he said aloud, but without conviction. He levered himself from the padded chair. For a long moment he stared at Hobsworth, at the fire lacing his head. Then he walked to the door of the Galichthouse, opened it, and went out.

It was an easy task to find FirstBred Pale. Stekoni were common enough in the Fringes, but not in the Holdings. There were restrictions everywhere for the aliens—if Pale was still in Christos and not elsewhere on Chebar, there were only a few places she could stay.

The hotel was nice enough, but it reeked of Stekoni musk. The human clerk wore prominent nasal filters and would not look at Colin at all after the first glance. His gaze circled uneasily about Colin's distorted features and never came to rest until it dropped to a paper on his desk. "Your name, sir?" he queried when Colin asked for Pale.

"My name doesn't matter."

The clerk shivered and looked over Colin's left shoulder. "I'm afraid it's required."

"Because of Pale?" Colin was suddenly afraid that the alien had been implicated in the bombing of the church. If so, Colin felt he might have just cast suspicion on himself.

"Because of the *law*, sir. Anyone wishing to see a Stekoni—"

"Fine," Colin growled, relieved. "It's not as if you're going to have any trouble describing me. Colin Fairwood, Galicht."

The clerk typed the name into his desk terminal. He waited, the colors of the monitors reflecting on his face, and he shrugged. "She's not currently in her rooms, sir."

"What's the number?"

Again the man almost looked at Colin. "We're not permitted—" he began.

"Never mind," Colin interrupted. "I'll wait here in the lobby."

FirstBred Pale arrived an hour later, rushing into the hotel in what seemed to be great agitation. Her golden eyes showed white around the pupils, the fingers moved ceaselessly near the young-pouches, her smell was tinged with a rancid edge, and her loincloth was soaked and discolored with secretions. "Galicht Fairwood," Pale said when Colin rose, her voice breathy with surprise.

"Let's go to your rooms, FirstBred Pale," Colin said, ignoring the polite niceties of Stekoni speech. "We have to talk. Now."

Pale's living area looked out on an array of government buildings set across a windblown square. Colin watched the movements of workers behind the lighted windows, waiting for Pale to settle herself. She had gone into the bedroom to change her clothing, apologizing all the time to Colin for the odor of her rooms. As she returned, Colin saw that she had brushed her fur, that her smell was milder and almost sweet. "This one is sorry, Galicht Fairwood—"

"What are you telling the MulSendero about me, Pale?"

She started at that, backing up a step and sitting carefully on one of the plastic chairs in the room. Her voice was very soft, very slow, almost without the normal Stekoni lisp. "This one searches for the Sartius Exori as you know, Colin Fairwood. This one spoke to you of that on Nexus. This one has hidden nothing from you. Roland Naley—"

"Roland Naley isn't important to me at the moment." Colin turned back to the window, stared a moment, and then swung around again. "Right now, I feel entirely selfish. I care about *me*. What are you saying about *me?*"

She did not answer immediately. One hand slid along the opening of a young-pouch, stroking the roll of muscle there. "When this one watched you and Mad One Naley, when this one heard that Colin Fairwood was of the Galicht as was Prophet Gelt, this one was struck by intense curiosity. The more this one could learn of you, the more that interest waxed. This one has also witnessed the reaction of Commander Blaine and listened to rumors of Colin Fairwood's hidden past." Pale's entire body quivered with a shrug-spasm. "Can Colin Fairwood tell this one that he is absolutely *not* the Sartius Exori?"

"Yes," Colin said quickly. Then he grimaced, his hands making a sweep of disgust. "No. I don't know. Listen, Pale, I'm not sure *what* is happening. I'm confused. I'm even a little frightened, and I'm feeling that I'm being pushed."

"This one would feel very frightened if MolitorAb spoke directly to her, if she were chosen for a task by Her. And as to the feeling of being pushed..." Pale's voice dropped to a whisper. "That is the hand of MolitorAb you feel, Colin Fairwood. This one is certain of it."

"It could as easily be the hand of insanity." Colin walked across the room and sank into a nearby chair; built for the thinner, lighter Stekoni, the chair groaned uneasily under him. "Pale—" Colin began, stopped, and took a breath. "You know, I thought that I saw my face yesterday," he said, and then it was all coming out, faster and faster: all his hidden fears and inadequacies, jumbled and dis-organized. All of it tumbling from his lips: Hallan Gelt, the veil-dreams, the tint of madness that he saw in his mind. Colin rambled for long minutes, talking more to himself than to Pale.

After a time, Colin became aware that Pale had stopped listening to him. He broke off the monologue in midsentence. An instant too late, Pale gawked at him. "Galicht Fairwood?"

"You weren't listening any more."

Yellow-flecked eyes blinked. "This one is sorry."

Colin sighed. "You were upset a few minutes ago, Pale. Is that what's distracting you?"

Silence. Then Pale nodded her broad head. "This one doesn't deserve your kindness after her impoliteness. You were being far more open than she could have wished and she failed you." Emo-tions tugged at the lines of her face; Colin could not read them. "Yes, Galicht Fairwood, this one has other worries. This one is very concerned for her friend Kiri Oharu."

It was as if the invocation of that name put the last piece of a puzzle in place in Colin's mind. His eyes narrowed, banding muscles down his cheeks; a sudden certainty gripped him.

"The destruction of that church—St. Alicia's. She was hurt during it, and she's asked you for help."

Pale looked more frightened now than Colin had thought pos-sible. She huddled in her chair and the fear-scent began to rise from her again. Colin could see the moistness as oils made her fur slick—already, the edge of the wrapping around her waist was touched by a spreading stain. "How did you know, Galicht Fairwood? Did MolitorAb—?"

"A guess, Pale. Nothing more. What about Kiri?"

"As you have . . . guessed, she is in trouble. Someone came up behind this one on the street before and told her. There was no note or anything, Galicht Fairwood, just a voice saying that Kiri needed this one's aid. It also whispered an address." Pale's look was bleak. "This one . . . can't help her, Galicht Fairwood. Even if this one were not simply . . . *afraid,* a Stekoni is too visible here on Chebar. This one would only draw attention to herself and cause Kiri Oharu more trouble. There is so much possibility of danger. She is Buntaro, and the Zakkaists . . ." Her head went down, her hands moved convulsively.

"I understand, Pale. It's all right."

She glanced up, the hope in her eyes almost painful. "Galicht Fairwood, you will help this one?"

He could have said no. He was very close to saying that, of choosing the path of isolation once more. Yet he had been treading those ruts for so long, and there was little joy in the scenery.

Maybe your God is still speaking to you, Colin/James. Maybe you're not mad.

Colin sighed. He nodded. "I'll help," he said.

Aaron Roberts watched the man advance from the alleyway. Aaron prayed to MolitorAb that he wouldn't need to use the ancient laser rifle strapped to his back. He'd gotten sick of the idea of killing—seeing Hawk trapped in the rubble of St. Alicia's yesterday had altered his outlook. Everytime Aaron had shut his eyes since, he saw that ruined body again, the rent torn in Hawk's stomach and the entrails spilled before the body. Hawk had been a lover, a friend. Now Hawk was dead.

If Aaron did no more killing, he would be satisfied.

The damn Church. The damn Church. All they gotta do is let us pray the way we want to. It ain't that friggin' much . . .

Aaron let the intruder get halfway down the narrow lane between the buildings before he unslung the rifle with practiced ease and pulled the trigger back to the first click. A tiny spot of brilliant red blossomed on the man's chest. Aaron smiled when the man noticed the dot of light and instantly stopped; this one was observant—most people simply wouldn't have seen it.

Still, the observation would have been far too late if Aaron had wanted to pull the trigger back all the way to where the rifle spat terrible, awful death. The weapon thrummed in Aaron's hand as the man below glanced all around for the source of that scarlet button.

Looks like Joshua was right; Kiri's got friends—which is fine, so long as the friends ain't cops. He peered down through the sights of the laser rifle. The man's face was turned upward toward the roofs, and Aaron nearly dropped the rifle in shock. *By Gelt! That's the one people have been talking about, the one without much of a face.* Aaron's finger trembled on the trigger; he reached with his other hand for the contact of his fibermic. "Got a man in the street, Joshua. And it ain't just anyone—it's the one Kiri was talkin' about."

Aaron heard the street door open below him and saw the man turn toward the source of sudden light. Aaron slid the rifle into his back-tether and scrambled down from the roof. Let Joshua be angry that no one was watching the alley—Aaron wanted to meet this one.

His first thought on entering the room was that this Pretender was the ugliest thing Aaron had ever seen. That face looked as if someone had peeled skin away with a dull knife and sprayed the result with a clear acrylic. Aaron looked away after a few seconds— *Ain't something you want to keep staring at. Makes you feel like you were some kind of pervert to keep watching him. Who would have thought that the Sartius Exori might be some freak?*

Aaron watched Joshua, who didn't seem to be having much trouble confronting the man, though Aaron could see that Joshua's jaw was clenched and his hand stayed near the holster at his belt. He didn't like Joshua much, but Joshua was the senior Buntaro on Chebar. The old man talked too much about commitment, about how you had to be prepared to die for MolitorAb. Sometimes Aaron thought that Joshua might think *he* could become the Sartius Exori and declare himself the Chebar Pretender. Aaron had as much faith as anyone, but Joshua...he seemed to *smile* when he preached about sacrifice and faith, as if he looked forward to dying for MolitorAb. Last night, Aaron had spent a lot of time wishing it had been Joshua who died in the ruins of the church and not Hawk. Joshua would have enjoyed his heroic ending; Hawk had just screamed.

Aaron didn't want to die at all. He wanted to be around to do to the Church what the Church had done to the Buntaro, to *all* MulSendero.

". . . by the Stekoni?" Joshua was asking the man. Joshua was using his preaching voice—*like he was leading a service, wanting everyone to see how holy he is.* "Otherwise, you've just made a mistake."

The man laughed. Aaron slid another glance across the man's features, the grotesque rash of blood vessels, the slabs of muscles, the gleam of silver bone. He looked at Joshua again and saw the old man staring back angrily. *So what? If this is the Sartius Exori, I want to be able to say that I met him.*

"I doubt that you think I'm anyone else, not with this face," the man was saying. His voice was full of self-mockery, with a hint of sarcastic laughter. "I'm Colin Fairwood, yes. Where's Kiri?"

Joshua was doing his best to stare Colin down, Aaron noted. It didn't seem to be working. "Answer my questions first, Galicht. Are you truly the Sartius Exori?"

It was difficult for Aaron to decide whether the muscles tugging at Fairwood's lips were shaping a smile, but the man answered easily enough. "I'm Colin Fairwood. That will have to do for the moment, Buntaro. If you want to call me anything else, feel free. Now, can I see Kiri?"

Joshua swiveled his head toward Aaron, glared, and motioned. "Take him to her," he said.

Aaron waved a hand to the door behind him. "This way," he said to Fairwood. The man followed Aaron two doors down the alley and into a small, dim room. The woman lay on a bare mattress in one corner, covered by a thin blanket that was stained with brownish red blood. The blanket rose and fell with her raspy breath, and the air held a sickly tang. Fairwood turned to Aaron, a question in his eyes. Aaron shrugged.

"She was tired and kind of sick when she got here. She helped us with the thing at St. Alicia's. We had some trouble with the explosives; the message packet went off while we were still placing it. Killed Hawk, threw Kiri here against a wall. Then the cops showed up and we just had time to get her and ourselves out. Didn't help her none, I guess, having to drag her out like that, but it's better than giving her to the cops. She'd've died in jail."

Fairwood went to her, bending down on one knee next to the mattress. His hand tentatively stroked her forehead. "They would have treated her. They're not all barbarians. You're beginning to believe your own propaganda."

Aaron shook his head, wondering that a Pretender could misunderstand so much. "She's *Buntaro,* caught blowing up a church. You think they're gonna waste their time? Not when Zakkaists died in the blast."

"Uh-huh," Fairwood grunted. "So what are *you* doing for her?"

"We got *you.* " Aaron grinned, an expression that faded when Fairwood turned and stared at him. *It's not just the face. It's something else. There's a power in him.* "Look, I'm sorry. Joshua really did all he could. We had to move quickly and we can't stay here very long—we have to get back to one of our safe houses. She wouldn't survive another move—you can see that, can't you? Joshua wants to leave in a few hours." Aaron jerked a thumb back toward the other building. "The Zakkaists are scouring the city for us. Joshua thought maybe the Stekoni could help her."

Fairwood snorted derisively. "Right. He thought he'd dump her on us, now that she wasn't any use to him. Let the Stekoni take all the risks. Your Joshua's a coward, Buntaro. And he doesn't understand the Stekoni at all. I'd think that a MulSendero would have more knowledge of the First Race."

Aaron didn't answer. He couldn't. After a minute, Fairwood turned back to Kiri. "Get your stupid leader," he said. His tone told Aaron that he expected obedience. Aaron shrugged, tugged the rifle onto his shoulders, and did as he was bidden.

When he and Joshua entered the room a few minutes later, Fairwood was still on his knees beside Kiri, a hand stroking her arm. He glanced back at them. "She was still bleeding. I stopped it." Then, seeing their faces: "I put pressure on the cuts and bound them up. I don't do miracles every day. I just did what you could have done."

"Hey, we were a little concerned about getting away, Fairwood. We didn't have a lot of time." Joshua's voice was loud with self-righteous anger. "We took enough of a chance just contacting the Stekoni."

"It's awful having to save your own skins, isn't it?" Fairwood retorted. "To hell with Kiri if she's a liability—the only thing that matters is that *you* escape. Hurrah for the revolution, but shit on the soldiers."

Aaron glanced sidewise at Joshua and saw the deep flush on his cheeks. *Now Fairwood's had it. Old Preacher Joshua's gonna give him hellfire.* The old man drew himself up. His shoulders came back and his chest expanded. "We fight for MolitorAb!" he roared.

"Our concern is only what is good for Her. We're just pawns, as is Kiri—"

"Right," Fairwood said. "And you're going to help me get this pawn moved to another square."

"You don't listen, Fairwood," Joshua spat out. "We have to leave. You can let her lie there or you can take her, but *we* have to move."

Fairwood stood, pushing away from the floor. He was a few inches shorter and much leaner than the barrel-chested preacher. Hands on hips, he glowered at the man. "And if I'm the Sartius Exori?"

For an instant, Joshua's tirade failed. His eyes widened. Then he canted his head. "Is that what you claim?"

"I claim nothing. I just wonder how history will view you, my friend, if you fail to help me. The tale of the Sartius Exori might always include the chapter on Chebar, where a fool of a MulSendero failed his faith. It's your choice—but I tell you that you *will* help me, for your own sake."

Silence. Aaron glanced from Joshua to Fairwood, awestruck. The man had as much as admitted that he was the Sartius Exori. Aaron knew that he wasn't simply another of the Pretenders: he had too much presence, and there were Kiri's tales about Naley's abdication . . . It was all Aaron could do to keep from taking the preacher by his shoulders, shaking the old man, and saying "Fool, can't you *see?*"

"I give the orders here, Fairwood," Joshua countered, but his voice had gone soft.

Fairwood said nothing.

"If you are the Sartius Exori, why don't you simply say so?" Joshua was almost pleading now, shaking his head. "Why do you play with us this way?"

No answer. Aaron could hear the labored rasp of Kiri's breathing.

At last Joshua turned away from Fairwood. His gaze fell to Kiri's huddled form. "What do you want us to do?" he said.

Aaron grinned.

This moment would be something he would tell his children about many times—the day he'd met the Sartius Exori. He, Aaron, had been there when the Black Beginning had come to Chebar.

CHAPTER NINE

They marvel that a prophet of their own should arise amongst them. "He is but a cunning enchanter," say the unbelievers. "Does he claim that all the gods are but one god? This is indeed a strange thing."

KORAN, Sad 38:3—4

There are a thousand reasons humanity is moved to grandeur or degradation: sex, politics, even the latest ball game can serve. All of them—mundane and glorious—arouse a surprising degree of emotional response.

One of the strongest of these reasons has been constant throughout human history: religion. People will fight for God, kill for God, love for God. Religion has been the most important single rationale for conflict since the first Neanderthal touted his Lightning Spirit over a Cro-Magnon's Fire Goddess.

It's indeed a pity that we find it so hard to gather up all this pious energy, this righteous fervor, and apply that power to fostering harmony rather than discord. That's all I wish to do, my friends. I want to make all religious people one with God. There's not much difference between us—Jew, Christian, Moslem, whatever. We all spring from the same source, we espouse much the same moralities. I find it hard to believe that God is pleased with our self-enforced segregation. Rather, I believe—no, I know—that He would want us to give Him praise together, as one voice.

—From Simon ben Zakkai's address to
the First All-Faith Conference.
Jerusalem, 9 August 2086

Colin's concern was that Kiri would not be able to move on her own. He could think of no way to hide her from the Chebar authorities if she had to be carried, no way he could easily smuggle her aboard the *Anger*. He crouched beside her in the shabby room and pulled back the covers, looking at her again and shaking his head. She was naked underneath the blankets. The bandages were dark with her blood, but it seemed that the bleeding had stopped. Her right side was one long mottled bruise just turning an ugly green brown—that alone would give her great difficulty in walking, but it couldn't be helped. Colin's hands probed her limbs—no breaks, only a few minor cuts sticky with congealed blood. He gently moved her hair back from her face, softly touching her all around her skull. A welt swelled under his fingertips at the right temple.

Concussion. That's why she's still out.

He sat back on his heels, pondering. The kid Aaron was still in the room, watching with an attentiveness that amazed Colin. "Can you get me a washcloth, Aaron? I could use a basin of cool water and a couple NoPain tabs as well."

The boy nodded and fled. He came back a few minutes later with the items. He handed them to Colin, stretching his arms out as if he didn't want to get too near. "Thanks," Colin said. The boy grunted something and wouldn't look at Colin.

Colin cleansed Kiri's face, mopping away the sweat and grime. He forced her mouth open and put the NoPain tabs under her tongue. There seemed little else he could do; he was beginning to regret his belligerent confidence with the old preacher. *Let her wake up and be strong, MolitorAb. Otherwise, I don't know how I can help her at all. Above all, don't let her die. Not here.* It was as near a prayer as he could manage. Her breathing had become shallower in the last few minutes—he wondered if all his attentions had come too late.

Colin took the cloth from her head, rinsed it in the basin, and leaned over her again.

His hand brushed her skin.

Something passed between them, a sharp jolt like a static spark. Colin grunted in surprise and Aaron's eyes widened.

Colin drew his hand back and then touched her again.

She moaned. From his station near the door, Aaron gasped in wonderment.

Kiri's eyelids fluttered. The motion startled Colin, made him shiver.

A pale tongue licked cracked lips. Kiri's eyes opened. She saw him and did not seem surprised. "Colin," she whispered, her voice broken and raspy. "I didn't think that you wanted to see me again. I'm glad I was wrong."

"Bad karma," he said. The jest felt leaden.

"MolitorAb's hand."

The comment would usually have struck reflexive anger from him, but this time the mocking response he might have made would not pass his lips. Colin glanced at Aaron and what he saw in the boy's face made him scowl. He turned back to Kiri. "I hate to ask you this. I know you're in a lot of pain, but you have to try standing. We have to leave here—your associates don't seem to think it's safe."

"All right," she said simply. Colin wrapped the blanket around her shoulders and helped her up. She grimaced and nearly fell when she tried to put weight on her right leg, but she stood. Alone. Then she sagged back into Colin's grasp. "My head's killing me," she said.

"You're in no position to complain about a headache. I'm surprised you're alive."

Her hair rustled against his shirt: a nod. From the doorway, Aaron spoke. "We thought you were going to die, Kiri. You didn't wake up, wouldn't respond at all..." He stammered, took a long, gasping breath. *"He* brought you back." Aaron jabbed a finger at Colin.

"I didn't do anything you couldn't have done."

Aaron shook his head. "Sir, we tried. Truthfully. We did all we could."

"It was just circumstance, then. If I were going to perform miracles, I'd throw in a flash of light and a heavenly choir." Colin's voice was freighted with disgust. Aaron's jaw snapped shut, and his knuckles whitened around the barrel of his weapon.

"Why do you make a mockery of yourself?" he asked Colin sharply.

"I mock what I know. It's easiest."

Kiri pushed away from him, wavering unsteadily. "Colin," she said, "stop denying your power." Her eyes, stark in her tired, lined face, searched his face. Colin wanted to step away, raging at the two of them for forcing him to talk about this, but he couldn't. He remembered the startling shock that had passed between Kiri and himself. *Coincidence. Static.* The words failed to convince him, but he fought them anyway.

"There's no power in me, Kiri."

"False humility doesn't change what I saw," Aaron interjected hesitantly.

Colin whirled on him. "You won't change any minds with that rifle either."

Aaron fumbled with the laser weapon, distressed. He began to sling it over his back again and finally let the weapon drop with a loud clatter. "Master, please ... I'm sorry. I didn't mean to get you angry."

"You see, Colin," Kiri said. "He's Buntaro, but he'll give up his weapon if you tell him to." Suddenly she sagged against him, all the strength gone from her legs. Colin clutched for her. "I need to sit down, I think," she said. "I'm just ... very tired."

Colin lowered her to the mattress. He paced the room, his back to them. "Rest for awhile. Then you can go with them when they leave."

"I intend to go with you, Colin. Pale will want to come as well."

"Why?"

Before Kiri could answer, Aaron cleared his throat. "Pardon, Master, Kiri, but you're not going to be able to walk through the port authority and get your permits, not with the Stekoni and not after what happened at St. Alicia's. You'll all be detained and questioned."

"He's right," Kiri said, all hope gone from her voice. "You might be able to disguise me, but you and FirstBred Pale ..." She lay back on the mattress. Weariness slackened her features.

The crossroads. Colin knew this was the moment he'd been anticipating. What he did now would shift the direction of his life. He could leave this room, leave Christos the city and Chebar the world. Alone, he could put it all behind him, could ignore the veildreams and the haunting of Gelt. He might always wonder, and he might always have to avoid flying because of the dreams, but the fantasy that surrounded him could be denied.

Or he could let it surge over him.

Who are you? God or MolitorAb or nothing? Hallan, did you truly believe, or was it just another game of power?

What happened to your faith, Colin-who-was-James? You were so certain once. Take what is offered before it is withdrawn from you.

Conviction came suddenly. He sighed.

"We'll all leave," he said to Kiri. "You, Pale, and me. Your friends will give us the help we need."

Colin expected to be stopped before they reached the port. Somehow they were not. As a trio, they were certainly conspicuous enough: Colin with his torn face, Kiri hobbling and leaning against the glossy fur of FirstBred Pale, whose fright at this adventure had turned her scent to a pungent bitterness. The port authority building was a huge glass and steel structure that dwarfed the people inside. An immense representation of the Zakkaist triangle swung below the distant ceiling. Through the floor-to-ceiling windows, Colin could see the spidery arms of the berths outside, most of them vacant, the beams gleaming with rain from the lowering, massed clouds. The *Anger* was nearby, two slips down from the field exits, the hull of the farship swathed in the magnetic pulsers that would heave her into the drizzling sky.

Very close.

Colin closed his mind to the nagging doubts. This had been too easy thus far—their success bothered him. He had smuggled often enough in the past to know there were usually more problems than anticipated, not fewer. He also knew that if he were in charge of such things, he would be very suspicious of a newly arrived Galicht ship, one of whose passengers had been a Stekoni. If he were looking for an odd coincidence to match up with the bombing of St. Alicia's, he would investigate the *Anger* and her passengers.

It was too early in the morning for the port to be crowded. Those few people in the building stayed well away from the three odd people angling toward the gates and the guards standing there. A buzz of conversation trailed them. Colin glanced back and saw a priest come through the street entrance, accompanied by four burly men. Colin thought the group watched the three of them too intently. A shiver of premonition ran through him. *Can't go back now. You can only go forward and hope that you've set it up well enough.*

There were two guards at the gates. Colin remembered both of them from his arrival on Chebar. They nudged one another as Colin approached. "Tell the Stekoni to keep her distance, would you?" one of them said. His companion laughed. "What do you want, Fairwood?"

"I'm going aboard my ship," he said curtly. "Taking these two visitors with me."

The guards grinned at each other. "What's the matter, Galicht? Need to hold a service and can't find a MulSendero church?"

"Just checking the ship. You can't trust the Holdings to take good care of Fringes equipment. *Our* stuff doesn't need a priest's blessing before it works."

One guffawed, the other shook his head. "You got the port master's permission?"

"Since when do I need permission to go aboard my own ship?"

"Since now, Galicht." The guards' gazes went past Colin. Colin did not dare turn around, but he heard the sound of footsteps. *Now. It had better be now or we won't make it.* "Look, Galicht, just go see the master, huh?"

"It's not as if I'm shipping out. I just want to check my property. That's my right, isn't it? You can't stop me from doing that." Desperation colored his voice. *Now, Buntaro. Please.* At his back, Colin heard Pale squawk in consternation. Kiri began a protest as the priest's hand touched Colin's shoulder. "Galicht Colin Fairwood, you're—"

There was the sound of a God's anger.

A red fury. A thunderclap. The explosion shattered the glass front of the port authority building, flinging pieces of the windows across the tile floor. Near the entrance, people began to scream. The concussion shook Colin, nearly sending him to the floor. Kiri staggered against him, and he reached for her as she fell. The priest and his entourage, the gate guards—all seemed to forget Colin and his companions in the confusion of the moment. They stood in shock, then began running toward the sound of the disturbance. A ground vehicle was afire near the doors; Colin could see injured people on the floor; others were wandering dazed, with hands held against bleeding cuts. Only the priest stayed behind as the others rushed to help, his hand still grasping Colin's shirt.

The priest stared; Colin shoved the man, who fell awkwardly. "Move!" Colin shouted to the others. Ignoring the priest, he began to run toward the *Anger,* half supporting Kiri. Pale moved with sleek power ahead of them—Colin had never seen a Stekoni run before. He was amazed at how quick and graceful Pale could be at need. The rain pounded at them, hard, cold droplets. Pale reached the farship well before them; she opened the hatch doors and let down the ramp. Colin shoved Kiri toward Pale and moved up the ramp himself.

He paused, his hand over the contact that would pull the doors shut again. Rolling, greasy smoke smeared the damp sky. Sirens wailed in the distance. A swarming shadow milled inside the shattered walls of the building.

It's all changed now, Hallan. It's as you wished.

"Forgive me," he whispered.

Colin touched the switch. The ramp slid up before his eyes.

Pale was scrambling into her acceleration webbing. Kiri was already slouched in hers, watching Colin with a calmness that dismayed him. "I may have been responsible for killing people back there," he said as he readied the farship. "And we're not at all assured of getting away yet. Doesn't it bother you that people may have died for nothing?"

"What choice did you have, Colin? If MolitorAb needs them to live, they will. If She had wanted no one to be hurt, She would have made our way simple and none of it would have been necessary." She shook her head at him sadly. "I can see the pain in you, Colin. I'm sorry. I wish I could take it all from you, but all you could have done to make it different was to forget me. That would have meant *my* death. Either way, it would have been your fault. I'm afraid that I can't be unhappy with your choice. Colin, you'll go insane trying to end strife — it can't be done. You're the Sartius Exori; the Black Beginning heralds death — Gelt says it."

"You sound amazingly like him, Kiri." *How did you phrase it, Hallan? "We can't erect a new faith without first destroying the 30old. What cannot or will not change must be taken apart."* The *old Obdurate credo that we both mouthed.* Colin slammed controls home. The *Anger* quivered in the pulser field while a slow keening moved upward through and out of the range of his hearing. An alarm wailed and they were flung into the sky like a rock from the fist of an angry child.

Kiri laughed. Pale hooted. "This one gives thanks to MolitorAb," the Stekoni cried. "And to you, Colin Exori." In the monitor, they could see the edge of Chebar becoming a curve, the blue green shoulder of the world.

"We're not away yet," Colin replied, tight-lipped, a little annoyed at his companions' good mood. His fingers tapped at the keypads of the controls, sending the *Anger*'s probes outward, searching.

For several minutes he said nothing, engrossed in his work as the curve of Chebar deepened. The continents turned slowly below, storm clouds making variegated patterns across the land. The farship moved steadily away from the world.

For a time, Colin thought that Kiri and Pale might have been right, that his premonitions had been only paranoia.

That escape could be too easy.

One of the sensors chirped an alarm. "Hell," Colin muttered.

"Galicht Fairwood?" Pale asked, her voice tenor with apprehension.

"Another ship, a big one. Just over Chebar's horizon." Colin looked at the figures being displayed in the monitor tank and leaned back in his webbing. "A naval cruiser, I think. She'll be a hell of a lot faster than we are—we'll never get far enough out of Chebar's gravity well to veilshift. She'll get to us long before that." He touched a key; the monitor spat light and then slowly darkened as it displayed a camera view of the void outside the farship. A fleck of brilliance was rising above the slope of the world, the flares of the cruiser's drive, enhanced by the farship's display monitor. As they watched, the light pulsed and several points broke away from it—missiles. "There," Colin said. "They've got us. The bastards aren't even going to give us a chance." He could not breathe; the closeness of death crushed his chest. "Two minutes, maybe a few seconds more. That's all we have. I'd recommend that you make your peace with MolitorAb—you'll be meeting Her soon."

"You're the Sartius Exori," Kiri insisted.

Colin laughed mockingly. "That doesn't seem to impress them at all, does it? What do you want me to do? Do you think I can wave my hands and destroy their weapons with my great wrath?"

The Sartius Exori is under the protection of MolitorAb," Pale answered, though her eyes were on the brightening spots in the tank. An electric blue shimmer was spreading between the points of light, a field of energy being strung between the *Anger* and escape. "MolitorAb will keep you safe."

"That fails to comfort me, Pale." Colin sighed, forcing himself to take a deep breath. "I'm very sorry, Kiri, Pale. I'm sorry that the two of you believed your delusions concerning me. I'm sorry that I wasn't strong enough not to be swayed by them myself. We're all going to pay the cost of fantasy."

"We're still alive," Kiri said.

"Only for seconds." Colin glanced back at the monitor and touched a key. The display quickly flashed descending numbers, then Colin switched it back to the camera view. Against the backdrop of stars, the translucent glow was pulsing, flowing like a milky curtain between the ship and the emptiness beyond. The field began to flare as it hurtled toward their ship, dark lightning lancing through the azure. It should have been noisy, a form filled with thunderous growling, but it was not.

Death was silent, waiting.

The *Anger* and the shimmering energy field converged. The lights of the missiles slid away around all sides of the monitor, leaving the tank a field of glaring blue. *I'm sorry, Hallan. Maybe when we meet you can tell me why this happened.* A primal urge made Colin want to shut his eyes, as if in denying vision he could deny this ending. He forced himself to watch, waiting for the instant when the *Anger* would plunge into the energy field and be torn apart.

The field *opened* as if a fist had punched through the shimmering death. Colin stared at the tank in disbelief. Stars beckoned beyond. Colin stared for a second, then hurriedly took the *Anger*'s helm, guiding the farship through that impossible rent.

The ominous sea tint in the monitor washed to the edges of the tank and disappeared.

As a miracle, it was almost anticlimactic.

Colin realized that Kiri was shouting. "Colin! You see, you see!" In the background, Pale was trilling in her own language, emitting quick, birdlike syllables that Colin, though he could not understand them, knew to be a paean.

"I saw," Colin replied. "By MolitorAb Herself, I saw it."

He began to laugh.

Ascendant Huan Su was on his knees in the dirt, his cassock streaked and muddy, his knobby hands stained with humus. He wiped his brow, smearing a brownish trail across his forehead as he leaned back on his folded legs in a *seiza* posture. He looked over his garden and was pleased—the emerald green of moss dappling the stones, the bright sound of the stream moving in its rocky bed, the plants swaying in a soft, fragrant breeze off the bay. Su patted the lump of rose quartz in front of him. It had taken the Ascendant a week to decide where to put this particular rock: just to his left, near the stream and away from the bonsai tree. There the crystal would catch the last beams of the afternoon sun and fling them back to the windows of Tokyo Cathedral. Someone glancing out at the meticulous little courtyard—Su's own small obsession—might see the delicate gleam like the winking of the sun's eye. Su nodded. Yes, this would be good. He leaned forward again, patting dirt around the base of the stone.

Absorbed in his work, he didn't hear Culper approaching along the winding gravel path until the man cleared his throat. "Ascendant Su?"

Su finished his work with slow precision before he glanced up, tapping the earth into place and arranging the sphagnum moss around the flank—green leading to the green of the bushes at his right hand. Then, groaning, he rose. His joints cracked audibly, nor could he straighten all the way. *The price one pays for age. I'm not complaining, my Lord—the cost is not much.* Su made no attempt to brush dirt from his hopelessly soiled robe. "Good afternoon, Joseph," he said. The man's presence spoiled his good mood, but he refused to allow the irritation to show. He made himself smile.

"Huan." Culper bowed stiffly. He glanced down at the quartz. "You could get one of your assistants to help you, you know. All that bending isn't good for you at your age."

"But the discipline does wonders for the soul, Joseph—and which is more important, neh? A soul at peace or a body that moves slightly better than it might?" His narrow eyes peered at Culper. His smile was a faint irony.

"The Church has need of your body, Huan. Someone else could do the maintenance on this courtyard for you and allow you more rest for the Church's work."

"Then it would no longer be my garden; I'd have no peace in its serenity anymore. That would be very sad, Joseph. Please allow me that small vanity." Su took a deep breath, tasting the salt tang of the sea breeze. It soothed him. *If you could only still the death in my gut, my garden. If only I could borrow your tranquility.* Then he laughed inwardly. *Yes, that tranquility will come soon. God will call you to Him and you will have all His peace. Soon. Be patient.* The words seemed to come from some mischievous spirit in his soul. Su chuckled outwardly and Culper frowned.

"Don't worry, Joseph," Su said. "I laugh at idle thoughts, that's all. I'm sure that I'm keeping you from some urgent business. You didn't come all the way out here just to tell an old gardener that he should spare his back, did you?"

"No," Culper admitted. "I've just received some news I thought you would want to hear." Culper frowned at Su. "It's done, Huan. We allowed Fairwood to escape Chebar. The manner in which we let him go will lend him the reputation that we desire."

"We?" Su stressed the word lightly. "I would like to believe that you didn't come out here to gloat, Joseph."

"Gloat?" Culper sounded hurt. "I know how you feel on this subject, Huan. I wouldn't presume to anger you by being childish. No, I wanted to be the one to tell you so that I could also say that I'm grateful to you for keeping the rules of the Conclave and maintaining silence concerning the Church's intentions toward this Fairwood."

"I've given my life in service to the Church, Joseph. I've seen her do some things that I've considered wrong, perhaps abhorrent, but my faith and allegiance have never wavered. The Ascendants' will was that we all remain silent—your plan would never work without that agreement."

"Sometimes people have felt that conscience is a higher authority than the Ascendants."

"We're all of us human, Joseph, me no less than you. I'm certain in my mind that you are utterly and completely wrong in this. I'll continue to oppose you in whatever way I can. I pray to God that we've not made an incredible blunder, but I've just enough humility to realize that there is a possibility—faint, as I perceive it—that your way might not lead to catastrophe. So I have done as I have said I would do."

Culper's heavy black eyebrows were twisted in a frown. "You puzzle me, Huan."

"I puzzle myself, Joseph. I'd rather shout my feelings to the world than keep this deception bottled up inside me. I pray every night that God will give me a sign to speak or to indicate that I'm doing the correct thing by being obedient to the will of the majority of the Ascendants." A bitterness rose in him, souring his stomach. He turned away so that Culper could not see it.

"Then you *would* speak if you thought God willed you to do so."

"I would." The conviction in his voice startled even Su. *And you ache to do it. It would be like spitting out bile. It would be a way to say "I'm sorry" to the memories of the Purge.*

"The MulSendero faith is the worst enemy that our Church has faced. The Stekoni heresy was tolerable when only a few were tainted by it. But now Hallan Gelt has turned against all humanity."

"Do you believe in the strength of God, Joseph?"

"Of course." The answer was pat and automatic.

"I don't think that you do. If you did, then you wouldn't worry about the MulSendero. You'd know that God will eventually triumph as long as we have faith."

"Faith sometimes requires action."

Su shook his head wearily. The sun, setting behind the steeples of the cathedral, threw shadows at their feet. "You have just said what all restless, impatient people say to rationalize their deeds."

Annoyance flushed Culper's neck, though his face remained blandly neutral. "You think that *I'm* impatient and faithless?"

"I think that you've fallen into the trap of listening to Satan's words, yes."

Culper's mouth opened, then shut. His eyes glinted, narrowing.

"I tell you that you're wrong, Ascendant, and I resent your arrogant superiority."

"Then we have nothing more to say, do we?" Su's answer was mild and gentle. He leaned over to pick up his trowel, patting down the moss around his stone. He heard Culper begin to speak, then evidently change his mind. Culper began to walk away. Hunched over, Su said softly: "Are you going to try killing *me* again, as well as your Fairwood? You might have to, Joseph."

The footsteps halted, scrunching on the gravel. Su continued to work. Finally, the footsteps began again, receding toward the cathedral.

The gold green light of afternoon turned ruddy with twilight. The dying rays of the sun struck fire from the quartz before slipping below the tiled, sway-backed roofs.

Su worked until the stars pierced the sky.

EPIPHANY
2559

. . . But I really have to tell you about Dridust. You've heard all the tales about Colin Fairwood going around the Fringes—I had a three-day layover before the Dridust Master could get a cargo for me, so I went down to the Flats to see him where he's been holed up. After all the wild talk about my old friend, I thought it'd be interesting to see the truth. The way I envisioned it, we'd talk, joke about the Chebar mess, and commiserate about the way the Holdings has been treating the Galicht lately. Hell, maybe we'd even go to bed later, if he wanted to. The poor guy isn't what anyone can call handsome or even friendly most of the time. You knew him; you know what I'm talking about.

I guess I should have known. You'd hardly believe it, Sarah. Fairwood has his own little town out on the Flats, with a few thousand people around: Buntaro, Galicht, even a few Stekoni, though most of them are the curious and the simple-faithful type. I could hardly get near Colin. There's an entourage around him to keep away the rabble—the Sabbai, they're called. One of them, a Buntaro bitch, screws him when he wants it, I heard. I tell you, it's a regular circus and Fairwood's in the center ring.

He's changed. A lot. I remember a confused and surly guy, but that person's gone. I think he's been to the Veils a few times too often. He's totally caught up in this Sartius Exori role. I thought I could talk to him, crack a few jokes, and he'd be telling me with that weird grin of his how this is the best sham he's ever managed to pull. But now I think that it's not an act with him. I think he believes it all . . .

. . . He saw me and came over, all dusty and windblown, with everyone gathered around him and gazing at him with smiles and nods. He shook his head at me and said: "I see that you still shut your ears to the Voice, Mari. That's a shame."

"Do I look like I'm crazy, Fairwood?" I told him.

"Poor Mari," he said with this damn pity in his voice, like I was some neglected pet he'd found. "We were so alike in our unhappiness. I tell you that we both held a chimera in our minds and we called it sanity. We were afraid to listen. Mari, reality is contained in the howling of the beasts in the Void. True peace is in the word of MolitorAb. The Galicht know, many of them, even if they won't speak it for fear of what others would say. You know it too."

I should have said something, but I couldn't. He had all those people around him, and he so obviously *believed*. How was I going to convince a madman? He stared at me for a long time with this sad little smile on his lips and that wrecked, awful face. I don't know if he thought I'd fall on my knees in front of him or what. Then he moved on. His disciples all looked at me as if I was garbage that should shrivel up in the heat and blow away...

...I watched him preaching. After his sermon, a woman came up to him, limping rather badly. He prayed over her for a time, and then she gave out a strange, small cry and jumped up, laughing. She danced away from Fairwood and everyone around me oohed and aahed at the supposed cure. I wasn't impressed, I'm afraid. It would have been too easy to fake. From what I understand, there are weekly miracles out here for the edification of the masses. I wonder if Fairwood is as duped as the rest.

If he is, then it's easy to diagnose his problem.

He's listened to the Veils. He's mad.

I used to like him. Truly. I don't think I like *this* Colin.

> —excerpts, letter from Mari Salay
> to Sarah Miller, July 6, 2559

CHAPTER TEN

For I know that after my death ye will in any wise deal corruptly, and turn aside from the way which I have commanded you; and evil will befall you in the end of days; because you will do that which is evil in the sight of the Lord, to provoke Him through the work of your hands.

OLD TESTAMENT, Deuteronomy XXI:29

And leaving Chebar in the wake of signs and wonders, the Sartius Exori came to Dridust and there resided for a time; his people flocked to him to listen to his words and follow his path.

THE TESTAMENT OF JOSHUA, 2:52

Kiri and FirstBred Pale watched the *Anger* ground in the Flats beyond the village of Genesis. The farship's descent whipped up swirling clouds of alkali sand—both Kiri and Pale wore the *thorbani* of the Dridust natives, a wrapping of thin cloth that draped their faces like gauze, protecting them from the abrasive, stinging sands. The ship's ramp slid down as the searing winds took the storm to the southeast and away from them. A figure stepped from the ship and waved at them.

FirstBred Pale laughed and ran toward him; Kiri followed more slowly. She watched Colin hug the Stekoni, then open his arms to her. Her lips tight, she let him embrace her without returning the affectionate gesture. "Well?" she asked.

"The Voice spoke to me again," he said. He stared at Kiri, an unasked question in his eyes. "I'll tell you about it later, when we've gathered the Sabbai together." He coughed as the wind shifted direction and cast a veil of sand over them. He shaded his eyes against the glare of Dridust's blue white sun. "You're angry with me."

"You knew that I'd be angry when you left," she answered. "You also know why. You shouldn't act so surprised."

99

Listening, Pale shifted her weight from foot to foot uneasily. Kiri saw the motion and sighed at the Stekoni's apprehensive expression. *Can she sense it, feel it the way I can? Sometimes I think she knows that there is life stirring inside me. I'm amazed that Colin doesn't know it as well—how can he not when the child holds half of his life too?* With that musing came the other thought. *I must tell him soon. A year ago, when we first talked of the possibility, he wanted this child... yet each day he becomes less my lover and more MolitorAb's possession.* "Colin, you know that I think you're taking unnecessary chances," Kiri said wearily, trying to explain. Again.

Tendons slid past each other in his transparent face. "You have to learn that MolitorAb protects me, Kiri. You've told me that often enough when *I've* been the doubting one."

Pale took a step closer to the two of them, her head down, her musky odor sour. "This one does not wish to intrude, Colin Exori, but she feels as does Kiri Oharu. Forgive this one her lack of faith, but she, too, worries."

"Am I Sartius Exori?"

"This one believes so, of course."

"Then there's no danger in meeting with my God. I must go into the Veils. I must hear what MolitorAb would tell me."

"Please forgive this one's presumption," Pale continued doggedly, "but then this one thinks that you should at least take Kiri Oharu or another of the Sabbai with you so that you may give your full attention to Her voice and not be concerned with bringing the ship from the Veils. Colin Exori, too many ships have been lost when—"

"—When their pilots went mad. Is that what you're saying?" Colin's mockery raked both of them. "I'm not about to go veilmad, Kiri, Pale. At least, no more than I already might be."

"Damn it, Colin, don't be such a son of a bitch," Kiri replied heatedly. "If genuine concern bothers you so much..." Kiri stopped herself, taking a deep breath and closing her eyes. She could feel the angry, frustrated tears coming and didn't want him to see them. *Colin, I love you, I acknowledge you as my spiritual leader, but you're still an asshole at times.* Colin was changing—they were all seeing it, all the Sabbai. Kiri and FirstBred Pale knew it best; they had known Colin longest. Aaron and Joshua, the Buntaro who had followed Colin from Chebar and had become part of the inner circle of disciples, they spoke of it as well, in whispered conversations. The remaining Sabbai, if they noticed, did not seem to mind. SlowBorn Brightness, a Stekoni priest who had joined them, articulated that position best. "This one would not question the methods of MolitorAb," she had said. "What She needs the Sartius Exori to be, he will be."

Perhaps. Kiri watched the growing power in Colin with unvoiced trepidation. There were times when she felt she preferred the old, unsure Colin to this confident Exori; it was easier to love his vulnerability.

Colin frowned at her anger. Then he tried to chuckle; the laughter had a ragged edge that tore at Kiri. "I've been touched by the hands of God, Kiri. Her touch is never gentle. Tell me, FirstBred Pale, didn't the Stekoni fear the insanity of the First Prophets?"

"Yes, Colin Exori, for sometimes they were violent, but this one..." Pale went silent. She could see that Colin had stopped listening.

Colin put an arm around Kiri; she shrugged it away after a moment. The sun's heat buffeted them, radiating from the baked earth. The *Anger*'s hull ticked and groaned as it shed its own greater heat from the long descent. "Let's get out of the light," Colin said, trying to end the argument that was so obviously distressing all of them. "We can talk better in Genesis, eh?"

He began to walk away. After a shared scowl, Pale and Kiri followed.

The village was not impressive. In the year and a half since Colin had come to the Fringe world of Dridust, this place had become more than just another oasis in the Great Flats, but it had yet to move much beyond being a motley collection of houses formed of mud bricks, baked white in the ferocious sun and set in a swarm of brightly colored tents and awnings. The former campsite of mineral caravans, the small area around the springs had become crowded with those seeking the Sartius Exori, with those who wanted to see the Dridust Pretender. As Colin approached Genesis, the faithful and the curious began to crowd around him, chanting "Colin Exori!" and reaching out with hands of sun-blackened skin or oil-slicked fur, most of the faces *thorbani*-masked. The majority were human, but now the occasional Stekoni walked under the sparse shade of the jug palms.

They had come following the trail of rumor and legend, the tales rippling outward from the events on Chebar. The Holdings press had said little, but the stories had spread despite the efforts of the Church to suppress them. The God-obsessed masses of the Fringes passed on the word, perhaps slightly embellished after each telling;

the Zakkaist authorities could not stop that. Buntaro leaflets circulated the rumors in garish prose, MulSendero preachers hinted of it from their pulpits.

Gelt's vision is about to unfold. He is here, among us. He has come. This is the One.

The government of Dridust had not seemed happy with Colin's choice of residence. They had also not been anxious to offend the newest and most successful of the Pretenders, but they obviously hoped to avoid the potential crises his presence might entail. They had hinted that the Great Flats that belted their world's arid equator might be a better site for Colin than the greener cities of the temperate latitudes.

Colin had laughed and gone into the sandy wastes, taking with him those closest to him—the Sabbai, now numbering seven—and a few hundred followers.

From that beginning, the settlement had grown. Its inhabitants pressed around him now. Colin smiled into the swirl of faces, touching the outstretched fingers, stroking the wind-dry cheeks. They gazed on him and did not turn away in distaste at the sight of his face. That unflinching adoration was something Colin had come to need, Kiri knew. The adoration itself was responsible for some of the changes in him. In this role, he'd found a niche where his appearance did not matter; in fact, it rendered him more visible and distinct. She could feel him feeding on the energy of the crowd, letting their power flow through him, soothing him. He began to smile, grinning as they walked slowly down the loud, dusty, hot street. He hugged Kiri to him again and reached out to stroke Pale's shoulder as if no disagreement had come between them.

"MolitorAb spoke very clearly to me this time," he said. "Her message was extraordinarily clear. I know we've talked of leaving Dridust, but we must stay. We must prepare for a visitor."

"Who?" Kiri asked. "Primus Keller, more of the Stekoni? Colin, Genesis can only expand so far, the resources here are so limited—"

"An Ascendant," Colin said. Kiri could not believe the calmness with which he said the word. "Huan Su, if my vision is correct." He came to a halt in the middle of the street, stooping to embrace one of the camp children. The onlookers encircled them, smiling at the scene. Colin glanced back and laughed at the expressions on Kiri and Pale's faces. "You doubt me?" he asked. He released the child, who ran giggling back to her father.

"No," Kiri answered. "Of course not. But why would the Ascendant come here?..."

Pale gave voice to the premonition that had caused Kiri to falter. "Does he have warships? Is that it, Colin Exori?" she said. "Then these ones must be made ready to flee, as this one had feared. They are in jeopardy."

"That's not certain," Colin said. He stood, brushing dust from his knee. "I wasn't shown such a thing, and in any case, it doesn't matter."

"How can you mean that, Colin Exori?" Pale asked.

"Do I need to placate the doubts of a disciple whose faith is weak?" The haughtiness was back in his voice, the jovial mood gone as quickly as it had come. The quilt of skinbase and flesh that was his face tautened. "Su's coming—that's the entire extent of my revelation. If it isn't enough for the two of you, then go into the Veils yourselves and tell MolitorAb that you're not satisfied with Her gift. I don't need your doubt clouding my sight."

Pale's mouth had dropped open. She glanced at Kiri, a look of silent pleading. Underlids covered her golden eyes in a reflexive fear response. Then she bowed deeply to Colin. "Sartius Exori, this one apologizes. Truly. She should let her faith speak and not her fears." Her fur shimmered in the sunlight, the folds of the *thorbani* falling over one shoulder.

"No," Kiri said. "No. You shouldn't need to apologize, First-Bred Pale. Colin, you've no one who believes in you more than FirstBred Pale, and she doesn't deserve your shabby treatment." Kiri rested her hands, balled into fists, on her hips, her eyes blazing above the *thorbani*.

For a moment she thought Colin would explode in a torrent of rage, but the lines of his face eased slowly as he turned to her. His hand came up and traced the steep fall of her cheekbone. He nodded at her, and she saw the affection in his gaze. "You're right, love," he said very quietly, then turned to Pale. "This one is also sorry, FirstBred Pale. My emotions tend to get a little ragged after I've been through the Veils. I shouldn't have let them get the better of me."

Colin bent down on one knee again and took a handful of sand from the lane. "You see this sand? Once it was part of those mountains." He nodded toward the distant blue peaks of the range. "The work of an age of wind turned those rocks to this. The sand itself will change in time. Each grain has its own purpose in MolitorAb's creation. So do we. The mountain shouldn't concern itself with the sand or the wind, the sun shouldn't wonder what the water is doing. All will be revealed as MolitorAb wills." He let the tiny granules drift between his fingers; they streamed back to the ground, glinting.

"My feelings bind me to you more closely than wind is bound to stone, Colin," Kiri said to him.

Colin said nothing as he stirred the sand with a forefinger. He seemed lost in his own musing. Pale raised her eyebrows to Kiri, who shook her head. They waited, and at last Colin sighed.

"I'm very tired," he said. "The trip was exhausting and the veildream . . . it was very draining. Let me go and rest—Kiri, would you wake me in an hour? I'll want to speak with the Sabbai after that, so tell them to gather in the temple."

Kiri hugged him, but her kiss was perfunctory and distracted. Colin didn't seem to notice. Again, she wondered when she should tell him her own news. Not now, certainly. Maybe not soon at all.

Colin smiled at them and moved down the lane toward the MulSendero temple where the Sabbai resided. He paused often to speak with those who came up to him. He joked with the children, comforted the sick, spoke with those who questioned him.

Kiri turned away finally to find Pale regarding her strangely. "You still smile when you watch him, Kiri, even though I know you are upset."

"My anger doesn't change my feelings for him." She shrugged. "I love him. Mostly, we're happy."

"This one can't help but be concerned, Kiri Oharu." Pale's wide mouth was twisted with distress. "This one worries for the Sartius Exori as you do. We both know that he goes into the Veils alone, with no one to aid him should he become lost and disoriented. You tell me that he does not eat well. He sometimes goes alone into the Flats for days at a time. He seeks visions and in seeking them he courts his own destruction, embraces insanity as a mistress." Pale kicked at the sand with a sandaled, bony foot. "Does this one say anything that Kiri Oharu has not already thought?"

A stab of fear had gone through Kiri at Pale's words. She shivered despite the heat. "No," Kiri admitted. "And I understand that he must do as MolitorAb wills. Sometimes I remember how troubled he was when we found him, and I'm amazed that I can be so afraid for us now that he has found his path. What of you, FirstBred Pale? You were searching for the Sartius Exori and you've found him. You should be grateful."

Pale almost smiled. "This one supposes so. And perhaps, as Colin Exori has accused, this one's faith is not as great as it should be. This one does not doubt him though. This one can believe that Ascendant Su is coming."

"He doesn't seem upset by the revelation."

Pale took a deep breath. "Kiri Oharu tells me, then, that she has also noted that complacency on the Exori's part. Does she also wonder whether that is...?"

"Is what?"

Pale hesitated. Her hands tugged at the knot of her loincloth, tapped at the seam of her young-pouches. "Sane, Kiri Oharu. Sane. The alteration of Colin Fairwood disturbs this one, jars her. It has happened so quickly. MolitorAb forgive this one, but she hopes that the Voice has chosen a strong vessel to be Exori. This one would not like to see him destroyed. You are his lover, Kiri Oharu, his confidant. You know him as none of the rest of us can. Please, talk with him; see what we must do to serve him best."

Kiri's mouth curved in a smile tinged with melancholy. Unbidden, her hands cupped the imagined swell of her stomach. "FirstBred Pale also knows that I've felt those same fears and that I've tried to confront Colin with them before. I sleep with him, yes. I can soothe Colin the man, but I'm afraid that I've little contact with the Mad One inside him. *That* one is married to MolitorAb, not me." She adjusted the ribbing of her *thorbani* as a gust of wind sprayed sand against the buildings.

"And if Ascendant Su is coming to destroy him and us? It is an unworthy thought for this one, but Gelt's scripture says that the Sartius Exori is under MolitorAb's protection—but Gelt says nothing of those around the Exori. This one speaks not only from personal fear, Kiri Oharu, but this one does not *wish* to die unless she must."

"We've both told Colin that we feel he should leave Dridust, for many reasons. This is simply another. If he wants to stay..." Kiri paused, glancing at the aching pinpoint of sun at the zenith. She continued with more confidence than she felt. "...then I will stay as well."

Pale sighed. Kiri could smell a sudden change in the Stekoni's scent, as if some inner decision had touched the chemistry of her glands. "This one is also a tool in the Sartius Exori's hands," she said. "This one only hopes she is not destined to be broken. Kiri Oharu, this one is afraid she wishes that Colin Fairwood had not been so touched by the Voice. Is that sinful?"

"I won't hide *my* feelings from him, FirstBred Pale. If I did, then I couldn't say that I loved him. You'll do the Exori no service by following blindly."

They walked slowly toward the temple as the crowds began to disperse. Many of the people nodded respectfully to the two First disciples. The sun gave eternal heat to the land; the winds blew sand at the distant mountains, shaping them with a centuries-slow hand.

There were no quiet gardens aboard the cruiser *Jehovah's Sword*. The best Su had been able to arrange was to fill his admittedly spacious rooms with a myriad of plants. Commander Benesch had looked askance at the fronds of greenery but had prudently said nothing, only ordering his ensign to make certain that all the pots were properly secured so as to be no danger to the Ascendant during any possible high-gravity maneuvers. Su tended the makeshift garden with devotion—it was his sole diversion during the long voyage. Dridust was several weeks and three Veil passages away.

After the second passage, Su called Mother Crowell to him.

He was disturbed. Even the feel of loamy soil could not soothe him. He had never been so marked by a veildream before; the images kept nagging at him.

Mother Crowell, or at least his mad image of her, attacking him with a carnivore's razored teeth. Her nails were bloody, a terrible smile was on her mouth. In that nightmare, she killed him, slowly and painfully, stalking him through the gardens of Tokyo, pouncing on him to tear the living meat from his frail bones and devour it.

Su had not wanted her to accompany him on this trip. He had been unable to accomplish that—ostensibly, she was aboard as an observer for the curator's office, Colin Fairwood being under formal charges in the Holdings. Su knew she was Joseph Culper's eyes, and he suspected she had other tasks as well. Su wondered whether, knowing what he intended to do on Dridust, she would make an attempt to stop him.

Mother Crowell entered his rooms with habitual deference, her eyes downcast, her stance and demeanor humble. She knelt before him and he held his hand out so she could kiss the ring of his office.

His hand trembled, palsied. She touched the ring with her lips and looked at him.

Su knew that he was not pleasant to look at. His limbs were afflicted with an eternal tremor. The progress of his diseases had left him skeletal, his skin drawn drum-tight over his skull, his eyes buried in cavernous dark hollows. His arms were splotched with ulcerous patches, some scabbed with a yellowish crust. He wheezed: even a short walk left him winded for minutes. Each night, David— for the doctor had insisted upon accompanying the Ascendant— tethered Su's life to machines that beeped and purred in his bedroom. "An immune-system deficiency," was all that Su knew or cared to know. Death hovered by him like a bright carrion bird—he didn't need to ask its name.

"Ascendant Su," Mother Crowell said, "you look well today."

Su laughed aridly at that. "Please, Anna, I'm well beyond expecting small, polite lies. I admit that I tend to avoid mirrors, but I'm well aware of my appearance."

"I'm sorry, Ascendant."

He waved a hand at her. "Don't be. I apologize if I sounded gruff." Su appraised her, kneeling before him. "How was your Veil passage, Anna?"

She shook her head and smiled wanly. "Tedious and filled with too many images, Ascendant. I'd rather not talk about it."

"Did the Voice torment you?"

"I've heard it before," she replied. "I try to laugh when it speaks. I think about it being the devil, trying to snare my soul."

The old man sighed. "I do see how we lose the faithful to MolitorAb, Mother. When we worry about the veildreams, I suspect that we only increase the likelihood of making our fears spring to life before us. MolitorAb, or whatever that Voice may be, senses doubt and forms it into a palpable shape. Or maybe MolitorAb is only our own lack of faith being shown to us. Well, we only have one more ordeal to face before we meet this Colin Fairwood. You've met the man, Anna. What did you think of him?"

"I thought him tormented, Ascendant," she replied without hesitation. "He put on a brave, stoic front, yet behind it you could see his soul cowering."

"That's very poetic, Mother, and very subjective." A dull pain spread through Su's chest. He grimaced, clutching his robes involuntarily. Seeing Mother Crowell rivet her attention on him, he forced his hands to relax, shutting off the feeling in his mind. *There is no pain—all you feel is life.*

"The description still seems apt," she was saying, standing firm against Su's gentle admonition. "Perhaps I was being a little too subjective, as you say, but I think you'd find that to be accurate as well."

"Is he still so tormented, do you think?"

"I believe that he has settled the war within himself."

"Given in to madness?" Su prompted. "That is what Ascendant Culper has said in his public statements on the Chebar mess."

The priest gave him a shrug. "Mad or not, Ascendant, he has come to terms with what troubled him, or he couldn't have begun to act at all. He was very indecisive when I met him. He blustered, but it was all a sham. He did what I told him to do. The person who escaped from Chebar had begun to fight back."

"What of his miracles? His powers? Colin Fairwood has healed, according to the reports—cured illness, produced signs and wonders, evaded at least one potentially deadly situation. By rights, Fairwood should have died on his farship, trying to escape Chebar." He knew that for falsehood; he wondered if she knew as well.

Her face revealed nothing. "He has benefited from the gullibility of the masses, Ascendant. They expect miracles of their Sartius Exori and shall have them despite truth. I don't think I need tell you that evidence doesn't mean anything to a person who is determined to ignore it."

"Some people would claim that *our* prophets can be explained away in the same manner, Mother."

"I don't doubt my faith, Ascendant," she replied. "Do you doubt yours?"

The impudence of the question nearly sent him into shocked laughter. He struggled to control his scorn, censoring the barbed reply he might otherwise have made. Instead, he cleared his throat warningly. When she only glared back at him, he knew that this priest considered herself immune to his wrath; that therefore she felt her mission for Culper made her invulnerable. Su determined he would try to keep her away from Fairwood if he could.

"Faith has been an excuse for many beliefs and actions over the centuries, Mother. Once I thought that faith allowed me to kill because that was the will of the Ascendants of the time." His eyes clouded with remembered pain and his hands became claws. "I paid for that faith with years of guilt. I'm still not certain that God doesn't continue to punish me for those days."

"Then you need to strengthen yourself, Ascendant. God can forgive anything and His demands on us can be mysterious. Isn't that what we teach?"

She was humoring him, he noted. Impatience sharpened her stare. He was tempted to rail at her, to see if she would react with sharp words in return. *Wanting to show off your power a little, Huan? Does she make you feel so puny you need to indulge your vanity? Or are you just wondering whether you ever had any hold on her at all?* He shook his head at his own frailty and noticed that she was watching him closely again. He knew, suddenly, that she considered him a doddering old fool. He told himself he didn't care.

He leaned forward and touched the fronds of a *Dracaena marginata*. The yellow-shot strands whispered under his fingers, the edges of the thin leaves sharp and rasping. The feel brought back images of the veildreams: Mother Crowell's hands on his throat, throttling him, the fingers cold as steel, her foul bitter breath on his face.

Su wanted her gone. Now. He was weary of her defiance, tired just from the work of concentrating. Soon, he knew, the weariness would swell and he would press the contact on his wrist that would call David. His friend would come and strap him into the embrace of the machinery once more. Su wanted to see Anna Crowell's face no longer, those features that his veildreams had distorted and made horrible. He plunged his fingertips into the cool soil of the dracaena. "We should give life back to life, Mother Crowell," he said, not knowing where the words came from or what they meant. "It's a humbling experience to work with this soil, for you learn that the earth has much still to teach us, even after our thousands of years of working with her. Sometimes I wonder if humanity looked in the wrong direction when we became entranced by the stars. Maybe we should have looked beneath our feet for enlightenment. After all, we are more earth than air."

"Yes, Ascendant." Politely.

Unsettled, he dismissed her then and watched the relief flood her face as she kissed his ring once more and rose. After she had left, he got to his feet groaning and shuffled around the room, touching all his plants and cleansing his mind of thought. The discipline of his soul came slowly back to him—a state in which he was simply an open vessel, a receptor and not a judge.

When the next Veil passage came, several hours later, he sighed and gave himself to it.

Again, the shade of Mother Crowell waited for him.

CHAPTER ELEVEN

Do not suppose that my mission on earth is to spread peace. My mission is to spread, not peace, but division. I have come to set a man at odds with his father, a daughter with her mother, a daughter-in-law with her mother-in-law: in short, to make a man's enemies those of his own household.

NEW TESTAMENT, Matthew 10:34–36

And even those who were his enemies sought to make peace with the Sartius Exori, and he spread wide his hands. Gladly, he embraced them as he would a brother or sister.

THE TESTAMENT OF JOSHUA, 12:1–2

The reactions to Ascendant Su's arrival on Dridust were as varied as the interests they reflected. Dridust's government erupted into near panic as the political factions of its parliament quickly polarized. The minority Zakkaist members allied with the out-of-favor Social Realists, whose cause was to bring Dridust into the ranks of the Holdings worlds. Together, the two factions nearly forced a vote of no confidence against the majority leadership, many of whom wished to forbid the intrusion of a Holdings naval cruiser into Dridust orbit. There was a certain false air to all the indignant cries in the stormy sessions—Dridust had only the barest semblance of a navy itself, its ships being mostly converted from the hulls of outmoded Holdings cargo ships. *Jehovah's Sword* would have been as little bothered by them as a wolf by mosquitoes. After a week of furious debate whose rancor destroyed more than one political friendship, the inevitable compromise was reached. *Jehovah's Sword* would be permitted to enter Dridust orbit. In truth, if that was what the Ascendant Su wanted, there was no way for Dridust to stop it. Since Su insisted that his mission was peaceful, the government could assuage its pride by gracefully "allowing" the cruiser to park in orbit.

It was not certain where the prayers of the Sartius Exori and his Sabbai went. The impending arrival had sown as much discord in their ranks as it had among the politicians: the Sabbai were not a unified group either. They had come to Dridust and Colin at the behest of a myriad of voices.

Amid the furor, only Colin seemed unperturbed. He smiled at all the impassioned rhetoric and kept his own counsel.

"How can you be so calm?" Kiri asked the night before *Jehovah's Sword* was to arrive in orbit. She lay curled against him, his arm under her. The open window of their bedroom gave no breeze—sweat trickled between her breasts and Colin's chest was slick. They had not made love, not for several days, nor had Colin eaten anything in that time. Kiri was used to his periodic abstinences; in those times, Colin said, the visions would come.

Denial opens the paths of the soul.

"'We need to speak.' That's what Su said in his message to me, Kiri. How can I deny that of a man? Why should speech cause me to worry?"

"You really believe that all he wants to do is talk?"

"In his heart he wants more, but he'll find another answer here."

"What does that mean?"

Colin shrugged and became silent. Someone moved in the street below them: a quick laugh, a voice blurred in the night. Kiri sighed and stroked the muscles of Colin's neck and shoulders. "Colin, if you're wrong, the price we'll pay is too great. That cruiser could destroy Genesis and everyone in it before we could run. In ten minutes. Less."

She could feel his amusement. "They could try. But Su won't allow it."

"You've never met the man. How can you be so sure of him?" She was upset with him; it sharpened her words. Then another thought occurred to her. "Unless MolitorAb has spoken to you again. Has She?"

"In which case you'd no longer be angry? Is that it, Kiri? Colin the man can make a mistake but Colin the prophet can't be wrong. So what would you have me do, Kiri Oharu? Should I hold the Ascendant hostage and demand a ransom as Aaron and Joshua wish, or do you preach Pale's argument and want me to flee screaming into the Flats?"

"Please don't mock me, Colin," she said quietly. "I don't know what I think. At one time, yes, I'd be with the Buntaro. Maybe a more aggressive stance would be better, lest we become victims."

"You'd risk the life inside you?"

His words were soft and even. They struck her like a blow. She pushed him away from her, sitting up in the bed and hugging herself. "How long have you known?" she demanded. "*How* did you know?"

"Ahh, Kiri, no matter how hard you try, you sometimes doubt me as much as I once did myself."

"You've no doubts any longer?"

In the darkness, she thought she saw him frown. She heard his fingers brushing the sheets, back and forth, restless; still he didn't answer.

"Colin?"

"If *you* doubted me, why did you allow yourself to become pregnant?"

"I've only missed one period. Nothing's certain yet—that's why I haven't said anything."

"It's certain," he replied. "*I* tell you that."

"The man or the prophet?"

The intake of breath was a hiss. One of the moons was up, silvering the walls. His head was a silhouette against it; a line of shifting light sliding across it as he turned away from her. She touched his hair with soft fingers. "Talk to me, Colin."

"I don't know what you want me to say."

"How do you feel, knowing you're going to be a father?"

Moonlight curved a cheek, gleamed in the hollow of an eye: he turned back to her. "A little scared. Maybe a lot scared. But I'm happy with it, Kiri. Very much so."

"Truly?"

"It's too important to lie about."

"I'm scared too, Colin. More than you."

"I know. I can understand that."

She shook her head. His hand stroked the swell of her leg under the sheet. "I don't think you can. I really don't think so. It has nothing to do with you as man or you as Exori either. I just don't think you can comprehend what this means to me. If you did, you'd see how hard it is for me simply to stand by and watch the Zakkaists come here."

"Back to that again?"

"Damn it, don't patronize me, Colin," she said heatedly. "Don't treat me like some nosy disciple. I'm carrying your *child*. I don't want to lose you now. I don't want to bear him or her in some Holdings prison. We've both said that we love each other. I think that gives me the right—no, the *obligation*—to ask you a few questions. If you're acting because MolitorAb insists that you do so, fine. But She doesn't determine all your decisions, does She?"

"I'm not a puppet. No."

"Then you could be making a mistake?" At the last moment, her voice tilted upward into a question.

He sounded weary when he finally replied. "MolitorAb told me that Su was coming. I saw him, walking on the Flats with me."

"If that was the extent of your vision, then Pale or Aaron or any of the rest could be right."

"Yes." Flatly. "And your advice is no better than theirs."

"Agreed," she said. *Don't be angry with him—he's hurt and striking back. You wanted him to show his vulnerability. Don't make him regret it or you'll never see him this open again.* "Colin, I just want you to be careful. People already see this as a conflict between our God and their God."

"MolitorAb *is* their God, remember."

"That's not how the Church perceives it."

Colin rolled away from her on the bed, the sheets rustling beneath him as they momentarily cooled despite the dry heat of the Flats. "I don't *know* what MolitorAb wants," he said, and his voice was choked with unusual confusion. "I feel like a piece in a game, Kiri. I may even be a relatively important piece—the king in chess, perhaps—but I don't control the game; I can't even see most of it. There's some player at my back that directs the movements. All *I* know is what the pieces nearest me would like me to do: you, Pale, any of the rest of the Sabbai." The words came faster now, tumbling out like driftwood suddenly freed in a swirling current. "You tell me to be careful; Pale just wants to worship me and would feel best if all the politics were simply ignored; Aaron and a few of the others want me to grasp at all I can. Some would have me be messiah—king. Others just want another prophet. You all want Jesus or Mohammed or even another Simon ben Zakkai."

She heard his frustration in his slow exhalation. "None of you seems to want *me*," he said.

"What are you then?" Kiri asked. She wanted to touch him but was afraid to break the mood. The facade was down, as it so rarely had been for the past year or more. *Fairwood now, not Exori. I can love this man; I can only respect the Prophet. He's gone so much of late, this Fairwood...*

He spoke as if he guessed at her thoughts. "I'm the father of your child."

That made her smile briefly. "Other than that," she prodded.

His ravaged, grotesque face turned to her, dappled with the moon's brilliance. "I don't know, Kiri. I *still* don't know after two years." His eyes were bleak and sad. He sounded so unlike himself that she reached for him, took his head between her hands. "Sometimes I'm so sure of things that I can't understand how anyone can fail to see them as I do; then I get angry. Or I'm so filled with MolitorAb that the power nearly burns me from the inside so that I'm afraid to touch anyone for fear it would strike them dead. And at other moments I'm standing entirely outside myself, watching Her move my lips and tongue, performing all my actions for me. I'm a length of oak in the hands of MolitorAb, Kiri." His voice was a whisper. "I don't know if I'm to be a rod to strike those standing against Her, or a support to build into a new house. Maybe there's no way to tell until both have been tried."

His words frightened her, she felt a thrill of anxiety that turned her cold, suddenly and inexplicably. "Is that what you wanted to hear?" he asked. He laughed once—scornfully—and she thought she had lost him again until she glanced at his face and saw the shattered expression there.

"No," she said. She turned her head, brought him to her. She kissed him, tasting his warm breath.

"Your Sartius Exori is just a person," he said afterward, cradling his head against her neck. "And, yes, just a little mad. No one can look at God and remain as he was. I need you to understand that, Kiri, and forgive."

For a long time, she simply held him.

Long after he was asleep, she lay beside him, watching the shadows move as the moons slid down the sky.

CHAPTER TWELVE

And Balaam said unto Balak: "Lo, I am come unto thee; have I now any power at all to speak any thing? The word that God putteth in my mouth, that I shall speak."

OLD TESTAMENT, Numbers XXII:38

The Sartius Exori replied, saying: "How can you say, 'This is the work of MolitorAb' or 'This is not'? For all things issue from Her—you cannot speak a word that MolitorAb has not heard before it issues from your mouth. So speak as you will, only remember that it is MolitorAb's purpose that you fulfill."

THE TESTAMENT OF AARON, 56:34–37

The media on Dridust were ecstatic. The news of the historic meeting between the Dridust Pretender and Ascendant Su spread slowly over the vast distances between the worlds—it was far too late for any other news networks to send their own reporters. The lag time between worlds was measured in weeks: it was left to the meager resources of Dridust's various media to give an accounting to the widespread billions. They did their best.

A hundred lenses swung in unison as the shuttle from *Jehovah's Sword* slashed through the heat-rippled sky above the Flats. A like number of devices recorded the face of Colin Fairwood as the Pretender watched the approach with the Sabbai ranked behind him. Colin's arms were folded passively over his chest; his *thorbani* masked the features below the high cheekbones. The shuttle touched sand and sent long plumes into the winds; Colin did not move.

The Sabbai were more revealing of emotion than was the Pretender. Kiri's stance spoke of feral, open antipathy; Pale moved with nervous, flitting unease; Miriam, Joshua, and Aaron all seemed to be attempting an imitation of their leader's stoicism, a pretense spoiled by their restless hands and feet. To the left stood Samuel Conner, barefaced and hawk nosed, his attention not on the shuttle but on the Sartius Exori, as if anything other than Colin was unimportant. A little way behind him, standing judiciously downwind, was SlowBorn Brightness, the first Stekoni priest to join Colin's ranks. Her head was bowed, and her lips moved in what might have been a prayer.

Behind them all, the population of Genesis packed the sunbrilliant streets.

A mournful wail came from the grounded shuttle as the flight engines were disengaged. The craft lumbered slowly toward the waiting group, turning to give its side to the waiting cameras. A ramp slid from the gleaming metal. A door opened.

Ascendant Su stood there, tiny without his ceremonial robes. The face that filled the holotanks was far thinner than the official portrait that hung in the Zakkaist churches. He looked ill as he moved slowly from the top platform of the ramp. He wore simple cotton pants and tunic, the ring of his office his only jewelry. The physician David was the next one from the shuttle, his attention given to Su rather than to the crowds; behind him came several priests of Su's staff and then Anna Crowell. No guards made an appearance, which perhaps appeased some of Colin's faithful, though all could see the gun turrets of the craft. All the armaments were judiciously lowered, turned toward the emptiness of the Flats, but the crowd knew how quickly that could change.

The protocol of the visit had not been arranged in advance. The queries from Su's staff had been given the same curt reply each time, relayed from Colin via FirstBred Pale. "I am here if the Ascendant seeks me," had been the message. "Let him come as he wants."

The eyes and ears of the press waited for the first movement, the opening words. The winds of the Flats hissed like static in the electronic ears they carried.

Su came down the ramp with an old man's shuffle. At its end, he stepped onto the sands of Dridust. Colin did not move forward, and Su continued walking slowly toward him, halting a few meters away.

He bowed. "I'm given to understand that we may have met before, Colin Fairwood," he said. His smile was gentle, melancholy. "For that, I've already prayed for God's forgiveness. Now I've come seeking yours."

The news holocameras panned to the Pretender. Above his masked visage, light eyes glinted. His robes slapped in the gusting wind.

He took a step toward the Ascendant and extended a hand. "You don't need *my* forgiveness, Ascendant. You need that of MolitorAb."

Su shook his head, but the smile widened, showing small, crooked teeth. "On that point, I think we must remain divided. But I would speak with you on the subject. I think we can save a great deal of strife between beings of all faiths. Will you talk, Colin Fairwood?"

"I will, Ascendant."

Su took Colin's proferred hand.

They walked toward the white-gleaming town.

The meeting that afternoon was informal. A large, open tent had been erected halfway between Genesis and the bare stone hills that sheltered the town from the scouring gales of the Flats. The reporters, at Colin's insistence, were kept back from the area. Other than Colin and Su, only the Sabbai and Su's staff were allowed under the canopy's shade. Once the meal had been served and all the flagons filled with cool wine, the servants were escorted away. Colin set his wine aside and made himself comfortable on the cushions placed on the warm sands. The roof of the pavillion swayed in the breezes, the cloth snapping in accompaniment to the conversations. The murmuring voices subsided as Colin faced Su and nodded. Su bowed back, smiling benignly, a frail hand toying with the brocade of his pillows, upon which embroidered animals leaped.

A premonition intruded upon Colin, an insistent sense of misgiving. *Something is going to happen. Here. Now. Soon.* He was certain of it. The feeling had the solidity of a veildream. He frowned at the scene around him, the two parties arrayed behind their respective leaders like massed armies. Colin took his goblet in his hand, swirling the dark liquid inside it. He sipped, trying to hide his unease.

"You've accomplished much in a short time, Colin Fairwood," Su said at last.

Colin traced the golden rim of the goblet with a forefinger, his eyes on that slow motion rather than on the Ascendant. "I would say that you have just helped me in that immeasurably, Ascendant Su," he answered softly. He set the goblet down on the sand and raised his head. "No Zakkaist official has ever deigned to visit a Pretender before. You've now done wonders for my little reputation."

"I think that you rank slightly higher than just a mere Pretender." Su chuckled, still oddly jovial despite the obvious pain he was feeling. Colin's information was that Su was quite ill, that he was constantly medicated to ease some of the suffering. He certainly did not look good—his face seemed like a skull, with just a few wisps of hair remaining. *Is it Su that is bothering me?* Colin wondered. *Is Su behind this prickling of MolitorAb's finger?* "If I'm wrong in that," the old man continued, "then yes, I'm certainly guilty of a costly mistake. I speak with the man most widely accepted as the legitimate claimant to the title of Sartius Exori, however. Certainly, you're the only one to have gained a reputation exceeding the simple local variety." Su stared directly at Colin, his oriental features crinkled with what might have been amusement.

Colin could not help liking the man—his self-effacing manner, his quiet politeness, his soft good humor despite his infirmities. He sat straight backed in his formal *seiza,* his legs tucked under him. Colin's mouth curved involuntarily into a grin; then he guffawed. Su laughed with Colin, and the tension Colin had felt momentarily dissolved. *Maybe it was nothing. Maybe I'm making more of the situation than it deserves.*

Behind the two, their followers smiled. Kiri came and sat next to Colin. He took the hand she put on his knee.

"More of the Ascendants should be like you," Colin said. "If they were, there'd be easier relations between the Holdings and the Fringes, between Zakkaist and MulSendero."

"You honor me." Su nodded.

Kiri's hand squeezed Colin's. From what he'd been told of Ascendant formalities, Colin knew he should now wait for a like compliment from Su. Instead Colin decided to forgo circumspect politeness—he felt Su would understand. Colin broke in bluntly with the question on which they'd all speculated. "Ascendant Su, why have you come here, to this place and at this time?"

If the abruptness of the rude query shocked Su, he showed nothing. "It's very simple," he said. A slight pause. Then he added the honorific. "—Sartius Exori."

"Colin will do, if the title bothers you."

Another nod. "Colin, then. And I am Huan."

"Huan. Let me be so forward as to place words in your mouth, Huan." Colin was suddenly sure. He spoke quickly, leaning forward eagerly. "Let me say that you came here because you wanted to know your enemy."

Su's fingers tugged a little too hard at his pillow's brocade. A thread pulled loose; Su studied it for a moment. When he looked up again, his smile was gone, his face composed and utterly blank. "You are indeed most surprising, Colin."

There's only the finest distinction between intuition and proph-ecy, Colin wanted to say to him. *It was only a trick. I knew, yes, but it was as much simple luck as inspiration from MolitorAb.* "Why else would you come, Huan?" Colin smiled to take away any offense from the words. He was still not certain he wanted to trust the man. If he had read Su wrongly . . . It would be so easy to shift the guns of the shuttle toward the town or to contact the cruiser lurking above. That sense of dread returned. Colin glanced over at Kiri to see if she felt it as well, but she was looking at the Ascendant with a polite smile on her face. Colin continued: "We're forced into the roles of enemies. The more information you possess concerning those set up against you, the better you are able to defeat them. I wonder, Huan—did you have a plan prepared against me? Did you need to see me to know that it would work?"

Su regarded Colin with that unreadable neutrality. Behind his back, Colin could hear the whispers of the Sabbai. He could see the priest frowning at the tone of the conversation. Su took a deep, slow breath; a flicker of pain seemed to cross his features—then the Ascendant shook his head. "I don't think in terms of victory or defeat, Colin," he said. "I fear the results of that mind-set: the loss in lives and property, the hatred that would consume each side when it thought of the other. No matter who was eventually the victor, there would always be between us the barrier of spilled blood, a buried rancor that would last decades, perhaps centuries. It would be passed from parent to child, becoming more rotten with each generation. Perhaps we must be 'enemies' of the mind, but I would like us to be like siblings who must disagree but—in their hearts—are tolerant of the family's errors."

Beside Colin, Kiri made a sound of disbelief. "Pretty words," he heard her mutter. "Speak if you want to," Colin said to her. She glanced at him, then nodded, her hand leaving his grasp to point at her chest.

"I am a Buntaro," she said. "What you ask of Colin Exori is to abandon the Buntaro, don't you, Ascendant Su? Does that also mean that the Church will free those you've imprisoned because they believe in the wrong God? Are you going to miraculously cure those the Church has maimed with torture, are you going to return the lost lives? Hallan Gelt would spit on your righteous pleas. I've been in the Holdings, I've seen what you will do in the name of your God."

During the outburst, Colin watched Su, expecting to see the old man grow angry or defensive. But Su listened quietly, motionless, only blinking once or twice. He made no attempt to interrupt or to correct Kiri. Su nodded to her when she was done, then addressed his words to her.

"In my past, I've been guilty of some of the atrocities you cite. But I still ask you to believe me when I say that I wish these things to *stop*—on *both* sides. The Buntaro have killed innocents too. I've seen priests tortured in the name of MolitorAb. Revenge does nothing but widen the gulf between us. We should build a bridge over that rift rather than continue to dig at its edges."

"That's all pious nonsense," Kiri answered. "Your idealism sounds very nice and you may well even believe it—I've no way of knowing. What of your Curator of Justice—Culper? Would *he* be willing to abide by this pastoral vision of yours?"

"Ascendant Su—if I may?" Mother Crowell interjected. Su bowed to her.

"Mother Crowell." Su turned to Colin. "She can answer better than I, as she is on the curator's staff," he explained.

"Ascendant Culper is charged with upholding the laws of the Zakkaist church," Crowell said, stepping forward beside Su. Her attention was more on Colin than on Kiri. "As curator, he is morally and legally bound to obey the will of the Ascendants. He would do as they order him to do."

Colin had not noticed the woman before now—she had simply been another of the robed group in the background. Now, as he listened to her, saw her, his memory was sparked. "I know you, don't I?"

"Yes." She hesitated as if she had been about to add a title but had changed her mind. "We've met." Her tone was scornful, disrespectful. "At that time, you didn't call yourself a prophet. You told me you didn't believe in MolitorAb. You denied Gelt's calling."

"At that time, the Voice was just beginning to summon me, Mother Crowell. I was a stubborn fool who wouldn't listen. Tell me, does your Ascendant Culper approve of Ascendant Su's visit here?"

She hesitated again and Colin saw her weighing the lie before she spoke. Su watched her as well; Colin wondered if he saw the deception in her. "No," she said at last. "He doesn't approve."

From the sour expression on her face, Colin judged that to be true—he would have been curious to see if Su would have corrected her had she said anything else. "The curator feels this trip is a waste of time," she continued. "It is also a drain on Ascendant Su's health."

"Ascendant Culper doesn't believe in understanding his foe?"

"I can't speak for him, obviously. But I'd speculate that he feels that he understands enough. You believe in MolitorAb. Your faith is misplaced. That's all he needs to understand."

And just like you, he's an arrogant bastard who thinks that's enough reason to hate a man. "Then I'm happy that Ascendant Su has come here rather than *your* superior," Colin told her. Even as he dismissed the priest, Colin felt the stab of his premonition again. He watched her as she slid back into the group behind Su, then forced himself to look away. "Do you feel the same as Culper, Huan? Is it enough to condemn me that I am MolitorAb's tool?"

"Are you, Colin? Are you MolitorAb's tool?"

Colin shrugged, mulling over the question. He took Kiri's hand again, intertwining his fingers in hers. With his other hand, he gestured to FirstBred Pale, immediately behind him. "This Stekoni saw me oust the Nexian Pretender when even I didn't know what I did or why I did it. Kiri feels that I saved her life on Chebar, that MolitorAb touched her through my hands. A Holdings cruiser fired on us as we fled Chebar, and its weapons were somehow turned away just as they were about to destroy us. Others here will testify that I've cured them of ills, made sense of their lives, eased their troubles. Listen to them as I listen to the Voice, Huan." He squeezed Kiri's hand and stroked Pale's slick fur. "Yes, Huan, I believe that MolitorAb moves through me. I denied it once, but Her choice was forced upon me. I deny it no longer."

"You refer to 'Her,' in the Stekoni manner."

"It's a convenience. I would venture, Huan, that a good part of the resistance of humanity to MolitorAb is the Stekoni insistence on using that feminine form of address. The Stekoni are matriarchal by biological necessity; despite all our efforts, humanity is still too much the other way. You invoke God as a Father. MolitorAb is All. We can call to the Voice as we wish: Him, Her, It. Gender doesn't matter. MolitorAb will respond—even *your* God is a shade of MolitorAb." Colin stretched his back; his muscles were sore with sitting. "Did you come to argue theology?" he asked. "What do you demand of me? More miracles? I'm afraid that I can't produce them on demand. I wish it were so; even if it were, would you believe them? I don't think so—it's too easy to deny such things and call them tricks."

Su's lips parted; his eyes narrowed as if something pained him. Then he smiled. "It *would* be a little too convenient, yes. In that you're correct, Colin. It's too easy to fake cures and the like. But no, I'm not here to argue theology, not at all. We're forever separated on that issue, Colin Exori. What I wish to do is speak of politics. The world of the body."

"You can't make that distinction," Colin argued. He waved a hand at the canopy above them, at the houses of the town. "When you live your life by your faith, those beliefs become your politics. As long as the Ascendants rule the Holdings, there are no politics that aren't marked by your religion, or vice versa. Believe me, I know this to be true, Huan. So do you, in your heart."

The point was taken, Colin knew: Su inclined his head. "I grant you that much. Let me amend my statement then. What I would like to discuss are the more mundane aspects of our religious quarrel. You asked me a pointed question when we began. Let me give you one in kind. What does the Sartius Exori intend to do with his followers?"

"I can't answer that," Colin said. All at once, he decided to answer honestly. "That's not from secretiveness or arrogance or anything else you might believe. I can't answer because *I* have no intentions for them at all. They came to me of their own free will, and that's all that keeps them here. We worship MolitorAb together. I'd be satisfied to continue to do that peacefully—within the Fringes *and* the Holdings." Colin paused, studying Su. *Yes, I like him. But please tell me, MolitorAb, can I trust him?* In the silence, Su suddenly coughed. A spasm of pain crossed his face. Sympathy for the man welled up in Colin. That empathy, as much as anything, prompted him to add one thing. "I'm not your enemy, Huan. Don't make me one."

"I'm not your enemy, Huan. Don't make me one."

In Su's rooms, in a small ornate chest, was a package. Wrapped in a parchment envelope were the statements of several people— Commander Blaine of the *Bright Faith* chief among them. Coupled with Su's own testimony, the statements were evidence that could well destroy this Pretender who sat before him. Ascendant Su could, by handing the package over to the waiting reporters, turn to rubble the pedestal of miracles that supported the Sartius Exori. Gone would be that glorious escape from Chebar: the little healings would be easy enough to lay at the door of hysteria.

Huan Su knew that he held the Sartius Exori in his hand.

If this Fairwood had been the arrogant, vain fool Su had expected to find, there would have been no hesitation. Even now he might gesture to David and tell him to bring the chest here and expose its contents before the cameras. Yes, he might, but the resolution to do so had wavered, its purpose had become diluted. There was an air about Colin Fairwood that made Su hold back and consider his options.

It would be so easy—the proverbial two birds with one stone. The false Exori would be gone; with it, Culper's sins would be exposed to the light of reason for all to see and judge. The uproar might shake the House of Zakkai, but we would endure. The changes that would follow would be good. The MulSendero might never survive the tumult, for any future Pretender would be suspect. Those whose faith wavered on the edge would be nudged back to the true God. My God. This God, not the Monster of Dreams.

That is what you want. Is it what God wants?

A new thought intruded. *This Colin seems reasonable. What if you fail, Huan? What if you're wrong? The next Pretender, the Sartius Exori that would follow, might be terror incarnate. This one is not a devil—what of the next?*

"I'm not your enemy." With Fairwood's last words, indecision wracked Su, an uncertainty that had blossomed when the Pretender had first begun to speak. *"Did you have a plan prepared against me?"* He'd spoken the deceit hidden in Su's breast. *"Did you need to see me to know that it would work?"*

The pain of his vacillation wracked Su as surely as did the unrelenting sun of this awful world; it was as constant as the ache in his body, which had not left him since the last Veil passage. Su considered his next words carefully. He wanted to lick his lips, cracking in the dry heat, wanted to stretch his cramped legs, wanted to have David plunge the syringe of blessed peace into his arm again. Su shoved all that into the recesses of his mind, willing himself to concentrate fully on Colin. "Do you see a way for us to be friends, Colin? Can we do that and still not believe in the same things?"

"Simon ben Zakkai faced that difficulty."

"He died for it," Su reminded Colin. The man was facile enough, if not particularly well schooled. His parables, his reasoning were all simplistic, but Su found his earnestness engaging. Su could not deny the hope he felt.

"Granted, Huan. But the problem is the same as that faced by Jesus or Mohammed or any of the prophets. I don't deny *them*. I know that they existed, that they were holy people. Why do you deny the same of the Stekoni Mad Ones, of all who speak for MolitorAb?"

"Colin, my heart and my teaching both tell me they worship the Voice of Madness. Answer me this: why would a God want his believers to become insane listening to him?" Su recalled the nightmares of his own veildreams and grimaced—it would be simple to succumb to them, he knew. "That's what happens to all who go too often to MolitorAb, who give themselves fully to the Voice."

His stomach knotted suddenly; his guts heaved and he almost cried out. *No! Not now, God. Please, a few more minutes and then I can retire back to the ship for a time. Please, my Lord.* Su clenched his sphincter, put his attention on the swaying of the canopy overhead. He could feel the sweat breaking out on his forehead. *Don't think of it—pay attention to the winds. Breathe. There, isn't that the smell of the Stekoni?* The spasm passed and he relaxed slowly. He'd missed some of what Colin was saying.

"... consider madness is thought to be a state of grace by the Stekoni. The words of the Mad Ones are holy. They're written down in books, studied, and revered."

"It's easy to find meanings in vague images and loose symbology. Even the mad can sound deep."

"Do you find *me* mad, Huan?"

Su studied that strange face, wondering what Colin meant—the Exori had not smiled as if his question were a jest, nor did he frown as if he were insulted. No, he sounded as if the question truly nagged at him. *Does the Pretender fear for his own sanity? Does he fight not to lose himself to the Voice?* "No," Su replied cautiously. "I think you're consumed by a passion. That's not necessarily crazy."

"Is it a terrible thing for us to worship MolitorAb?"

"It's a terrible thing for your soul, Colin. You jeopardize your eternal life and that of your followers. The actions of the Buntaro"— he glanced at the woman beside Colin, at the other two Sabbai whom he knew to be of her sect: Aaron Roberts and Joshua Benoit. They all gazed at him placidly, smiling. Smug. "If we're to have any hope of coming to an agreement, a reconciliation, you must disavow the Buntaro. Cast them out, Colin. They stain you."

Colin's reply held mocking laughter. "Cast them out? Will you do the same with Culper, with all the Ascendants who agree with his policies?"

I wish that were possible. The thought came unbidden. With it, as if in response, the pain tightened in his gut once more. He kneaded his stomach with one hand, angry that he was forced to show his torment. Su could feel all their eyes: Colin, the Sabbai, Mother Crowell, David, his own priests. The doctor came forward, touched Su on the shoulder. "Huan?" he whispered.

"It's nothing new, David," Su answered, waving him back. "A twinge, that's all."

"You're getting weak. Tell Fairwood that you need to rest. If he has any goodness at all, he'll agree to that. You can continue this later."

"No."

"Then I'll tell him."

"No!" Su said more forcefully. "Please, David—I know what I can do." David sighed loudly and returned to his place. Su composed himself, using meditation techniques he'd learned long ago. He saw that Fairwood was waiting patiently but was not giving Su the chance to excuse himself. He wanted an answer. The Pretender's expression, if such could be read into that ruined mask of a face, seemed kindly enough, but not so kind that he would ask if Su wished to retire. The Ascendant took a breath; as ever, he could not draw the air deeply into his lungs without pain.

Su knew he had little time left to him. If he hoped to accomplish anything with the Pretender, that agreement had to come with this visit—Su could not be certain he would return to Dridust again.

Now. The decision must be now. Expose the man, or work with him.

Please, Lord, give me a sign in this. Let me know Your will, though I know that I don't deserve such favors of You.

Nothing. The wind tumbled grains of sand before him.

"I don't think that we can reconcile our Gods, Colin," he said at last. "Your MolitorAb is not my Lord. I'm certain of that. The Voice does not speak the words of my God, of Allah. But..." He paused and caught the Pretender's eyes.

"I don't believe that we should let that stop us from learning to tolerate each other's ways," he went on. "Please, let us start to work toward an understanding, you and I. Let's devise some plan that will point us toward peace." Su turned to David and beckoned the doctor closer. "David, there's a package in my room, in the lacquer chest. Please bring it here." He turned again to address himself to Colin. "I had other uses for it, but I give it to you, Colin."

Su nodded to himself. The decision felt right. "David, bring the chest and give it to the Sartius Exori."

* * *

"... give it to the Sartius Exori."

With Su's words, Mother Crowell knew she could delay action no longer. Joseph Culper had been right—the Ascendant Su had planned treachery against the Church, would sign an unspeakable alliance with the MulSendero. She had not suspected herself how crucial her presence might be. The hand of God had guided Culper, and she gave thanks.

He has the proofs that I allowed him to have, Culper had said. We must know if he will use them. That's your task, Mother Crowell. Watch him. If Su uses the statements, either to depose the Pretender Fairwood or to join with him, then you will do as I've instructed.

The curator's suspicions were correct—Su was a traitor. He would strike his own deal with the heretics. She could understand the old man's sentiment, but she despised his weakness.

Your actions will have two results, Mother. First, it will cement the Pretender's fame, giving him another miracle like that of Chebar. Second, and more important, it will make Fairwood cocky. From that day forward, he'll be careless of himself. When we make our final move, perhaps he'll be an easier target. I don't like doing this, Mother Crowell; you must understand that. But we've learned of Su's plans too late to do anything but take the quickest, easiest course. We trust that God will make it work.

It was almost too bluntly simple. The weapon she pulled from her robes would have been recognized by any person of the last several centuries. It had one task: to deliver a lethal blow to a body, doing as much damage to the soft tissues as possible. Humankind hadn't been able to improve much on that method of easy destruction since the invention of gunpowder. Mother Crowell's gun was small, made of plastic to enable her to avoid quick detection, and unreliable beyond a range of a few meters but effective despite its limitations.

With one difference. The first cartridge was indeed genuine. The next two in the chamber were not.

She would miss with the first, then fire quickly two more times as close to Colin as she could get, preferably pointblank. Anyone firing the gun after the third shot would find all the remaining cartridges to be live. It was a simple deception, as Culper had said.

The Church has need of a sacrifice, Mother Crowell, perhaps even a martyr. There's no possible way for us to know what will happen after you fire on the Pretender Fairwood. You may be killed. You will in all probability be jailed, with whatever consequences that may entail within the Fringes. Knowing there are Buntaro in the Sabbai, you cannot discount the thought of torture. You must

*give all your suffering to God and know that if at all possible, once
the life of Fairwood has run its short course and the MulSendero
are crippled or gone, we will come to rescue you.*

Mother Crowell stood, the pistol in her hand. As she raised the
weapon, time seemed to slow around her. She could see everything
with incredible clarity—

—the woman Kiri's mouth open in a scream of warning and
rage even as she started to lunge for the weapon.

—the Sabbai, drawn back from their Pretender in attitudes of
horror or fear, frozen.

—Fairwood, looking directly at her, staring, that ruined and
incomplete face far too calm.

—and Su. She had not thought the Ascendant could possibly
move so quickly. Even as she touched the raised stud that triggered
the weapon (her aim slightly high and to the right of Colin), he
came at her, springing from his seated position with an awful shout.
The pistol bucked in her hand, surprising her, and she saw cloth
tear on Su's tunic as the impact of the bullet spun him around.

Even as she cried out in horror at what she had done, she stepped
around the sprawling form and pointed the weapon into Fairwood's
chest, fired. Fired again. The reports were loud in the stillness that
surrounded her; her eyes shut in response.

The Pretender winced, looked down as if to see the blood spurt-
ing from him.

The Buntaro woman hit her then, knocking Anna onto the grating
sand, wrenching the gun from her hand. Others gathered around
and hauled her roughly to her feet. She stood pinned in their grasp,
slack jawed, playing her part even though she wanted only to twist
away and look at the Ascendant. She thought she was going to be
sick, and she retched dryly.

It was easy for her to fake astonishment.

*Oh God, that wasn't supposed to have happened. Please don't
say that I killed him. Let him live, let him live.*

Someone struck her hard across the face.

She screamed as a dark mist rolled over her.

CHAPTER THIRTEEN

The unbelievers say: "This is but a forgery of his own invention, in which others have helped him." Unjust is what they say and false.

And they say: "Fables of the ancients he has written: they are dictated to him morning and evening."

Say: "It is revealed by Him who knows the secrets of heaven and earth. He is forgiving and merciful."

KORAN, Al-Furqan 25:4–6

They will say that what I have written here is madness and lies. There is a simple reply that you should make to that accusation.

You are wrong.

For what I have written is truth, and you are bound forever to the words.

GELTIAN SCRIPTURE, 105:24–26

David was the first to reach Su. He propped up his friend's head with slow tenderness, gently straightening out the twisted legs. Su's eyes were open but clouded with suffering. "You'll be fine, Huan," David said, taking a small knife from his pocket and slicing away the bloody shirt. "I'm here. Just relax."

Su's head moved in a slight nod. The pupils of his slitted eyes were dilated with shock and his skin had an alarming pallor. David peeled away the shirt and probed the wound quickly. The entrance wound at the shoulder was badly torn and speckled with powder burns. Blood oozed slowly from the puckered gash in a dark and steady flow. David sighed, his exhalation laced with relief—the arterial pulsing of blood that he had dreaded was absent. He gestured to a priest; together, they turned Su's body so that David could examine the exit wound, halfway down the back but well away from the spine. David nodded, biting his lower lip with his teeth. "Fine. Let him back down now. Gently, gently. Good."

Engrossed in his work, he noticed little of the tumult around him until a shadow fell across Su's face. David turned his head to see Colin standing beside him.

"How is he?" the Exori asked.

"He's ... in trouble." David hesitated, wondering if he should say more. "With a younger man or someone in better general health, this wouldn't be critical, but—" David shrugged. "I need my kit and a litter of some sort."

"I've sent for help from your shuttle. Also, one of my own doctors is coming—she's had surgical experience and will assist you, if you wish."

"Thank you." A frown tightened David's mouth. "How are *you,* Colin?"

The smile was faint. To David, the Exori seemed distant, stunned. He moved like an automaton. "I wasn't hit."

"God," David breathed. There was wonder in his voice. "I can't believe that. She was so close to you ..."

"Believe it," Colin answered softly in a strange, bland tone. *In that instant, when he'd seen the muzzle of Crowell's gun pointed at his chest, when he'd seen her touch the trigger and watched the quick flame spurt from the muzzle, when he'd realized that—incredibly—he was still alive, it had come. The Change.* Colin wandered in a shouting, screaming nightmare. He was frightened. The world lay shattered before him, melting and dissolving, then snapping back into strange shapes. Colin saw David kneeling beside Su, but in that instant when the physician had glanced up, the flesh of the doctor's face had slid on the bone like warm putty—aging, sagging, until it was an ancient's sad face staring up at him. *MolitorAb, you have marked me.* Colin shook his head, and the image was gone. He could hear his breath, ragged and fast, and nausea made his stomach heave. *Show none of it, man. Wait; it will pass.*

The blood-stained sand under Su seemed to writhe, as if fingers of grave worms were wriggling just beneath the surface. Colin turned his head away.

Huan Su stirred under David's hand. "Colin," the Ascendant whispered. Colin looked back, and the sand was still. He took a deep breath. "I'm here, Huan."

"Colin, forgive me," Su rasped. "Believe me, I knew nothing of this." As Su spoke, his face shimmered, and there was only a bone-white skull, the jaw working obscenely. "Please tell me that you know that," it said.

Colin closed his eyes. "There's nothing to forgive, Huan," he whispered. Opening his eyes, he saw only Su once more. He glanced down the body to the wound, at the splintered bone showing inside the torn skin and muscle. A thought pounded at him: *Your face might have once looked like that—raw, bleeding meat.* "I know this was not your doing. Tell me if I can help you."

"NO!" The word shrilled from Su's throat before Colin could turn to go. The Ascendant began to struggle up; David pushed him back onto the sand. *For an instant it was not just David and Huan but two demons locked in awful embrace. Then the dream-flash was gone, and Dridust returned.* "Colin, stay away from me. Don't touch me." Su's eyes were wild as his head moved violently from side to side, the wispy, silver hair tossing. He groaned against David's restraining hands. Colin drew back.

"I wasn't going to..."

"You'll stay away. I don't want your healing!" he screamed. "David, get me back to the ship. Please!" The Ascendant swallowed and cleared his throat with a liquid rattling.

As Colin stood, watching and not responding, David touched his shoulder. "Please, Exori. The man's very sick and confused. I must get him into surgery. The stretcher's here."

"Did you see his face?"

David looked at Colin strangely, and he knew that the doctor thought him mad. "His face?" David asked, bewildered.

"And yours too. They were all changed," Colin persisted, not certain why he was saying these things. He shook his head again, forcing his mind to clear. "I'm sorry, doctor; the shock, perhaps..."

"Yes," the man said. "I have to go. Please, your own doctor will see to you..."

Colin stared down at Su as they lifted the Ascendant onto the makeshift stretcher. He flexed his fingers into a fist, wondering if Su were right, if he could send that flaring power through his hands again as he had on Chebar. The air of a Presence surrounded Colin; the landscape turned and wavered unsteadily. Some of Su's party stared at Colin with open hostility and even fear as they took Su away toward the shuttle. Reporters crowded around the stretcher as it left the pavilion, and to Colin they seemed as carrion birds around a downed animal. In a delirium, Colin walked slowly over to where Anna Crowell was sprawled in the center of a shouting group of Sabbai and Zakkaists.

Aaron's foot was swinging back, ready to kick the downed woman. "No, Aaron!" Colin shouted. They all turned to him, moving aside as he thrust his way into the center of the group. "Get her up," he said.

Aaron and Samuel took the woman under her arms and hauled her to her feet. Crowell's dark hair was tangled and matted with blood and sand. A nostril trailed a rivulet of blood across one cheek; a long, deep gash on her right temple spread a fan of scarlet. She seemed disoriented. Colin stared at the woman, thinking that he should be feeling hatred, yet he could feel no spark of rage in himself at all. He seemed to have gone dead inside. Some reflex mechanism was working his body, and MolitorAb laid Her veil over his eyes.

"Mother Crowell," Colin said. He repeated the name, taking her chin in his hand and forcing her to look at him. "Mother Crowell." She averted her eyes. When Colin let go of her chin, her head dropped to her chest.

One of the Zakkaist priests held her pistol. "Give it to me," Colin heard himself say, as if from a long distance. From some vantage point in his mind, Colin watched the priest back away a step, a flush of anger rising on the man's cheeks. Kiri stood near the man; she glanced worriedly back at Colin as if she saw his distress. She moved to take the weapon away from the priest herself, but Colin waved her back. "We've enough problems at the moment, Father," Colin's voice said. "You're on a Fringe world, not in the Holdings. Here, MolitorAb rules, and I am Her voice. You will give me the weapon."

In dreamtime, Colin held out his hand, seeing it as if through a distorted lens but knowing he would be obeyed. None of this was real. None of it. Not the sun's pounding heat, not the crowd around him, not the battered woman before him. The priest hesitated, the flush on his face deepening; then he handed the gun to Colin with a breathy curse. Colin turned the pistol over in his hands as if it were a lump of quartz, touching the smooth grip where several more cartridges could be seen under the transparent plastic. It seemed incredible that this toy could have done so much damage to Su. Colin sighted down the short barrel, pointing the muzzle at Crowell's head. He seemed to see her with too much clarity; the pores of her skin were sharp in the glaring sunlight. His tongue moved unwilled. "Tell me, Mother Crowell," he said. "Can you think of a reason why I shouldn't kill you here and now?"

Her head lifted slowly as a heavy drop of blood fell from her chin to the sand. Her mouth was slack, working soundlessly. She cleared her throat. "For what I did to Ascendant Su, there's no reason that you shouldn't," she said. "For that, you may punish me as you will."

"I intend to do that."

He felt his hand tighten around the grip. Colin, suddenly a spectator in his own body, willed his hand to loosen, to drop the weapon, but he could not.

None of this is real. None of it matters.

Abruptly, he jerked the weapon up and fired.

A sharp report echoed from the hills. A hole appeared in the canopy above them; through it, a wedge of sunlight sparkled against the sand. Colin felt a warmth near his side: Kiri. "Colin, are you all right?"

"I'm fine," he answered, while he shouted denial inside. He could smell the characteristic fear odor of the Stekoni, though it seemed there were overtones in the scent that he had never sensed before—if he wished, he knew he could read the emotional matrix of Pale, open and unmasked.

Pale's worried face nodded at him from beside Kiri. "This one wonders what the Sartius Exori will do now, and if it is also what Colin Fairwood would do."

"Isn't Colin Fairwood the Exori," Colin stated rather than asked.

"The Sartius Exori knows what I mean," Pale said.

Colin stared at the column of sunlight streaming through the bullet hole in the canopy.

"You're going to kill me now?" Crowell asked, only half in question.

"You tried to do the same to me."

Her features twisted with some emotion that passed too quickly to be read. She seemed resigned, almost sad. "You're the Sartius Exori," she said, her voice toneless. "You can't be killed that way."

"Then why did you make the attempt?" Kiri asked angrily.

"Because..." She looked from Kiri to Colin, then at the other faces around her, full of hatred and fury. "I had to know," she said to all of them.

Kiri made a sound of disgust. Colin laughed, sharply and without humor. "That isn't all of it, Mother Crowell."

Crowell's eyes narrowed. She started to shake her head in denial. The grip on her arms tightened, as if Aaron and Samuel thought she might rush at Colin with her bare hands. "I'm a Zakkaist, Colin Exori. I've no faith in MolitorAb to sustain a belief in Hallan Gelt's prophecies or in you. I needed some other proof. Now I have it."

There was no intensity in her voice. The words were uttered

flatly and without inflection. Colin found he did not believe them, and he knew the Presence in his body did not believe them either.

Crowell continued in the same monotone: "I would beg forgiveness of the Sartius Exori. Please understand why I did this. You live, Colin Exori, yet you should be dead. When others hear of this, they'll begin to believe. I've helped you."

"That's all of it?"

"I risked my eternal soul for you, Exori. Does it mean nothing?"

Colin held the gun out in his palm. As he stared at it, he became aware of a sense of conviction, a glimmering of purpose awakening in him. He clung to that and spoke the words that came to him. "You couldn't have killed me with this."

Her eyes widened wildly. "I know that now," she said.

"You knew it before. Were I you and your precious soul, I think I'd be praying for the health of Ascendant Su. He's the one you've harmed. He will die."

His words were like a physical blow. Her sullen defiance broke and tears started in her eyes. Her knees buckled beneath her, and she hung limp in the grip of the two men. "That was not supposed to happen," she cried. "Believe me, Exori. He . . . he threw himself in front of me . . . just as I shot . . . I didn't aim . . ." She took a sobbing breath. "He's dead?"

"He will die," Colin repeated. *This is true. I know it is true. She has killed him; if not now, then soon.*

"No harm was intended him." Her sorrowful gaze searched Colin's face with its smooth bundling of muscles under the skinbase. "What are you going to do with me?" she asked.

He looked at her and the world swayed around him again. He saw her, saw himself standing beside her in the landscape of some other world, and he knew he was not permitted to kill her. *She is part of your future. MolitorAb does not want her soul. Not now. Not here. As you are MolitorAb's, so is she.*

"I'll do nothing with you," Colin said.

"What!" The protest came simultaneously from Kiri, the Sabbai, and the Zakkaists.

"Nothing," Colin repeated. "She's offended MolitorAb, and she'll find punishment or solace only from Her. As to the rest—Dridust hasn't any extradition arrangements with the Holdings that I'm aware of. If she wishes to claim asylum here, then . . ." He shrugged.

"She tried to kill you, Colin!" Kiri insisted. "She's a Zakkaist assassin."

"If the Church had wanted to kill me, there's a few thousand more effective ways of doing it, Kiri." He knew he sounded pomp-ous and unfeeling, but he could not help himself. "This was clumsy and stupid, an amateur's work. I've no anger toward her, none at all. MolitorAb has none either. Why should she care that a fool attempts the impossible? Aaron, Samuel, let her go."

"Exori—"

"Let her go!" Colin shouted. He stumbled as he flung an arm at them, and Kiri moved closer to him.

"You can't do this." The protest came from the priest who had picked up the gun. "We can't allow it. She must go back to the curator."

Colin wheeled on the man, kicking up sand. A bloody haze seemed to film his eyes, a scrim through which he viewed the world. "You *dare* to oppose MolitorAb's will? I tell you, man, that her fate is not her own. Nor mine, nor yours."

The priest's face had gone a bright vermilion. He glanced at his companions; then, sensing their lack of support, he seemed to shrink back. "She's sinned against the person of the Ascendant—she must be tried by the courts of the Church," he insisted, though not quite so loudly.

"She has sinned against your God, who is only a shade of MolitorAb, whether you know that or not. I speak for MolitorAb, priest. If you or any of your people have a quarrel with that, then I will show them God's anger!"

Fury blazed in Colin's voice. He watched himself speaking, the words tearing at his throat. The priest backed quickly away as Colin raised his fists in the air and the Sabbai frowned in sympathy, ready to defend their prophet. The Presence in Colin waited, and Colin felt that It almost hoped the man would defy him. Power filled Colin, waiting to be unleashed, and he felt his body was a frail vessel for that anger. It would consume him.

The priest lapsed into sullen silence. At last Colin's hands came down to his sides, the fists relaxing. "Let her go," Colin said again. Aaron and Samuel stepped away from Crowell. She staggered and then caught her balance. "What should I do?" she asked Colin.

He waited for the Presence to answer and It would not. He spoke for himself. "Do whatever you must do, Mother Crowell. The Sartius Exori has freed you. Go into the desert, surrender yourself to Su, go to the commander of your ship, walk to my temple and pray—I don't care. I've no use for you and no fear of you."

Colin moved into the sunlight piercing the canopy roof. The bolt of sun touched his shoulder, slid down his body and onto the sand.

Colin hefted the gun and tossed it casually into the brilliance. Its plastic case spat highlights back at him.

"Sartius Exori, I don't understand," Anna Crowell said.

He seemed to smile for an instant.

"I know you don't," he said.

Colin looked at Kiri, who was watching him worriedly, and the nightmare shift of time and place fell around her. For the space of a breath, Colin saw Kiri's body, twisted, broken, and lifeless, and himself standing beside her, motionless in horror. He could feel the pain of loss, the warm blood slick on his hands as he cradled her, moaning. And then the vision was gone, and Kiri stared at him in concern.

"Kiri," he whispered.

"Colin, what's the matter? Please..."

"Kiri."

She came to him then, pulling him to her fiercely, whispering as he felt his strength leave and he sagged to the sand. "I love you, Colin. It's all right. I'm here."

He nodded, letting the words and her soft hands and her affection caress him and soothe him into sleep.

CHAPTER FOURTEEN

For, lo, I will command, and I will sift the house of
Israel among all the nations.
Like as corn is sifted in a sieve,
Yet shall not the least grain fall upon the earth.
All the sinners of my people shall die by the sword,
That say: "The evil shall not overtake nor confront us."
In that day I will raise up
The tabernacle of David that is fallen.

OLD TESTAMENT, Amos IX:9–11

MolitorAb moved in the Sartius Exori, and like all the prophets
of God, he did not truly comprehend what he did or the reasons
for his actions. For God is not understandable even by Her chosen
ones, and the prophets as often speak with their own words as with
Hers.

The Sartius Exori said: "This one will not punish you, Great
Traitor, for that is the domain of MolitorAb. Go as you will, for
She has no more use of you." Colin Exori thought he spoke truth,
but he had not listened to the Voice within himself.

THE TESTAMENT OF
FIRSTBRED PALE,
150:12–14. (Generally considered
apocryphal by Exorian scholars.)

In the loud darkness, she held him.

"Colin?"

"Just hold me for awhile, Kiri. I need to feel you. Please."

Outside, the temple water-giver passed with his night call, sand
shushing under his sandaled feet. From across the Flats came the
faint, hooting challenge of a whiptongue. A breeze wafted in the
window, carrying some small relief from the heat still radiating from
the sands.

"Love, you scared me today. I thought..." Kiri could not finish.

"I scared myself. Kiri, there was a frightening, powerful Other in me. I was full of MolitorAb—I thought Her energy might destroy me. She moved my hands, my mouth."

"You were gone, Colin. I wondered what I would do if you had moved to hurt me, to hurt our child, to hurt Pale or the other Sabbai."

"You doubt your faith that much?"

"I doubted then." Her arms tightened around him. "I would have tried to stop you."

"You would have failed. It was terrifying, yes, but yet... In some ways, it was exactly what I've sought, to be an instrument of MolitorAb—fully, completely. Do you see?"

"I see that I worry for you and myself. And not only for your possession. You've also thumbed your nose at the Holdings by letting the Crowell bitch go."

"You saw her choice. She went into the desert. We all watched her leave. She'll die there."

"Perhaps." He could feel her chest moving, as if she were choking back tears. "If she'd hurt you or moved against any of the rest of us, I'd've killed her there, no matter what it cost me. And— may MolitorAb forgive me for saying this—I don't want to lose you to the Voice either. I'll fight that as well."

"Kiri..." His voice came quiet, soothing. "I want you. I want our child. Believe that."

"Then tell me what you saw just before you fell, Colin. You looked at me, and all the muscles in your face leapt as if you'd been slapped. You cried out my name. What did you see?"

He didn't answer at first. He lay there on the bed, cuddled into the crook of her arm, one leg over her hip. He listened to the velvet brush of the palm fronds moving in the gardens outside, to the ebb and flow of conversations in the houses around them.

Her blood dappling his arms and chest, everyone roaring around him, her lifeless eyes open and staring at him in mute accusation.

"I don't remember," he lied. "Just hold me awhile longer."

"Huan."

The summons was a bolt of arc lightning in an ocean of drifting quiet. The afterimage of the word dazzled him, stirring memories of heat and sand and white light, of a weapon in a traitor's hand.

Grains of harshness.

He shook his head, denying it all, willing the sea of gentle solitude to cover him again. He would stay there, in the soothing, warm, lemon-scented swells.

"Huan."

The voice was insistent. He could not remember if it came from a veildream's madness or some nightmare of his own mind.

"He's coming out of it now. Huan. Open your eyes, Huan."

He felt the brush of eyelashes against his cheek, and then there was a blur of images and light that made him squint. His mouth was cotton dry, the tongue swollen; as he licked his lips, he could feel deep, swollen cracks and taste stale gumminess. He blinked once, and the blur before him resolved itself into a montage of faces, only one of which he recognized.

"David," he tried to say, but all he heard was a breathy croak without syllables in a voice he didn't know.

"Easy, Huan," David said, leaning over so that his face was very near Su's. "You were in surgery for two hours, then out of things for more than a day. You'd better be damned grateful that I badgered you into giving me those tissue samples last year. Their offspring are working to patch you together now."

"How . . . long?" Su concentrated on making the words distinct.

David glanced away and Huan caught a glimpse of monitors and the drifting bulk of gray machinery; several people in hospital blues huddled alongside them. "A local day—a little more. Maybe a day and a half, Old Earth time."

"How . . . am I?"

"About as well as you can expect."

The seriousness of David's features made Su want to laugh and cry at the same time. He struggled to sit up and found he could not. His body would not respond. He could move his fingers, but he felt little else. Panic began to rise in him—*a cripple, then? God, please, no*—and he forced his mind away. "That is . . . an evasion, David. You can't . . . fool a preacher." He wrestled with the words, forcing them out. His tongue felt huge, cumbersome. His lips stuck together.

"You're right." The face slid away to glance at a display above the bed. "And that's all you're getting from me too."

"Have to . . . get up. Have to see . . . Colin."

"He'd like to see you as well, I'd think. Huan, he's let Mother Crowell go. Commander Benesch is furious." David's own anger put an edge on the words. "If you'd died, I think he'd have destroyed Fairwood's settlement."

Huan sighed. He found that he could move his hand now, lift it slightly above the cool sheets. He held it in front of his face, turning it so that he could see the ridges of veins, the furrows of dry skin. "I didn't think . . . I'd wake up again, David. Forgive me. A person who . . . expected to see his God . . . is a little slow . . . responding. Tell me . . . what's happened."

"You should rest."

"No." Su's answer was firm, if not loud.

David glanced at the monitor again, then nodded. "Let me give you something for the pain then." He touched the mednurse at the foot of the bed and a needle pricked Su's arm, cold and quick. Su heard the sound as David dragged a chair to the side of the bed and sat. "There's a lot of tension, Huan. Fairwood's defied all of Benesch's ultimatums to turn Crowell over to us. He insists that Crowell is in the hands of MolitorAb—that *he* doesn't control the woman or hold her. From what we've heard, she's disappeared into the Flats, which means she's most likely dead already."

David glanced at Su, and Huan could see the weariness in the dark pockets of David's eyes. *He's been here all along, if I know him. Probably hasn't slept.* "If Fairwood forces matters," David continued, "there could be bloodshed. If you had died, there wouldn't have been any doubt of it."

Huan tried to smile. He covered David's hand with his own. "Your skill prevented . . . that. Thank you . . . David."

"Thank your own stubbornness. I was certain that I'd lost you."

"Do you think . . . Benesch could have killed . . . Colin Exori?"

"The Pretender, you mean?" David spat out the title.

Su chuckled and moistened his lips again. "Call him . . . as you wish. Tell me, did we . . . witness a miracle?"

David caught his upper lip between his teeth and stared into some unseen distance. He started to shrug, stopped, and leaned back in his chair. "I don't know, Huan. I don't know. I can think of several ways to fake what we saw—and it's suspicious to me that Fairwood is so insistent on keeping Crowell out of the hands of our people. Assassinations can be made to fail deliberately. God may intervene on His own too, I suppose—and I don't mean MolitorAb." David sniffed and rubbed at his bloodshot eyes with the back of his hand. "No, I wasn't convinced. My faith isn't so easily shaken. And you didn't see Fairwood after you were shot. Huan, the man had some type of psychotic episode. I swear. Others here will tell you the same. He had a fit, and he collapsed. Fairwood's a lunatic, Huan. A madman."

"Aaah." Su nodded. He brought his hand back to his side. "You

will . . . get me ready, David. You and these . . . machines which are
. . . your faith. Send for . . . Colin Exori."

"Huan—"

"What, my friend?"

"I . . ." David halted, and Su saw that he didn't want to say more.
At last David seemed to shake himself from reverie. "I should tell
you that I won't be able to take you off these . . . machines, as you
call them. Not this time, at least not until we get back to Old Earth.
Not yet. Maybe never."

Shock made Su close his eyes; he felt momentarily dizzy and
nauseous. *She's killed you, then. If this is all the life left to you, it
might have been better to bleed to death on the sand.* Then guilt
crushed the thought. He pursed his lips, grimacing. *No. You've been
saved for something, Su. The Lord will show you what it is.*

Huan opened his eyes and felt moisture on his cheeks. He had
not realized that he was crying.

"You have done . . . the best . . . you could do. It doesn't . . . matter, David. Send for the Exori. We need . . . to complete our talk."

When David had gone from the room, he turned his head away
from the figures tending the machines. Then, as silently as he could,
he let the inward sorrow run its course.

Colin could smell death as soon as he entered the room. The
lights were dim, though bright lamps illuminated the figure lying
on the bed: Su. The Ascendant seemed to be held in the embrace
of brooding metal. A thick band straddled his chest, alive with
flickering, shifting points of light. Another device hovered at his
feet, and several more stood at attention alongside. The monitors
pulsed; the slow, rattling breath of the man was accompanied by a
sympathetic, mechanical wheeze. Huan Su looked *old,* impossibly
old, the skin shrunken on his cheeks and pale under the spots. His
eyes opened; only *they* seemed to have any energy or life. A hand
fluttered above the smooth coverlet and fell exhausted. "Exori," Su
said, his voice a throaty whisper.

"Ascendant." There was a chair to the left of the bed. Colin
went to it and sat. "I prayed for your recovery."

"Then you prayed . . . to the wrong God. I feel awful." Su tried
to smile and instead coughed. "For the second time . . . in my life
. . . I've had the last rites . . . performed over me. The last time . . .
I cheated death. God wanted . . . me to stay." Su's speech was slow
and weak. Colin leaned forward in his chair to hear the man. "This
time I . . . don't know that . . . I'll be so fortunate."

The Ascendant gasped, four quick, shuddering breaths. His hand trembled as he lifted it; then it collapsed again. "Tell me ... Colin Exori," he said. "Could you ... cure me?"

"You didn't want that, I thought."

"Could you?" Su insisted. His eyes held Colin, reflecting as they did the intense, multicolored points of light of the displays. Colin flexed his hands, remembering the power that had flowed through him on Chebar with Kiri, conjuring up the wave of Presence that had beaten inside him after the shooting. There were others who claimed to have been healed by the Exori's touch, but Colin didn't fool himself. *Most of those cured themselves— "Go, your faith has saved you."* Psychosomatic illnesses, neuroses, or simply the placebo effect: that was the bulk of his healing. He was tempted—to be able to say that the Exori had been the salvation of a mortally wounded Ascendant ... *It would mean you could not be denied. It would mean you could go back into the Holdings with impunity.*

"I don't know," Colin answered at last. "When it happened, perhaps yes. I felt full of MolitorAb at that moment, under Her hand. But now ..." He shrugged. The ends of the white *thorbani* he wore lifted, sliding down his chest.

A bell chimed. A light on the monitor display went from red to pulsing amber.

"You're honest ... and a hard man ... to dislike."

"Do you want me to try to heal you? Your doctor thinks I'm dangerous, if not outright insane."

A long pause. Su's eyes closed, the eyelids fluttering. Colin wondered if the man had fallen into a drugged sleep. He wanted to reach down and touch the emaciated hand on the sheet but did not. He watched, and Su's eyes struggled open once more. "I've wrestled with ... my own devils now." His gaze found Colin, and he smiled. "No, Colin. I don't want ... you to try. I am in ... God's hands."

"So am I, Huan. I wish you could understand that. MolitorAb is your God too. Why can't you see that it's the same as when Simon ben Zakkai proclaimed that Allah, Yahweh, and the Lord were all identical? That's all the MulSendero ask. Half of our problem is just semantics. We're not that far apart if we admit that."

"Far enough ... apart."

"Why?" Colin persisted. "Huan, my God is more visible than yours. That's one reason the Church is jealous, and that's also why you'll eventually lose. You can feel Her presence in the Veils; God touches you personally as your God has never done except for a privileged few. Yes, the Stekoni speak of Her as feminine, but that's for the same reason that we tend to use the masculine for *your* God. You fight and threaten and kill because you think that to acknowledge the truth threatens your power. You're simply blind to the visions: you've covered your eyes and ears and noses, dulled all your senses, and said, "I can't find God here." Yet you *have* to go into the Veils or give up the empire you've carved. You can't escape the Veil Presence, but you'll deny it. It's stupid and vain, Huan."

Colin had risen from his chair and was pacing the confines of the room. His voice thundered, his arms beat air, he shook his awful head at Su. He could feel that sense of unreality coming over him again, a smoky pall over his vision.

"Your creeds . . . are different," Su was protesting, but the person who now controlled Colin's tongue would not let him stop speaking.

"Our creeds are no more different than Jew was from Christian or Christian from Moslem, Ascendant. Most of the differences are superficial. No one claims that humans must follow the ways of the Stekoni. MolitorAb knows that we're separate—though look well at the Stekoni. No one has heard of Stekoni killing their own kind: is that such a terrible example for us to emulate? If our pride holds us back from God, of what use is it? Don't let *your* pride speak for you, Huan Su."

Abruptly, the passion left Colin like a dying breeze in the sails of a ship. He blinked and felt himself returning. Su watched him, a strange note of caution in his voice. "Because one is . . . possessed of a voice . . . doesn't mean that . . . the voice . . . is God." A swollen tongue traced his lips. "Do you hear me . . . Colin Fairwood?"

"I hear you. But you haven't listened to the Veils as I have, as Hallan Gelt did."

"For that . . . I think I'm . . . grateful. You know the . . . Veils as a Galicht. I would look . . . to myself . . . first as the . . . source of . . . my visions."

I am not mad. The old refrain, now slightly altered. *I am not mad, for it is MolitorAb that speaks in me and that is not insanity.* "Years ago I knew Hallan Gelt. I've talked with his soul in the Veils, and I'm certain that it is the same Hallan I knew."

"You think . . . it is him . . . because your memories . . . can make him real." The speech tired Su. He sagged back against his pillow, eyelids drooping, his breath frighteningly shallow.

"I'm tiring you, Huan, and the argument can't be ended. I know that now. Should I call for your doctor?"

"No. Please." His voice was barely audible. "There are things . . . I must know. Is Mother Crowell . . . your agent?"

"No." Quickly.

A rustle—Su's head on the pillow. "Then she is Culper's . . . and only she . . . holds the truth." Su gathered what little energy he had left. "David . . . will give you . . . the proof of what . . . I tell you now. Colin . . . you have been duped. Set up by . . . the Ascendants. We manufactured . . . you."

Colin laughed scornfully. "You've never felt what I've felt, Huan. You can't know what it feels like to have a Presence moving within you. There was nothing false about it, and you could not have 'manufactured' that."

Su's hand lifted, and Colin let him speak. "Please . . . I tell you . . . the truth. There was no . . . miracle escape . . . on Chebar. The navy was . . . instructed to let . . . your ship pass . . . so it would appear . . . to be more . . . than it was." Eyes closing, struggling to open. "I have . . . a tape of . . . a conclave . . . during which Culper says . . . these things. He seeks . . . your death and . . . with it the end . . . of the MulSendero."

Colin had not thought that he could feel doubt again. He was surprised at the rush of anxiety that Su's words engendered. He thought back to Chebar, to the certainty that had been fixed in his mind after the *Anger* slid through the field that had trapped them. *It can't be a sham, not all of it.* "What does your tale matter?" Colin protested. "A miracle isn't less a miracle because MolitorAb forced your Culper into doing Her will."

"One expects . . . direct intervention . . . in miracles."

"You haven't seen the healings, felt the power that I've felt. I keep telling you that—those aren't false feelings, Ascendant. And what of this last thing? Mother Crowell's bullets were certainly real. You're the proof of that."

Su didn't reply. He seemed to be taking his time, drawing on his reserves of strength so that he could speak. "Yes. I can't . . . answer that. But Crowell . . . is on Culper's . . . staff."

"Innuendo." Colin's arm stabbed air. "That's all you have. I'm the prophet of MolitorAb. Sartius Exori. You can't make me doubt myself."

(He could feel the stirring again, deep within him. The underpinnings of reality quivered, loosened . . .)

Lights flashed along the display girdling Su's body, pulsing quick numbers toward Colin. Su shifted weakly in his bed. "Colin . . . I grew up . . . Chinese in . . . Japan. You can't know . . . but I do . . .

understand cultural ... hatred. I understand ... prejudice. Yes, the Zakkaist church ... has shown that same ... blindness toward the ... MulSendero. Humans have done ... the same to Stekoni. None of it ... is right."

"And you can't change it. I can't change. Not with words, Huan." (Shifting, rumbling ...) "I agree with the Buntaro in that. There's nothing to build upon. We need to construct some new foundation."

"Colin, I ... can expose you. Or I can ... work to see the ... MulSendero worshipping ... freely in ... the Holdings."

"Like your Chinese in Japan? I suspect that the Zakkaists have long memories also."

Colin could feel himself pulling away from his body, growing smaller as the Presence made Itself known. He could feel the bright spot of his anger, the cold nodule of doubt, could feel all of his doubts sliding under the power of Her. He gave himself to the intrusion, let Her take him. He listened to his own voice wonderingly as he uttered that last statement.

"I offer ... a chance to make ... peace between us," Su insisted.

"You offer blackmail to the Exori. You don't offer equality, simply a truce under your terms. MolitorAb is all: human, Stekoni, and races yet to be discovered. My God doesn't hide as yours does, Ascendant. She's visible to all who travel the Veils; a living being."

"Her prophet ... is a fake ... conjured by the Church."

Colin simply laughed. The Colin inside laughed with him. The image of Su slid into that slippery half-dream, and Colin saw the Ascendant here, on that bed, but now writhing in the grip of a veildream as the monitor light changed from amber to red. His breath rattled and stopped, and his chest no longer moved as alarms began to shriek. Colin could see the soul stealing from the husk of the body, a vaporous, wavering entity. He knew then: Su would not live to see Old Earth again. He would die during the first Veil passage. "You can't help me, Huan Su. Even if you wished it. Tell me, why wouldn't you let me touch you when you lay on the sand? I can answer for you, for I saw the truth in your fear. You thought that I might heal you, and that would mean that all your protestations are just wind. Tell me, would you like me to pray over you *now,* Ascendant. Are you willing to face the proof that *your* God is false?"

Fear made a mask of Su's face, more terrible than Colin's own. The distant-Colin felt a wave of pity for the man, but he could also feel the Presence exulting. *So terrified that he might be wrong and so afraid of the coming darkness that he's blind to the salvation in front of him. He came to Dridust to assuage his guilt, not to do justice. It was all a sham that fooled even himself.*

"I trust...in the Lord," Su declared.

"Your God will let you die before you ever reach Old Earth," Colin's voice said. "That's why I can't ally with you. The truth is before you, Ascendant. You know that I can't stay here on Dridust much longer. The very pressure of my success is forcing me to leave—even now I can barely support the people who have come to me. You would see the Sartius Exori caged safely within the confines of the Fringes and controlled by the Holdings. I tell you that you cannot shackle the beast that I will become if I must."

From a distance, Colin felt his hand going into his pocket and bringing out a small knife. He watched himself as he opened the blade and ran a finger along its honed length. "I give you one last chance to see, Ascendant. I am the Exori, and the Exori can do things no man can do."

Before Su's apprehensive stare, Colin plunged the blade deeply into his own palm, dragging the blade viciously from one side to the other, laying the flesh open to the bone. Colin gritted his teeth against the searing agony as deep lines creased the skinbase of his face. Blood poured, a thick torrent, down his wrist and arm, as he held the mutilated hand out toward Su. Large, wine-red drops spread on the sheets that shrouded the Ascendant. "Could I have cured you, Ascendant? Watch."

The Presence rose full in him, shoving aside the Colin-ego, and he felt a distant warmth in his hand. Slowly, impossibly, the edges of that horrible wound began to close, knitting together once again, the flow of blood becoming turgid and finally stopping. In a minute, Colin lifted his hand high and closed it into a fist. He felt himself laughing in triumph, and he was frightened. The fist opened before the startled Su like an ugly, red-stained flower.

There was no sign of injury except for the tracks of blood.

"You see!" Colin heard himself shout. "Can you still deny me?!"

A relay clicked on the monitoring devices. Lights went amber in a serried row across Su's chest. His weak hands grasped at the sheets.

David burst into the room. *"Get the hell out of here!"* he screamed. "You fool! You're going to kill him!" Then he saw the gore covering Colin's arm, and he stopped. His eyes went wide and then narrowed. "Get out," he said, very softly and very coldly. "Get out or I'll have the guards take you."

Colin laughed. "You'd punish me for giving your Ascendant a chance for life?"

"*I'm* his chance. Not you. Now, get out!"

With no warning, the Presence left Colin. He nearly fell from the suddenness of it. His mouth hung open, he blinked and looked down at the knife in his hand. "You're condemning him to a useless death."

Su's voice grated harshly. "David. The devil . . . had him."

Colin pressed against the top of the blade. It swung back into the case with a solid click. He put the knife back in his pocket, his fingers trembling. His hand felt cold. "Not a devil," he told Su. "You saw salvation and refused it. A devil would have been more handsome and tempting than I. The Zakkaist church would not have destroyed the devil's face."

"Get out," David repeated.

This time, Colin nodded. "I'm sorry for you, Huan," he said as he passed the foot of the bed. "You're basically a good man. MolitorAb will be kind to you in the afterlife despite your sins."

The shuttle's guards stared at him as he walked from the room—the red-drenched shirt, the spattered *thorbani*. Colin could feel their hatred as if it matched the sun's heat.

CHAPTER FIFTEEN

Because of these words, the Jews were sharply divided once more. Many were claiming: "He is possessed by a devil—out of his mind! Why pay attention to him?" Others maintained: "These are not the words of a madman. Surely the devil cannot open the eyes of the blind!"

NEW TESTAMENT, John 10:19–21

"I fail to see the philosophical base of your preachings, the concrete morals and codes by which you want your people to live their lives. Isn't that the essence of any religion?"

He laughed at me, a sound as ugly and open as his face. "It's never the responsibility of a prophet to formulate codes. My disciples will do that—I merely form the vessel they will later decorate. It's enough for the prophet to shape the outlines, the broad brush strokes. In any case, what do these rules you want matter, except to the followers? To me, they're nothing. Nothing at all. I do as MolitorAb wills, whatever She wills. The Ascendants pursue the identical philosophy of pragmatism and act as they see fit without worrying about morality. Morals are for sheep and philosophers."

—From a disputed "interview" with the
Sartius Exori by Everett Hodgson,
February 27, 2560.

The Stekoni sectors of the MostHidden Cathedral of MolitorAb varied greatly from the areas in which Primus Jasper Keller dwelled. Here the light was tinted an aquamarine hue, the corridors were lower and wider, sloping gently and branching at odd, acute angles. The walls were a mottled gray stone, the knobby texture polished to a satin patina by the touch of a multitude of hands over centuries of use.

Exactly how old the deepest wings of the cathedral were was not known, for the foundations predated the time of QuietCry Moon-shade, the first of the Mad Ones, who began the preaching of MolitorAb the Voice. Originally, these altars had been dedicated to StormBringer, chief goddess of the fallen pantheon. Her worshippers had laid these stones in place, bolstered by the euphoric false strength of their ritual wine—*injusae*—and unable to sense the exhaustion of their muscles until their bodies slid helpless to the ground.

Those useless carcasses had been thrown into the hollows of the foundations and cemented into place.

It was said that their ghosts would forever guard the temple from enemies. Their blood had given an ochre hue to the mortar; the chill movements of air that wafted down the corridors were said to be the SpiritBreath, the immortal souls of the sacred workers.

A human would have said that the place reeked. To the Stekoni, the temple corridors offered a wealth of informative scents—subtle and flavorful, a shifting, elusive miasma of the past. Here was the scent of a fledgling's newFear; here a ManyMother's distant aroma of confidence, heavy with pheromonal calm. Hurried anxiety, irritation, religious awe: one could stand in this place and sense it all—trapped, drifting, and slowly fading as newer and stronger feelings overpowered the old. This air, this air was *alive*, a celebration of being.

Not empty and lonely as were the winds outside.

Even Primus Keller, on those rare occasions when he walked here, would always first stopper his nostrils with plugs. The Stekoni would shake their heads sadly at that—why did he not put out his eyes and puncture his ears as well? So stupid. This was a realm of shifting beauty, a still place. Here, one could listen and feel and touch history. It did not so much amaze the Stekoni that the humans could not understand as that they didn't even make the attempt.

ThinShell Third Darkness knew that wonder well. Her nestkin, GoldenShell, was highest aide to Primus Keller. She had heard her nestkin speak scornfully of the Primus's ignorance, as she did now. "He believes that he knows this one so well. Can you believe, nestkin beloved, that he would place manstench on his body after his toilet, so that our Primus Keller smells like a neutered low-caste offal worker? Or that he will pass a woman newly mated and *never* compliment her on the odor of her passion, or even give a bow of acknowledgment? All he needs to do is *nod*, as any priest would for the least servant in her household. This one, beloved, wonders whether humans are worth the effort we have put into them."

"The humans are predators always and only, nestkin beloved," ThinShell reminded her. "Thus they have the predator's blindness."

"Yes, this one knows," GoldenShell sighed. The subtle under-scent of hostility emanating from her dissipated, leaving only the base of purelove that enveloped her like an embrace. "And this one knows that you have preached patience to her. This one apologizes for her continuing lack of that virtue."

Then, responding to GoldenShell's compelling musk and her accepting stance, ThinShell opened her arms and gave out that most private pheromone, her small lower tongue flicking. Their scents mingled and altered as they came together. The Stekoni passing their alcove smiled at the aroma and politely averted their gaze, giving the two privacy...

Afterward, they rejoiced in shared warmth and listened to the chuckling words of shared joy from those passing the niche.

"You please this one, nestkin beloved."

"And this one."

ThinShell detected the tang of her nestkin's shifting mood a moment before she spoke. "This one wonders if the Sartius Exori is to be like the other humans. This one dislikes the race, nestkin. Yes, we must use them as we did Hallan Gelt, but to admit them to the faith...this one wonders if that is right."

"GoldenShell can think such thoughts after coupling with her beloved?" ThinShell chided her gently, amusement in her voice and an ironical heaviness to her odor.

"This one begs pardon, but yes. With apologies, this one deals much with humans, while her nestkin beloved can stay with the SpiritBreath here, in the company of those like her."

ThinShell stroked the oil-slick fur of her lover, enjoying the smooth gliding of her fingers and lightly tracing the closing edges of her vaginal slit, still engorged with remembered passion.

A chattering of greeting and empathetic joy came from the dim corridor as another Stekoni passed. ThinShell pressed GoldenShell's head to her chest; her nestkin's hands stole inside one of the young-pouches to stroke the nipple there.

"Nestkin, what can be better for Stekoni than to have the human-predators with us in MolitorAb?" ThinShell asked. "This one re-members the lifestorms of the WaterMother on the nesting world. Does GoldenShell recall the rumbling darkness on the horizon and the ManyMother's call to run/flee/disperse as the rains began? This one was often too slow, and the pelting water would sting her back and wash away the scents until she smelled like a dead thing. And afterward, the nests would have to be repaired and the world smelled like the mud below the tides, with ripworms wriggling on the surface, a danger for unwary feet. But always, a few weeks after, the plants would rise and this one would work in the fields alongside the others, gathering for the dry times."

ThinShell paused. Her scent became sweet with the memory of old happiness. "That's what the Sartius Exori will be for us, GoldenShell nestkin," she continued. "A lifestorm whose fury will be terrible but in whose path will come sustenance. Safety."

"Colin Fairwood sits on Dridust, beloved. He sits and does little."

"He is the storm on the horizon, then—the bulwark of massing clouds, gathering energy. SlowBorn Brightness will see to that as priests of a generation past saw to Hallan Gelt. He will not sit for very long. Already he grows discontent."

"Still, he does not seem passionate enough for a storm, according to all this one has heard."

ThinShell smiled, her long mouth yawning. Minty breath enveloped them both. "Oh, his passion comes, nestkin beloved. His trial and his agony wait for him. Of that this one is certain. Ascendant Su is there now, or possibly gone already. Perhaps Huan Su will be the spark that ignites the storm. The Exori will move. Soon."

She leaned toward her nestkin and hugged her. "Let us forget the humans for a few more hours and rejoice in ourselves, beloved."

Her scent was warm and tinged with the hint of something bittersweet.

A Stekoni's shrill voice chanted the FirstHour devotions, the quavering descant cutting through the hiss of sand sluicing against the windows. The sound stabbed at Kiri even through the walls of the temple, bringing with it a shaft of apprehension tipped with guilt.

Colin was out there. Somewhere in the Flats.

She unpolarized the window, watching fingers of liquid purple black dissolve; and gazed out at Genesis. Not much could be seen of the settlement because of the erratic funnels of sand that danced through the streets. She could see people hurrying about their business, *thorbanis* flapping. Kiri cupped the soft curve of her belly. "He'll be all right, little one," she whispered. "Your father is the Exori—he can't be hurt." She'd been sick that morning, the first time the nausea had reached her. She could see the pregnancy was just beginning to show when she looked in the mirror of her bedroom.

"Colin, you can't go chasing this ghost, damn it! You're needed here. To have you wandering the Flats isn't going to do any good."

"You don't tell me what to do," he'd shouted back at her. "Something is waiting for me out there. MolitorAb tells me that."

The other members of the Sabbai would arrive in a few minutes for the weekly meeting to arrange the worship schedule for the temple and to deal with the problems of the town. That latter item had become more tedious in the last several months: as Genesis grew, the logistics swelled with complications. Arguments were becoming heated among the Sabbai, even in Colin's presence. Kiri didn't look forward to the next few hours at all. She wished Colin had returned, if only because then the quarrels would be aimed at him, not at Kiri. That tendency was one of the things she hated: because she was Colin's lover, even those who knew her well usually assumed she always thought as Colin did. In fact, she was often in disagreement with him.

It had been simpler a year ago, two years ago, when it was only Colin and Pale and herself, along with the few followers impelled as much by curiosity as faith. Kiri stared out the windows and whispered a prayer for Colin's safety, trying to forget the rancor she felt when he'd insisted on going.

"I have to find that Presence, the visions."

"Colin, why won't you listen to me when I tell you that you're driving yourself too much? By MolitorAb, I don't want to lose you, not now."

"I have to know how to deal with this situation. MolitorAb will tell me."

"She'll tell you even if you stay here. I hate arguing with you like this, but I know that I'm right."

"And I know that I'm right. So who am I supposed to believe, Kiri? You or myself?"

She heard the door open and polarized the window again—a wash of inky purple trickled down the pane. FirstBorn Pale and SlowBorn Brightness moved together into the room, shuffling toward a rear corner as if there were an isolette set there, as if they wished to avoid offending the humans with their strong odor. Both bowed to Kiri, though Pale used the lower, more respectful bow while the priest merely nodded, her bright eyes peering at Kiri. FirstBred Pale smiled as her head came back up. "How is Kiri Oharu?"

"I'm as well as I can be, FirstBred Pale," Kiri answered, bowing in return. "This one is touched by your concern for her, and she would tell you that it is good to be swelling with this new life." She touched her womb, cupping it gently.

"This one shares that joy, and she hopes one day to experience it herself."

Miriam Hall strode in then, her *thorbani* crusted with sand. She was a slight woman, tall and angular, with a complexion that Dridust had turned to warm oak. She held herself as if she took for granted the stares she received from the people in the camp, as if her striking appearance were something due her. She nodded to the Stekoni and ignored Kiri completely, brushing her clothing and taking a seat on one of the stone benches. She slid a flatscreen from a pocket and began to study the rows of figures scrolling down it. She alone of the Sabbai was a Dridust native, the guide who had first shown Colin and his paltry entourage the spring-fed anomaly that would become Genesis. Kiri knew Miriam had propositioned Colin a number of times. He had declined the offers; strangely, that seemed to have inflamed Miriam against Kiri but hadn't affected her feelings toward Colin at all, as if she felt that Kiri were responsible for his refusals. Miriam had left Genesis for a time, following the caravans, but had returned in a few months, moving quickly to her current position as treasurer for the group.

"Kiri!" Aaron called from the doorway, pulling her attention away from Miriam. "Is Colin Exori back yet?"

"No, I'm afraid not."

A frown appeared between the young man's brows. "He's holed up somewhere waiting for the wind to die down, I'd guess," he said, but worry pinched the corners of his eyes.

Samuel Conner entered behind Aaron, his habitual smirk neatly arranged. He slid to the rear wall of the room, his arms crossed in front of his chest. Like Colin, he was Galicht; like the old Colin, he was the skeptic of the Sabbai. Kiri had never been able to understand why Colin tolerated the man, why he'd drawn him into the inner circle of disciples: if there was one of the Sabbai she totally distrusted, it was Conner. He nodded to her, and she gave the slightest movement of her head in acknowledgement. He seemed to shrug and propped one foot against the wall.

Joshua was the last to arrive, swinging the door open breathlessly. "Sorry to be so late," the oldest of the Sabbai said. He shook sand from his *thorbani,* dusting the floor. "I was coming across the square when a half-dead band of supplicants staggered in from the storm.

I had to find them room to sleep and arrange to have them fed."
Joshua's gray green eyes were restless. Unlike the leader Kiri had
known on Chebar, Joshua the Sabbai was nervous and restless,
talking as much with his hands as with his mouth. His acceptance
of Colin as Sartius Exori had destroyed his arrogance and confidence, and he moved like an unsure colt. "Has the Exori returned?"
he asked, holding his arms out to show his wind-tousled appearance.

"No," Kiri answered again.

Joshua's gaze moved helplessly to the window. "You shouldn't
let him wander about as he does," he declared. "We've enough
difficulties without adding to them."

Kiri tasted sourness in the back of her throat, the foul remnants
of her sickness that morning. Already the bickering had begun. "*I
don't control the Exori, nor can I dictate to him what he should or
shouldn't do. He already complains that all of the Sabbai try to
bind him too closely.*"

"Then you should communicate his concerns to us, since you
hear them first. None of the rest of us sleep with him." That was
Miriam. She would not look up from her flatscreen, and her words
were carefully stripped of any inflection. Kiri swallowed, tasting
bile.

"He's concerned with Ascendant Su, with that Holdings cruiser
above us—he needs our total support." She said the words, trying
to shove the memory of her own argument with Colin to the back
of her mind. "He'll do as MolitorAb tells him to do. God doesn't
speak to the rest of us, does She?"

"Kiri Oharu is correct," FirstBred Pale said. "Listen to her.
Ascendant Su is a good man, and he gives us hope of compromise
with the Church. Together, he and Colin Exori could save us much
bloodshed and horror." A surge of cinnamony sharpness came from
her as her mouth twisted in what might have been a grimace.

"Su's just a Zakkaist." Aaron twisted in his seat to make his
retort to Pale. "Can't you see the bloodstains on his hands? Use
your eyes and not your nose."

"This one refuses to believe that, Aaron Roberts. Huan Su has
offered us a chance to meet with the Church, and even a Buntaro
should not defile that with blind hatred. Nor should he let his dislike
for the Stekoni color his judgement."

Aaron scoffed. "Yeah. Right. FirstBred Pale, you're the most
naive being I've met. Ask your own priest about Su if you want—
SlowBorn Brightness would agree with me, wouldn't she?"

Before the priest could answer, Kiri flung up her hands. "Please!"

she shouted. Most of them turned to her, though Miriam didn't glance up from her display. "Colin would be most disappointed with all this sniping. If MolitorAb called one of us to be the Sartius Exori rather than Colin, then that person would leave and seek his own fortune. We're not supposed to be minor Pretenders; we should be an aid to Colin Exori. Let's see what we can do about the concrete matters that face us. Let's deal with the overcrowding or the food. Each week Genesis spreads a little farther—already our water's in danger of contamination from waste. We're choking on our own success."

"Meanwhile, Colin Exori goes seeking visions under the shadow of a Holdings cruiser," Samuel commented sourly from the back. He hadn't stirred; his eyes were half-closed. "How will he know whether what he meets is MolitorAb or just the ghosts roaming his head?"

"You disagree with what Colin has done?" Joshua commented.

"He hasn't *done* much since Su was shot." Samuel pushed himself off the wall. "What are we trying to accomplish? Does the Exori want to move to the cities of Dridust and become a businessman like most of the other Pretenders and all of the Zakkaists? Is that why Su's here—to offer a business proposition? Or does Colin want to remain a vital, active force?"

"You indicate your preference with your choice of words, Samuel," Kiri snapped.

"I'm not used to hiding my feelings."

"'Exori, do this. Exori, do that.'" Kiri mocked all of them. *And yourself. You're as guilty as the rest.* "We have to stop. All we do is make him angry, make it more difficult for him to hear the Voice."

"Does that mean that Kiri Oharu has abandoned the aims and methods of the Buntaro that she once espoused?" SlowBorn Brightness inquired. Her young-pouches were hidden beneath the loose yellow wrapping of her formal vestments. One hand made a mound underneath the robes, which were splotchy with her secretions. "Does she feel that no violence is needed to overthrow the Zakkaists?"

Kiri's surprise must have shown in her glance, for SlowBorn gave the shiver-shrug of the Stekoni. "This one is merely curious," she said. "She certainly would not care to be part of such aggressiveness."

"What I'm thinking isn't important," Kiri said evasively. "We're not here to offer opinions, revered one. We worship MolitorAb and we do as the Sartius Exori would have us do. Isn't *that* our task?"

The Stekoni priest drew back slightly at the verbal challenge. "This one is sad to hear the sharpness in Kiri Oharu's voice. Perhaps she is more upset at this situation than SlowBorn Brightness is herself."

Kiri sighed, shaking her head. She ran long fingers through her hair, snagging them on a tangle. "Yes. Yes, this one apologizes to SlowBorn Brightness. She is affected by everything at the moment."

"Hormones," Miriam muttered.

Kiri began an angry reply but smothered it, realizing that the meeting would then dissolve into chaos. From the corner of her eye, she saw Samuel slouch against the wall once more.

"It doesn't matter what we do in this room," he declared. "In that you're right, Kiri. Genesis is finished. It's gotten too big; so has Colin. He needs to decide what we do next."

"If we're allowed to do anything," Joshua interjected. "Benesch still demands that we turn Crowell over to him. If *he* gets too irritated, he could make the whole discussion moot."

"Still," Samuel answered, "we have to move. All of us know it, and each has his own preference in how we'd like Colin to do that. Su's cruiser is ready to squash us like some insect: if I were the commander, I'd already have done just that to be rid of the threat. We've all known that we can't stay on Dridust forever— we might as well paint a big target on the temple square. Aaron, Kiri, and maybe you, Joshua, would like Colin to be the Buntaro leader, wielding his sword against the enemy. Miriam and FirstBred Pale want him to move slowly and carefully, if for entirely different reasons."

Miriam looked up from her flatscreen, eyebrows raised. "Do you realize what he could do if he wished? There are enough faithful on this world to form a good financial base in any of the northern cities. He could head the largest MulSendero sect in the Fringes within two years—without danger and without any grief." She put the flatscreen down on her lap and sniffed. "So what do *you* want, Samuel?"

"I want to go someplace where there are no sandmites to nip at my ankles and the air doesn't steal the moisture from my mouth. I'm a simple man, Miriam. I'll follow the Sartius Exori and not worry about the rest."

"We should all think of doing exactly that," Kiri said loudly. "Colin Exori has given us the responsibility of dealing with Genesis at the moment. Let's do that without any more pettiness."

"This one agrees with Kiri Oharu," FirstBred Pale said. "Until Colin Exori returns, let us deal with the smaller tasks."

"So the two First Disciples are going to assert their dominance." Miriam laughed. She took up the flatscreen again, her classic features relaxed as always. "Then I'll bow to their leadership and listen to this futile exercise. What we might want the Exori to do is an academic point at the moment."

Kiri heard the winds buffet the windows. She laced her fingers over her stomach and nodded. "Then the first order of business is the food supply," she said.

Hours later, after very little had been accomplished, she went back to her rooms, hoping that Colin had returned in the time she'd been away.

He had not.

He'd wandered into the Flats searching for power. MolitorAb had not come to him when he'd taken the *Anger* into the Veils the day after he'd spoken with Su, nor had he felt the touch of his God in the weeks of tension that followed. As the ship *Jehovah's Sword* continued to prowl in Dridust orbit, anxious messages went from the Dridust government to both Colin and Commander Benesch. Benesch's reply was simple: Return Mother Crowell. Colin's answer was as brief: She is in MolitorAb's hands.

Ascendant Su had slipped into a coma, and the tension notched higher. Colin had thought the Presence would direct him again, move him in the proper direction. Instead, as no message came, he made no move at all, and he'd had to confront the growing uneasiness in the settlement and the grumblings of the Sabbai.

He'd gone into the wastes as much to escape them as to find MolitorAb.

Colin had been three days without food and hours without sipping from the canteen in his pack. His face was stubbled where there was skin and smooth under the skinbase. His hair was matted and filthy, and sandmites had made a pocked, angry rash of his legs. Rimed with a crusted seepage, his eyes were nearly swollen shut. The winds had begun in earnest hours ago, but Colin had laughed at them—MolitorAb's breath.

Visions had swayed before him since he'd awakened the night before. The rest was only an uncomfortable intrusion: the sand, the heat, the gales. Huan Su walked beside Colin, limping and wheezing. The Ascendant brushed green fronds of plants with his withered hands, his white robes iridescent in the sunlight.

"You can't stay here, Colin. You must leave." Su's voice was gently chiding.

"I know that, but were do I go? Who do I take?"

"I can't answer that."

"I don't know what I'm supposed to do."

"That isn't known to me either."

"You owe me the answer. I killed you, Huan. I let you die when I might have saved you. Tell me."

But Huan had left. The cool air, the greenery dissolved before Colin and the sun lashed at his face, glaring on the sand. Colin stumbled and felt gritty dust fill his outstretched hands. He struggled to rise but fell again. Heat burned the length of his side.

"Get up," a voice said.

Colin turned his head, the crystalline Flats sandpapering his cheek. He spat grit from his mouth. "I can't, Hallan," he said.

"You're not allowed to die here. That's not the prophecy."

"Then you must help me."

"Can't you make your own decision?" Hallan held a drink in his hand, sipping from it as ice cubes tinkled in the sweating glass. Colin yearned for it; his hands dug soft grooves in the sand.

"I'm MolitorAb's tool, Hallan. The decision isn't mine to make."

"Of course not." Hallan laughed. "Your faith is weak, Colin. Would MolitorAb have chosen you if you'd do anything against Her? You're Her vessel because you're made the way you are. You were always a good follower, Colin. You followed me when we were Obdurates, you follow me even now." Gelt turned toward Colin and the shirt he wore gaped open. Colin could see deep cuts on his chest and stomach, all of them oozing slow, bright blood. "Your decision will be Hers: She'll let nothing else happen. Your hesitation is only your own pride." Hallan sipped at the drink again, and his image began to waver. Colin levered himself to his elbows, shaking his head.

"No!" he tried to shout. "Hallan, why can't She do all this by Herself? She could change things with Her own power."

"You think that you can understand God, Colin?" Hallan's face blazed with sudden radiance. "If so, your arrogance surpasses mine. I don't question Her will. Get up, Colin. Get up."

Colin sobbed. With all his remaining strength, he braced his knuckles against the shifting sand and brought his legs beneath him. He knelt in the swirling, dry storm. His thirst tortured him. When he coughed, it tore at his throat. He reached for his pack and canteen, but the straps were gone from his shoulders, the comforting weight missing. He looked around but could see nothing through his slitted eyes. "Hallan, why did you take it?" he screamed. The shadowy ghost only laughed again. "Give it to me!" Colin gasped. He leapt at the mocking Hallan. They rolled in the sand, grappling, Hallan's drink spilling unheeded. Colin had his fingers around Hallan's throat; he leaned on the bigger man, bearing down.

Hallan disappeared.

His support gone, Colin toppled headfirst onto the ground again. "Exori, get up."

Colin shook his head, his face grinding into the sand as he refused to look up. "Go away," he said. "Leave me alone."

"You must get up."

Colin knew that voice. He rolled to his side and saw the figure wavering like a heat demon before him. "Go away, Crowell. I don't need to see you. Go with Su and Hallan to hell."

"Exori, let me help you."

"You're dead like all the rest of them. You can't help me any more than they could—you'll just pour empty advice into my head."

"Please, sit up." He thought he felt a hand cradling his head, and then a cool, bitter, blessed moisture trickled along his parched lips. He sucked at it greedily.

"Thank you, phantom. You may leave now."

"I'm not a phantom."

He tried to bring her into focus and couldn't. The sunglare formed a halo around her, and the sand-laden winds shimmered through her body, twisting the ragged *thorbani* she wore. Colin chuckled and dropped his head back on the sand. "I want MolitorAb, not a bad assassin."

"I can't drag you by myself, Exori. If you want to go back to Genesis, you'll have to help me."

"Why? In half a minute, you'll be gone and some other restless soul will want to talk with me."

"You're delirious, Colin Exori. You're mad and you're going to be just a pile of sand-scraped bones if you don't get up and move."

"Why would *you* help me? Isn't my death what you wanted?"

"Think of this as penance for a grave sin, Exori. Or consider that the simple disappearance of the Dridust Pretender would mean nothing as far as proving Gelt wrong."

"Why don't you mention that to him? Let me get him for you— he was just here." Colin coughed again. "Hallan! Hallan! Come here, I've got a friendly spirit for you!" Colin's hands formed into fists: the skin at his knuckles was torn and bleeding. He pushed himself up and felt Crowell's hands under him, helping. He staggered to his knees, then to his feet; lurching, he leaned against her. "Don't you have advice for me, ghost?" he asked her. "All the rest did. Where should I go, what should I do?"

"I'll tell you that if you stay here, you're dead. Come, we have to walk. I've found some shelter from the storm."

Colin giggled, swinging his arms wildly. "You'll go with me? That's fine, spook. Let's go back to Genesis and show the rest how well my visions talk."

He put his arm around her. They began moving, one slow step after the other. The wind shrieked invectives at them; buff sand filmed the sun. Leaning like drunken companions, they moved into the face of the storm.

CHAPTER SIXTEEN

If Allah punished men for their sins, not one creature would be left alive. He respites them to an appointed day; when their hour is come, not for one moment shall they stay behind: nor can they go before it.

KORAN, The Bee 16:60–61

What must I do to prove to you what I am? If you doubted that I were living, would you ask that I tear open my chest so you may see the beating of my heart? If you say that I am not a man, must I bare myself so that you see my manhood? Why can you not simply look upon me with the eyes MolitorAb has given you, with the faith She has placed in your breast?

Then you would see that there are no lies within me. I am the Sartius Exori, the one filled with Her rage and Her joy. I am the fisted hand nested in velvet, the rending claw clothed in soft fur. My way leads through sorrow and pain, but beyond it is the glory of MolitorAb.

THE WORDS OF THE SARTIUS EXORI,
Despair 8:73–75

FirstBred Pale, in the seat beside Kiri, saw them first. "Kiri Oharu, *there!*" she cried, pointing down into the seething glare of the Flats to the southwest. Kiri, piloting the tiny hovercraft, craned her neck to see, peering through the sand-scratched glass. Yes, there were two figures plodding through the drifts, both wearing *thorbani,* one of them Colin's height and build. Kiri swung the controls over and the balky vehicle banked into a groaning, shuddering turn. They were near the limits of the broadcast power from Genesis; the craft, never responsive, was annoyingly sluggish. "This one feels that it must be him," FirstBred Pale said excitedly.

"Pray that it is," Kiri answered, then pressed her lips together. She fought to hold back the rising hope.

The storm had subsided two local days before, dying in the morning light as the winds slowed and shifted to the west. When Colin still had not returned by late afternoon, Kiri found FirstBred Pale and took the hovercraft from the temple garage. She and the Stekoni had been crisscrossing the Flats since then, finding only emptiness and a few supplicants trudging toward Genesis. Kiri would not let herself believe that Colin was dead. "I'd know," she'd said to Pale when the Stekoni had hesitantly broached the possibility. "I'm sure that I'd know."

The smaller of the figures waved as they passed over them. The other glanced up—there was a glistening skinbase, a layer of plast-alloy muscles.

Colin.

Kiri gave an involuntary sob of relief. Pale sighed. Kiri set the craft down as quickly as she dared and ran toward him, her feet sinking into the loose sand.

He looked terrible. His skin was dry and cracked, his hair matted, his eyes glazed. His lips were dark with dried blood. "Colin, you bastard!" Kiri hugged him to her, uncaring of his filth. His arms came around her weakly; his companion took a step away. The motion drew Kiri's attention. "Crowell," she hissed, suddenly angry. She held Colin as if he were a treasured possession. Mother Crowell only stared.

FirstBred Pale came hurrying up. "This one will help, Kiri Oharu." The Stekoni glanced at Crowell with suspicion but said nothing. "Colin Exori, this one has water for you."

At that, Colin seemed to stir. His puffy eyes squinted at them. "Is Crowell's ghost still here?"

"Ghost?" Kiri breathed.

"Can you see her?" Colin's voice rasped like sand. "She was the best of the visions I had."

Kiri turned her head to Crowell. Their eyes met, antagonistic. "I see her," Kiri said.

"A good vision, isn't she?" Colin said huskily. "I kept her here to show you. I've been telling her about you, about the child we'll have."

The priest endured Kiri's stare. Crowell had lost weight since Kiri had last seen her—she was a skeleton over which someone had pasted loose flesh. Her appearance was more ravaged than Colin's: her features were parched, broken, and caked with grime; her soiled clothing was in rags. Kiri felt a stab of pity and did not want to. She stroked Colin's hair for a moment and then took the jug of water from Pale, spilling some of the cool liquid into her palm and rubbing Colin's face with it. Colin shook his head, stumbling away from her.

"The ghost first," he said. "I have to feed my visions so we can take them back to Genesis. Let her drink, FirstBred Pale. Do the dead still need to drink, Mother Crowell?"

"They do, but they can wait, Exori," she answered.

The Stekoni looked at Kiri, who shrugged. Pale was slow in obeying Colin, but at last she nodded and padded over to Crowell. She held out the jug with the water gurgling inside. "The Sartius Exori would have Mother Crowell refresh herself," she said.

Crowell's nose wrinkled at the closeness of the Stekoni, at the reek of the creature. She took the water, hands trembling, the joints of her fingers swollen and cracked open. Greedily, she tilted the jug and sucked at the water.

Kiri watched Crowell, though she spoke to Colin. "You can't take her back, Colin."

"She's my vision, not yours."

"Benesch thinks that she's dead or lost. Bring her back to Genesis now and you'll have that cruiser down on us."

Colin laughed. "What does MolitorAb care about a cruiser?" he flung out, scoffing. "To Her, it's less than a flea." He weaved in the sun; Kiri saw the madness in him and knew that the sun and thirst had taken his wits.

"Kiri Oharu, we can't leave her here. We can't abandon her," FirstBred Pale objected. "This one could not leave her to die."

Mother Crowell still said nothing. She held the jug out to Kiri. "He needs this," she said.

Kiri glanced from the jug to Crowell. "You tried to kill him," she said. "Why would you care now?"

"I also saved his life. It was MolitorAb's will that I find him." A muscle jumped at the corner of her jaw. "He is the Sartius Exori."

Kiri couldn't tell if there was sarcasm in her voice or not. "If he brings you back, he'll get nothing for it but trouble."

"He is the Sartius Exori," Crowell replied, her voice suddenly bold. "He'll do what he needs to do. Do you doubt him?" she challenged.

"Bah!" Kiri spat out. "Get into the hover, Mother Crowell. I suppose I owe you that much."

Commander Benesch wasn't a man given to subtlety. He ran his ship with the expectation of instant obedience. When such was denied him by those under his yoke, his reactions were harsh and instinctive. He did not think.

As a military man and a devout Zakkaist, he was used neither to heretics nor to open defiance. As part of a navy that had seen almost no action for his entire career, he had yet to find a situation where his instincts were put to the test. None of his decisions had ever been crucial, none were ever anything that the regulations had not adequately covered.

He also tended to brood. A more decisive, experienced officer might have made his or her decision days earlier, but Benesch had remained in Dridust orbit, fretting. His procrastination worked to his benefit.

Mother Crowell had returned to Genesis.

Benesch told himself that the event was vindication for his un-acknowledged expertise. He told David as much when, for the hundredth time, the physician had begged the commander to return to Old Earth. Su would have ordered the return himself, David claimed—but the Ascendant was still lost in a coma. The ship's surgeon, perhaps knowing her superior's temperament, had dis-agreed with David, saying that Su's condition was at least stable and that the Veil passages could endanger Su more than the wait. The chance was not worth taking, she said. Offers of help from Dridust medical facilities (prodded by their anxious government) could be taken advantage of if things suddenly turned critical.

The cruiser had hung there, a carrion bird waiting for prey.

It surprised no one that Commander Benesch himself took the shuttle down, nor that a full platoon of the cruiser's complement of marines was included in his contingent. When the shuttle grounded, Benesch immediately strode down the ramp into the waves of heat. He flicked a glance at the Pretender's farship sitting nearby. There were people waiting for the commander near the settlement. Benesch recognized only one of them, the Buntaro and member of the Sabbai known as Aaron Roberts. Colin was not there, nor any of the rest of the Sabbai—not the Stekoni nor the woman who carried the Pretender's bastard child. Benesch's mouth tightened.

Aaron stepped toward the commander and dipped his head in that half-Stekoni gesture Benesch hated. "Commander," he said. "I regret to tell you that you're not welcome here without the per-mission of the Sartius Exori."

"Don't give me that crap, Buntaro," Benesch snapped. "I don't want to listen to your prattle. Give me the priest Anna Crowell."

"I can't do that."

Benesch gestured toward the shuttle as its turrets eased around to aim pointedly at the MulSendero temple. Marines filled the entrance to the ship. "I don't intend to give you a choice, Buntaro."

"You've no jurisdiction here, Commander. You'll do nothing but create an incident that will destroy your career."

"That's the argument your Pretender used with Ascendant Su. The Ascendant may have been fooled by that bit of sophistry, but his wisdom is no longer available to us. The priest Crowell has sinned against the laws of the Church and the Holdings. I *will* take her to the Holdings's judgement." Benesch drew himself up, a vision—in his mind—of the ramrod-straight officer. "You can tell the Pretender Fairwood that. I'll wait for him to bring Crowell here, but tell him that my patience is very short."

The Buntaro grinned. "I'm afraid that you'll need more patience than that, Commander."

"You have about five minutes to change your mind."

"Commander Benesch, Colin Exori is no longer here in Genesis, nor is Mother Crowell. They're no longer on Dridust at all, in fact. I'm in charge of this encampment, and I can't comply with your ... orders."

Fury surged through Benesch, mixed with fear—he'd bungled, if what the man said was true. "His farship's sitting right there," Benesch said. "And I know that no other farship's left this miserable hole."

"Colin Exori found passage with a Galicht in one of the northern cities, Commander."

Benesch snarled at Aaron. His left arm shot out and his forefinger jabbed at the town. "Search this place," he barked to the marines. "Don't be gentle, and do it thoroughly. If Crowell's hidden here, bring her to me."

"Commander," Aaron shouted. "We must protest this treatment. A report will go to the Dridust Council and the Conclave of Ascendants." Benesch was glad to hear the apprehension that shook the young man's voice. He smiled at the Buntaro and nodded his head to the platoon lieutenant.

"Do it," he said.

Hours later, sand-caked and weary, the marines had found no sign of Crowell or the Pretender. Two of the buildings were burning; smoke smudged the sky and sparks leapt to the roofs of neighboring houses. The population was in panic, fleeing into the desert along the pathways to the hills or gathering in a crowd near the shuttle.

Aaron sat on the sand before Benesch, flanked by guards. After the lieutenant had made his report to Benesch, the commander strode down the shuttle ramp and halted before the Buntaro. The crowd watched apprehensively from the edge of the settlement, a soft wailing coming from them. "Get him up," Benesch said. The guards hauled Aaron to his feet. Before he could catch his balance, Benesch cuffed him across the face, sending the man sprawling.

"My patience is now gone, Buntaro," Benesch growled, glowering down at him. "Tell me where Crowell is and where Fairwood and the rest have gone."

Aaron wiped at his mouth and spat blood. The wind shifted, sending the smell of burning wood toward them. "I told you, commander. They're not on this world. They went into the Veils."

"You're lying to me."

"I'm not."

Benesch exhaled angrily. He glanced about—at the watching, waiting crowd; at the pall of smoke sparks coiling upward; at the silly little village stuck in the middle of nothing. His frustration, alloyed with despair, boiled inside him.

The whole affair had gone so badly.

"Pull five people from that mob, Lieutenant," he said. Marines leaped to obey. The crowd screamed, and they all tried to run. The effort was futile. The marines dragged the unlucky five to Benesch. "I will have them shot before your eyes, Roberts," Benesch said to Aaron. "I'll put the muzzles to their temples and you'll see their brains spill out on your lap. If you want to see them live, you'll change this stupid tale of yours and finally tell me the truth. Your choice, Buntaro."

Aaron's eyes had gone dead and dull. There was an air of passive acceptance about him. "I've told the truth as far as I know it, Commander. Their blood will be on your hands alone when you go before MolitorAb. I've nothing more to say." He looked at the five. "I'm sorry," he said. "Take comfort in your faith. Pray. Your souls will find peace."

Benesch closed his eyes and pressed his lips together. He made a gesture to the marines and they lowered their weapons. The five ran, unbelieving, back to the settlement. "Shoot the Buntaro traitor instead," he said. He began walking up the ramp toward the ship.

He heard the shot before he had left the oppressive heat.

CHAPTER SEVENTEEN

Moses said: "Pharaoh, I am an apostle from the Lord of the Creation, and may tell nothing of Allah but what is true. I bring you an undoubted sign from your Lord. Let the Children of Israel depart with me."

Pharaoh answered: "Show us your sign, if what you say be true."

Moses threw down his staff, and thereupon it changed to a veritable serpent. Then he drew out his hand and it appeared white to all who saw it.

KORAN, The Heights 7:104–109

Was Colin Fairwood a madman? No one can say unless he or she is sure of the faith transcending death and the truth behind the Veils. If he was mad, then he was also incredibly fortunate. If he only followed the will of MolitorAb, then we cannot hope to understand God. Perhaps he was both, and only those whose souls have been torn and bloodied by life can be fully open to the hands of the Diety.

So you may ask your question, but expect no answer except the sad wailing of the wind or the silence between the stars. If you can hear the words there, you will know.

And humanity will also call you mad.

—from the introduction to COLIN EXORI:
A LIFE OF CONTRADICTION, by S.N.
Soellner-Federle, Zakkaist Press 2615

Moving from Nexus Port into the interior of that enclosed world-let, one is transported from nature's silence to humanity's cacophony, from open space to claustrophobic canyons of streets, from loneliness to jostling, faceless crowds. The elevators from the port down to the hollow ball of rock empty into a plaza where the newcomer—usually—can see the tunneled city stretching before him.

Usually.

As Colin, FirstBred Pale, Kiri, and Mother Crowell stepped from their elevator compartment, they were greeted by a pressing, insistent mob. Thousands were crammed into the plaza, a vast sea of bodies through which there was no path. They faced Colin, a blur of flesh. As soon as the door to their compartment had hissed open, hands stretched out to him, pulling and tugging; he could hear the ragged chant that welled from their throats: "Colin Exori! Colin Exori!" The chant slammed against the walls and shuddered back at the crowd, rejoining and swelling. "Colin Exori! Colin Exori!" Thunder in a world that had never known weather.

He'd seen nothing like this before. On Dridust, there was always room enough. If crowds came to hear him speak, to see him, there was always the equivalent of an escape route. Afterward, he could always move away from them.

Colin felt fear, a sense of being trapped. He almost turned to go back into the elevator, but the doors slid shut behind him, and eager hands pulled him forward. Suddenly there was nowhere to go, nothing he could do. People: a montage of terrifying faces—they surrounded him. That chant battered the walls: *"Colin Exori! Colin Exori!"* Colin began to struggle. He screamed and could barely hear his own voice; he lashed out at those nearest him, twisting to be free of the hands that everywhere touched him. He couldn't see the short form of FirstBred Pale at all, could not smell her. Mother Crowell was off to his right, separated by a wall of supplicants. And Kiri...

Someone had shoved her aside in an effort to be nearer Colin. As Colin watched, he saw her face compress in pain and anger— she struck back at the man, open palm to his nose. Colin saw the nose flatten, thought he could almost hear the cartilage break. Blood smeared across her palm, across the man's cheek. Then the man's companion pushed at Kiri and she stumbled. People pressed into the opening, uncaring.

"NO!" Colin bellowed. He thrust his way to Kiri. *"Damn you all! Don't hurt her!"* Startled faces gaped at him, a few even tried to give him room, but others pushed back from behind. Colin thought they might both be trampled under and cold fury rode in him, twisting the muscles in his transparent face, a flush deepening the ruddy lacework of vessels.

"YOU CANNOT DO THIS!"

The scream savaged his throat, tearing and rending it. He had not thought his voice could be so loud. His anguish, impossibly, carried over the roar of the chanting, the chaos of the city. All around him, the crowd went quickly silent. Kiri staggered to her feet. He pushed through the last people between them, caught her, and hugged her to him. He glared at those nearby.

"How could you think that I would be *pleased* by this!" he bellowed. "Did you think that being near the Sartius Exori would *save* you? *Fools!* I BRING YOU ONLY PAIN AND DEATH!" His eyes blazed, his hands sliced air. Slowly, all around him, the mob was going to its knees, forming a widening circle. Colin was standing in an ever-growing valley with Kiri beside him; his hands were doubled into fists at his sides as the rage still coursed through him. He scowled down at them.

They knelt, abject.

Frightened eyes were fixed on him.

He could feel the fullness of MolitorAb in him. He waited until the rage had died to glowing coal inside him, and then he began to preach.

"How do you know, Exori? How can you be sure?"

"Mother Crowell, I know that I'm the Sartius Exori the same way you knew of *your* faith. Would you have become a priest without belief? Yet you had no proof—you had only the certainty in your soul."

Colin looked down at the cavern-world from the window of his hotel. Through the field charge, he could hear the faint clangor of the city: the ground vehicles making their way through snarled streets, the hum of the generators, the bass drone of the McCarthy enhancers, the soughing of a billion humans speaking and laughing, moving from place to place. As an undertone to it all, there was the low chant of the faithful who still gathered around the entrance to the hotel, waiting for him to emerge: "Exori! Exori! Exori!"

"My faith proved to be false," Mother Crowell said behind him.

"Not entirely false." Colin took a deep breath and lifted his gaze. Far in the distance, the Barrens clambered drunkenly up the walls of the world. The Galicht-house was out there somewhere, lost among all the buildings. And everywhere there were the crowds, moving through the eternal fungal light. "You're now exposed to the entirety rather than simply a part," he continued. "Your faith was never incorrect, only incomplete."

Colin turned back into the room.

Mother Crowell sat on one of the ornate chairs, listening to Colin attentively. In her simple robes, she didn't seem to fit. The rooms were too luxurious—Colin didn't feel comfortable there either. The rug seemed to slosh around his ankles, the chairs appeared to be borrowed from a museum. He felt like an intruder despite the fact that the suite was paid for, in scrip, in advance—a gift from an anonymous donor. Colin was no longer poor; he'd seen the money placed on SlowBorn Brightness's offering plates on Dridust, and he knew that Miriam had channeled some of that money into an expense account for the use of the Exori. Colin might have been able to afford these rooms himself.

He would rather have stayed in the Galicht-house, but that would not have been safe.

"Then how can we ever trust faith, if it's so fallible?" Mother Crowell asked.

"The problem isn't faith, Mother Crowell. True faith isn't mistaken. It's the people who are fallible—they believe too easily in what they want to believe without examining their hearts."

There was a soft knock at the door. "Come in," Colin said.

Kiri entered. She glanced at Crowell sourly. "Roland Naley's in the outer room, Colin. He wants to see you."

"What's the matter, Kiri?"

"You'll have to ask him. I don't read minds."

Colin shook his head. "Not with Naley. With you."

"Does the Exori demand that I shrive myself in front of strangers?" Her voice lashed at him. Mother Crowell rose from her chair. "May I talk with you later, Exori?" the priest asked.

"Certainly."

Mother Crowell nodded to Colin and walked toward the door. As she came near Kiri, the two glared at each other. Kiri did not move; Crowell brushed against her as she left. Colin knew he didn't need to ask what bothered Kiri.

He scuffed at the carpet with a foot; it hushed back into place, uncaring. "I don't understand, Kiri. You won't give her any pardon at all. She saved my life."

"After trying to take it."

"Granted—but you're a Buntaro. People have died at your hands as well. Should I send *you* away?" He tried to say it gently and knew that she misunderstood. Her mouth twisted into a thin line and she shook her hair from her face. Its glossy black strands swayed.

"You don't need to talk down to me, Colin. I understand what you're saying and it doesn't alter anything. I won't talk about it if that's what you want, but I tell you that Crowell's going to cause you—us—grief if she stays. I'm asking you now to send her away."

"Or?"

Kiri's oriental features went empty, all emotion hidden. She canted her head, studying him. "I've never demanded anything of you, Colin. I've taken what you've been willing to share and given you as much as I could. I love you. Sometimes though, I'm not certain that I like you. I wasn't delivering an ultimatum. When that time comes, I guarantee you that you'll know."

She went to the door, her hand on the knob. "You want Naley?"

"I'd rather talk with you."

She didn't smile.

He knew he couldn't win. "Send him in." He sighed. "You and FirstBred Pale should be here also, I think."

"Not Crowell?" Her eyes flung window light back at him.

He didn't answer, and she left the room.

Roland Naley looked much the same as he had a few years before. He no longer claimed to be the Sartius Exori and now headed the MulSendero church on Nexus. He retained the piercing quality of his stare, the fanatical glare, and his loosely reined violence. He entered the room quickly, aggressively, and gazed at Colin without offering his hand or bowing, without any greeting at all. At last he nodded his shaggy head at Kiri and FirstBred Pale came in behind him.

"You're still damned ugly, Colin Fairwood. I detest looking at you. But MolitorAb moves in you—no one else could have done what you did yesterday at the port plaza. I still think that you're the Sartius Exori."

"I am," Colin replied. "I've no doubt of that."

"You didn't believe that when we first met."

"At that time, we were *both* mistaken."

Naley scowled at that. Colin wondered whether Naley was actually angry or if this was simply the way he reacted to bluntness. Then the man grinned, an ugly, feral thing. "I came here for a few reasons, Colin Exori. First, I have information for you." He paused. "Ascendant Huan Su is dead. That was confirmed at the first stopover of the cruiser *Jehovah's Sword*. He didn't survive the Veil passage."

FirstBred Pale sighed. The odor of the creature changed, became touched with some fleeting sweetness. "This one is sad at the Ascendant's passing, but Roland Naley should know that Colin Exori foretold the death of the Ascendant."

"Yes," Naley answered. He wrinkled his nose as he glanced at the Stekoni. "But I don't think he foretold this. The Veils were good coming from Dridust, and a message was passed to me an hour ago from a Galicht in from that world. You have your first martyrs, Exori."

"What?" Kiri said suspiciously as FirstBred Pale gave a soft wail and exuded a bitter odor.

Naley almost smiled. "I didn't think you'd know," he said.

"What happened?" Colin took a deep breath, his teeth clenching. *Aaron, Aaron! You knew there was danger, but you said that you would stay and hold Genesis for me. May MolitorAb be kind to you, may I see you in the Veils to tell you that I am sorry.*

"Benesch didn't care to be duped," Naley continued. "I've only gotten a sketchy report, but it seems that he ordered Aaron Roberts shot, ostensibly for obstructing his pursuit of Crowell. When that happened, several of your followers rushed the shuttle. The marines weren't gentle with them."

"How many?"

Naley peered at Colin appraisingly. "My report said twenty-three, and there were several more injured. And Genesis was torched, burned to the ground. The final tally could be higher."

"All for Crowell," Kiri muttered.

Muscles went taut under the skinbase. Colin cursed under his breath and went back to the window, suddenly sick to his stomach. He stared down to the dirty vista below and up at the mottled expanse of rock that was the Nexus sky. He thought he should feel sorrow, that tears should be in his eyes, but there was only resentment and a yearning for revenge. He wanted to drive his fist through the wall, to scream his fury to all of Nexus. He could feel the others in the room watching him, gauging and judging, and he wanted to turn and shout, to vent some of the emotion. *Aaron, I am sorry. I stayed too long on Dridust, as you told me. I didn't use the power MolitorAb has given me, and it cost you and others your lives. Too high a price to pay for me to learn my folly.*

He slammed his hand against the painted wall, hard enough so that he yelled as much in pain as in anger. "Damn them!"

He heard the click of the door and turned to find that Kiri had gone. Naley still watched Colin, a sardonic smile on his bearded face. FirstBred Pale was agitated. Her scent was strong, deeply musky, and her loincloth was darkening with secretions. "This one ... would go with Kiri Oharu," she said.

"No," Colin replied. He knew he spoke too harshly and tried to soften his tone. "Let her go."

"This one fears that Mother Crowell and Kiri Oharu..."

"She won't hurt her. She's upset with me, not Crowell. I think she realizes that."

FirstBred Pale nodded, her delicate hands moving near each other like moths circling a light. She backed away from Colin until her spine was against one of the walls.

"What was the rest of what you wanted to say to me, Naley?" Colin asked brusquely.

Naley sniffed. He drew a sleeve across his nose. "I thought that I'd offer my temple to you to preach in while you're here—it wouldn't do any harm to my contributions for the Sartius Exori to give a sermon or two, eh?" He chuckled, deep and low. "But now I see that I'm too late. You're not going to stay, are you?"

As the man said the words, Colin felt the truth of them. *No, you're not staying. You've taken the easy path for too long, the way of reconciliation. You're the Sartius Exori, and you have a task.* "Back to being a prophet, Naley?"

Naley snorted. "The gift never leaves you, Exori. And I'm not wrong, am I?"

"No," Colin replied simply.

"I thought not. In that case, I'll take my leave." He nodded, as if an inner voice had spoken to him. "Yes. I'll keep you informed if my sources tell me more of Dridust." Naley strode to the door as quickly and purposefully as he had entered. As he opened it, he glanced back at Colin. "I still pity you," he said. "I thought that the burden was to be mine. I never realized how little I actually wanted that load until you took it from my shoulders. You can't see your soul being bent under all that weight, Exori, but I can. You'll never know until it's broken you entirely." He grinned and closed the door behind him.

Colin shuddered.

"This one has never liked that man."

"Does FirstBred Pale like the Exori she has chosen instead?"

Pale didn't seem to know how to answer that. She began to reply and stopped. Her bare toes pulled at the thick pile of the carpet. "Sometimes," she said at last. "This one is sad to see Colin Exori and Kiri Oharu at odds with each other. She bears your child, Colin Exori, and needs your affection."

Colin shook his head. "Odd for a Stekoni to say that—your males are used only for breeding. The rest of the time you pen them up like animals."

"They *are* animals," FirstBred Pale insisted. "This one is not so foolish as to think that humans must be like Stekoni."

"Kiri has my affection and my love, FirstBred Pale. And I look forward to the time when we can be with our child. She knows that."

"Colin Exori is certain of that?"

"Yes."

"Then there is nothing more this one can say." Pale shuffled over to the door. "This one grieves with Colin Exori for the loss of Aaron Roberts and others of the faithful. She will pray for their souls."

"I will do more than that," Colin replied. "More than that."

CHAPTER EIGHTEEN

It was then that certain Pharisees came to him. "Go on your way!" they said. "Leave this place! Herod is trying to kill you." His answer was: "Go tell that fox, 'Today and tomorrow I cast out devils and perform cures, and on the third day my purpose is accomplished. For all that, I must proceed on course today, tomorrow, and the day after, since no prophet can be allowed to die anywhere except in Jerusalem.'"

NEW TESTAMENT, Luke 14:31–33

I cannot tell you what to do. Only MolitorAb may do that. So I say that you must listen to the whisperings of the Voice in your heart, and do as that Voice says. If it is your task to heal, then sell your possessions so that you may buy medicines. If it is your task instead to destroy, take the hammer in your hand.

—From the sermon of Colin Fairwood
to the congregation of the Nexian
Temple of the Voice, June 3, 2560

In the month following the Dridust Confrontation (as it became known) tensions grew between the Holdings and the Fringes, between Zakkaist and MulSendero. The news, appropriately trimmed and tinted to fit the audience, spread slowly through the Veils from world to world. Where the Galicht carried the tale, Benesch was pictured as an ogre-puppet at the end of whose strings curled the hands of Ascendant Culper. Where the Zakkaist church could control the press releases, the focus was the attack on Su and Colin's subsequent refusal to hand Mother Crowell over to justice, along with the crowd's attack on Benesch's shuttle.

The details varied and were never afterward clear, diffused as they were by anger and frustration and by reprisals against all factions. The Buntaro redoubled their terrorist activities within the Holdings. Churches burned as Genesis had burned, rioting scarred

174

the cities. In retaliation, the church became more oppressive: mass arrests, executions, curfews, harsh sentences, and torture were the order of the day. Invariably, that meant that the moderates, those MulSendero (actually in the majority) who had no real quarrel with the church other than their right to worship as they pleased, found they too were harassed and subjected to what they considered unfair treatment. Some of them were jailed, a few were killed. The sides quickly became polarized. The cycle continued: harsh reactions by the church, more Buntaro revenge that engendered stricter countermeasures...

The secular governments within the Holdings appealed to the new Pretender Fairwood to speak, to stop the spreading violence. But in the time it took those appeals to reach his last known residence on Nexus, he was already gone.

Gone, it was said, into the Holdings.

Medee was often called the Fringe world of the Holdings. The veilpaths to Medee from Old Earth and the other Holdings worlds were rarely good, making travel and communication between them slow and tedious. The Veils into the Fringes proper were far better. Medee had a large MulSendero population—it took so many passages to reach Medee that the natives joked that all immigrants were half converted by the time they arrived.

Sympathies toward the MulSendero aside, Archbishop Mueller of Medee wasn't happy to learn that the Pretender Fairwood had chosen Medee as the site of his first venture back into the Holdings. The visit presented the archbishop with logistic and legal problems that she frankly would rather not have faced. Colin Fairwood was officially under indictment in the Holdings for the bombing of Chebar Port and his illegal flight from that world. Yet the archbishop knew that to arrest him on his arrival meant a risk to the precarious position of the Holdings government on Medee—the threat of a violent coup from the large MulSendero factions on her world was very real.

The Archbishop was a Medee native. She knew too many MulSendero too well to feel she could ignore them. Medee could not survive without their support. She realized that the balance of power was delicate, and she was aware that was exactly the reason Colin Fairwood had chosen to come there. Someone in the Sabbai had advised him well.

Mueller didn't think Fairwood was the lunatic he was sometimes painted to be. She thought him all too shrewd.

If Colin hadn't given advance warning of his intention to visit Medee, she could have had him arrested and shipped to Old Earth and the curator. But Fairwood made every move of his a matter of public record. He never said anything explicitly, but the message was clear: *I am coming. Arrest me and your cities will erupt like volcanoes too long capped. Medee will become an inferno.*

Mueller waited as long as she dared, hoping that someone would arrive from Old Earth or that definite orders would be issued from the Conclave—anything to take the responsibility from her. Nothing arrived but the farship that brought Colin. Archbishop Mueller prayed and examined her own conscience. She was independent, used to political infighting, and was that still rare phenomenon: a woman in a male-dominated theocracy. Medee was like her, aligned but stubborn where her own customs and rules were concerned. Archbishop Mueller would ignore the warrant against Colin in the hopes of avoiding greater problems.

You may land, Colin was told. One false step and you will be arrested, but you may step on our soil and attend to your flock here. There was a private communiqué appended to that official notice.

Don't make me look foolish in this, Colin Fairwood, or I can ensure that I will redeem myself.

Archbishop Mueller watched the first meeting from her offices, her advisors arrayed around the shallow well of a holotank, full-sensory headsets looped over the arms of each of their chairs. The tank was already lit. In it, like a set of clever miniatures, figures swayed around a stage on the floor of Calvert Arena, a continent away. The crowd was held back from the risers by static repellers, and several of the Pretender's group were already on the stage. Two of them were Stekoni, oiled fur gleaming under the harsh lighting and seated carefully in the square of the required isolette. Of the others, Mueller recognized only the woman big with Fairwood's child: Kiri Oharu, a Buntaro wanted on the same warrant as Fairwood. A gray-haired man was addressing the crowd, his hands weaving patterns in the air as the tinny trickling of his voice came rasping through the speakers.

Archbishop Mueller turned slightly in her seat to her security advisor, Hal Woodward, a balding and embarrassingly devoted man. "Is one of his people the renegade priest Crowell?"

Hal shook his head. His frown was more serious than it needed to be. "No, Archbishop," he replied. Unlike the others of her private staff, he never called her by her given name, Kathlyn. It was always the polite, correct "Archbishop." She had never been able to break him of the habit. "Most of them are the Sabbai—they all gathered on Nexus following the trouble on Dridust. Crowell is still there, as best as we can determine. She certainly wasn't on any of the three farships Fairwood arrived with. The others are local Mul-Sendero leaders—you'll recognize Rafel Mendez to the left and Carl Sabini seated beside Oharu."

"How's the crowd?"

"Larger than we would have liked. The arena's full and a little more. Maybe fifty thousand or so."

Applause and cheering pattered like hard rain from the speakers. The crowd rippled in the tank, a blanket of humanity, an ant swarm around the stage. Colin Fairwood stepped into view from behind curtains across the rear; a spotlight bathed him in brilliance, and the noise redoubled. He walked quickly to the front of the stage and stood there, absorbing the praise with his arms outstretched. The cameras zoomed in toward the Pretender. His face stared back at Mueller and her staff.

"Allah, he *is* ugly, isn't he?" the Archbishop breathed. "I don't know that I'd ever get used to looking at that face." She shook her head as Colin lowered his hands and the crowd quieted. "How many cities do we have scheduled for him?"

"Ten over the next few weeks, scattered around the globe," someone answered from down the row.

"Can they all handle crowds like this?" Her attention was fixed on the Pretender, who began to speak. She toyed with the light band of her headset, yearning to put it on so that she could experience him as one of the crowd.

"I don't know," the same voice replied.

"Then we'd better find out now. Hal, you'll check on that for me?"

"Yes, Archbishop."

She nodded to Hal and leaned back in her chair. She took the headset and pressed the film contacts to her temple. The room faded in a showering of electronic noise and then she was *there*, a spirit hovering over the crowd seated along the walls. She moved with the cameras as she wished, floating around the arena, seeing Fairwood and feeling the heat of the enclosed room. The reverberations from the walls beat at her chest. She was part of it, flowing in the currents of the arena.

The Pretender was good; she admitted that after a minute. He had a natural presence that was somehow enhanced by his savaged face. His movements were overlarge, well suited to this large gathering, and his voice was a resonant baritone. She listened to the inflection more than the words as the Pretender spoke of MolitorAb, his Voice. Fairwood had a trick of dropping the volume of his voice abruptly for a sentence or two and speaking with an intimate huskiness that pulled the crowd forward in their seats to catch all of his words. Then they would be startled and overwhelmed as he roared the next line. Mueller suspected that Fairwood had never been taught to speak publicly: he was simply one of those with a natural flair for preaching. She envied him that gift—she knew from sad experience that her own sermons were dry and academic. As she hovered in the crowd, an insubstantial part of it, the Pretender's words sparked and flared. He prowled the perimeter of the stage, all eyes riveted on him. Below Mueller, the crowd shouted and howled the MulSendero responses back to him when he paused. They waved books of the Geltian Scripture; those standing in front of the rows of arena seats pressed forward to the limit of the static barriers, wanting to be near him.

Yes, he's good, she thought. He's *very* good.

The substance of the text was standard MulSendero fare, however well seasoned. *MolitorAb is the true manifestation of God, human and Stekoni. Those of you who worship the Zakkaist God, that of Christian and Jew and Moslem—you worship only a portion of the total.*

Heaven and hell both exist, and we travel their boundaries in the Veils, where time is shattered and broken.

And, to her mind, the worst of the heresies: *Humanity isn't special, favored, or chosen. MolitorAb doesn't care whether or not you reach salvation—it is there if you desire it, but MolitorAb won't weep if you choose hell instead.*

Lulled by the standard recitation of the MulSendero creed, she didn't immediately notice when Fairwood suddenly whirled about and peered into the lights of the arena. Into the cameras. Into *her* eyes. His gaze seemed to bore through Archbishop Mueller, as if he saw her spirit hanging there in the air. "You live in the Holdings," he said softly. "You dwell under the oppressive yoke of a false religion worshipping a shadow god. Archbishop Mueller—" Fairwood paused and Mueller started, shivering. It was as if he addressed her, as if he were in the room beside her. Delicate bands of muscle worked in his cheeks and around his eyes—he was a vision from her nightmares, a demon of Shaitan, speaking to her.

"Archbishop Mueller," he continued, "would have you remain docile, following the mandates of her church and praying to MolitorAb in squalid hovels, always afraid that, should you cause too much trouble, she will invoke Holdings law and forbid you to pray openly at all."

The Pretender stalked along the stage's edge, shaking his awful head. Mueller willed herself to move to a different camera viewpoint while he no longer stared at her. She went stage right. The arena spun around her, but Colin had somehow turned with that same motion. He pointed into the camera and his finger was aimed at her. A fierce passion shone in his eyes. "Archbishop, you watch me now and you want *me* to be docile like your cowed people. You want *me* to go meekly from city to city, to preach the doctrine of MolitorAb to my people and my people only, and then to leave. You know that if you put me instead in one of your Holdings prisons, I would burst out as if it were made of paper. You cannot hold me there. I tell you now:

"I—HAVE—*POWER!*"

Fairwood flung his arms toward the ceiling. The crowd screamed with the gesture. Slowly, he lowered his hands and faced the cameras again. "MolitorAb is my power!" he shouted. "My *people* are my power!"

They howled at that, surging. Sparks ran along the static barrier. The Pretender continued to stare at the Archbishop, impossibly, as she moved from stage right to stage left. She began to drift along the row of cameras and always he moved with her. Always those mad eyes were there; that twisting, shifting worm-mass face of tendon and muscle, of silver bone. Archbishop Mueller was caught in some strange distortion of reality, like the nightmare one knows is a dream but from which one cannot seem to wake.

"No one escapes MolitorAb!" Colin roared, and the crowd howled in response. "Not while I have my people. Watch!" He glared at Mueller with those lunatic eyes. His smile was vicious. The Pretender leaned toward the seated masses, his arms wide. "Answer for me!" he said. "Am I the Sartius Exori?"

"Yes!" they shrieked. The affirmation rocked the walls.

"Will you do as the Sartius Exori bids?"

"Yes!"

"If the church would take me prisoner, would you tear down the bars that hold me?"

"Yes!"

"If MolitorAb willed you to take this very city, would you pull it down brick by brick?"

"YES!"

The Pretender's voice was torn, ragged. "Then *rise! Get up! All of you, on your feet!*"

They rose as one. A tumult they were, a thunderhead waiting to be riven by the lightning's flash. Their voices alone threatened to pull the arena down around them. "You see!" Colin exulted. "They are *mine,* and because of that, *you* are mine!" Fairwood turned, and his stare found Mueller once more—that burning stare!

Archbishop Mueller tore the headset from her temples and flung it away.

Her advisors stared at her.

For she was standing, standing in her office with the image of Colin Fairwood laughing at her from the holotank.

"I'm not afraid of your church," he jeered. "I've my own path to follow, and it leads inward, Zakkaists. Inward."

He began to laugh again, a cold, chilling sound.

Slowly, feeling very old and tired, Archbishop Mueller sat.

Within three weeks, in the wake of long nights of violence and days of bitter fighting, the Medee Council let it be known that it was the will of Medee to resign from the Holdings.

By then, Colin had returned to Nexus. "Where do you go next?" the reporters clustered around him had asked.

"My people know," Colin had answered. "For the rest of you, you will know that I've arrived by the shouting of the faithful."

They're mine." Colin waited. Scheffer's mouth opened—well he was about to speak, and Colin held up a hand. "I'll see to it, do

CHAPTER NINETEEN

And ye shall chase your enemies, and they shall fall before you by the sword. And five of you shall chase a hundred, and a hundred of you shall chase ten thousand; and your enemies shall fall before you by the sword. And I will have respect unto you, and make you fruitful, and multiply you; and will establish My convenant with you.

OLD TESTAMENT, Leviticus XXVI:7–9

Colin Exori said: "This one knows that he does not show Kiri Oharu the full depth of his feelings. It is a fault he would correct if he could. The words will not leave him; they stay trapped in his throat while the moment passes." Then the Sartius Exori shook his head and admonished this humble one. "Strange it is that this one can feel the power of MolitorAb but cannot rule his own life. See that you do differently."

THE TESTAMENT OF FIRSTBRED PALE, 175:40–43

Colin could see Jasper Keller appraising the room. The Primus wore his full regalia; the gray, aristocratic head perched atop flowing yellow satin robes brocaded with gold thread, the MulSendero circle set off center in contrasting bright scarlet. Colin, who had seen the man only in holos, found that in person Primus Keller moved as if he was unsure of himself. His gaze slid all around the room without coming to rest. His long, well-groomed fingers were clutched at his waist, and he hummed tunelessly deep in his throat. Colin simply watched the man, waiting.

"I'm happy to see you," Keller said finally.

"And you, Primus. Will you sit, take some refreshment . . . ?"

Keller's eyes found Colin, then darted away again. "No," he said and cleared his throat. "I, ahh, won't be able to stay. I have other matters to attend to after our business is concluded."

Colin watched patiently as Keller made a circuit of the room. The realization came to him that Keller was uneasy, as if Colin's very presence unnerved the man. "I never thought that I would be the one in whose time the Sartius Exori came," Keller continued. "I thought that Gelt's prophecy concerning the Sartius Exori was a euphemism, that the 'soon' he used could as easily be two hundred years as the present moment."

"Hallan Gelt was always a man to use words exactly," Colin said.

Startled, Keller raised his eyebrows. "Yes," he said. "I've seen enough Pretenders fall though, as did my two predecessors. Answer me, Colin Fairwood: before MolitorAb, are you another Pretender, or are you the Sartius Exori?"

It might have been more dramatic if Keller had been able to ask that question while looking Colin in the eyes. The Primus tried and failed; Colin found himself almost angry at the man's timidity.

"Is that how you examine all your Pretenders? I'm not one of them," Colin said curtly. "You know that already, or you wouldn't have come to Nexus to see me."

Keller nodded too quickly. "Yes," he said again. "I've prayed to MolitorAb and sought Her in the Veils even as I came here. All the signs tell me what I realize intuitively. You are the Prophet."

"You'll acknowledge that publicly then?"

Again the quick nod, the nervous pacing. "Yes. Tomorrow. In Naley's temple. At that time, I will announce you as Sartius Exori and give to you the reins of the MulSendero Church."

The manner in which he said that last revealed to Colin the reason for the man's nervousness, his sad moodiness—Primus Keller was simply upset at having to hand over the temporal power he had gained. Colin almost laughed.

"I will still need you, Primus Keller. I'm not a man for running the day-to-day affairs of the faith. You've done that well for this long, and I would have you continue in that capacity as Primus. The Sartius Exori is not Primus; his task is elsewhere."

Keller could not keep the relief from his face. He smiled. His hands dropped to his sides, and slowly he knelt. "The Sartius Exori's will is my will," he said.

There should have been relief, a burst of elation—some feeling of joy and accomplishment. Colin was surprised at how empty Keller's words left him. He tried to smile for the Primus and couldn't. Keller glanced up at him and a hidden shred of vanity came to the man. "You think I had no choice," the Primus said.

"How do you want me to answer, Primus?" Colin shrugged. "Get up, get up. Forgetting any modesty that I might once have had, I tell you that eventually you *would* have had no choice. None at all."

"Yes," Keller replied softly, standing. "I thought you might say something like that."

There was something else troubling the man, something beyond Keller's simple concern for his status. Colin moved in front of Keller, forcing the Primus to meet his eyes.

"What else, Primus?" he demanded.

Keller blinked. He looked down at his chest, at the symbol on his robes. "I've read Gelt extensively," Keller said. "You were a person of his times, so you claim, and I thought that seeing you would help me understand Gelt."

"Does it?"

"No." Keller tried to smile. "And..." He paused.

"And?"

Keller smoothed the front of his robes. "I've lived with the Stekoni for the last several years," he said. "I've become sensitized to their way of viewing the world. They're a very intuitive race, you know, very subtle. And ever since I walked into this room with you, I've noticed something." He licked his lips; Colin could see him arranging the words in his head. "There's a scent to you, Colin Fairwood, and it comes from your soul, not your body. You smell of the charnel house. Despite Gelt's words, I wished there would be hope in the Sartius Exori, a certain lightness.

"Yes, you're undoubtedly the one. But there's nothing but death around you. I wish MolitorAb hadn't given it to me to announce you."

The ruins of Manhattan formed a backdrop to Culper's office as they had once to Su—draperies of vine over crumbling walls.

Culper's back was to the scene, but even if he had been facing the expanse of windows, it was doubtful he would have noticed the view. It was like a painting seen too many times on a familiar wall—he would have seen it only if it had changed.

In a few minutes, he would go to the subbasement where the blessed fool Benesch was jailed and there perform his duties as curator. The worst of the charges against the former commander were involuntary manslaughter and negligence in the death of Ascendant Su, who now lay in a crypt in Tokyo Cathedral. Su's physician was insisting that Huan Su might have survived if Benesch had left Dridust immediately. As penance for Su's death, Benesch would die. The other Ascendants would see to that, and Culper would gladly help them.

Now there was a simple task to perform. There was a wafer-sized rectangle set into Culper's desk, keyed to respond only to his thumbprint. Culper touched the pad of his thumb to the wafer. It pulsed green and he pressed twice more. The wafer went utterly black.

A bank in Los Angeles received a shielded, coded message at that moment. Deep within the cold liquid memory of that institution's data bank, a large sum of money was transferred to a numbered account in a small European country, there to be encoded again and placed in a courier bag to be shipped to another Holdings world entirely. Neither of the account numbers was directly traceable to Ascendant Culper or any Zakkaist organization. The account in which the money was eventually deposited was handled by a firm quite used to dealing with substantial transactions and which held the names of its accounts in strictest confidence.

On yet another world a few days later, a woman would be informed of the deposit. One local week would pass, and when no signs of any untoward interest were noted as a consequence of that transfer, she would make arrangements for passage to the world Horeb.

But all that was yet in the future. On Old Earth, Curator of Justice Culper walked slowly down to the sublevels of New York Cathedral, there to teach an erring naval officer of the temporal consequences of sin.

Kiri stood naked before the mirror, her hands cradling the swell of her belly. Her breasts were enlarged and her nipples were large and dark against her oriental skin. The long scars on her body stood out along its changing lines, furrowed reminders of her long-past ordeals. She pursed her lips, examining herself critically and wondering at her body's slow alteration. The baby turned in her womb, and she saw the movement outlined by the stretched skin of her abdomen.

She laughed in delight. "Little imp," she whispered, stroking her stomach.

Hands came around her waist suddenly. Startled, she began to turn, then she gasped. "Colin! You scared me."

"Sorry." He laughed. "You were all caught up in your reflection."

"I've turned from just plain to ugly," she said.

"You've changed to beautiful." He pulled her back against him, still hugging her from behind. He kissed the back of her neck, the skinbase of his face warm and smooth against her. "I mean it."

"The glow of motherhood, Colin? Don't be silly," she said scornfully. "I don't need any false flattery. All I want is for you to love your child."

"I love the child. I love the mother."

She leaned her head back against his shoulder. "You're sure?"

"Don't you know?"

"Not always."

She knew he was considering his answer to that; his hands moved restlessly. "I wish that wasn't true," he said finally, stroking her, "but I see how it could be. I wish you knew all the time."

"You're too busy to love me all the time. You're too obsessed and too driven. We're too different as well, you and I."

She could see him in the mirror, his face puzzled and contemplative. "I won't tell you that it's not true," he answered. "I don't want to lose you to doubt, Kiri. I want you to know—I love you."

"Does the Sartius Exori love me?"

His head rose, and in the mirror their eyes met. "The Sartius Exori must love MolitorAb first."

"Are you telling me that I have to be content with that? It's not a full relationship, Colin."

"It's all I can offer." He brushed his lips against the fall of her hair, his hands cupping her breasts. "It's all I ever offered."

Kiri sighed. Her hands came up to cover his, and she moved them down to her stomach. She shifted her weight, and they both felt the child kick.

They chuckled.

"Tell me, prophet," Kiri said. "Boy or girl?"

"The doctor knows. Ask her."

"I'd rather be surprised."

Colin kissed her neck again and Kiri turned to him. The kiss was tender. After a lingering moment, they began to pull apart. Then Colin inclined his head toward her once more, his mouth open and hungry.

"Would you like to be surprised now?" he asked.

"I already am," she answered.

She took his hand and led him toward the bed.

CHAPTER TWENTY

"What are we to do," they said, *"with this man performing all sorts of signs? If we let him go on like this, the whole world will believe in him. Then the Romans will come in and sweep away our sanctuary and our nation."*

One of their number named Caiaphas who was high priest that year, addressed them at that point: "You have no understanding whatever! Can you not see that it is better for you to have one man die for the people than to have the whole nation destroyed?"

NEW TESTAMENT, John 11:47–50

If they had wanted to love me, then I would have made them love. Since it is their wish to hate, I will give them hatred in full measure. They will know that MolitorAb returns what is offered to Her in kind.

THE WORDS OF THE SARTIUS EXORI,
Fury 12:1–2

The woman named Jaimi stepped from the farship into the chill of Horeb Port carrying her suitcase. Outside the windows, a sullen sky threw sleet across the field; it seemed not much warmer inside. Horeb was playing the coquette with her sun, and her natives flaunted their indifference to the cold. It was said that the only reason their buildings were heated was so the plumbing would not freeze.

Jaimi was a plain woman with a wide face. Her coloring was dark, her hair long and an undistinguished brown. She was full breasted, a little too heavy by current ideals, and her clothing was cheap and ordinary.

Quickly, yet without seeming to hurry, she made a circuit of the port building as if looking for someone who was to have been there to meet her. Her hands on her hips, she frowned and then went into a com-booth, pulling down the privacy shield. When she came out a minute later, she seemed irritated—her mouth set and a flush colored her cheeks. She glanced around the area once more and went into a public restroom.

Jaimi never came out again. Janice did: she was more slender than Jaimi, smaller breasted; her hair was shorter and lighter, her eyes green rather than brown, her skin lighter by a shade or two. Janice wore a suit cut much the same as that of her predecessor, though patterned differently. Jaimi now inhabited the suitcase (now plaid), which contained an innocent collection of makeup, wig, and pads. Janice went to the luggage area of the port and watched as the bags from her flight were processed. She was most interested in a large blue suitcase. A burly man snatched it from the rack and began walking away with it. Janice watched as he walked unmolested to the door and left the port. She followed behind him a few minutes later.

She had packed that suitcase herself but had neither checked it onto the flight nor been associated with it in any way. She was very good at what she did, painfully methodical even when circumspection seemed unnecessary.

Janice went to a hotel.

The next day she traveled to a particular open square in the city of Alexandria. While sitting at the edge of a grimy fountain eating her lunch, she studied the square and especially the buildings around it. Then she strolled through the area, musing in the bitter wind.

That evening, Judith left through a back door of the hotel; she was a stout, blondish woman with the slow, weary walk of the tired matron. She was evidently an older woman trying vainly to appear twenty years younger. Judith spent much of the early part of the night in a small, noisy tavern in one of the poorer sections of Alexandria. She found her quarry soon enough—a sallow-faced young man named Robert with the smirking confidence of the professional hustler. She courted him openly, letting him know that she had money. Judith was satisfied to see the greed that was evident in Robert's smile. He was pliable and willing. She gave him a small roll of the local currency, an address, and a piece of paper on which she had scribbled a few words, all with the promise of more money if he brought a piece of luggage to her. Robert agreed. Judith watched him leave the tavern for the frosty night and ordered food.

An hour later, she pushed the plate away and paid her tab. She went outside to wait for Robert. He arrived ten minutes later, carrying the blue suitcase. There seemed to be no one following him down the long street, and there was no sign of nervousness in him when she stepped from the doorway to greet him. She motioned him into an alley and gave him the money to count while she examined the seals on the case. All were intact and untampered with. Judith allowed herself a smile. "It's all there, lady," Robert said. "What say we go back inside for a drink?"

"In a moment," she answered. Setting the case on the ground, she lifted the cover, facing it away from him. "What's in there?" he asked, leaning toward her.

"This."

Robert had only a glimpse of metal nestled in her palm before there was a small puff of air and he slapped at his neck as if an insect had bitten him. There was the smallest trace of blood on his fingers. "What . . . ?" he began and then slumped to the cold stones of the alley.

Judith made certain he was dead, then rifled his pockets to make it seem more like a simple robbery. With any luck, the bored officer who found the body would pursue it no further than the report he had to write.

Judith closed the suitcase after a brief inspection of the weapon inside, cradled in foam. She left the alley unhurriedly.

For the next day, she was busy. As Joliet, a nervous and obviously distraught woman fleeing a broken marriage, she rented a room in a dingy apartment building a block from the square. She took a room on the seventh floor despite the manager's good-natured efforts to talk her out of it. "Those seven flights'll kill you," he said, perspiring despite the Horeb cold. "Think of lugging your groceries up here."

Joliet glanced out the grimy window streaked with bird droppings from the roof sill above. She could see fully two-thirds of the square. "It doesn't matter," she said in a tenor voice whose accents were very close to the manager's own inflection. "I like it."

One of the first things she moved in was the blue suitcase. The disassembled weapon went into her mattress, and the suitcase was repacked with secondhand clothing purchased by Jill.

Joliet/Jill/Judith/Janice/Jaimi studied the newspapers and listened to broadcasts on the local stations. Horeb was alive with talk of the impending arrival of the Sartius Exori.

She endured the next few weeks, mostly living a meager life as Joliet. Finally, she saw a party of workers beginning to erect a stage in the square, working in a cold, slanting rain. Joliet nodded, pleased. The information she'd received from her connection to the Exori was correct. Her employer had assured her that this particular area would be the site of the Sartius Exori's first speech on Horeb. Joliet had not questioned that; her price was too high for anyone but the rich and powerful—those in a position to know such things—to contact her. In any case, if the information was in error, the employer had only wasted his or her own money: Joliet would have lost nothing. She had been years gaining her reputation. She was no unreliable criminal, no simple finger to pull a trigger.

She was surprised the Horeb government had even permitted the Sartius Exori to come here: not after Medee, after Dridust, after Chebar. But she was glad it was true. In her career she had killed a few highly visible people, but none had been as well known as this Colin Fairwood. Her peers would know, and those who hired people like herself would know—they would know who had done this thing.

Joliet reached into the slit under her mattress and took out the sight for the weapon. The piece was not what she would have chosen had she been given the option. Pulsed-laser weaponry was ancient—accurate enough, but crude and messy by her standards. Joliet would have preferred a slowdart, which would have let Fairwood continue his sermon until, several hours later—when she would be long gone from this world—he would collapse and die in a matter of seconds as the dart released a few molecules of antimatter deep in his body. The resulting small explosion would ensure that nothing could be done to save him.

But her employer wanted this killing done publicly. Wanted it done, as the filtered and unrecognizable voice had told her, *ugly.*

Fine. Joliet cradled the sight and brought it to her left eye. Through the eyepiece, she could see the grain of the wood of the platform and the nap of soiled rough cloth over a workman's shoulder. Zooming back, she could see the entire stage. She touched a contact on the back of the sight and glowing cross hairs appeared. She smiled.

She placed the sight back in the mattress.

The anticipation was almost too much to bear at that moment; it was a fever that was sexual in its intensity. It would be with her now until the Exori was dead. She lay back on the bed and closed her eyes.

The crowds began to gather early that morning. Joliet watched the square fill throughout the day until, by the swift, chill afternoon of Horeb, the area was full. Food and drink vendors moved through the press that spilled back onto the streets leading into the square.

Joliet knew the Sartius Exori had arrived when she heard the whining shrill of the hovercraft the inhabitants of Horeb seemed to prefer. The hover landed in a cleared space behind the stage. Joliet couldn't see who left the craft, but she knew. She could feel him in the sudden heat of her body.

She turned out the room lights.

Joliet began slowly, carefully to assemble the laser weapon as spotlights raked the sky and centered on the stage. The chant began to swell: *"Exori! Exori!"* The last piece snapped into place. Joliet laid the weapon on the bed beside her and looked around—a distorted negative of her window was thrown across the wall by the stage lights.

"Exori! Exori!"

Joliet watched, sitting to one side of the window. When the Sartius Exori stepped into view, the uproar surpassed anything she had heard before. She hadn't thought there could be so many MulSendero on Horeb. All of them must have come to this city at the call of the Sartius Exori, must have come from every Holdings world within a Veil passage.

The woman who now called herself Joliet didn't care. She was that rare entity—she believed in no God at all.

She brought the laser weapon up and hugged it to her.

Through the sights, she could clearly see Colin Fairwood. He stood motionless, hands upraised, as he basked in the crowd's adoration. The cross hairs glowed on his chest like a brand. The laser thrummed under her hand, a live thing, emitting the angry purr of the feline hunter.

Joliet smiled.

She could not miss.

She touched the trigger and the feline howled.

Afterward, she would always contend that what happened then was flatly impossible.

JIHAD
2560

From her isolette, FirstBred Pale listened to the cheers of the Horeb crowd, blinking into the blinding spotlights that swept over the stage. She could see Colin standing there, a silhouette to her, lost in the acclaim, a long shadow of himself stretching out behind. Alongside him stood Kiri, who glanced back at Pale and grinned. FirstBred Pale knew Kiri was sharing the exhilaration he felt, and she wished the scene was not so incomplete to her. Behind the isolette's insubstantial barrier, the odors were lost: the pheromones of that excitement, the reek of the crowded city, the metallic tinge of Horeb's air with its gritty aftertaste of volcanic ash. Even the blessed chill of the wind was gone. FirstBred Pale could smell only herself and the strong scent of SlowBorn Brightness beside her— the priest seemed unusually stimulated by this gathering as well: her loincloth and ceremonial robes were soaked with secretions and the mottled pattern of her fur was shimmering with oil. Pale could sense an underscent of nervous anxiety in SlowBorn Brightness; she wondered at it, for there seemed no reason for apprehension. Everything had gone well since their arrival on Horeb. Amazingly, the Horeb authorities had been gruff but pliant.

Now the crowds that had come to hear Colin surrounded the stage, and he fed on their energy. In a minute he would begin speaking, and all of them—Sabbai, MulSendero, and Zakkaist— would witness again his undeniable power. Pale waved a hand at Kiri and Kiri turned back to the crowd, a hand on Colin's shoulder, waiting for him to begin

Something flashed out beyond the thousand-scented crowd, something more intense than the spotlights. It lasted only a second, even as Pale winced and felt her underlids flick over her eyes. Because of that instinctive motion, she saw what most humans— blinded by afterimages—would never see. She wished, afterward, that her eyes had instead gone blind at that instant, that her nostrils had been sealed.

In a moment that would linger in horrible detail, FirstBred Pale saw Kiri sliced open as if by some awful invisible sword, her body ripped and laid open from neck to waist as gore splattered everywhere on the stage. She was gutted, everything tumbling out and even as she fell dead, Pale thought she saw her hands moving, pitifully trying to do the impossible and close that terrible wound. FirstBred Pale could see Kiri's face in the glare of the spotlights, her eyes open and empty, her mouth wide in a soundless scream. Everything was red as Kiri toppled to the stage, and FirstBred Pale could see all too well the shape of Kiri's unborn child in the tangle of entrails.

Pale vomited, a wrenching heave that soured the air, and then she screamed, the high trill of Stekoni fear. Instinct powered her leap from the isolette to the stairs at the rear of the stage. She pushed aside the security people who were running onto the stage. Everything was confusion, a roaring horror that stank of outrage and terror. FirstBred Pale was on the pavement and halfway to the hover transports before she could control her fear and turn. It took all her willpower to press her way back into the mob that milled around the stage and climb the stairs again. She stopped as soon as she could see, peering over the lip of the platform. The Sabbai blocked her view behind the swarm of police—the spotlights had left the stage and now illuminated the crowd beyond. SlowBorn Brightness was there, having somehow controlled her reactions. She still knelt in the isolette, gawking and motionless. Seeing the MulSendero priest, FirstBred Pale forced herself to climb the rest of the way, to step gingerly between Samuel and Joshua.

She nearly ran again.

Colin was hugging Kiri's head to his chest, cradling her as he rocked back and forth on the wooden planks. Pale felt the panic sweep over her again: Kiri's torso moved, but the rest of her lay motionless, a ruin. Colin's shirt was splattered with her blood, soaked in it. Pale could not believe how much blood there was. Steam rose into the cold night air. Pale swallowed her bile and went to the child; the scent of the blood, the stench of Colin Exori's grief was almost unbearable. Pale reached out and turned the infant on its—no, *her*, Pale saw—back. She moaned in grief as she did so, seeing the mutilation that had been done there. Pale felt for a pulse, a breath, knowing she would find nothing.

She drew her shaking hand back and looked at the stains on her fingertips as she knelt in the pool of Kiri's life. "Colin Exori," she whispered.

Colin glanced up at her and Pale felt the urge to flee again. There was only madness in that face. He was no one she knew at all. Colin stared at Pale, tears beaded on the skinbase, and suddenly he roared his pain and sorrow.

Miriam came slowly over to them. She put a blanket over the

bodies. Colin scowled at Miriam, at Pale, and then he whipped the blanket aside. "No!" he shouted. "I'll save them. No one can steal her from me! No one can take my lover, my child!" he raged. Colin placed a hand on Kiri's lifeless, staring head, the other on the child's. *"MolitorAb will move in me!"* he screamed to all of them. "You'll see! Kiri Oharu, I command you to return to me!"

Pale would never forget that scene: Colin huddled on the stage in his horribly stained clothing, lost in despair, desperately searching for the power that never came as everyone watched. It began to rain—a frigid, pelting shower, and still Colin sat there, inconsolable. Pale could only watch with the rest of them, mute and helpless, seeking help in the faces around her: Miriam, Joshua, Samuel, SlowBorn Brightness. They all reflected her own agony.

"Kiri Oharu," FirstBred Pale wailed as Colin began to rant, a blaring tirade as the rains gentled the scent of violence.

Gingerly, always watching the furious insanity in Colin's face, Pale bent down and closed the eyes of her friend. "MolitorAb take you, Kiri Oharu," she whispered brokenly.

FirstBred Pale could stand it no longer. She rose and walked quickly from the stage. The odor of her pain lingered after her.

CHAPTER TWENTY-ONE

Allah revealed His will to the angels, saying: "I shall be with you. Give courage to the believers. I shall cast terror into the hearts of the infidels. Strike off their heads, maim them in every limb."

Thus We punished them because they defied Allah and His apostle. He that defies Allah and His apostle shall be sternly punished. We said to them: "Feel Our scourge. Hellfire awaits the unbelievers."

KORAN, The Spoils 8:12–14

Culper fails to realize that he dances on the edge of a precipice. One misstep and he will plunge utterly into the abyss. My fear is that he will drag the Holy Church after him in his panic. Colin Fairwood is dangerous, and Culper refuses to see that. The Lord sends this new Pretender to me in tormented dreams—surely that must be some sign? Yet I can't find the way to convince Joseph Culper of my belief.

I fear that I'll need to take some action myself against the oath of the Conclave. I fear, also, that to do so will cost me more than I might wish to pay. And I would have to act knowing there would be no guarantee that my mission would succeed.

I wonder what the cost of failure would be?

—From the journals of Huan Su,
Book 5, page 126, undated entry.

"Crowell!"

With FirstBred Pale and the rest of the Sabbai in flustered pursuit, Colin plunged through the room of his Nexus suite, tearing open the doors and flinging furniture out of his path.

"*Crowell!*" he shouted again, enraged, with tendons cording his neck.

"Here, Exori." She stood at the door of the common suite, gazing at Colin with a look of deep pity. She might have been crying. Her

196

skin was puffy and discolored under her dark eyes. It was late at night on Nexus; she wore only a simple robe, as if she'd just awakened or had not been able to sleep. "Exori, I heard the news only a few hours ago. I'm very sorry."

Colin lurched to a halt, glaring at her, every muscle in his body tensed. His hands were clenched into fists at his sides, and he breathed heavily and fast. With no warning, he lashed out at her, a blow that snapped Crowell's head back against the door frame. They all heard the muffled thump, and the priest crumpled wordlessly, her eyes rolling back in her head. FirstBred Pale leaped to grasp Colin's hand as he drew his fist back again, leaning over the woman.

"Please, no, Colin Exori! This one begs you..." The rest of the Sabbai watched, clustered in the hallway.

"Out of my way, Pale," Colin grunted. He yanked his arm away from the Stekoni and Pale staggered against the wall. "You heard what they said on Horeb—it was a professional job. Someone knew that we were going there, and only the Sabbai had that information: the Sabbai and Crowell. So, was it you who told the Zakkaists, Pale?"

FirstBred Pale shook her head vigorously. "Of course not, Colin Exori—"

"What of the rest of you then?" he blared, swinging about. "Was it any of you?"

Heads moved side to side; they muttered denials. Colin turned to face Crowell. She was sitting now, one hand at her bloodied, torn mouth, her head back against the door frame. "No, it was *you* who told them where I would go, wasn't it, Mother Crowell? You were always the Zakkaist in your heart, always the treacherous one. Was I to be the one killed, or was Kiri always the target?"

"I know nothing about it," Crowell protested. Her voice was slurred by her hand, and blood dripped onto her robe.

Colin laughed without humor, a mad roar. FirstBred Pale shuddered to hear it. She could smell the violence in him, an odor that made her want to put her back to him and run—the primal instinct. She saw SlowBorn Brightness at the rear of the Sabbai, taking a few slow steps away.

Colin hammered the side of his fist into the wall. "No!" He pointed to Crowell with a trembling forefinger. "It had to be you. No one else. You've taken Kiri and my child from me, traitor. You owe me life for life."

Mother Crowell's hand dropped into her lap between her sprawled legs. She seemed dejected, resigned; only her eyes were still alive. "I've sinned against you and MolitorAb before, Exori," she said. "For that I deserve whatever you do now. But I still deny *this* accusation."

"How else could it have been, traitor-priest?" he said scornfully. "Do you expect me to take the word of Culper's agent?"

They all saw her eyes widen at that, and Colin smiled in vindication. "Yes, I knew. Huan Su warned me about you, and I didn't listen. Do you expect me to believe anything you'd say?"

"No," she said, very softly. A spot of scarlet fell from her chin to her robe. "Exori, what will you do to me?"

Colin's eyes narrowed, and muscles worked in his face. He spat at her. "I will hate you and curse you, Anna Crowell. I'll degrade you and use you. You took my wife and child; you'll give me back the child I lost and I—I will give you *nothing*. Nothing."

"Colin Exori." Pale was beside Colin again, her scent troubled. The touch of her hand on his shoulder left a streak of pungent oil, and her golden eyes beseeched him. "This is not a thing that Kiri Oharu would have you do. Punish her in some other way if you must."

Colin raged back at Pale. *"How can you* dare *to tell me what she'd want!"* he shrieked. Pale cowered, retreating from his fury. "The Sartius Exori does as he wishes!" Colin bellowed. "Your task is to obey, Stekoni. Be a good sheep and do that. If you can't, leave me."

"Colin Exori—"

"Get away from me, Pale." Colin's voice was ominously low. "Your scent disgusts me."

FirstBred Pale looked from Colin to the Sabbai. She saw no sympathy in either place, not even from SlowBorn Brightness. Pale blinked, feeling the racing of her heart and smelling the scent of her own panic and repugnance. Yet she felt that she had to protest, had to voice what she knew would have been Kiri Oharu's feelings. She did not understand the Exori, could not fathom what he was thinking. But even as she began to speak, Anna Crowell stopped her. "No, FirstBred Pale," she said. "You'll only harm yourself. Thank you for your concern." She touched her swollen lip with a finger. "Colin Exori, I tell you you're wrong."

His voice was freighted with hatred. "I don't believe that. I can taste your guilt. Your soul's stained with it."

"If you believe that, Exori, nothing I can say matters." For a second, her chin came up in defiance. "I've sinned enough against you—I suppose that I shouldn't be angry that you're choosing to punish a phantom sin now."

FirstBred Pale could not stay to hear more, to see what the Sartius Exori would do. She drew herself up and pushed past the Sabbai. Of them, only Samuel showed her any sympathy, giving her a brief glance of understanding and a touch on the arm. The others—Miriam and Joshua and SlowBorn Brightness—simply let her pass and gave Pale no more notice. Colin stared at the departing Stekoni with a twisted and ferocious grimace on his face.

FirstBred Pale simply shrugged at him.

"I tell you again, Pale," the Sartius Exori growled. "Your duty is to obey me, not to question me. You should learn to understand that."

"This one knows her duty, Sartius Exori," she replied. "She will do it even when it leaves a bitter stench in her nostrils."

She wondered how long the Sabbai would stay and watch.

For the first time in his memory, Joseph Culper was genuinely frightened. He was utterly fascinated by the recording that showed on the wall grid, fascinated in the way a deer might be transfixed in a flashlight's beam, or as an innocent adolescent is drawn to the mysteries of the flesh.

Culper understood how the early church fathers had come to the conclusion that knowledge was evil. They had confused simplicity and ignorance for holiness, but there was a certain logic to their mistake. Those who were in the night, unaware, couldn't be tempted. What Culper had just seen stirred all the doubts he'd left buried outside the temple of his faith. Joseph had thought himself a devout, staunch Zakkaist, firm in the conviction that his faith was the only true faith. That certainty had sustained him in his tasks as Curator of Justice. No matter what he had felt compelled to do, he had told himself that it was for the good of the church. For the church, Joseph Culper could cause pain; for the church, Joseph Culper could kill.

The means served the ends.

The visicrystal sent from Horeb had cracked the underpinnings of the faith that had shaped him. Culper's soul still reverberated with the blows.

He'd received the crystal the day before. In that time, he'd already reviewed it perhaps fifty times, with each playing hoping he would see something new in it, something that could crush his sudden doubt. One well-manicured finger again circled the crystal, set in its viewing mechanism. Culper pressed one of the crystal's faces: the wall grid went transparent.

Culper looked out over the Horeb crowd and faced Pretender Fairwood. The man, with his obscene mockery of a face, stood at the edge of the stage with Kiri Oharu beside him. The crystal had been recorded in an extremely rapid sequence—the result was a highly detailed slow-motion image of a few seconds of real time. Culper had intended to use this recording to view the moment of the false Exori's death: it was to be a graphic depiction of the MulSendero falsehood, the refutation of everything Gelt had prophesied.

Culper would ensure now that no one ever saw it. The crystal would reside forever in New York Cathedral.

The crystal was sensitive to a far greater range of light than was the human eye, and it had captured what no person could have seen: the beam of the pulsed laser. The searing light entered the holotank from above; it was a flare of painful brilliance heading directly for the Pretender. With the beam's appearance in the image, Culper adjusted the crystal to slow the projection speed even further. As he had every time he'd viewed this sequence, Culper leaned forward intently, holding his breath. The crystal expanded microseconds into visible time. The pulse of energy slid unerringly toward the Pretender.

There. Culper slowed the projection even further, and the scene broke into discrete still images. There. There were those distressing, incomprehensible few frames of intense overexposure through which the Pretender could hardly be seen. Three bare frames, a splintered fragment of time. When the wall dimmed again to normalcy, it was already over. The laser beam had, somehow, been deflected even as the crowd and Fairwood reacted belatedly to the flash.

Culper touched the crystal. He had no desire to watch the quick, cruel dissection of Oharu. The wall grid went dark; the crystal was warm under his fingers.

For a long time, Culper sat in the dim light. He brooded, hands steepled before his handsome face.

At last he lifted his head. He ran a finger through his graying hair and bowed his head at the Zakkaist triangle on the wall. Slowly he prostrated himself before it, lying full length on the carpeted floor. "Forgive me, my Lord," he prayed. "I can see now that You have sought to test Your servant. You wished to see if I would fall to a lie that would tempt all those with no faith in their hearts. You have decided to see who will remain faithful to You despite the challenge. Lord, You can see there is no fear in *my* soul."

Culper sighed. He raised his head so that he could see the triangle with the smaller shapes of the three faiths set inside it. "I am not deceived," he said.

"What do you want, Pale?"

FirstBred Pale shuffled gingerly into the dim bedroom. Colin, naked, was at the window lost in the panorama of Nexus. He didn't even turn to look at the Stekoni. Anna Crowell sat on the bed that dominated the room—Kiri's bed, Pale thought—covered to the waist under the sheets but unclothed above. Pale tried to smile at the priest, willing her scent to go bittersweet in sympathy. The woman only stared at Pale blandly, passively. Crowell's umber eyes were darkly circled and dull. The marks of rough fingers mottled her shoulders, upper arms, and heavy breasts. Pale could scent a smouldering resentment in Crowell: it was bottled up, hidden away, but the taint of it leaked from every pore.

Colin turned. It was the first time Pale had seen Colin completely nude, and she saw that the skinbase covering his old wounds trailed down onto his chest in a ragged curve, showing strands of bunched pectoral muscles. As Colin swung about she thought she saw a glimpse of pain in his face, and she caught an underscent of inward revulsion; then the mask of his face shifted and the Sartius Exori stood there: the Mad One, not the hybrid she called Colin Exori. There was nothing of Fairwood in this person. The dangerous bright madness of MolitorAb shone in the depths of his eyes, and that horrible brilliance frightened Pale.

Yes, he is a Mad One now, in the hands of MolitorAb.

Pale hesitated near the doorway, wondering whether she should simply go. She took a long breath, tasting the aroma of the room— the heavy odor like ripe cheese that was the afterscent of human intercourse, the tang of sweat, a faint smell of panic that must have came from Crowell—all were fading afterimages. Pale did not enjoy the sensations.

Mad Ones were frightening. FirstBred Pale remembered a pilot who had returned from the Veils infused with the unbridled power of MolitorAb. That Mad One had gone on a rampage through the nesting grounds and finally entered the males' pens. From her mother's young-pouch, the fledgling Pale had watched, eerily fascinated, as the Mad One attacked the larger, stronger males. The Mad One had killed two and left most of the others unfit for mating before the priests could be summoned to subdue her. FirstBred Pale had chaotic memories of bloody fur and shouting, of her mother's hands pushing Pale deeper into the young-pouch as the Mad One tore apart the bodies in a frenzy. "Why is she doing that?" Pale had asked. "She cannot help herself," her mother had replied. "This one would be acting in the same manner if MolitorAb chose to come fully to her. Do not blame the Mad One; she sees another world."

Mad Ones were dangerous among the Stekoni. FirstBred Pale could not imagine the potential violence of a human one.

"What?" Colin demanded brusquely.

Pale blinked, trying to control her nervousness. "This one is doing as the Sartius Exori asked. He said to notify him when the *Anger* would be ready. The Sartius Exori may board when he wishes."

"Tell the other Sabbai then. I'll be leaving as soon as I can. You'll go with Crowell and me in the *Anger;* the others will take another farship. I'll tell them where we're going after we've come to the first Veil passage."

Pale tugged at the knot of her loincloth—it would have to be changed after this meeting, she knew. This exchange with the Sartius Exori made it reek of stress. "This one apologizes, Sartius Exori," Pale said, "but she would prefer to travel with the other Sabbai and not the Sartius Exori."

She knew she'd made a mistake. Colin's eyes narrowed, and the veins under the skinbase swelled. Taking a step nearer the Stekoni, he glowered down at Pale.

The odor of her apprehension filled the room.

"What the hell do you mean by that, FirstBred Pale?"

Underlids flickered anxiously over golden eyes. "Sartius Exori, the *Anger* will always remind this one of Kiri Oharu. This one would prefer to be elsewhere." Pale's gaze went involuntarily to Crowell, and Colin noted the motion of her eyes. He laughed and went to the bed.

"And Crowell isn't Kiri, is that what you're saying, Pale?" He snorted his derision. "Well, you're right. She's not much like Kiri at all." He touched Crowell's cheek with mock tenderness. "Are you?" he asked her. When Crowell didn't look at him, Colin reached down and roughly ran his hand in her hair, jerking her head back against the headboard. Crowell gasped and pressed her lips together; the tendons of her neck made ridges under her pale skin. "Yes," Colin said. "You'd rather that I kissed you, caressed you, teased you into heat as I did with Kiri. But all I'll ever do is spread your legs and take you." He shoved her head down and away and Crowell fell sideways on the mattress, where she lay, eyes closed, rubbing her neck. Pale could taste her pain in the air, but the woman did nothing; she passively accepted Colin's brutalization.

"Kiri Oharu would have taken your manhood if you'd treated her in this fashion. She would do it now if she saw what the Sartius Exori does here." The defiance in Pale's voice surprised even the Stekoni. Her repugnance lent a smoky cast to the words.

Colin drew himself up, his chest expanding and his eyes widening. FirstBred Pale thought she had misjudged Colin's tolerance. She could feel the intense energy in the man, the power that surged in him. It seemed that if he chose to unleash it now, here, there would be nothing left of Pale but ash, so potent was the flame that maddened him. She was caught in his fiery regard. She could only wait and accept what he would give her. In that moment, she thought she could understand the odd indifference of Crowell to her situation. FirstBred Pale breathed a quick prayer to MolitorAb.

His voice was dangerously quiet and ominous. His rage burned in her nostrils. "You didn't know Kiri as I did," Colin said. "Compared with me, you lost nothing when Crowell had her killed. Nothing."

"This one feels that you should not treat people like animals," Pale insisted, knowing the words would damn her. "And Kiri Oharu was the closest friend this one had. She was nestkin as no human could have been before. There was no one closer to this one than Kiri Oharu, and this one is shamed to hear the Sartius Exori belittle her relationship this way."

She waited to be struck down. But the Sartius Exori inexplicably retreated, and she saw the lines of his face smooth out—saw Fairwood appear. Colin inhaled deeply and his jaw unclenched. Unsmiling, he nodded.

Thank you, MolitorAb, for letting this one see him again. This one had thought him forever lost.

"You're right, FirstBred Pale," Colin said, amazingly. Then the scowl returned and Fairwood seemed to retreat. "But that doesn't alter much, does it? Will you obey your Sartius Exori or will you leave? Know this if you decide to go, FirstBred Pale: once away from my side, you'll never return."

"FirstBred Pale—" Anna Crowell's voice pulled Pale's attention away from the confrontation with Colin. "He needs you. He simply can't ask, not any more."

Colin whirled around. "You don't know me at all!" he railed.

Crowell shook her head. "I know you all too well. I don't even have any anger toward you, I know you so well." Her gaze slid back to the Stekoni. "Please. Go with us on the *Anger*. He does need you, and I think that I might need you as well. Please."

FirstBred Pale watched the Exori as Colin stalked away from the two, going around the foot of the bed to the windows again. The glow of phoslamps brushed emerald light over his thin body and the slight roll at his hips.

"I look at him," Mother Crowell said, "and I see that the Church has made its own destruction. That's when I sense MolitorAb the most, FirstBred Pale, when I see that in following our hatred, we did Her will. We forged the very weapon that will strike us dead. I knew what the Church intended—not where or when, but I *knew* and I said nothing. Half of my guilt is in seeing how deeply we hurt him, and the rest is in the knowledge that the very pain he feels has given us what we wanted least." Crowell sat back against the headboard, knees up, pulling the sheet tightly around her as if she were cold. She stared at something Pale could not see. "I wish I knew why MolitorAb did this. I wish I felt that I understood. What gives me any hope at all is that someone like you will be with the Sartius Exori. Let me still have hope, FirstBred Pale."

Pale heard only genuine sadness in Crowell's words. She shrugged, not knowing what to say, as she ran her tongue along the flat ridges of her teeth. Her odor changed slightly, and she knew she had made her decision. "This one will come with you," Pale said. She bowed to Crowell and to Colin. The Sartius Exori waved a hand at her, not even bothering to look back.

"You had no choice," he said. "You've never had any choice."

CHAPTER TWENTY-TWO

Serve the Lord with fear, and rejoice before Him; with trembling pay homage to Him, lest He be angry and you perish from the way when His anger blazes suddenly.

OLD TESTAMENT, Psalms 2:11–12

MolitorAb will come to the worthy in two ways. In the first, She is gentle and caring, like a lover, wrapping you in Her arms with a supple tenderness. She holds you at a distance so that Her warmth will not burn your flesh. When this happens, you have indeed been gifted, but there is little power in that favor.

When MolitorAb truly favors you, She comes as She comes to me. She is powerful; there is no gentling Her. There you truly find the adamantine bones of God. Her touch is painful and harsh. Your time with Her is more hell than heaven.

Yet it is there that MolitorAb gives Her power almost in full measure—She must always hold back lest She destroy you. She will bring you to the brink of your existence and leave you balanced there, ready to fall screaming. Your body is full of MolitorAb and there is nothing else in you. You see the world with Her eyes and it is strange and awful.

Your soul sits inside the cage of your body and howls like a lost child.

THE WORDS OF THE SARTIUS EXORI,
Faith 5:1–4

The veildream came upon him suddenly, like the slap of a hand across his face. The *Anger* was gone, FirstBred Pale and Anna Crowell were gone, the trailing presence of *Gelt's Dream,* the other farship, was gone as well. There was only a cold wind and a thin, high screaming like the tearing of velvet.

The dream frightened Colin. Even the Presence that had dwelled in him since Kiri's death was frightened here; he felt it cowering behind his own ego. The passages from Horeb to Nexus had been full of this same dream, this same place.

There was nothing of comfort here. Even the Voice was gone.

"MolitorAb? Hallan?" Colin called out into that frigid void (noticing now that he had no body here—he was as formless as the ether in which he floated). He heard nothing but the faint, mocking echoes of his call.

Blue. He began to see the walls that held this place were the blue of polar ice. As Colin drifted, the air around him seemed to lighten (as it had in every passage recently) and again he saw the vast, curving ribs that supported the place—white, long hills in the blue that slid into haze on either side. There were no other forms here, but Colin knew he would find that impression to be false— four times now he'd been here, asking for the Voice that never answered. Colin waited.

The currents of this void wafted him toward the walls. As he came closer, he could see shapes in the walls, in its supports: distorted faces screaming as they pressed against the walls as if trapped behind clear ice. The Presence hiding behind him dug razored claws into his back as if frightened at the sight. The trapped ones' torment showed in their twisted, open mouths, in the pain lines at the corners of their mouths. They were in anguish, these ones: human, Stekoni, other races Colin didn't recognize. "MolitorAb, what is this place?" Colin asked again and gasped as the claws drew deep, burning lines across his back again. He could feel the warm blood trickling down his spine. "Hallan, where are you?"

Faint screams answered, muffled behind the walls.

There was no Hallan. No MolitorAb. Colin was bereft. The Presence shivered behind his back as it huddled there.

"What have I done that You've left me?" Colin sobbed, and the tears that gathered in his eyes were as cold as the air. "What do You want me to do? I need to know; how else can I serve You? Send Hallan to me. Speak."

"Vector 4.3," a voice said.

"You must listen!" Colin demanded, trying to spark the Presence, to use the power. He was cold, so cold. Fingers of lacy ice were coating the walls of this prison, masking the tortured faces. "You have to lead the Sartius Exori. How else can I know Your will?"

"Vector 4.3. Imperative."

The ice was expanding quickly, coating the walls thickly, and now Colin lay within a long tunnel of deep glacial azure. "Imperative," the voice repeated. "Vector 4.3. Imperative."

There was only one path of escape now. Colin must move or be trapped forever in that frigid embrace.

He willed himself to slide down that narrow opening. Sharp knives of ice gouged and tore at him.

Worlds shuddered into place around him once more.

The *Anger,* with *Gelt's Dream* linked to her, careened from the Veils with a severe yaw and pitch. FirstBred Pale cried out as the tumbling flung her from side to side in her netting. It took several disoriented minutes for Colin to stabilize the two craft and a while longer for the navigational systems to determine that they were in Kellia's star system, though that world still lay several days ahead of them. The farships were out beyond the orbit of a gas giant, circling forlornly around the distant sun flare like a petulant child.

The Veil passage had been a shoddy performance for any experienced pilot. Colin's ineptitude dismayed Pale, who had seen his skill within the Veils many times before. No matter how troubled Colin might have been in the past, he had still kept his proficiency.

It was as if the beast inside the Exori had drained Colin of his prowess. For the first two days afterward, Colin seemed withdrawn and troubled. Pale felt a waxing hope that perhaps the shock of the passage had caused the Sartius Exori to withdraw, that Fairwood would return. It was obvious to the Stekoni that both the humans—Colin and Anna—had experienced passages laden with portents, that the Veils had marked them both. Yet both remained silent for the most part, keeping their thoughts to themselves. Pale ached to be able to force them to talk. Their moodiness colored the air of the cramped farship; empathic, Pale became listless herself.

The disc of Kellia's sun grew large and bright. Colin wouldn't answer the com—he ignored queries from an anxious Kellian government and concerned questions from *Gelt's Dream.* Secundus Schaeffer, the MulSendero leader of Kellia, begged FirstBred Pale to be allowed to speak with Colin, but the Exori only shook his head at Pale's mute supplication. Colin sat brooding in his seat, tethered to the *Anger* via the nerve links.

Later that day, he disconnected himself from the farship and stalked over to Crowell's bednetting. There, uncaring that Pale would and must see, Colin took the woman, quickly and without passion. Pale turned in her own netting and put her face to the hull.

That helped little—the mingled scents and sounds were worse than the sight.

Afterward, Pale heard Crowell's choked whisper as Colin left her. "Never again," she said and then spoke louder. "The Veils have told me what I needed to know, Colin Exori. You have what you've demanded of me. I don't intend to let you touch me again."

Colin laughed. "You can't threaten the Exori, Crowell. Remember? You tried to kill me at Horeb and it didn't work."

Her reply was a whisper that only Pale could hear. "I don't intend to kill you, Colin Fairwood." Pale shivered at the words—she could smell the resolution there. Netting rustled as Crowell turned. Colin still laughed. Pale heard him putting his clothes on once more, then the metallic clicks as Colin reattached himself to the ship.

"This one could not have tolerated the Sartius Exori's abuse even this long," Pale whispered to Crowell when Colin was asleep. "She would have found a way to end it sooner."

Crowell plucked at the hem of the simple robe she wore. Her sunken, bloodshot eyes were hooded. The whine of the *Anger's* system drive nearly hid her answer. "He won't do it again."

"This one heard Anna Crowell threaten the Exori," Pale replied. She was silent for a few moments, listening to the ship and Colin's slow, deep breathing. "This one would wonder what Anna Crowell saw in the Veils."

"What's the matter, Pale? Don't you feel I deserve this treatment? Don't you still want vengeance for your beloved Kiri?"

"This one is not the Sartius Exori. This one also does not have the guilt of Anna Crowell."

She heard a sharp intake of breath, and Crowell turned over in her netting, giving Pale her back. At another time, Pale might have been cowed by the priest's hostility. Now she blinked heavily but forced herself to speak with embarrassing, impolite directness. "This one might have wished that Anna Crowell had been punished, yes. She would not have protested if Anna Crowell had been taken to prison or even quickly executed if Colin Exori had demanded such. But this one is sickened by the Exori's degradation of you."

"Surely you've figured it out by now, Pale," Anna said in a mocking, spiteful voice.

"This one desires understanding."

With a rustling of cloth, Crowell turned back to Pale. With the interior lights dimmed for Colin's sleeping period, Pale could see only the outlines of her face and the reflections of panel lights in her dark eyes. "You know. You said it a moment ago."

"This one said that she did not have the guilt of Anna Crowell."

Crowell nodded. "I helped to kill Oharu and her child, however indirectly. I think that also drove Colin into his rage. I never intended that, FirstBred Pale." Crowell took a deep breath. The darker shape of her hands passed in the air before her face. "I've been devout and obedient all my life; I've even seen people hurt as a result of my obedience. But I'd never killed, and before this there was always the excuse that the small evil I might be doing would result in a greater good." Her words were coming faster, as if they had been held back too long. "After I killed Ascendant Su, I came to realize that I couldn't use that rationale anymore, that such a judgment wasn't mine at all but God's. If Colin had asked, I could have told him that the Zakkaists hoped to kill him; I just didn't think that the information would be helpful to him—not knowing where, not knowing when or how, just that it would be soon. So I said nothing.

"That's my guilt, FirstBred Pale. I've felt it every waking moment since I learned of Kiri's death. It's haunted my dreams. I don't think it is strange to want to make amends for that." She paused, and there was pain in her voice. "If he wants a child of me, I will give him that. I saw . . . I saw the child within me as we passed through the Veils. I saw the life there, huddling in my womb."

"Anna Crowell," Pale said softly, "this one feels your torment."

For a long time, Crowell made no reply. Her indistinct shape was still; Pale thought that perhaps the priest had drifted into sleep. Then the faint smell of human anguish came to her and Pale heard the muffled sound of weeping. She listened, sympathetic oils glossing her fur. If Crowell had been Stekoni, she would have sensed Pale's sharing and would have gone to her companion for mutual comfort. They might have cuddled together as Pale and Kiri had often done, soothing each other.

Crowell did nothing. Pale could see her thin shoulders lifting with quiet sobs.

Firstbred Pale could not stand the sight or smell. The sorrow in the woman compelled Pale to leave her bednetting and move over to Crowell's. The Stekoni placed a hand on the priest's shoulder, her warm fingertips soft with fragrance. She pressed gently, marveling at how emaciated Crowell had become. At the touch, Crowell's head came up. Her eyes were puffy, but there was no wetness on her cheeks. "Get away from me," Crowell said.

"This one—" Pale began. She moved her hand away. "Anna

Crowell said that she would need this one. That is why this one comes to you now."

"Leave me alone."

"Anna Crowell, you cannot hide your pain from me. Not from any Stekoni."

"I don't want your damned sympathy. Do you understand that?" Crowell's voice broke and she swallowed heavily. Her expression was bleak—frightened rather than angry. "Please, go away." The words were punctuated by a shuddering breath.

Shiplight glinted on the smudge Pale had left on the woman's shoulder. Pale stared at it rather than at Crowell. "This one will be here if you need her," she said. She started to turn, then paused. "This one would like to fully understand you, Anna Crowell. She still does not know why you follow the Sartius Exori. She knows too little of your feelings. Is there more you would share with this one?"

Crowell didn't answer. After several seconds, Pale walked away. She lay down in her netting.

She prayed to MolitorAb, formless, silent pleas. She didn't even know what she asked.

It was a long ten days more before they reached Kellia orbit.

Kellia was a wet world. Two long, straggling continents held back hemispheres of vast ocean. The huge expanse of water was the wellspring of a monstrous heat engine that spawned titanic hurricanes. When those gigantic systems rolled over the land like enormous, angry beasts, the inhabitants of Kellia took cover and prayed. There was nothing else for them to do. Nature ruled Kellia, and she was an unkind dictator. Even when the motherstorms stayed well out to sea, small subsystems drenched the land. Kellia was always warm, always damp. Lush vegetation greened the flanks of the mountainous continents, forming dense rain forests through which brightly colored amphibians roamed.

The first Holdings colony had been established here to harvest those forests, to take the wood and the herbs and the molds, to leach the plentiful minerals from its soil, to plant tobacco and teas. Most of the colonists soon left when they discovered that Kellia was too harsh, not caring at all when those who remained declared Kellia a Fringe world. There was little here for the Holdings that could not be taken from some easier world.

Kellia proved again that human worlds must always in some manner resemble each other—the parameters within which hu-

manity can comfortably dwell are narrow. Kellia crowded the edges
of those restrictions.

The *Anger* and *Gelt's Dream* sliced down through a thousand
meters of cloud before their passengers glimpsed Loris, Kellia's
main city. When the farships finally burst from the bottom of the
storm, a wind-driven mist sheeted the hulls and blurred the view
from the ships. Colin and his party expected to see only the puddled,
gray expanse of the city. Instead, stretching out into the haze, they
saw people. The entire populace of Loris, of Kellia, covered the
landing field, making it look, at such a distance, like a meadow of
colorful grasses. At the appearance of the farships, the people began
moving back from the landing slings and a dais that sat beside them.
Police vehicles drifted above the throngs with their lights flickering
like quick lightning.

The pulsers caught the farships. The *Anger* lurched and began
to drop toward the canted gantries. With the ship's drive shut down,
the drumming of the gale-driven rain against the hull was clearly
audible. Under that sound, fainter, there was another—the booming
of a gargantuan, multivoiced throat: "Exori! Exori!"

FirstBred Pale glanced at Colin, still wrapped in the coils of the
nerve links. The Exori smiled smugly. "They are eager to see the
Sartius Exori," Pale ventured.

Muscles glided around bone in Colin's face. He pulled the links
from his neck. "They'll lose their eagerness soon enough," he answered. "Does it frighten you, Pale, that even though MolitorAb
wouldn't speak to me in the Veils, I can still feel Her inside me?
Look at the crowds down there." Colin gestured to the holotank.
"I could make them do anything." He held his hand out, palm up
and fingers extended. "They are my hands, FirstBred Pale. My
hands and God's hands. There is nothing I can't accomplish with
them." Slowly, he curled his fingers into a fist. His knuckles went
white with the pressure. Then he laughed and let the hand fall.

"Am I being overly dramatic for the two of you?" The smile
was back as he glanced from Pale to Crowell. Pale could see the
strain in Colin's face, the warring emotions—Fairwood struggling
against the VeilBeast of MolitorAb.

Struggling. And losing.

The com-unit chimed as the *Anger* docked and mated with the
port facilities. Colin spun in his chair and touched a contact; the
wall near him flickered and the picture changed from a view of the
crowds to a close-up of the head and shoulders of a man in ornate,
bright clothing. His auburn hair was sleeked down on a balding

head as if the man had been out in the storm. He had protuberant eyes the emerald green of a stagnant pool, and two small aquamarine gems dangled from the left nostril of a hooked nose. Suspended on short silver chains, they danced on his upper lip as he spoke.

"Sartius Exori, I am Secundus Schaeffer."

"I know of you, Secundus," Colin answered. "What do you want of me? I've come to address my faithful on Kellia. Do you have an objection to that?"

Schaeffer smiled quickly. He squinted at Colin, studying the Exori's face, and then averted his gaze. The gems swayed on the ends of their chains. "No *objections,* of course, Colin Exori. Primus Keller has made his choice quite clear to all MulSendero. But my— our—government here is understandably concerned. After Horeb..." Schaeffer faltered. His eyes bulged and their thick lids blinked. His wide forehead creased in folds of consternation. "... after your great loss there, we thought..." He came to a struggling halt.

"Thought *what?*" Colin spaced each word carefully. Pale hated the arrogance she heard in that voice, the sick, brooding violence of the VeilBeast. Colin's tone grated—he didn't sound like himself at all.

Schaeffer grinned nervously. The wide, oval face glanced back at someone who stood to one side of the com-unit. The Secundus nodded his head, setting the gems fluttering and bouncing softly. "Exori, we've set up a dais so you may speak to those who've come to the port. You've no idea how much difficulty your arrival here has caused. If you'd given us sufficient warning, better arrangements could have been made. We've very inadequate security for you, by my standards, especially after..." Again the hesitation. "... after your trouble on Horeb. The logistics of handling a crowd of this size has given the port master a very large headache, to say the least, not to mention that all traffic to and from the port is at a standstill." Secundus Schaeffer had a tendency to whine, Pale noted. His petulance made his voice rise and added a grating, nasal tone.

"You haven't answered my question, Secundus Schaeffer," Colin said, interrupting. "Since you've bothered to contact me, I assume you've something more on your mind than simple complaints about your own problems. What do you want?"

Schaeffer brought his treble chin up. Small flecks of light from the gems trailed over his cheeks. "I would like to know what the Exori will be saying to my people."

Colin barked laughter. With the sound, Pale got a whiff of the scent of the beast. "First of all, Secundus, they're not *your* people.

They're mine." Colin waited. Schaeffer's mouth opened as if he was about to retort, and Colin held up a hand. "I'll damn well do as I wish with my people. Second, I'll say what MolitorAb wills me to say. Even if I could, I wouldn't preview it or censor it for you."

They could all see the flush rising on Schaeffer's high forehead. The secundus moved his head to one side and the focus shifted as he leaned back from the camera. There was stubbornness in the man's polite response—FirstBred Pale could see that the secundus was not accustomed to assaults on his authority. "I'm responsible for the MulSendero of Kellia, Sartius Exori. I must do my job—I have my responsibility to Primus Keller and to MolitorAb. The Buntaro element, for instance, is very small within my flock. Your Sabbai are more infested with that disease than I'd prefer to see."

"The Sabbai follow the Sartius Exori, not the other way around," Colin answered. "Secundus Schaeffer will do the same. I've been given my title by your superior, Secundus." Colin leaned forward in his chair, lifting his body by bracing his arms. His voice lashed out, cutting and strident. "I am MolitorAb's prophet! I am our Messiah, our leader, and our king!"

Colin was shaking as he sat back, his fingertips trembling on the armrests.

"I've come to take your flock from you, Secundus," he continued. "I've come to take them to Old Earth."

For long seconds, Schaeffer gaped in shocked silence, the gems swinging wildly above his open mouth, while static hissing issued from the speakers below the screen. Pale could smell her own rising panic and she held her young-pouches as if she were physically threatened. *MolitorAb, you cannot mean for the Exori to do this thing. We cannot go to Old Earth without an army behind us. This one knows that we will all die. What would that accomplish for You?* Pale glanced at Anna Crowell, but the woman's face was shuttered and blank. If the priest felt that same thrill of fear, she did not show it.

"You're a madman!" Schaeffer burst out, as if he could contain his thoughts no longer. His eyes seemed about to burst from his face, and his brow was deeply ridged. His nostrils flared over the gems. "I won't allow this, not at all! You're leading a pack of fools to their imprisonment or death."

"I'm the Sartius Exori," Colin replied. Veins swelled like a rash under the skinbase. "You've read Gelt's prophecies, Secundus; you know what I portend. You're absolutely right, even if you're a pompous ass yourself. I'm tired of idiots like you expecting me to be pliant and kind, to waste my powers healing the sick. I'm not weak! Christ said it—there will always be the poor, the sick. I intend to use MolitorAb's power fully. The Black Beginning has come, Secundus Schaeffer—your words won't hold me back. You're raging uselessly into a bitter wind."

"I won't let you speak to my people," Schaeffer blustered.

"You can't stop me."

"In that, you're wrong, Exori." Schaeffer's hand plunged down and the wall went dark.

In the sudden twilight, Colin roared his amusement. The spice odor of the presence inside Colin was overwhelming. Pale retreated from it, going to her netting and moaning softly to herself. When Colin's awful face swiveled around to look at her, she cowered.

"Fools, indeed," he muttered. She could see his muscles, knotted and contorted. "FirstBred Pale, get up. You'll tell the other Sabbai that I'm going out to see my people. My little flock of sheep."

CHAPTER TWENTY-THREE

Behold, I have given him for a witness to the peoples, a prince and commander to the peoples. Behold, thou shalt call a nation that thou knowest not, and a nation that knew not thee shall run unto thee.

OLD TESTAMENT, Isaiah LV:4–5

Understand God? What vain nonsense! Yet both Human and Stekoni are vain and the history of both races has been caught up in that futile struggle. What does God mean by this action? we ask. Is that MolitorAb's hand? At least the Stekoni have not fallen into the pit behind this trap. Where humanity fails to see God, it thinks it glimpses the face of the devil. The Adversary. The Stekoni know the truth: the mask of MolitorAb has two sides.

How can you ask me to tell you what MolitorAb intends?—I am the Sartius Exori, not the Voice Herself. I understand Her less than anyone. If there is a devil, I tell you that his name is Reason. Cast him out, all of you, for there are no answers to his questions. He will drive you mad more surely than the Veil Voice.

There is only faith. Belief and acceptance. That is all the Voice demands of you.

THE WORDS OF THE SARTIUS EXORI,
Mocking 12:7–12

"I'm not handing over my charge to a raving lunatic!" Schaeffer declaimed. Alison heard his pulpit voice in the statement, a stentorian basso throbbing with passion. The Secundus slammed his open hand down on the panel of the com-unit; one of its glass panels cracked with a sharp report. Alison nodded mutely. As Schaeffer's attendant for the past Flood Season, she'd seen enough of his moods to know that he was lecturing himself. Alison could well understand the emotion in her usually quiet and forgiving superior. The Sartius Exori had made her shiver: that horrid face; his arrogant, flat stare;

his belligerence—Alison was not certain that a MulSendero church under guidance of the Exori was an institution she wished to be associated with. Alison's own faith was simple and unquestioning. She was not one of those who wrestled with inner demons to arrive at the conclusion that MolitorAb was her deity. She had been into the Veils four times now: each experience had reinforced her belief. There was Something there, and She whispered to Alison in that all-pervading Voice. Alison's parents had been Zakkaist, but the Patriarch God (as Schaeffer liked to refer to it) had never been so visible to her.

She preferred a God who manifested Herself.

Alison shied away from the political arguments, the controversy surrounding accusations of torture and imprisonment by the Zakkaists, the pragmatic terrorism of the Buntaro. Alison prayed and listened to the Voice. She had often thought that after her time with Secundus Schaeffer was over, she might join one of the contemplative orders.

But the Sartius Exori had come to Kellia. She was very much afraid her faith would never be so simple again.

Through the long, curved windows of the port terminal, she could see the impatient crowds milling around the twin spires of the Exori's farships. Alison shook her head—she understood everyone's fervor but didn't share it. Yes, the Sartius Exori was obviously the Chosen of MolitorAb. Like the rest, she'd seen the Horeb film, where the Hand had swept aside the deadly laser beam. She'd heard the tales of Dridust, Chebar, Nexus, and Medee.

There were large flatscreens tethered about the field, placed when it had become apparent that the audience for the Exori's arrival would be far too large for all of them to view him easily. Now the screens shimmered into life and became sparkling rectangles filled with that face, the face she'd seen everywhere in the past several days. Alison's stomach fluttered and her mouth turned down in a sour grimace. She'd heard the other tales as well—how the Exori had been captured by the Zakkaists after helping Hallan Gelt to escape Old Earth; how the Ascendants had peeled his flesh back from his skull as the Exori screamed in his cell. They'd left him to die, but MolitorAb had placed Her protection over him. He'd survived, leaving the terrible damage to remain forever visible, to show graphically the evil of the Zakkaists.

Alison wished that the Exori had died. Strands of blood-red tissue writhed like fat snakes in his cheeks and around his jaw. The Sartius Exori was grotesque, like a hell-sent demon.

And yet . . . there was an attraction to him. Even Alison could feel it, pulling at the strings of her faith.

"Alison, please. Did you hear me?" Schaeffer's strident voice pulled the woman from her reverie. "Tell the master to cut power to those screens—the Exori has already begun speaking."

"Secundus . . ." She had not often dared contradict the man before, and she did so now only hesitantly. "If you do that, we'll have a riot out there."

"Better that than what that madman would have them do. We can handle a riot; I've called for troops from the nearest marine post." Schaeffer rolled his eyes and sighed. A stubby finger flicked at the blue facets of his nasal rings. He toyed with the jewelry as he glanced out to the field where several Colins spoke. From the terminal, they could not hear his words, only the faint growl of his speech. "Get that power cut, Alison. Then we'll go out there."

As Alison contacted the master, Schaeffer tugged an oilcloth over his silken robes of office. Together, he and Alison walked quickly down a hallway to a service exit to the port field. At Schaeffer's gesture, the ground doors rumbled open and a cool mist enveloped the two. With the weather came the Exori's voice, like the bellowing of a distant giant.

". . . LEARN THAT YOU MUST OBEY NOT YOUR LEADERS, NOT YOUR PRECIOUS CONSCIENCE, NONE OF THOSE YOU'VE BEEN TOLD WERE IN AUTHORITY. THERE IS ONLY ONE AUTHORITY. SHE CAN BE HEARD IN THE VEILS, AND *I AM HER PROPHET!*"

"You hear him, Alison?" The mist beaded on his oilcloth covering, while a droplet shivered at the end of his nasal gems. Schaeffer's forehead was shiny with moisture, but he ignored the rain as any Kellian would. Angrily, the Secundus shouted to one of the port workers to bring a hover. "He's going to serve them fiery pablum and tell them how MolitorAb will guarantee his victory. Half of them will probably believe him, and they'll join his insane crusade."

Schaeffer clambered heavily into the hovercraft, which dipped under his weight. He rapped his knuckles impatiently on the side' of the little craft as Alison stood there. She was transfixed, caught in that voice. "Alison!" The command made her shake her head, flinging water from her short blond hair. She clambered into the pilot's seat, whipping the hovercraft around as the worker backed away, startled. The static shields came up, protecting the two from the wind-tossed rain.

They careened above the mobs into the thunder of the Exori's rage.

"I TELL YOU TO COME WITH ME! I WILL LEAD YOU, AND TOGETHER WE WILL CRUSH THE TYRANNY OF A FALSE GOD! LISTEN TO MY WORDS, ALL OF YOU FAITH-FUL—MOLITORAB ABHORS THE WORSHIP OF THE ZAK-KAIST GOD, THIS MOCKERY OF HER TRUE SELF. SHE IS FURIOUS AT THE WAY IN WHICH THE TRUE FAITH IS TREATED. SHE WILL TOLERATE THEIR SCORN NO LONGER. *I AM HER FIST!*"

Below them, the masses screamed back at the Sartius Exori, their hands upraised and stretching out toward his tiny figure.

"He'll give them shortened lives. Pain and loss," Schaeffer muttered. "Alison, I thought you told the master to shut down those screens."

"I did, Secundus," she replied simply. She wished Schaeffer would be quiet. Most of her attention was on the nearest screen, on the strange and angry visage of the Exori. Alison wondered how the Secundus could fail to be caught in the outpouring of the Exori's fury. His words were molten lava, scorching her soul and faith, burning all before it. Swelling emotions flared from the man, incandescent fires. Alison was not surprised that the screens were up. She could not have moved to stop that voice either—MolitorAb would have struck off her hands at the impertinence. The Exori, full of Her, would have leaped from screen to screen despite such a move.

It didn't matter that only a few minutes before she had thought she might hate the Sartius Exori. Then, she had been an apostate. She had not heard. The Voice came to her now in the person of the Exori.

The Exori called. The faithful must answer. That was as simple as her earlier faith.

"THOSE OF OUR TIME WILL COME TO HATE ME. *YOU* WILL HATE ME."

His eyes stared at her. Only at her. His regard seared her and she could not breathe. He had singled her out; she was at once exhilarated and afraid.

"ONLY YOUR CHILDREN'S CHILDREN WILL SEE THE GIFT THAT I BEAR. YOU CANNOT, FOR THAT GIFT IS SHROUDED IN PAIN, BORNE BY DEATH. I PROMISE YOU THE AGONY OF BIRTH, THE BIRTH OF A NEW PEACE! WILL YOU DO AS I DEMAND?"

The shout that answered him shook rain from the brooding clouds. The drizzle became a downpour that soaked those below and slammed the hovercraft sideways. They's drawn near the dais now, with the farships towering behind. Alison could see the Exori and the Sabbai flanking him. Two Stekoni stood on the stage as well, the harbingers of MolitorAb. The Sartius Exori looked almost normal standing there, too far away for the vestiges of torture on that ruined face to be seen. Yet his voice was supernaturally large, amplified and reverberating over the field. "FROM THE ROTTING CORRUPTION OF DEATH I WILL BRING THIS LIFE. THE ZAKKAIST CHURCH GIVES US NO FREEDOM—I SAY THAT WE WILL SIMPLY COME AND TAKE IT FROM THEM!"

The multitude roared affirmation.

"WILL YOU BE MY MARTYRS IF I ASK IT OF YOU? WILL YOU HAVE THE FAITH THAT AARON ROBERTS HAD, THAT KIRI OHARU HAD? I WILL NOT DECEIVE YOU—I DO NOT BRING JOY AND FLOWERS. THE FLOWERS WILL INSTEAD BE PLACED ON YOUR GRAVES. WILL YOU STILL FOLLOW ME?" He paused, gathering his breath, and then he shouted the question once more. "WILL YOU DO THIS?!"

His body shook from the effort. The masses pressed around the stage, shouting back at him with a howling that raised the hair on the back of Alison's neck. White knuckled, she gripped the hover's wheel as the craft dipped low. The excitement made her want to yell with the crowds.

The face of the Exori swiveled in the screens as he spotted the hovercraft, and he pointed. "THERE!" he proclaimed. "THERE IS AN UNBELIEVER. HE DOES NOT HAVE MOLITORAB IN HIS SOUL. HE CANNOT HEAR THE TRUTH OF MY WORDS, ONLY THE WHISPERING OF HIS OWN PRIDE. WILL YOU LET HIM LIVE?"

The denial was louder than anything Alison had ever heard. She mouthed it herself, staring at Schaeffer. She felt only loathing for the Secundus, a slow-burning hatred. How could she have missed seeing the stain on his soul? The heat of the Exori's passion filled her. Alison leaned forward against the seat restraints and flicked a toggle. The hover's shields dissipated and the hard-driven rain pummeled them. Schaeffer brought up his hands to protect his face. "Alison, what in MolitorAb's name are you doing?" he shouted.

She didn't answer. She turned the wheel hard over; the craft tilted alarmingly, the motor groaning as the gyros struggled to keep the craft from tumbling. Alison brought the wheel back, and Schaeffer lurched heavily back into his seat.

"YOU MUST SMASH THE ENEMY EVEN AT THE COST OF YOUR OWN LIVES. YOU WILL DO THAT KNOWING MOLITORAB WILL TURN HER BACK ON THOSE WHO FAIL. YOU CANNOT FAIL! YOU ARE THE SALVATION, THE POWER!"

Alison smiled. The Exori smiled with her. She listened to the Exori's words even as she pointed the hovercraft's nose toward an empty gantry. Schaeffer shouted at her, grasping for the controls. Alison slapped him back with a strength she'd not known she possessed.

"THOSE WHO OPPOSE ME WILL DIE IN FLAMES!"

They passed over the dais. Alison glanced down to see the Exori pointing to her. From all the screens, she could see him nodding, satisfied. His pride was a warmth, a balm that sustained her as the hover slammed into steel girders, as the craft's fuel tank ripped open and spilled its volatile contents over the engines, as the slow, rippling explosion tore the hovercraft apart and sprayed burning debris over those unlucky enough to be near the gantry. Alison felt neither the heat nor the torn support that sliced her from crotch to breast.

The hovercraft fell, taking her broken, smiling body with it.

CHAPTER TWENTY-FOUR

First you must understand this: there is no prophecy contained in Scripture which is a personal interpretation. Prophecy has never been put forward by man's willing it. It is rather that men impelled by the Holy Spirit have spoken under God's influence.

NEW TESTAMENT, 2 Peter 1:20–21

What was least understandable about the Zakkaist-MulSendero confrontation was the fact that there was little conflict between their moral codes. Both ascribed to certain basic tenets regarding social behavior (which the humans, at least, of both sides have more often than not ignored). In fact, in considering the similarity of Stekoni beliefs to our own, there is a compelling argument for the existence of God, in whatever form She may take. How could it be that another race, arising separately from our own and having a divergent evolutionary background with grossly variant influences, seem so damnably human?—*if there were not a guiding hand behind the creation of both species.*

The conflict, we feel, is rooted in the Zakkaist church's inability to change. Ossified since the time of Prophet Simon and perhaps too largely burdened with the remnants of the old Roman bureaucracy, it could only react to assault with brute force and steadfast denial. There was no suppleness in the body of the Church. Once pushed off balance, it could only fall. The only hope for the Church was to see that weakness before it was toppled.

From MASKING GOD: A STUDY OF
RACIAL CONFLICT, by Arlin
Webbe and
Chaim Goldblum, University of
Kellia Press, 2575

FirstBred Pale reeked.

She'd washed three times before coming across the linktube to

Gelt's Dream, and already her nostrils were clogged with the out-welling of her emotions. To another Stekoni, that complex mix was an open confession of her soul written with the oils that turned yellow brown on the folds of her body wrapping.

Samuel Conner, being human, merely wrinkled his nose and coughed softly. Pale's expressive eyes berated him.

"I'm sorry," he said. "You want me to tell you how lovely you smell?"

Underlids blinked at the sarcasm. Pale brushed a hand over the wall screen that dominated Conner's sleeping room. *Gelt's Dream* was larger than the Galicht craft *Anger;* Pale envied Conner his privacy.

The screen shimmered and the brilliant curve of Kellia appeared. Through the haze of the world's atmosphere, Pale could see the beacons of ships. She knew that over a hundred were out there, though only a few could be seen. The rest were points of light moving among the stars or hidden beyond the horizon—a ragged fleet of crowded farships vaulting into the sky at the Exori's urging.

"The Sartius Exori will return from Loris Port very soon," Pale said. "He was arranging for supplies to be ferried into orbit."

Samuel said nothing. At last Pale gave the breathy explosion that passed for a sigh among the Stekoni. "The Sartius Exori killed Secundus Schaeffer and twenty-three others," she said, her gaze still on the screen. She pointed to the image of the closest ships—her fingertip brushed the screen, leaving a long smudge. "Yet *they* went with him. This one does not understand that, Samuel Conner. The Sartius Exori revealed the VeilBeast inside himself and *still* they followed him. Stekoni would have run screaming from the Mad One. This one does not comprehend humanity."

Samuel grunted at that. He reclined in his bednetting, long legs dangling over the side. His feet swayed in the scant enhanced gravity of the ship. "That's bullshit, Pale. There were two Stekoni present, you and SlowBorn Brightness. Neither one of you ran. Hell, you saw your priest, didn't you? I thought she looked rather pleased that her pet prophet made such a powerful showing."

"Samuel Conner, this one did not come here to joke."

"Oh, I believe *that,*" Samuel said. He sniffed for effect. "What's the matter, FirstBred Pale? Don't you like your prophet now that you've found him?" He chuckled softly.

Samuel Conner always confused Pale. She never knew when he was serious. She hesitated, wondering whether she should simply return to the *Anger* and wait for Colin to return. Yet the opportunity to speak alone with Samuel might not come again for some time; of the Sabbai, he was the only one who might understand her dilemma. She ran her tongue along the ridges of her teeth. "This one is not certain," Pale answered. "This one has always felt that she trusted you, Samuel Conner. You have always been the one among the Sabbai who would question the actions of the Sartius Exori and the others. Yes, this one has doubts, may MolitorAb forgive her."

Pale's attitude was downcast. The mood had turned her oily fur dark and musky. She plucked forlornly at the cloth around her thin hips. "The human religions have devils and demons, Samuel Conner, and your people have been possessed by them, it is said." Slowly, she gave that inner blink, then opened the underlids to show her burnished yellow eyes. "MolitorAb contains all—all your evil spirits as well as your gods."

"And you wonder which part of Her has chosen to take residence in the Sartius Exori. Is that it?"

Pale's head inclined in what might have been a nod, might have been a twitch. "This one would prefer the Sartius Exori to be more gentle and caring. She would like to see more...compassion. In your race, that has happened with prophets, has it not?"

Samuel laughed. He swung slowly to his feet, drifting to the floor like a thin, sagging balloon. "You want Jesus Christ, FirstBred Pale? Then you're mistaken—it was Christ who invented hell and eternal torment. Christ had no compassion at all for those who failed to follow his ways. Devils danced behind all his pretty words, and his disciples brought them out regularly to frighten the masses. You don't want Christ, FirstBred Pale." Samuel rubbed at the side of his nose with a forefinger, squinting his eyes and yawning. "You don't want Mohammed or Moses or Ezekiel or even Simon ben Zakkai. They're all human, just like Colin. When God spoke through them, you could see the shadows of their faults in the radiance."

"Colin Exori kills and he does not care, Samuel Conner. He holds a sickness within him—this one smells its foulness every time the Sartius Exori speaks."

"That's religion you smell, Pale. Fanaticism. It's what eats the souls of your Mad Ones as well."

"That is simplistic, Samuel Conner. This one does not think that you believe your own words—you argue only to argue."

Samuel stuck out his lower lip in an exaggerated pout. "Ahh, Pale, you perceive things so well. One wonders why *you* aren't the Exori."

Irritation gave an acid edge to her scent. "This one perceives the universe well enough to see MolitorAb's handiwork. You speak as if you do not believe in Her at all, Samuel Conner."

He gave a barking laugh, his thin face lean and taut. He slouched against the wall screen, a bony finger tracing a slow-moving arc of light. "God's handiwork, Pale? Oh, I see it too, in the evil as well as the good. Yes, I've felt MolitorAb in the Veils—a vast, living intelligence that notices us the way we'd notice an annoying bumblebee. I believe in Her, and I acknowledge Her as my deity. I can well believe that She created your race and mine, that Her hands shaped all the worlds. I'd even say that She has the talents of a true artist, for what She's made is incredibly beautiful at times. I've no choice in believing, Pale. But sometimes She's hard to *worship*, when I see the horrors we're capable of."

"When we do that, we do not do Her will."

"No? Then how do you explain Colin? Mohammed? Christ? Take your pick of prophets, FirstBred Pale. Tell me which of them hasn't the ugliness inside."

"Stekoni commit no horrors, no murder," Pale insisted.

Samuel pressed his fingertip hard against the screen, as if he would crush one of the ships like an insect. The farship's beacon glowed ruddily under his nail. "I question that, FirstBred Pale. I won't let you hide behind that myth. Your priests do nothing to stop the Buntaro, for instance—wouldn't you cast them from the church if you truly abhorred their actions? No. Instead you slap their wrists gently now and then and spout pious lectures in their direction, all the while smiling as they do the drudge work in the war against the Zakkaists."

"The Buntaro believe in MolitorAb..." Pale began, but Samuel lifted a finger to his lips, his mouth tight in a mocking grin. "I'm not done," he said. "You came to me with your problem, so listen. I also see *you*, FirstBred Pale, following Colin's bloody trail. Your presence lends him veracity—'Look,' the people say, 'he has Stekoni with him. He must be the one.' So I think that your hands are tinged pink because of that. Even better, let's look at Kiri's death. That's troubled me for the last few months, and I still haven't quite decided how I feel about it."

Samuel went back to his netting. He sat on the edge of it, swinging slowly, and took a deep breath. "Let's take it as a given that someone within the Sabbai gave needed information to the Zakkaists. The assassination attempt was too well planned for anything else. Who do we have as suspects?" He lifted his hand, counting on his fingertips. "Miriam? Admittedly, she doesn't care for the direction of the Exori's teaching—it doesn't lead to wealth. Still, the woman's idea of violence is a subtraction error in the books." A second finger came up. "Joshua? No, he's Buntaro and he'd dearly love to see Colin descending on the hordes of unbelievers: the angry messiah-king. He'd have arranged it only if he could have stepped in front of Colin at the right instant to become another blessed martyr like Aaron."

Three fingers. "I'll even count in Anna Crowell, the obvious suspect. If she could have known that Kiri would be the one killed, she might have done it—but that was coincidence. Kiri wasn't the target at all. I know how you feel about Crowell's innocence, Pale, and I'm inclined to agree with you now." His little finger joined the others. "Then there's you..." He glanced at Pale. She took a step back, her hand covering the openings to her young-pouches.

"This one did not," she gasped.

Samuel nodded. His thumb opened from the palm. "And I tell you that it wasn't me—you'll have to take that on faith." He smiled. "That leaves only one other name."

FirstBred Pale shook her head violently, then gave the wriggle of Stekoni negation. *"Arryzk,"* she said in her own language, forcefully. "No, Samuel Conner. SlowBorn Brightness is a priest of MolitorAb and a Stekoni. She would not order his death. She would not wish to harm the Sartius Exori."

Samuel shrugged. The netting twisted under him. He put his feet on the floor to stop the motion. "So you say."

"It needn't have been one of the Sabbai, Samuel Conner. There could have been other ways."

Again, the shrug. His hand dropped to his lap. "I'll grant you that. But certainly it's the simplest explanation: Occam's razor. I'd bet that one of the Sabbai played Judas. Now we humans know that tale well—we all know what betrayal cost Judas. I wonder if any one of us would even take that chance. Look more closely at your priests and your religion, Pale."

The turn of the conversation was as unsettling to FirstBred Pale as her fears concerning Colin's madness had been. She'd come to Samuel Conner seeking commiseration and solace. She'd felt that the man was as disturbed by the Exori's path as she. With Kiri gone, Pale had no confidants among the Sabbai—she'd hoped... But now she had no more hope.

"This one will leave you, Samuel Conner. She thanks you for taking the time to speak with her."

"Not yet, Pale." When she started to shake her head, Samuel held his hand out to her. "Please. Tell me how the Stekoni deal with threats."

"That is simple, Samuel Conner. You know it already. The Stekoni do not oppose force with force. They will move aside until the threat is no longer present."

He simply gazed at her. For all the time she'd spent among humans, Pale had never learned the subtleties of their expressions— how to interpret stance and demeanor, all the small signals they used in place of their other atrophied senses. "Almost, Pale," he said. "In truth, the Stekoni are like the old Jesuits—you hold yourselves at a distance, you whisper this and that. You take your influence wherever you can find it, nudging this event, shaping that decision. And then you wait. You wait until the odds have turned back in your favor." He seemed to listen to a thought inside himself and chuckled. "I've wondered if we're not all caught up in Stekoni intrigue now. Your race has always been strangely subservient to humanity. When the Zakkaists banned you from the Holdings two centuries ago, you went peacefully, without much dissent at all. When they shut down the companies you'd established to sell your technology, you let us have the buildings, the books, the money, the warehouses. You acted proudly sad and went into your exile. You could do that because you'd already given us the one thing we couldn't do without—the farships. They were the key."

Samuel laughed. He pointed to the screen where the ships drifted, waiting for the Exori to guide them. "Humanity had to have the farships or give up the stars. Any other way of traveling is too slow. So we built our own ships using the engines stolen from you, and with them we could have our empire, only at the cost of always being forced to confront the existence of MolitorAb every time we went into the Veils. You let the Veils do your work for us. You knew that the Zakkaist church could never stand before that slow, steady assault. One by one, we'd begin to come to your God. You'd erode the Zakkaists until they were no longer a threat to you."

"Samuel Conner makes the Stekoni sound far too devious," Pale insisted. "If your hypothesis were true, then we would have no need of a Sartius Exori. We would only have to wait."

"*Yes!*" Samuel hissed. He nodded. "By that theory, the Sartius Exori is actually another threat—he could rule the MulSendero church—a human. But what if all humanity quickly becomes MulSendero, before their dislike of the Stekoni has dissipated? If that happens, then it doesn't matter that we use the farships, for we believe in the Voice. It would do the Stekoni good to kill this Sartius Exori before he becomes too powerful."

"That is not true, Samuel Conner," FirstBred Pale protested. She knew that her body cloth was hopelessly stained with her anxiety. She could feel the pounding of blood in her temples; her flight reflex made her legs quiver with the desire to be used. She forced herself to stay and confront Samuel. "The Stekoni have actively searched for the Sartius Exori," she said. "This one has been part of that search. Also, the Stekoni sheltered Hallan Gelt when no human world would do so. Primus Keller dwells with us, and through him the Stekoni have spread the word of the Sartius Exori to come. This one tells you that you have let paranoia and xenophobia blind you, Samuel Conner. You are plagued with phantom plots and theories."

Abruptly, Samuel guffawed, emitting a loud burst of amusement. He stood up and came toward Pale, who retreated until her back touched the ship's hull. Samuel hugged FirstBred Pale even as she twisted to move away. Uncaring of her smell or the oil that stained his own clothing, he embraced Pale, still roaring with laughter. Then he stepped away.

FirstBred Pale gawked at him.

"My, isn't this touching?" Pale and Conner turned to see the gray-haired, gaunt figure of Joshua at the door. The Buntaro flicked his gaze over the stains covering Samuel's shirt and trousers, and the lines around his eyes creased deeper. "The Exori's back on the *Anger,*" he said flatly. "He wants you, FirstBred Pale. While the two of you were . . . *playing* up here, the Exori was advancing our cause." An inner satisfaction tugged at his face and drew his shoulders back. "Colin Exori's forced the Kellian navy to agree to send three of their cruisers with us. We're armed at last. And Colin Exori will do the same at every Fringe world we visit."

The import of the words chilled Pale, deepening her confusion. "Samuel Conner," she began—at the least she wanted to understand his sudden, odd amusement of a moment before.

"Later, FirstBred Pale," Conner said tautly. "I was trying to point out that as poorly as you claim to understand humanity, we have just as much difficulty with the Stekoni." He stared at the smug Joshua. "And there are times when I'm simply mystified by everything. Go back to Colin, FirstBred Pale. Maybe you can talk sense into him."

Joshua stepped well back from the door as the Stekoni passed the older man. In the next compartment, SlowBorn Brightness was just entering her isolette. She lifted her head as FirstBred Pale moved toward the linktube.

Behind them, they could both hear Joshua speaking angrily to Samuel. "What's the matter with you? Surely you can see that this is the best news we've had in months. With the Exori, we'll force the Zakkaists down."

FirstBred Pale and SlowBorn Brightness stared at each other. Without the cues of the priest's odor, FirstBred Pale found she had little sense of the other's thoughts. Pale wondered how long Joshua and SlowBorn Brightness had been aboard, how much they might have heard of her conversation with Conner.

Miriam stepped through the linktube. She seemed distraught, her face blanched. FirstBred Pale ducked behind the woman as the lock door cycled shut. The Stekoni touched the contact to open it again.

As the linktube opened, they heard a long, high shriek of pain.

The agonized voice was Colin's.

In the nave of New York Cathedral, a group of young children in long white robes practiced a hymn before the critical scrutiny of the choir director. High, gentle harmonies drifted along the vaulted ceiling, leaving crystalline echoes. Ascendant Joseph Culper smiled briefly at the sound and touched the arm of the man walking beside him. "You hear that, Phillip? Simon's 'Praise God, All.' I've always loved that melody."

Ascendant Phillip Sterling, lately elevated to his current rank after the tragic death of Huan Su, glanced down the aisles to where the choir was assembled. The director waved his hand at a sharped passing note, cutting off the music. A finger pointed at the offender, and they heard his scolding tones. The children tittered and then became silent as the director raised his hands again.

The hymn began once more.

Sterling pursed his lips at the song of praise. He was absolutely tone deaf—he could not have said whether a melody was well sung or not; most music was simply caterwauling to him. High frequencies bothered his ears and buzzed like hornets in his skull. The pitch of the children's voices made a rude, clashing noise in his head. "It sounds like dishes breaking, Joseph. I've never understood the need for music in God's house. I find that it's only a way for certain people to preen themselves before the congregation. They're singing to hear *our* praise afterward, not to give glory to God. I would think He prefers one genuine prayer to a thousand hymns."

Pompous ass. Culper hid the thought well—Sterling was an ally to be cultivated in the Conclave. Culper gave a broad smile and clapped his companion on the shoulder. "Well put as always, my friend. That's why I value my time with you. I need your unique way of seeing things."

The stout, dour Sterling gave a grudging nod. "Glad you think so."

I don't. Still, I need your vote on my side. "You've no idea how I value your input," Culper said, and had to smile at the evasiveness of his reply. *Another small lie of omission, Lord.* "Tell me, Phillip, what are your thoughts on the Sartius Exori, now that we've had that disturbing report from the Fringes?"

Sterling's grimace told Culper more than any words. "This is the Church's most serious threat in centuries, Joseph, and I'm pleased that the Lord has considered me worthy of the challenge. The Sartius Exori is no less than the Adversary given form and breath—you were a fool to think you could defeat him with a simple subterfuge, Joseph."

Culper's breath was a hiss. *You'll pay for that remark and others like it, Sterling. On that day when I no longer need you...* He smoothed his face into bland neutrality. "Perhaps I was guilty of underestimating our enemy, Phillip. But I'd remind you that I was the first among the Ascendants to see any threat at all in the Geltian prophecies—Su would have had us treating the MulSendero as equals. He'd have forgiven the Buntaro all their crimes. I'd hoped to make Fairwood our puppet with which to deceive the heretics."

"You forgot that the MulSendero and the Stekoni are the devil's tools. They wouldn't be dangerous at all if they were so easily deceived, or if they were so obviously evil that all humanity would instinctively rise against them. It was only the wisdom of the Church that noted the Adversary's handiwork in the Stekoni and banned them from the Holdings. I've always been of the opinion that, from a historical perspective, that was a mistake. We should have done as we did with the Obdurates and obliterated the Stekoni entirely."

Culper was truly shocked at Sterling's comment. To hide his distress, he stared at the distant choir, nodding his head absently in time to the hymn. "I can't agree, Phillip. No one in the Conclave would advocate genocide. That's barbaric."

"It's a solution," Sterling said heavily. "There are all types of barbarism, Joseph." Sterling raised his eyebrows. "Some might think that what the curator of justice does is also barbaric. I think *you'd* also call it necessary, no? One doesn't have to *enjoy* such necessities." There was a soft emphasis in his words that pulled Culper's gaze around. Sterling cocked his head at the other Ascendant. "All you need do is acknowledge that such pragmatic decisions do the most good for the Church," he said.

"That's all past, Phillip. We can't do anything about it. My interest is in the Sartius Exori. Now. If you were Joseph Culper, what would you say to the Ascendants when the Conclave is called this week?"

"It would depend upon my options. What of this Mother Crowell who is with the Pretender?—Is she of any use?"

Culper shook his head. "No," he said definitely. "She may even be a liability. She's not made any of the contacts we'd set up for her to pass information to us."

"Then cut your losses. If she's a potential threat, remove her."

"That's under consideration," Culper said. "But all that is minor. The Sartius Exori will be here in a year, here in this system: I would put my life on that bet. I think that we should thank God that he'll only have a disorganized mob at his back."

"If the decision were mine, I'd mobilize our navy and wipe out the threat forever."

You have only one tactic, don't you? And you call me a fool. You don't even see the ramifications of your suggestion. "You'll never convince the Ascendants of that—Destroy the innocents? They'll cry. We can't do it. The protest that would follow would destroy us more certainly than the Exori's threat. In any case, there are those who will say that no matter what we do, we cannot kill the Pretender."

"*Cannot*, or *should* not?" Sterling's face was a blotchy red. He sniffed. "It's obvious the man's a rogue mutant—everything points to it. Telekinesis, telepathy—a few latent psi powers and you can explain away every one of this Exori's miracles. Take away the ones *you* provided for him and there's nothing left."

"Unless he's exactly what he claims to be."

Sterling's color brightened, pleasing Culper. "Rumor has it that you've a detailed recording of the Horeb snafu. Have you been watching it too much, Joseph?"

"You're new to the Conclave, Phillip. You can't feel the mood shift that has come over the assembly since Su's death, since Horeb. They're a lot more inclined to be conciliatory toward the Mul-Sendero: that's one of the reasons I pushed your nomination so hard. I wonder if one or two of our peers might not be having a minor crisis of faith. They might even wonder if this Colin Fairwood might not be another Simon ben Zakkai, come to make us all one faith again. You heard Jordan last session, muttering that there was little enough difference between MolitorAb and God. They're all a little frightened, Phillip. I can't blame them."

"Are *you* frightened, Joseph?" The flush crawled higher on Sterling's cheeks.

Culper's fine, aristocratic features went hard. "Only a fool wouldn't be a little frightened. It doesn't matter whether you believe in MolitorAb or not, or whether Fairwood's actually a prophet or some rogue telepath—*every*one's frightened."

"I'm not."

The struggle was visible on Culper's face. He turned to the choir again as the last refrain of the hymn began to fade. "Then I wish more of the Ascendants shared your opinion," he said over his shoulder.

Sterling seemed mollified by that. The choir had ended practice. Robed children stood in groups at the end of the nave. "What do you intend to do, Joseph? He *is* coming here, in that I agree with you. We can't sit and pray like monks. I've too little experience yet in the Conclave. The true faithful of the Church look to you as their voice."

Culper indicated the children with his chin. *"They* are my concern: the Church to come."

"A fine sentiment." Sterling smirked. "But sentiment won't stop the Sartius Exori."

"Doesn't God protect His flock, Phillip?"

Slowly, Sterling grinned. It did not seem to be a comfortable expression for him. "Of course He does. That doesn't mean that we should expect Him to act for us."

Culper laughed, a deep, rich baritone. "We will act, Phillip. Believe me. Just give me your vote when the time comes."

And afterward I'll ensure that you pay for your boorishness as the Exori will pay for his presumptions.

The two Ascendants clasped hands.

Giggling, the children began to depart the nave. They fell silent as they passed the Ascendants, glancing their way with shy smiles.

CHAPTER TWENTY-FIVE

Can he who shall face the terrors of the Resurrection be compared to the true believer? To the Wrongdoers We shall say: "Taste the punishment which you have earned."

KORAN, The Hordes 39:24

"How can you ask me whether or not I worship this man?" Samuel replied to them. "No, I do not worship him. You've made the mistake that too many have made if you can ask that. I worship MolitorAb, of whom the Sartius Exori is the prophet. This prophet is but a man as you named him—no man is worthy of worship. I tell you that I follow him because MolitorAb has bid me to do so, but my prayers go into the Veils. Are you such blind fools that you would deify the axe that fells the tree? Axes do not move of themselves; they are due no blame or praise."

THE TESTAMENT OF SAMUEL, 32:5–7

Blood, bright and an impossible scarlet, fountained from the Sartius Exori as he writhed on the floor. Anna Crowell sat in her bednetting, still holding a double-edged dagger in her hand. She had sliced Colin from his right hip to his crotch, digging deep into the abdominal cavity; her hand was stained to the elbow. Colin's pants were covered with a spreading darkness and he clutched himself desperately, blood cascading over his fingers. He moaned horribly, a keening wail, rolling from side to side with his eyes wide and bulging. Veins were collapsing under the skinbase.

Anna Crowell stared at him. There was no compassion in that gaze. She might have been watching the death twitches of some insect.

"Exori!" Pale screeched. The blood scent was overpowering, a thick, cloying odor. Pale retched, briefly nauseous. Miriam and then the other Sabbai pushed past Pale as she doubled over, helpless. "Oh, my God," Miriam breathed as she took in the brutal scene.

She immediately went to Colin, kneeling beside him. Joshua plunged past the woman and snatched the dagger from an unresisting Crowell. Anna gasped in pain as he twisted her wrist viciously to release the weapon.

"You fucking bitch!" he howled. He reversed the blade. Pale knew he wanted to plunge it into Crowell's heart—the Stekoni could see muscles shift in Joshua's forearm but stood frozen, able to do nothing.

"No!" The cry came from Colin. The word halted Joshua in midblow. The blade slid to one side of Crowell and slashed netting. Colin struggled to sit; Miriam held him down, her face white. "Exori, please," she protested. "Please, lie back. We'll go to the port, to a hospital..."

"Leave Crowell alone, Joshua," Colin grunted through clenched teeth, ignoring Miriam. Samuel pushed his way into the crowded compartment and stood beside Pale; down the linktube flowed the sweet scent of SlowBorn Brightness. "All of you—let her be," Colin ordered. "She hasn't harmed me."

They all looked. Already, the flow of blood had gone sluggish and dark, and the puckered lips of his wound were folding together under the ruined clothing. Colin's face was still bloodless though, and his hands trembled with shock. Sweat gathered on his brow and rolled down his face.

And his voice...His voice was Fairwood's. Pale almost cried out in joy to hear it.

"Exori, this bitch tried to kill you," Joshua insisted.

"She was protecting herself. You'd do the same, Joshua—any of you would." Colin's gaze swept by them all as he levered himself unsteadily to his feet. Miriam aided him, bracing her arm under his shoulder. The flow of blood seemed to have stopped, though his clothing was soaked with it and an irregular, thick puddle spread at his feet. Crowell's mouth opened in a half-sob at the sight of Colin standing. To Pale, Anna's emotional pattern hung in the room like a ruby fog, obscuring everything else.

"Why do you follow me?" Colin demanded, and it was only Fairwood speaking. The power was gone from his voice; it was only a man's anger, freighted with deep weariness. "You're all fools, every last one of you. Sabbai! Hah!" His scorn brought color to Joshua's cheeks. Colin berated them like an apparition from a nightmare. "You're feeding on my power, that's all. You know that my time will pass soon, and you all want your precious little hands in the building of what will follow me. You're waiting like vultures beside a dying man."

As Colin spoke, Pale could hear the Presence in him beginning to reassert itself until an uneasy balance seemed to be reached. The faint hope the Stekoni had felt began to dim—if the Exori had remained Fairwood, she might have been able to speak with him, to show him there must be some other way than the path he had chosen. *Not to Old Earth,* she would say. *Not to confrontation.*

"Colin Fairwood," she began, hoping she could still reach him before the VeilBeast fully shared him. She stopped as Colin held out red-dripping fingers to the Stekoni. The scent made her back away.

"I know what you'd ask and this is your answer, FirstBred Pale," Colin said. "This is the ultimate answer to everything I do. I am *HATRED!*" He bellowed the word, leaning his head back so that the tendons bulged taut against the skinbase. "Hatred, intolerance— the parents of all religions. They are *my* tasks. I might wish to perform a few tricks and preach a nonviolent gospel, maybe spice it with sex and visceral pleasure and sit back while I filled all our pockets with gold. But I *can't.* She won't allow it. She bends me to Her will—I am the Black Beginning. The Zakkaists have had time enough to come to MolitorAb and the reward they've earned is now due. If they'd listened to the Voice whom She called, if they'd even allowed the MulSendero to flourish alongside their own religion, then no Sartius Exori would have been needed. Hallan Gelt would have brought back no prophecy. But . . . They—did— *not!*"

Across his open patchwork face slid the traces of his inner struggle. Pale wanted both to run and to reach for Colin. The man trembled with his internal passion; he seemed about to weep with the pain of it. Helplessly, Colin rubbed his hands, further staining them, on his pants. He swung about, flailing his arms, and then leaned heavily against his pilot's chair for support. "Get out!" he shouted. "All of you! Go!"

"As the Sartius Exori wills," SlowBorn Brightness said behind Pale. She shuffled back across the linktube, trailing a miasma of satisfaction that puzzled FirstBred Pale. The Stekoni turned to follow her priest, but Colin's voice pulled her back. "Pale, no. Stay." His face was blank, his eyes closed under knotted muscles. "I don't order you to do that, but I'd like it. Please."

The rest of the Sabbai stared at Pale as they passed, each with his or her own thoughts carefully masked. Only Samuel, last of them, smiled, his expression tinged with mockery. "How's it feel to be the chosen disciple, Pale?" he whispered as he slid by the Stekoni. Pale caught a pungent whiff of jealousy with the words.

"Colin Exori?" Pale asked when they'd gone and the linktube locks had cycled shut. Colin's eyes opened and the VeilBeast glared out from them.

"Sever the linktube, Pale," he snapped.

"Let this one clean your wounds first," Pale offered. "She will get you some medicines for the pain."

"Sever the linktube and tell the others that they can follow if they must. Then you and Crowell can do as you wish yourselves. Leave me, stay here at Kellia—I don't care. I'm going to veilshift when we're far enough away from this place, so make up your minds now."

Pale swiveled her head from the stern eyes of the Exori to the bitter, harsh glare of Crowell. She found no sympathy in either place.

Crowell spoke first. "If you try to touch me again, Fairwood, that next time I'll know to use the knife on myself," she said flatly. "I'll do it. If you want this child from me, you'll stay away."

Colin's reply was cold. "I've no use for you in that way anymore, Crowell. None at all. You needn't worry." He glanced at Pale.

She shrugged, a quick spasm. "This one has been given the task of following the Sartius Exori. That is what MolitorAb has said to her. She will do that."

Colin laughed. He swung stiffly into the pilot's chair and took the thick cable of the nerve links in his hand. He attached the leads to his skull and the back of his neck. The *Anger*'s system drive flared and trembled under their feet.

After that, for long, painful hours, there was only silence.

Four of them sat around a circular wooden table of polished oak. FirstBred Pale sat across from Colin, smelling of a salt sea and morning. To his right was Anna Crowell, smiling as he had only rarely seen her do, strangely attractive in a way that puzzled him. It was with a start that he saw Crowell was of the same body type and coloring as Kiri—he had never noticed such a resemblance before. He reluctantly tore his glance away to regard the fourth member.

The last guest, seated to Colin's left, was an enigma, a man-shaped darkness. Colin's eyes blurred when he glanced at the silent apparition, as if the thing were a hole in reality that a human's eyes were not truly able to see. The figure's outline was shifting, elusive. Colin noticed that the others avoided glancing at the murky shade as well.

Colin had not noticed before that the table was set as if for a formal dinner, though there was no food on it. The dishes were gleaming bone china with rims of gold, the tableware was sterling, the goblets before them (filled with a red wine, he saw now) were purest crystal. Nor had Colin noticed the room: Edwardian, a stage setting from some pre-Zakkaist play. Heavy, brocaded drapes were pulled across the windows, their folds of burgundy velvet trimmed with gold fringe. Through a gap at the center, Colin could see the same disturbing nothingness filling the windows, the mind-jarring emptiness that composed the creature beside him.

FirstBred Pale raised her goblet to Colin in an oddly human gesture, though he saw that her wine was now a light, effervescent aquamarine. "This one would propose a toast," she said, though her voice did not sound like the Stekoni's. Habit made Colin take his own goblet in hand; at the edges of his sight, he could see Anna Crowell and the apparition do the same. "To understanding," Pale intoned, and they all echoed the sentiment: "To understanding."

Colin sipped the wine. It was dry and tart, like a young Cabernet. He set the goblet down on a lace tablecloth that had not been there when he'd lifted his glass.

"Fine, Pale," Colin said as he leaned back in his ornate, massive chair. "I would like some of this understanding. Do you know who *that* is?" Colin nodded his head toward the brooding, strange form beside him.

Pale would not look at the specter. Her delicate fingers tapped the rim of the goblet, creating a soft chime. "That is the VeilBeast," she answered. "That is MolitorAb's hand, all of Her that mortals are ever permitted to see."

Colin sent his awareness probing within his own mind, seeking the presence that had been a part of him since Chebar, and he found that part of him empty. Relief made him smile and almost laugh. "The thing has left me," he said. He tried again to regard that aching nothingness and once more he had to move his gaze away from it. Perception reeled when he looked at the VeilBeast, and his eyes felt like liquid fire. "That is the Presence?"

Pale nodded, her scent overlaid with a gingery sharpness. "Humanity has always had a part of the answer, Colin Fairwood. Your God was a branch of the Many Paths, and you mistook it for the only Way. Your fault lay in the perception of the universe as deministic, Newtonian, with everything proceeding in an orderly fashion. You believed that every action caused one inevitable reaction, all of creation linked together in one enormous clockwork mechanism that God wound up and tinkered with every so often. You even kept that model when the physics that gave rise to the vision was destroyed. You clung to your God as if he were the *only* God, as if you had created *him*. Simon ben Zakkai took you a step away from that, yet you would go no further. You held on to your poor observation of MolitorAb as if it could save you."

Pale shook her wide head, the fur on her face glossy in the light of the ornate chandelier laden with dangling crystals. "When your scientists finally broke into the subatomic world, they expected to find obedient, peaceful, billiard-ball mechanics ruling that world in the same fashion as those same laws seemed to govern the macroscopic universe. Instead, you found strangeness, found that these particles ceased being definable 'things' and behaved capriciously—indistinct wave functions, a part of them always hidden. You found you could not accurately predict where and how such beasts would interact in any experiment that was set to measure them. Instead of the sharply defined certainty that A would cause B, all that could be said was A *usually* caused B. At the best, you could define probabilities, you could predict density or location in most cases, given enough sampling. You found uncertainty."

This was no longer FirstBred Pale speaking. Somewhere in that speech, her form had shifted and coalesced again. Now it was Hallan sitting across the table from Colin, shaking his head at his old friend and grinning. "Here in the Veils, you're sitting at the true nexus, Colin. This is where all probabilities rest—Heaven, Valhalla, Nirvana. Even Hell." He chuckled, showing his teeth. "All of it's here. You're touching the core, from which all the Many Paths begin."

"You promised me understanding and I still don't understand, Hallan. I don't see the truth. I don't much care about all your fancy explanations—they're not important. All I want to know is *why* MolitorAb tortures me. Why does this . . . this *beast* sit inside me?"

Hallan snorted with laughter. "*I* certainly don't know. Aren't you listening, Colin? I've been telling you that MolitorAb is simply beyond your comprehension. Humanity could fall away from God when He was still Newtonian in scope, when understanding the universe was simply a matter of uncovering all the variables, all the multitudes of possible reactions to specific events. God was still immense, yes, but the outlines could be faintly seen. But what the Stekoni had . . ." Hallan shook his head sadly. "A God who must juggle all the infinite possibilities in a random world—now *that's* staggering. And yet She is interactive as well. Anyone can hear Her by stepping into the Veils—there's no restriction to saints and mystics. Colin, all your personification of MolitorAb is just so much bullshit. All your ranting about how She must care for you is just bullshit too. She doesn't. She's using you, as She used me. As She uses all of us."

"Why?" Colin demanded.

"You're the prophet." Hallan shrugged. "You tell *me.*"

"I'm more puppet than prophet, Hallan. And you did it to me."

"You're no puppet at all, Colin. That's the false deterministic universe again, the billiard-ball galaxies. You always have your own choice to make—and that's why you're also wrong in accusing me. If the VeilBeast inside you demonstrates its own terrible ego, it's because it's feeding on yours. *You've* given it life, Colin. I tell you that even MolitorAb can't fully control you."

"Then She isn't God."

There was the smell of basil to his right, and Colin looked to see FirstBred Pale seated between himself and Anna Crowell. As Hallan snickered, the Stekoni touched Colin's shoulder. "'God' is only a term, Colin Fairwood, not a definition. If 'God' controls all, why did She bother making this universe? Certainly She would have no challenge."

"Now who's imposing a personality on God," Colin retorted. Pale withdrew her hand, blinking.

Hallan leaned forward, elbows on the table. "I'm telling you that MolitorAb has a destiny in mind for you, Colin. I'm also saying that there's no certainty you can fulfill it."

"Tell me what it is, if you have such an insight into Her, Hallan. Quit being so vague."

"I don't know what it is, Colin."

"Then let me talk with Her. Let the Voice speak. She has said nothing to me at all since Dridust." Colin could hear the pleading tones that pitched his voice high. He didn't care—his hands were two fists on the lace, and the distorted face he saw reflected in his goblet was desperate. "I thought that She might have abandoned me. Please, Hallan, tell Her to speak. Tell her!"

Hallan's smile collapsed. He looked very sad. The features of his face were wrapped in a webbing of dark lines. His body shimmered and began to fade like windblown smoke. "She won't speak with you, Colin. I'm sorry; I don't know why. She won't speak."

"She must!" Colin shrieked. He lurched across the table, sprawl-

ing, but Hallan was gone; Colin's grasping fingers found nothing. There was only the ghostly silhouette of a shape. "I'm sorry, Colin. Her back is turned to you. I'm sorry." The voice was a gravelly whisper.

Colin grasped the tablecloth and roughly flung it aside. The goblets toppled and crashed to the floor; dishes and place settings cascaded down. "Speak to me!" he shouted.

There was no reply. He stood, hands on hips and breathing heavily. He could see FirstBred Pale and Anna Crowell staring at him, could see the VeilBeast still sitting calmly in its chair. Colin slowed his breathing. His fisted hands unknotted. He sighed and ran a hand over his face, feeling the satin texture of the skinbase. The others watched him like actors waiting for their cues.

"She won't talk to me, FirstBred Pale," Colin said, and he realized the wetness he felt on the patchy skin of his cheek was his own tears.

"This one feels sorrow for you, Colin Fairwood."

Colin nodded, a strange catch in his breath. He wiped back-handed at his eyes and turned to Crowell. "Anna," he said. The name tasted strange in his mouth—it was the first time he'd ever spoken it. "I deserve nothing but your hatred, yet you've stayed." He hesitated then, biting his lower lip, not sure what it was that he wanted to say to her. "Anna, did you tell the Zakkaists about Horeb? Was it you who caused Kiri to die?"

He saw the truth glowing in her. "It was as I told the Exori from the first," she replied haughtily. "No. I was not your Judas."

"Can you forgive what I've done to you?"

"No," she said again, and that was also truth.

Colin shifted his weight and broken china clattered around his feet and became tangled in the folds of the wine-stained lace tablecloth.

"Vector 3.1," the VeilBeast said.

"No!" Colin raged suddenly. "I won't leave until MolitorAb speaks to me."

"Vector 3.1," the VeilBeast repeated impassively. "Imperative."

The return to reality was a twisting shock. Colin sat in his seat, stunned, as the familiar stars swayed on the screen before him. His pulse pounded in his temples as he steadied the *Anger.* When it was done, he swallowed hard, closing his eyes and willing the last of the dizziness to pass.

The VeilBeast chuckled deep in his head, back in its familiar lair. *Be silent,* Colin ordered. *If you must be with me, at least leave me alone.* The scolding did little good; the thing radiated amusement at Colin's efforts.

Colin swiveled in his chair to see Pale just beginning to sit up in her bednetting. He could smell terror in her, and her wrappings were drenched in secretions. He knew that whatever she had seen in the Veils had frightened her deeply. "FirstBred Pale, are you all right?"

"Yes, Colin Exori. In a moment...this one will be fine." Her lambent pupils contracted, and she stroked the wet fur of her chest. "Colin Exori, you were with this one in her veildreams."

"You were all in mine as well," Crowell interjected. "A strange dinner party."

"Anna—" Colin began, and he stopped as her face distorted into a snarling rictus.

"Don't call me that," she said slowly, her voice trembling. "Don't you dare give me your guilty affection." Her fingers were curled into claws that snagged the netting. "You set the parameters for our relationship, Exori. You judged me guilty and meted out my punishment. So now you can stay the hell away from me."

Within Colin, the VeilBeast howled with glee. "Anna, I can understand your feelings..."

"No, you *can't.* There's no possible way." Colin could see the moisture welling up in the corners of her eyes, and Crowell pawed at them with angry forefingers as if she hated them for betraying her emotions. Colin would have disconnected the nervelink, would have at least risen to speak with her, but her posture forbade it.

It was FirstBred Pale who moved, who took Anna's hand. The woman turned her head from Colin and buried herself in Pale's encircling arms. There she wept.

Colin sat, his own turmoil creating a sour knot in his stomach, with the VeilBeast giggling inside like an insane thing.

CHAPTER TWENTY-SIX

We know who said "Vengeance is mine; I will repay" and "The Lord will judge his people." It is a fearful thing to fall into the hands of the living God.

NEW TESTAMENT, Hebrews 10:30–31

You ask: "How can you regret a life that has allowed you to carve your name on the very faces of the worlds?" I tell you such a thing is easy. Never envy the powerful person, for that one has climbed to the heights on a ladder strung with those less fortunate. Every rung is a body.

THE WORDS OF THE SARTIUS EXORI,
Questions 27:2

Three weeks later, on Abijam, Colin acquired another two hundred farships, three of them old naval patrol ships crudely converted to Veil travel. The news from Kellia had preceded Colin by a week, and the ships were waiting for him already in orbit around the world. He left Abijam without ever setting foot on the planet.

On Lachish, his party survived a bomb attack by a fanatic whose explosives erupted while the terrorist was still at the edge of the crowds milling about the Exori. Thirty-two people were killed, another ninety-seven injured, and one hundred seventy-five ships joined the growing fleet. Lachish was pleased to see the Sartius Exori depart, for feeding the Exori's disciples and resupplying the farships placed a genuine strain on the world's marginal resources after two full seasons of drought. Several more ships—carrying the faithful from various Fringe worlds who were unwilling to wait for the Exori's arrival—joined the fleet before it broke orbit. Seen from the moons of Lachish, the array of craft was rapidly becoming impressive: it resembled a sea of new, shifting constellations.

Mizpah, Antioch, Seraph—the pattern was much the same at each. The worlds grumbled at the temporary invasion and the upset it would cause and then bowed to necessity. Their governments made the best of the situation; the officials would smile bravely and pose for pictures with Colin as the flotilla sucked at the resources below. Though laughably small in comparison to the Holdings's navy, the meager firepower of Colin's army of the faithful was enough to outweigh most of the individual Fringe worlds' navies; after all, what kept the Fringes free of any invasion threat was the paucity of their land. What no one had any great reason to covet, there was no need to protect.

When the Exori left Lysia, he departed with eight thousand farships at his back. Most of them were unarmed except for personal weapons; most of them were filled with simple MulSendero faithful who had hearkened to the call of the Sartius Exori and had no experience of war. They followed because the Sartius Exori had requested they do so. If these people feared his eventual destination, they said nothing. The Sartius Exori led them, said the rumors that flashed through the fleet, to a better land. They would take from the Zakkaists the wealth that had been stolen from the MulSendero. There was nothing better for them in the Fringes, on their dreg worlds. If the Exori would hand them the riches of the Holdings, they would proffer cupped palms and let the gold be placed there.

They knew the Sartius Exori was pleased at the sight of the faithful massed behind his own craft.

He was not. In their tour of the Fringes, there were eleven Veil passages. From each of them, Colin emerged more sullen and troubled than from the last. After the third, the *Anger* was connected to one of the Galicht farships in the group and towed. All of Colin's attention was on his dreams; he no longer cared about returning from the Veils.

MolitorAb would not speak to him. His God ignored Her prophet.

"She tests me," Colin muttered. "She wants to be certain that my faith is unshaken and so She turns Her back."

"Perhaps She does not approve of the Sartius Exori's actions," Pale ventured.

"No!" Colin roared. His anger drove Pale back. From her netting, Crowell glanced up. "I still have Her power in me, FirstBred Pale," Colin continued, forcing his voice back to calmness. "That wouldn't be so if She'd abandoned me. I'm not surprised that She doesn't speak. She would rather that I not have to do this thing."

That was all he would say.

They gained ships. Life quickened inside Anna Crowell.

At last they made passage for the final time, back to Nexus and a last gathering. The trail of farships slid into the Veils behind the *Anger.*

There is an aura of stateliness about the Ascendants. Their image is that of a group of elderly, robed men removed from the grime that flaws the souls of most people. When the Zakkaist faithful thought of the Conclave, the conjured picture was of an assemblage surrounded by a holy radiance, speaking in hushed and reverent tones as they discussed the issues. Disagreements, unlikely as they might be, would be delicately couched in polite and reasonable phrases. Certainly the few recordings of the Conclaves that the Ascendants had made public over the centuries had sustained the belief that the gathering was an ordered parliament.

A meeting of gentlemen as like unto their patriarchal God as humans could manage.

"I'm amazed that our esteemed colleague could be so stupid as to propose such an idiotic course of action." Ascendant Dmitri Vesilov thundered that statement as Joseph Culper began to take his seat after his opening statements. Since the death of Huan Su had left the moderate faction of the Conclave in disarray, Vesilov had emerged from the loose coalition as the new leader. A stout, balding man of Ukrainian descent, Vesilov sensed that Culper had overstepped his ability to control the Conclave. He had been waiting for this opportunity since the debacle on Horeb. Now that it had come he felt the adrenaline surging through his system. If Culper could be brought down, that slippery path to power in the Conclave would open before Dmitri. He remembered Su and how that frail man had for so long been the dominant force within the group, and how Su had made the mistake of allowing Culper to rise and threaten his hold. Dmitri Vesilov would not make that mistake: he would fight and claw to remain at the top.

Vesilov shook his head in mock sadness and regarded the Ascendants arrayed in their tiers. The Conclave was in Tokyo this month, and Vesilov vowed that if Culper lost this vote now, he would give his thanks in Su's garden. "I repeat: I am amazed. I can't help but recall that this Conclave was once convinced by Ascendant Culper to agree to another proposal—to place Colin Fairwood on the throne of the mythical Sartius Exori. I know that most of us would now argue that doing so was a crucial mistake. Ascendant Culper also used his persuasive voice to convince us to remove Fairwood. We all know how *that* failed. Since Horeb, Fairwood has become bitter and vengeful—God has punished us for our meddling. He has punished us with the specter of a heretic prophet. With the rioting and death caused by the Buntaro in every one of our cities. With the fear that afflicts all our faithful. With the increasing number of people who have turned away from the true faith to embrace the MulSendero. With the deterioration of relations between the Holdings and all the Fringe worlds.

"None of us is untouched. We have driven souls away from God with our actions, and He will judge us. Yet Ascendant Culper would *dare* to stand before this Conclave and propose even more drastic 'solutions' to our difficulties. I tell you that Joseph Culper sees the universe only in black and white. I tell you that he can conceive of only one solution to any problem: eradicate it." Vesilov paused for breath. He glanced at the Ascendants around him—yes, they were nodding and attentive. He filled his lungs. He shouted.

"I tell you that Joseph Culper is wrong! I tell you that this Conclave *will not listen!*"

Vesilov took his seat as a grumble of approval swept the hall. Culper, across from him, smiled indulgently, as if Vesilov's words were nothing more than the ranting of an errant child, to be listened to patiently and then forgotten.

Culper sighed theatrically. He rose again as the muttering began to quiet. For his part, Culper was aware that Vesilov lacked the personal charisma of Huan Su, that the man was a poor speaker given to empty thunderings. Culper also knew that the sympathies within the Conclave had swung away from himself since Horeb—any vote would be close. He could no longer so easily sway the Ascendants who inhabited the middle ground between the moderates and Culper's own conservative faction. Culper fully expected to lose this vote; he had planned for just that eventuality, but he could not afford to give it up easily. Vesilov, to Culper, was like most of the moderates—a man whose view of religion was spiritual and diffuse. Culper's faith was as strong as theirs and far more pragmatic.

His peers certainly did not think of Joseph as a saint. Still, he wondered if history might not judge differently. Even at the cost of his reputation, Culper would save the Church from itself—God would be the one to gauge his soul, not the Ascendants.

If they would be blind, he would ignore them.

Culper gazed down at the three empty chairs between the tiers, at the Zakkaist triangle glimmering on the wall. "I have always been very slow to call a man stupid," he said carefully, and his gaze was on Vesilov. "I'd fear that when God called me before him, he would brand that word on my own head." Culper heard stifled laughter at that, and he smiled inwardly at the sour expression that twisted Vesilov's thick lips. "I didn't doubt that when I stood to advocate using our navy to disperse this threat of Fairwood's, that I would meet strong opposition from my fellows. I'll fully admit that the events on Horeb couldn't have gone more wrong." His voice was full of bemused honesty, rich and deep. "I'll agree that we—*I*, rather—underestimated Fairwood's power. You have all heard the testimony from Ascendant Sterling's experts."

Culper nodded his iron gray head at Sterling, seated to his right. "They agree that Fairwood is most likely telekinetic, that possibly he doesn't even comprehend the fact that his powers emanate from his own mind. In short, we're dealing with a rogue, an accident of genetics. We have no prophet from the false Stekoni God. I am chagrined that such a possibility did not occur to me sooner—how else could it have been that Fairwood, with his hideous injuries and no skill at all, escaped the Obdurate Purge with Hallan Gelt? In retrospect, all of it makes sense. Had we known then, certainly my plan for dealing with him would have been radically different. All I ask is that you do not automatically discount this proposal because the last failed. It failed because our information was invalid.

"I contend that force must be met by force. I don't claim that my proposal involves no bloodshed; I would hope we can avoid that, but if one man's death prevents a thousand, which is better? We are talking realities here, Ascendants, and none of us is stupid enough"—he used the word deliberately, with an inflection that made Vesilov raise his head and glare—"to think that any major decision we make won't affect lives or lead to death. Our laws are *full* of death. We execute murderers in the name of God—we do that because in killing them we've done the greatest good for the largest number of people. Because we have done *our faithful* the most good. Colin's followers are not ours. Let them come here and *we* will be the ones who suffer."

"It's illegal for the Holdings to send a force into the Fringes, Ascendant Culper. As curator of justice, surely you know that." Vesilov's eyes glittered at his own riposte, but Culper only shrugged.

"I'm very much aware of that, Ascendant. I'm also aware that if Colin Fairwood decides to bring his fleet to *us,* we're left with no effective way of stopping him short of the violent confrontation you claim you're trying to avoid. Once he's within the Veils, we have no way of predicting where he will arrive within the Sol system."

"The man will have no more than ten thousand ships by the end of his gathering." Vesilov spread his hands wide, palms up. "That's according to our worst estimates. Let's be reasonable, Ascendant. Very few of those ships would be capable of dealing with one of our cruisers, and the largest number of people that could possibly be involved in this 'invasion force' would be in the neighborhood of seventy thousand. That is *not* a significant force, Ascendant, not when they must go up against the resources of Old Earth. They are untrained fanatics—like medieval peasants armed with sticks trying to storm a castle. It can't be done. We've nothing to fear from them at all, ultimately."

"Yet we all seem to persist in worrying about it, don't we?" Culper's smile brought an angry flush to Vesilov's face. "I see the fear in your eyes, all of you. One of the arguments presented against my proposal is that you're afraid the Church and the MulSendero might come to blows again and that we'll find Colin Fairwood is impossible to harm. First, I'd point out that *even if* that were the case, it's obvious that Colin's compatriots have no such immunity— witness Kiri Oharu or Aaron Roberts. Second, we won't offer the first blow in any battle. I am aware we could not afford such bad publicity. We won't confront Colin violently unless we are first attacked. The intent of sending portions of our navy to Nexus is to create a blockade around her gravity well and thus keep any farships from entering the Veils. And last, we're simply enforcing Holdings law by not allowing Fairwood and his followers access to our areas of influence: Stekoni are forbidden without first obtaining specific permission, and the worship of MolitorAb is illegal. We can't place a fence around the Holdings, Ascendants. If we wish to keep Colin Fairwood's fanatics out at all—and I tell you *now* that seventy thousand Buntaro are not to be scoffed at—we must go to them before they make Veil passage."

Culper's backers among the Ascendants applauded that, and he noted that some of the undecided members of the Conclave suddenly looked very thoughtful. Vesilov had evidently noticed as well, for he quickly stood up and pointed across the hall at Culper. "There *is* no threat, Ascendant Culper. Fairwood holds a toy gun in comparison to our navy. You propose a drastic action unwarranted by circumstances. You want to meet fanaticism with a fanaticism of our own."

Culper laughed at that. "Exactly, Ascendant. Exactly."

"I would be ashamed to admit to such arrogance. I say that we need to approach Colin Fairwood with reason on our side. Our best course is to send a diplomatic mission to Nexus—let us deal with his threats as rational people."

Phillip Sterling rose to speak, and Culper grimaced, wishing he could have stopped the impetuous man. "Then it's a pity that Huan Su is unavailable for the task," Sterling said. Culper grimaced again as Vesilov bared his teeth with a hissing intake of breath.

"Your comment is disrespectful to a revered, deceased member, Ascendant Sterling, especially in his own hall," Vesilov said in rebuke. "In any case, Ascendant Su was murdered by one of our own—the curator's agent."

"Anna Crowell is not ours," Sterling said heatedly. "Not any longer. She is bearing the Exori's child, as you all know. *I* think it likely that she deceived the curator from the start, that she was always a double agent." Culper closed his eyes at that. *I'll tear your fucking tongue out by the roots, bastard. Shut up. Can't you understand what you're doing?* "The assassination of Su wasn't an accident, but murder," Sterling continued. "That is how Fairwood would deal with *you.* "

"I'm certain that there are compromises we can reach with the man," Vesilov insisted. That brought Culper out of his chair. He did not even need to pretend to be aghast.

"You do not *compromise* for *God,* " he snapped. "I'll take no *compromise* for my faith, lest God decide to *compromise* when He comes to judge me. What I believe and what Simon ben Zakkai believed is not open to concession." Disgust freighted his words.

As Culper had known it must, the argument raged on for another hour and more. In the end, the vote was much as he had feared. His proposal was narrowly defeated. Despite his expectations, he felt genuine anger when the tallies were read. He thumped a fist on the railing before him and stood up once more, uncaring that there was other business the Conclave had yet to cover. "This is on your heads," he spat out.

Then, gathering his magisterial robes around him and with as much dignity as he could muster, the curator of justice left the hall.

From his room, Colin heard the sudden wail of the child. He could feel the VeilBeast laughing at the surge of emotion the sound engendered in Colin. A flood of images—memories—surged through his mind as he stood at the windows of his old rooms inside Nexus, seeing nothing of the city spread below him. Instead, Kiri's face was there; smiling, almost fierce in her love for him. Colin saw her as he often had in those frantic last months, her body swollen with life. He remembered how it felt to place his hand on the hard mound of her belly and feel the shape of the child.

Unbidden tears filled his eyes. He wanted to reach out and take hold of that phantom Kiri, to lose himself in her touch. He blinked and she was gone. There was only Nexus and the stone flanks of the Barrens.

Colin tried to bring back that memory, yet he could see only Horeb and Kiri's mutilated body sprawled at his feet. Distantly, he heard again the sound of the crowd's horror and his own helpless wail.

The VeilBeast chortled.

"Colin Exori?" came a soft voice behind him. He hadn't heard the door open, but he knew the muskiness.

"Yes, Pale?"

"Anna Crowell has given birth, Colin Exori. You have a daughter." Colin could hear the accusation in the Stekoni's voice: *You should have been there. You raped her and abused her and you wouldn't even give her that small comfort. Do you wonder why she would not forgive you when you asked?* The VeilBeast growled in quick anger at that. Colin forced the rage down, knuckling his hand against the windowpane. "Will you come with this one to see her, Colin Exori?"

Colin ignored the request, ignored Pale. In the window he saw nothing but his own faint reflection. "How is the child?" he asked.

There was the faintest shift in odor. "She is normal, Colin Exori. Dark hair and eyes. Healthy." The curtness sounded so odd in the Stekoni that Colin turned. Pale stood near the door, as far from Colin as she could be in the room. Her fur was uncharacteristically matted and dull. The golden eyes were half closed and the long, wide mouth was opened slightly, showing the flattened crowns of her teeth. A suspicion came to Colin.

"How is Crowell?" he asked. "Anna?"

"This one wondered if you would care." Underlids blinked, laying a satin glaze over the pupils. "She is exhausted and tired, as you might expect." There was the slightest emphasis on the "you." "Otherwise it was a normal enough delivery. The doctors all say that the many Veil passages have given neither mother nor child any apparent damage."

"I wasn't worried about that."

"This one had worried. Anna Crowell had worried, even if she said nothing."

You bastard. You bastard. The unspoken words hammered at

Colin and the VeilBeast reared against its restraints, howling to be loosed. "Tell Crowell that . . . that I'm happy to hear the news."

"That is all Colin Exori would say?" He could hear the caution in that question, balanced precariously between servility and scorn. "Will the Sartius Exori wish to see the child?"

"Later, Pale. Later."

FirstBred Pale sniffed and bowed. Hands slid over the young-pouches. "As the Sartius Exori wishes."

She moved toward the door. Colin could see the hurt in her demeanor, and he called to her. "Pale, please. I . . . I'm very grateful to you for all you've done. I hope you know how much I've needed your loyalty. A lot of others would have left me."

"The Sartius Exori has his own needs. This one understands that."

"When all this is over, Pale, what will you do?"

"This one has no thoughts on that at all, Colin Exori. She does not look to the future at all. The Voice decreed that this one must watch for the Sartius Exori. Now that she has found him, she was asked to remain. Beyond that, she has little curiosity."

"Is that because you feel there's not much of a future?"

"The child is a guarantee of a future, Colin Exori."

"I wish that I had not let that happen."

Pale blinked. Her delicate fingers smoothed the fur on her stomach. "Yet the Sartius Exori did so. It is finished. A fact. The birth of one's child should be an occasion for joy. It would have been so for Colin Exori if Kiri Oharu had been the mother."

At that admonition, the power within him stirred, snapping its bonds. Colin could not fully hold it back. "Don't preach to me, FirstBred Pale," he snarled. "The woman was never *held* here. She could have left. She brought this upon herself as her *own* punishment."

"This one believes that a child is not punishment." Pale quailed before his shouting, raising her hands as she retreated.

"Then that one should keep her beliefs to herself. Go attend to your precious child, Pale, and leave me alone." Colin pivoted away, hating the way he had reacted so harshly and wishing he could take back the words. But he could not, and the VeilBeast struggled against the apology he might have made. It was easier to give in, to pretend to stare down at the canyoned streets.

"This one will do so," Pale whispered. Colin heard the door open, then click shut.

He slapped his palm against the window, making the pane shiver.

"Damn," he muttered in a choking voice. He laid his head against the cool glass. "Why did You ever choose me? I don't want this at all. Let history hate someone else."

Above the stone sky of Nexus, the ships circled, waiting for him to lead them.

Her scent: an abiding satisfaction overlaid with a patina of caution, marbled with pride. In the darkness of the chapel, it was all ThinShell Third Darkness could sense of the newcomer. It was enough; she felt her own body odor shift in response. She shook herself from the half-trance of prayer. "The word from Nexus is pleasing then, nestkin beloved?"

The warmth of GoldenShell Third Darkness settled beside her. A hand touched her intimately. "This one has been told that all the pieces have been placed. She prays to MolitorAb that all proceeds as has been foretold."

"GoldenShell Third Darkness has done all she can. Her nestkin beloved is proud of the honor she has brought to our name. Would she pray with this one?"

"Only if she will promise to join her nestkin later in her rooms."

ThinShell Third Darkness leaned her head on GoldenShell's shoulder. That was answer enough.

Their scents mingled and fused.

CHAPTER TWENTY-SEVEN

If there arises in the midst of thee a prophet, or a dreamer of dreams—and he give thee a sign or a wonder, and the sign or the wonder come to pass, whereof he spoke unto thee—saying: "Let us go after other gods, which thou hast not known, and let us serve them"; thou shalt not hearken unto the words of that prophet, or unto that dreamer of dreams; for the Lord your God putteth you to proof, to know whether ye do love the Lord your God with all your heart and with all your soul.

OLD TESTAMENT, Deuteronomy XIII:2–4

The word came unto the Sartius Exori, who was sitting with the Harlot. The disciple FirstBred Pale bore the news, and her countenance was troubled as she spoke: "An ill thing has happened to the Ascendant Vesilov."

Yet in his power, the Sartius Exori was already aware of this. He turned to FirstBred Pale with a laughing mockery and said: "You who are least of my disciples should still know that what has happened is not an ill thing at all. It was as I wished. When one wants peace, he prepares for peace. When one desires war, he prepares as for war."

THE TESTAMENT OF JOSHUA, 81:12–14

The security for Ascendant Dmitri Vesilov's mission to Nexus was as good as it could be, given the circumstances. Vesilov's own people would have been far happier if Colin Fairwood could have been induced to come aboard the Holdings cruiser that ferried the Ascendant from Old Earth, but all efforts to bring that to pass had been futile. Colin would not meet with Vesilov on any naval ship. The message from the Holdings embassy was almost whimsical: "Mohammed insists on the mountain coming to him."

The Nexian ambassador had been appointed by Joseph Culper. Hearing that Vesilov would be entering the city-world, Greg

Mahring smiled to himself and patted the leather case in front of him. Vesilov's arrival indicated that the widespread gossip circulating through Buntaro circles was true: the Sartius Exori had caused the Ascendant to come to Nexus so that he might be destroyed. From what Greg had heard, one of the Sabbai was the source of that statement: not that it mattered. The Ascendants were, without exception, vermin; it would please MolitorAb to see them eradicated. Greg intended that Vesilov would die by his, Greg's, hand.

He was twelve, a thin and scrawny towhead whose voice had yet to fully change. This deed would mark his entrance into manhood, Greg knew; it would be a foreshadowing of future greatness. He dreamt that one day he would be among the Sabbai, close to the Sartius Exori as Joshua was now, as the martyr Aaron had been.

The Nexian police forces had been working overtime for more than a month, ever since the Exori had returned. The population of the worldlet had been significantly increased by the influx of his followers; more arrived each day. With Vesilov's arrival, the workload doubled. Security around the Cathedral of Simon, which was also the Holdings embassy and where Vesilov would stay, was increased. Everyone going onto the cathedral grounds was, without exception, searched. All those on Nexus who had Buntaro affiliations—especially those suspected or convicted of illegal activities—were interviewed and warned. The officers assigned to escort Vesilov from the port to the cathedral were familiarized with their faces, while several of the more potentially dangerous of the fanatics were arrested on minor and sometimes wholly falsified charges, to spend a convenient day tucked away.

Greg Mahring was not in any of the dossiers, not among the multitude of photographs, not on any of the records. He was far too new in Buntaro circles.

There was no way to move Vesilov from the port to the Cathedral of Simon without some minimal exposure, even if the man had been willing to submit to all the security requests. But the Ascendant adamantly refused most of the precautions. "I won't be bullied," he told Eric Shore, head of the unit in charge, during their holowave conversation. Vesilov's chins bobbed with fervor. "I am an Ascendant, not a parcel. I've no reason to fear my people or the ones who have fallen from the path. We're here to create a new peace; God will not allow anything to interfere."

At which Shore had winced unhappily. "He might as well tell them to take aim and fire," he muttered to himself after Vesilov had terminated the contact. "He's got a hell of a lot more faith in God than *I* have."

Most of the difficulties lay in the form of Nexus itself. There was finite room in the cavern-world—only so much space that could be utilized, so much expansion that could be done. Certain areas had to remain solid for structural purposes, and upward and downward room was limited. In addition, the mining tunnels had been there long before the settlers; their layout had been a major consideration in the plans for Nexus. The areas that worried Shore the most were the port elevators (for even the Exori had been caught there) and the exiting from the car that would transport Vesilov from the port to the cathedral. There were few ground vehicles in Nexus, and most of them were used for public transportation. None of the buildings had facilities for cars such as Shore had seen on other worlds: elaborate underground complexes with shielded entrances where diplomats could exit with impunity. Here, Vesilov *could* be driven onto the cathedral grounds and the gates shut behind him (though a distant sharpshooter might still be able to attempt something), but Ascendant Vesilov would not even allow them that small luxury.

He insisted upon addressing the crowd before the cathedral gates. He insisted that the shields that protected him from attack while in the car be dropped so he could "fully commune" with his people.

"He's more likely to 'fully commune' with his dear departed ancestors," Shore commented. "But let him go."

Shore sat in the car beside Vesilov, who in turn was seated alongside Senator Marie Belham of Nexus. Shore could have stayed behind at the communications center, but he'd given that task to his lieutenant. It felt better to be active, riding with the Ascendant from the port and personally overseeing all the arrangements. The car was cramped and slow; the shield generators hung from its sides like pontoons and shrilled with an annoying midrange hum that he quickly came to hate. It seemed that all of Nexus was watching for Vesilov, for the streets were dense with onlookers, strangely muted through the shielding. "Any problem, Chris?" he subvocalized. Her voice trilled in his right ear.

"Nothing, Eric. Carter pulled some would-be hero from one of the buildings along your route—the idiot was going to use a laser gun. Said it would be payment for Horeb. Wouldn't have gotten through the screens, of course. Any of the Buntaro on the 'Watch' list we'll move back away from you. Keep your eyes open, boss, but everything looks fine so far. You've done what you could; what more could they ask, right?"

"Yeah," he growled back. "Just take my job and pension plan."

She laughed.

Scanning the streets, Shore could spot his people scattered through the crowds, noticeable because their attention was not on the car but on the people crowding the pavement between the barricades. He tried to relax a little—there was nothing he could do at the moment; anything that got past the shields would likely fry him at the same time. Vesilov was nodding and waving to the faces sliding past despite the fact that most of them seemed neutral or even vaguely hostile; Senator Belham slouched in her own seat, looking uncomfortable and a little pale. She smiled wanly at Shore, who shrugged massive shoulders and smiled back.

"Uh-oh." Chris.

"What, lady?"

"Somebody blew it, down by the cathedral—let the crowd through the barricades. There's a small mob milling around by the gates; we're trying to move them back again, but you might have to wade on through them."

"Carol's in charge there, right? Tell her to get her ass in gear. Slipups like this shouldn't happen. I don't want Vesilov surrounded in that place—I want an open way out if we have to make a fast break. And make double sure she's got people up on the roofs."

"Already checking, boss."

Shore noticed that the senator was watching him nervously. He gave her a reassuring smile that had no feeling at all behind it. "Details," he said. She nodded back.

The Cathedral of Simon was large and rarely more than a quarter full. More people swirled around the ornate iron gates to the grounds than had ever worshipped within the church's Gothic-style walls. It was situated in the center of the largest cavern in Nexus; the ceiling hung only fifty feet above the tallest steeple. The edifice was designed to dominate and it fulfilled that function magnificently, overshadowing the clean and low lines of the nearest buildings. Isolated, vain, it brooded over on Nexus, glowering like an old man trying to shame his grandchildren.

People were scattered along its flanks. The crowd wasn't as large as Shore had expected—a thousand, perhaps less—and the majority of them wore prominent triangles proclaiming them to be Zakkaist. The Holdings guards standing on the far side of the closed gates seemed relaxed enough. Shore frowned—Carol still hadn't managed to get everyone cleared away from the gates. There would be a delay here even if Vesilov had not wanted to flap his mouth at the people.

"Tell the driver to stop now," Vesilov said ponderously. A stubby hand smoothed his golden robes and patted the tracing of hair on his balding skull. "And please get those shields down, Captain Shore. I told you they wouldn't be necessary."

Shore sighed inwardly, squelching an impulse to inform the Ascendant of the laser gunman. "As long as you understand that it's against my better judgment, Ascendant Vesilov." He waited, but the man said nothing. Shore tapped the communicator to the driver's compartment. "Put this thing as close to the gates as you can and keep her powered. Then drop the shields."

He loosened the flap of the holster under his jacket.

The annoying whirr of the shields cycled lower. The car shuddered to a halt. Vesilov stood up to the sound of scattered cheering as Shore and the senator flanked the big man. Shore switched channels on his throat microphone. "Carol?"

"Everything's fine, boss."

"Not until those gates are clear, they're not."

"It'll be done in a minute. Promise."

"Any faces?"

"Not in this crowd. Not a one is on the list."

"Good. Keep 'em back anyway."

"You got it."

Vesilov had launched into what was obviously a prepared speech, droning on about brotherhood and hands extended across the Veils. Shore heard it all distantly. His attention was on the perimeter of the audience, on the sea of faces. He scanned them, trying to spot anything before it became a problem.

He nearly missed it despite his vigilance.

He'd seen the boy a few times in his survey of the crowd. The youngster wore the Zakkaist triangle; if his attention was too much on Vesilov, that could be expected in a devout follower. The boy hadn't moved; if he had, Shore might have noticed how one leg was held stiff and immobile. Shore's attention was on the other spectators when the blond kid reached into a slit in his pants leg and pulled out a thick metal rod. The boy was already sprinting the five meters toward the open car when Shore caught the motion in his peripheral vision. The boy was about to leap, the end of that stick pointing straight at Vesilov's left side; the Ascendant hadn't seen the disturbance yet, though faces were turning from him and a shout rose from the crowd.

Shore knew what the kid held—an altered crowd-control prod, overcharged and set to deliver its full load as soon as it touched. The thing would scorch right through clothing, delivering a searing, lethal current that would send its victim into immediate cardiac arrest.

Shore dove for the boy.

They collided in midair, the prod arcing by Vesilov and missing him by centimeters. Shore lost his grip on the boy as he struck the pavement, dazed. He saw the boy swing the prod around toward him and rolled as he reached up, somehow finding the boy's wrist. Ungently, Shore used the momentum of his attack, swinging up to his knees and propelling the boy into the gates. The prod rang on iron; quick sparks sizzled, crackling as the prod welded itself to the gate. The boy screamed and let go of the weapon, his hand blistered; he huddled on the ground in a fetal position, howling. Two guards wrestled the child onto his stomach and pinned him there.

Vesilov gaped at it all. Shore waved his arm at the guards. "Get those damn gates open!" he shouted. "Driver! Move it—and get those shields back up!"

The kid screamed as the car accelerated past him. "I did it for the Sartius Exori! Someone else will get you, bastard! Bastard!" One of the guards cuffed him silent.

Shore waited until the car was through the gates and Vesilov relatively safe on Holdings grounds. Then he got to his feet groaning and moved over to the knot of people around the boy. Carol came up beside him as Shore shook his head at the youth. "Just a baby," she said.

"So much for suffering the little children," Shore said. He glanced toward the cathedral, where Vesilov was jogging with undignified speed from the car to the main doors.

Shore tugged at the handle of the prod. It was warm to his touch, firmly affixed to the gates.

"Okay," he said. "It's over. Now let's get the mess cleaned up."

Colin wasn't certain of what he'd expected to see or what he'd expected to feel. The VeilBeast was coiled in his gut, watching but quiescent for the moment. He cradled the baby in arms that were suddenly clumsy and leaden, and brushed back the coverlet around her face.

The baby was a fragile bundle of unexpected, active life, a

pouting midget full of sleepy animation. Her mouth was too tiny, fine sculptured like the rest of the round face. She wriggled in the crook of his elbow; startlingly blue eyes fluttered open and gazed up at him. Colin knew the effect of his face too well: he expected the child to pucker her face and wail.

She did not. She only stared at the gliding muscles and the net of veins in open-mouthed fascination. Her mouth twitched, and her breath was warm and sweet.

Colin smiled. When he touched her, the miniature fingers closed around his thick forefinger. Her grip was surprisingly strong, and Colin nearly laughed.

Your daughter. Your child. Rachel, Rachel. Even the VeilBeast would not mock the emotions that were racing through him. Colin sighed deeply; he was aware of a gathering pressure at the corners of his eyes. Without looking away from his child, Colin spoke to Anna Crowell, who was sitting on a windowsill in the nursery. "Rachel. The name suits her, Anna—a good choice." The infant's gaze roamed Colin's face, her eyes wide and very large. "I see a lot of you in her."

He glanced at Anna then and saw an unexpected fragility in her. Anna's lower lip was caught between her teeth, and one hand toyed with the lacing of her collar. The emerald glow of phoslamps gleamed from the cityscape behind her, making it difficult to see her face clearly, but Colin thought her features seemed drawn, more strained than ever before.

"Please don't try to be kind to me, Colin. I don't need the confusion and I don't need the lies." Her voice was soft and weary. Her dark hair hung in dull strings over her shoulders, and her skin was colorless against the scarlet cloth of the robe she wore. She pulled the robe tighter around her and rubbed her temples, looking away from Colin. "I've lost everything I had, being with you. I've lost my vocation as a priest, lost my faith, lost my respect. You've left me empty and used, Colin. When I decided to give you the child I'd lost for you, I told myself that I'd leave as soon as it was over. I was going to walk out and try to put something back inside my soul."

Her hands dropped to her lap like helpless birds. Her chin lifted. "Now I don't know," she whispered. "I don't know if I have the strength to leave her."

Colin hugged Rachel, swaying her gently. The huge, azure pupils moved, blinking. "There's no reason for you to leave, Anna. Stay. I won't drive you out."

Her inhalation was nearly a sob. "You don't understand at all. *She* holds me. Rachel holds me; nothing else. All along, I told myself that this wasn't *my* child. I was a breeding machine for your use. Nothing of *me* was involved at all, just my body. Yet..." Another breath. Anna leaned her head back against the window. Her eyes were closed, her hands knotted in the lap of her robe. "If I stay with you, I'd stain her with my hate, Colin. I'd poison her with all the bitterness in my heart and turn her into something dark and awful and empty like myself. She'd always see that her mother and father had no affection for each other at all, that she was the product of revenge and loathing. Not love, not even lust: nothing good at all. I don't want her to know that, Colin. I don't want her to hate us both or have to turn to one and abandon the other."

"Anna..." Colin sat on the bed near her. Their bodies were close and Colin saw Anna shift her legs so that they would not touch. "I *did* use you, and I've asked you to forgive me for that. I *did* hate you because of what I thought you'd done, and now I've found that I can't hate you anymore. Can't you believe that the same might happen for you?"

"No." Her reply was firm and so quick that he knew she'd already formed the answer before he finished the question. Her head came down and her dark pupils met his gaze. "*I* hate *you,* Colin. There's no affection in me for you at all. Nothing. You've destroyed Anna Crowell completely, broken her down just the way you'd intended. I don't know *what* I believe anymore. I don't know that I can worship a God who would do to someone what She's done to you or me, and I certainly can't condone all the killing done in your name. I know," she said, anticipating his protest, "I know that I've caused death myself, and I know that my old church is responsible for its share as well. None of that matters. I don't want to be known as the Sartius Exori's consort or for Rachel to be the hated Exori's daughter. Damn it, Colin, I didn't even want to *care* about her, but I do. I look at her and sometimes I start to cry; I feel her sucking at my breast, taking her life from me, and all I can do is hold her and whisper to her that I love her. I didn't want that. I didn't want it at all."

Rachel tugged at Colin's captured finger. He pulled back, but she wouldn't release him. He touched the fingertip to her mouth instead and she began to suck reflexively. He could feel the hard ridge of her gums. Colin looked up and found Anna staring at the child. "Anna..." The VeilBeast rose, and Colin felt its presence in his words. "Take her with you. Go away from here."

"No!" Anna sat up, hugging herself with thin arms. Her hair lashed her neck as she shook her head. "I let this happen so that I could give her to you. There was no other reason."

"Then stay. We could—"

"Could *what?* We've nothing at all to offer her. We'd tear at each other if I stayed, and all that would do is hurt her. If you wanted us to have a relationship, you should have thought about it a hell of a lot earlier. The best I can say now is that I feel very sorry for you. You might have been a decent person before MolitorAb took you. Now you don't control things at all. You can't make any decision without first praying to your God to see if it's allowed and then checking with the Sabbai to see if it's fine with them as well. You can't make me like you, Colin. That's too much of a miracle to ask."

The VeilBeast uncoiled, exerting its familiar pressure in his mind. Colin listened and found himself melding with the Presence. "If you truly thought that I was a monster, you wouldn't consider leaving Rachel behind, Anna."

She sighed. "Yes. You're right. You're not entirely a monster, and there are a few good people with you: FirstBred Pale, Samuel. They'll look after her if you can't or won't. I don't think you can escape what MolitorAb desires you to do. You can't escape war, Colin."

Then Anna's control broke all at once and she was crying unashamedly, her arms wrapped tightly around her, her knees drawn up to her chest. "Colin, don't you see how this is tearing at me? I don't have any options at all that I like. All I want is what's best for her. You can't bear a child and give her life without becoming attached—at least I've found that *I* can't. The child was my payment to you, my payment to Kiri's soul. Now the debt's paid." Anna took a deep breath. Her cheeks were wet and smeared with green reflections from the phoslamps. "In the week since I gave birth, I've almost taken my own life. Two times I've almost done it."

"Anna—" Colin reached out to touch her; the VeilBeast tried to stop the motion but Colin forced his will through the resistance. He stroked her cheek, cradling the child in his other arm. He expected Anna to turn her face from him, but she didn't. He felt a shiver as his finger brushed her skin.

"I'm serious, Colin," she said. "If you doubt it, feel under the pillow—the knife is there. I was always told that suicide was a sin, that a suicide's soul would never find God. That wouldn't stop me. I don't think I'll ever find God now; that's a guilt *your* soul will have to share. It was just that I was too much of a coward to take that way out. I didn't want to leave her that way, even if she would never know or understand."

Anna nodded at Rachel.

Colin was empty of words. Even the VeilBeast was silent. *The great prophet, so full of MolitorAb's chaos and destruction, and so fucking helpless before this woman's agony. Where's the comfort, Beast? What can you give me for this?* Colin pulled his finger away from Rachel—too hard. The child whimpered. He rocked her against his chest until she was quiet.

In the silence of those moments, the decision came to him. Colin wasn't sure if the resolution had its genesis in him or in the lurking presence inside. He glanced down at the baby and knew. Gently, he lowered his head and kissed her forehead. *The Sartius Exori must be the Black Beginning,* the VeilBeast whispered to him, *but black is the melding of all colors. You cannot have darkness without first having light.*

He tucked the covers around Rachel, then handed his daughter to Anna. Holding the child, Anna stared at Colin as he rose and walked to the door. His hand on the knob, Colin turned back to them. "If I died, would you come back for her?" he asked.

"Yes," Anna said immediately. "Yes."

Colin nodded. With the VeilBeast peering out from his eyes, he could see the emotions in her—the deep aquamarine of her bond with the child and the surging, sick yellow of her hatred for him. The truth of her answer were two bright darts of silver. "Then take her now," he said. "Take her before I have a chance to love her too. The Sartius Exori is only a beginning. I'd have to leave her too soon. She needs you more than me."

Anna only nodded. Her arms tightened around Rachel protectively.

"Just tell her . . . tell her that her father wished it could have been different," Colin said.

Without waiting for a reply, he wrenched open the door.

FirstBred Pale was waiting in the corridor outside. Looking at Colin's face, she saw the odd sadness there; she smelled the VeilBeast and was surprised at the sweetness of the Presence's odor. "Colin Exori," she said.

Colin swung around to face her. His face was touched with deep weariness; his smile flickered, pulling coiled muscles through his cheeks. "Yes, Pale?"

"This one was sent to give you news," she said, deciding not to question him about his meeting with Anna and his daughter. "This one is sorry to disturb you so soon after ... after your visit, but Joshua insisted that you would need to know." She knew that Colin saw her nervousness. She forced her hands to stop moving near her young-pouches. "Ascendant Vesilov has left Nexus."

The VeilBeast snarled into quick rage. "What?" Colin snapped. Pale stepped a pace away from him.

"Yes, Sartius Exori," she answered. "There was trouble on his arrival—one assassin was taken from a rooftop, another attacked at the gate, and a crude bomb exploded on the cathedral grounds an hour later. All were Buntaro caused, and all those arrested claimed that they were fulfilling the will of the Sartius Exori."

Pale caught conflicting scents: Colin's confusion, the VeilBeast's exultation. "Vesilov has left without talking? He believed that?"

Pale nodded sadly. "This one regrets that it is so."

"Can we contact him aboard the cruiser?"

"This one attempted to do so over Joshua's protests. She hoped that the Sartius Exori would wish to reopen negotiations..." Pale paused, uncertain.

"And?"

Her long mouth twisted, her body jerked with a shiver-shrug. "This one could see that the Ascendant Vesilov was truly frightened by his experiences. The Ascendant would say only that if the Sartius Exori desires war so much, the Holdings could oblige him."

Pale cast her gaze to the floor as the VeilBeast grinned in triumph. "Then the Ascendant broke contact," she continued.

"Let him stew a few days. It's just a trick to get me to come to him. He's just trying to save some of his pride."

"That is what this one thought at first," Pale answered. "But Nexus Port has told us that the Holdings cruiser has left its berth and is moving away under system drive. They have said that they will return to Old Earth."

"It's a bluff, Pale, They won't jump."

Pale glanced up, hopeful. "Then the Sartius Exori will call them?"

"The Sartius Exori will call the bluff."

"And if the cruiser jumps?"

"Then we'll go after it, Pale," Colin said, and his voice was strange. "All of us."

CHAPTER TWENTY-EIGHT

*The believers who stay at home—apart from those that suffer
from a grave impediment—are not equal to those who fight for the
cause of Allah with their goods and their persons. Allah has given
those that fight with their goods and their persons a higher rank
than those who stay at home. He has promised all a good reward;
but far richer is the recompense of those who fight for Him: rank
of His own bestowal, forgiveness, and mercy.*

KORAN, Women 4:95-96

*I wish that I could promise you riches and rewards. I wish that
I could say that you will all be housed under roofs of gold, that
the treasure plundered in the name of a false God shall be placed
in your hands, that MolitorAb will enter into every church of the
Zakkaist shadow-God. But I can't promise any of that. I will say
to you that the Voice placed within me by MolitorAb tells me that
I must go to Old Earth, that I must call on all those faithful who
will follow me. Many of you may well die in this venture; to those
I say that MolitorAb will greet you in the Veils with Her arms wide
to embrace you. For those of us who live, MolitorAb has blinded
my eyes to our road. I pray to Her, I place my trust in Her: you
must all do the same.*

*We will seek our fate within the home of our ancestors. All the
old gods that MolitorAb contains will watch us.*

THE WORDS OF THE SARTIUS EXORI,
Farewell 172:5-7

The mathematics of Veil passage are neither tight nor rigorous.
In the Veils, the dice roll of the universe can be heard, introducing
chance into every equation. Every passage through this nether region
contains its own possibility of failure; a great deal of chance enters
into every vector calculation. This gross margin of error is designed
to prevent a ship from coming back into everyday reality too far

262

within a planetary gravity well: tidal fluctuations would shatter a craft as if it had been hit with a cosmic hammer.

It is a very messy way to die.

Joshua was the first to suggest that Colin ignore the usual built-in leeways. As the only one of the Sabbai to have much understanding of strategy and tactics, Joshua had become de facto commander of Colin's ragtag fleet; the few naval personnel within the group were placed under his leadership. As Joshua explained to the Sabbai and Colin, the plan was dictated by circumstances.

Though naval warfare with farships of necessity took place over thousands of cubic kilometers, with most of the ships out of visual contact, there were still similarities to the days of sailing ships. Position was often the determining factor in success. Given a parity between any two ships' weapons and defenses, the better-placed ship would emerge the victor. In addition, the Veils maintained relatively stable entrance and exit points into real space: on quantum levels, the Veil pathways were snarled and intertwined, yet for practical purposes a pilot moving from Nexus to Old Earth had only a few options for emergence. Given that, it was Joshua's belief that a gamble had to be taken and normal precautions ignored. In that way, their ships, defenseless before the Holdings navy, might come out behind the expected bulwark of Holdings ships. Close to Old Earth, the more maneuverable and smaller ships they possessed would have a slight advantage in speed.

The suggestion caused heated, rancorous discussion among the Sabbai—Samuel and FirstBred Pale especially insisting that the plan was not sane. In the end, Colin railed at them. "I was born on Old Earth," he told them. "It's my right to worship MolitorAb there, and I will *have* it. I'll see us in New York Cathedral, where I once prayed. I'll go alone if I have to; if none of you have any faith in me, then leave now."

That had ended the argument; Pale could only nod at him. Joshua beamed and began to finalize plans.

Kathy Mayer was a Galicht-pilot, sane by her guild's standards but also a devout MulSendero. It was to her ship, the *Luckstone*, that the *Anger* was tethered. The rest of the fleet would follow her through the Veils. If she had doubts concerning Colin's instructions to her before the Veil passage, she didn't voice them. She nodded, she went back to her ship, and she spent the remainder of the time before the passage in prayer.

By all standards, the passage itself was a miracle.

It is not recorded if such a sight was ever seen before—fifteen thousand farships and more shimmering into reality from the distorted landscapes of the Veils. They slid into real space not two days from Old Earth, gleaming in the yellow sun and just beyond lunar orbit. For all of them, this was a moment for prayerful thanks and a stolen glance at the viewscreens, where the bright half-sphere of Old Earth floated.

There was a primordial response to that image, an adrenaline charge. Old Earth. Home. Awe was mixed with a certain fear, for this was also the seat of the Church, the very soil on which the great prophets had walked. Hallan Gelt, even Colin, had been born here. Grandparents and great-grandparents had walked under that sun, beneath that sheen of arching clouds. Seeing Old Earth was like glimpsing a family house long abandoned but still alive with memory.

It was a place at once strange and familiar.

The system drive of the *Luckstone* flared, and the lead farship began to move away from the rest, pulling the *Anger* with her. They all followed after, a small galaxy of beacons drifting inward.

"Hello, *Anger.*" The call was from *Luckstone;* it was Kathy's voice.

FirstBred Pale was the first to stir. Colin, the only other person on the farship, had yet to move within his cocoon of coils formed by the *Anger's* nervelinks. "Colin Exori?" Pale called softly. Colin's eyes flickered open; his tongue licked at dry lips. "She still wouldn't talk," he said. "I could hear Her speaking to all the rest of you, and She would say nothing to me." His voice was rough with phlegm. He coughed, clearing his throat. "I'm doing as She wills and she ignores me."

"Colin Exori, the *Luckstone* is calling you."

"I don't understand, Pale. What more can She want of me? Hallan mocks me when I go into the Veils. He says that I've always wanted reassurance." Colin didn't seem to have heard Pale at all. He stared ahead with unblinking, unfocused eyes. Random ligaments and tendons moved in his transparent face.

"Colin Exori?" Colin didn't answer. He remained sitting, the cable of the nervelinks draped over his shoulders. Pale unstrapped herself from her netting and pushed off toward the control module. She had never been good in freefall; she wrenched her shoulder as she tried to stop. Her body oils smeared along the cabinet's face as she fumbled for the controls. "Galicht-pilot Mayer, this one is FirstBred Pale."

"Yeah, I could tell. Where's the Exori?"

Pale glanced back at Colin. He was unresponsive, still lost in the remnants of his Veildream. "The Sartius Exori is yet with MolitorAb," Pale replied. "This one is afraid to disturb him, but she would offer Kathy Mayer congratulations on her passage."

"Uh-huh. It's not something I'd want to try again." Something in the woman's voice narrowed Pale's eyes. "Look, Pale, I think you'd better rouse Colin. Take a look at the sensor reading I'm sending over to you now." Numbers flickered green on a screen to Pale's right. "Those are what I'm getting from outward, where the damn Holdings fleet should be."

The array meant nothing to Pale—just a random jumble. "This one doesn't see anything—" she began, but the pilot broke in again.

"Damn right. Nothing. Nothing at all. There should be hundreds of those bastards out there waiting to turn us into plasma, and I don't see but one or two. So what's going on?—Joshua's over here muttering to himself."

"This one would not know," Pale said helplessly. The faint tug of the ship's movement twisted her; she clung to the module.

"Check inward toward Luna, Kath." Colin. Pale let her body drift up and around—Colin was awake and alert in his seat, the VeilBeast peering eerily behind his eyes.

"Just a second, Exori...oh, hell." More numbers flickered. "Christ, there they are." They heard both her sigh and Joshua's exclamation in the background. Then Joshua's excited voice shrilled in the speaker. "Exori, this shouldn't be—it would be madness to have deployed the fleet so near the world, unless—"

"Unless someone told them." Colin said it very calmly. "Or unless one of them is also a prophet." His laugh was cold.

"What should we do, Exori? We can't avoid them, and we can't fight them. Should we back out through the Veils again?"

Kathy answered before Colin could speak. "Nope. Not without new calculations and not this close in—the only way into the Veils is too far outward."

"She's right, Joshua," Colin said. "We keep going, that's all. We've come to worship here, to establish MolitorAb on Old Earth. Ignore them."

"And if they fire on us, Exori?"

Colin shrugged, the heavy cables of the nervelinks lifting away with his motion. "Then do what you can," he said. "And pray that you're favored by MolitorAb."

* * *

"I've never seen such a collection of junk, Commander. There's maybe a hundred ships in the group that have any military capability at all, and most of those are so old they creak." The ensign's voice was laden with scorn. He glanced up from his screens to Commander Ericson. Seeing the frown on the officer's wide, flat face, the ensign turned back hurriedly.

"You trust your instruments too much, mister," Ericson said. "You look at them and you don't see the significance of things."

The ensign looked bewildered. "Yes, sir," he said automatically.

Ericson shook his head. He couldn't truly blame the young man; his own temptation was to laugh at this 'invasion.' The devil Fairwood had ships enough, yes, but it was a collection of old derelicts, Galicht-type freighters, and pleasure craft. Firing into the pack of them would inflict terrible and certain damage. . . . It would also mean a lot of useless death, and Ericson was not happy with the idea. The sight of this motley armada on his screens made him hate the ugly Fairwood all the more—for shielding himself with innocents. It was one thing to kill a Buntaro who would gladly kill you first; it was another entirely to do this slaughter.

Still, the curator's instructions had been specific enough. Culper had given Ericson coordinates for the likely arrival of the Exori's ships, and the Ascendant had overridden the protests of all the naval commanders at the idea of concentrating their forces so near Old Earth, where they each would hamper the other. Yet the Sartius Exori had taken the gamble that none of them had believed he'd take. As a military man of long, if pacific, experience, Ericson would never have attempted the stunt himself, but he admired Fairwood's audacity. The commander shuddered to think what might have happened had the normal patrols been out, had the fleet been arrayed in its standard sectors. They could never have caught the farships before the invaders reached Old Earth. Even now the cities might be burning from a near-orbit bombardment.

No matter what the appearance of this fleet, no matter how his stomach recoiled at the thought of ordering his people to fire on the poorly shielded craft, he agreed with Culper's words: "At all costs, keep Fairwood's force from engaging the planetary defenses. Don't let them get that far."

There were three thousand cruisers in the Holdings navy stationed here, hulking behemoths bristling with firepower and heavy shields. The majority of them were in a position to engage Fairwood's group. There were hundreds of other lightly armed, smaller ships available as well. It was a monstrous chess game, and all the heavy pieces were ranked behind Ericson, waiting to swoop down the board. Yet... yet inside that swarming mass of lowly pawns that comprised Fairwood's force there were lurking rooks, and the king itself was disguised as one of the pawns. Ericson was quite a good chess player himself, and he'd often seen the slow, inexorable advance of the pawns. He knew that they had their own danger; that they could hem pieces in, that they could even kill. Ericson was not one to underestimate pawns. Let them get too close and one of the rooks would sweep past. Outmoded as they might be, one of the Fringe cruisers could reduce any of the Great Cathedrals to slag before the satellite defenses could destroy the attacker. Ericson knew the Ascendants—they would not have moved to safer quarters, most of them. Most of them didn't take Fairwood's threat seriously at all.

Ericson liked none of his options. That made his dislike of Fairwood deep and abiding.

"Contact all fleet captains, Ensign," Ericson said. "Keep pace with the farships; don't let them get in front of us, and be ready to engage. Try to disable those that you can, but don't worry about being too fine about it—I don't want anything to get past: is that clear?"

"Yes, sir."

Ericson took a deep breath. He was a burly man; his chest strained at the jacket of his uniform. He let his breath out explosively as he laced his fingers behind his back and then pressed his thin lips together. "Now," he said at last. "Contact this Fairwood for me," he said. "Let's see if he'll take an out."

"Colin Exori, what happened in your veildream?"

Colin brooded in his seat; his head hung down on his chest as his hands idly stroked the smooth casing of the nervelink cables. Fairwood the man sat there, not the Sartius Exori: Colin's scent was that of a troubled mind. The pall of his mood infected FirstBred Pale; her body wrapping was edged with dark oil. She glided in front of Colin, forcing him to look at her, to answer her question.

"Nothing happened, Pale." His heavy-lidded eyes flickered open. His pale eyes were bloodshot. "I asked for a vision and didn't get one, that's all. Hey, I'm a damn prophet, right? It wasn't too much to ask for. I wanted to hear Her voice telling me that all this would turn out well. I wanted to know that what I'm doing would lead to something good in the end." Muscles bunched along his arm as he gripped the nervelink cable tightly. "Pale, am I a monster?"

"This one would not follow a monster, Colin Exori." His pain filled her; she drifted closer and took his hand in her own, staring up at him. "You are the Sartius Exori; that is your conflict."

"They detest me, Pale." This close, she could see the jagged line of scars where flesh met skinbase in his face. She could not imagine how he might once have looked, if he'd been handsome or plain. "Even among my followers, the best I can hope for is fear," he said. "None of you trusts me, none of you feels safe near me. I can see that when people speak to me; they're always on edge, always ready to apologize or back down. Even you, Pale. Even Samuel, who pretends that he doesn't care."

"You are the Sartius Exori," Pale repeated. She didn't know where to begin, didn't know what to say to Colin to ease his torment. She glanced at the viewscreen where Old Earth hung like a mottled ornament and found no inspiration there. If he had been Stekoni, she would have known what to do, how to respond . . . "You are the Prophet. In twenty-five years, in fifty, in a hundred, no one will remember exactly what you were, Colin Exori. You will only exist in tales and legends that have their own truth."

"I'll be the Reviled One, you mean."

"You will be whatever your followers will have made you to be. You will be whatever faith is left behind you, good or ill. This one knows that FirstBred Pale is a different person to each individual who knows her—which is the true FirstBred Pale? But this one thinks that not even Anna Crowell would be without sympathy for you."

"You make it sound so false, Pale."

"No history that is meaningful can be—"

The *Anger's* com-unit chimed, cutting off Pale's reply. "Yes?" Colin said.

Joshua's voice came over the speakers—Colin still had the visual links off. "Colin Exori, there's a transmission for you being broadcast from Commander Ericson of the flagship *Viceroy*. If you'd like to speak with him, I can route it through some of our other ships so they can't pinpoint the *Anger.*"

Colin nodded wearily. Pale released his hand and pushed herself away toward her netting, watching Colin. "Fine, Joshua. I'd like to talk with him. Acknowledge his message and set up the call."

"It'll take a few moments, Exori."

There was the angry hissing of static, followed by a harsh burst of interference tracking across the wall flatscreen. Then the lines resolved into a face: hard, thick boned, darkly tanned—the face of a person who spent more time on a world than aboard a ship. His shoulders were wide and well muscled, the neck thick and corded; Colin immediately had the impression of someone who enjoyed challenging himself, who would climb a sheer rock face just to see if he could do it. "Colin Fairwood, this is Commander Ericson," the man said. "You and your ships are in violation of Holdings law. You are creating a navigational hazard and are currently within a restricted sector. I would point out that regulations allow me to open fire on your ships should you ignore this warning. I do not wish to go that far; if you will leave this sector and the Holdings, I will take no further action."

Ericson had deeply set brown eyes; they glimmered under the shadow of his brows. "I don't have much desire to end your little expedition, Fairwood," he continued. "It would be too damn easy, by God. But I'll do it if you don't back off. If you have any concern for your people's lives, you'll leave."

Colin flicked a toggle, activating the camera under the flatscreen. On the flatscreen, Colin could see the illumination as a screen in front of Ericson brightened in response. The man scowled, seeing Colin's face. The lines deepened in his rugged face. His response stirred the VeilBeast, which chuckled its amusement far down inside Colin. "What's the matter, Commander? Aren't I as pretty as you thought I'd be?" Colin glanced at FirstBred Pale, and Pale caught his thought: *Monster. You see?* "Well, I remember how my face came to be this way, thanks to the tender mercies of the Zakkaist church."

Colin knew the conversation was being monitored everywhere within the two opposing groups. It was also likely that the wideband broadcast was being relayed to Old Earth and the Ascendants as well. That didn't bother Colin—there were representatives of the Fringes press aboard the farships, and each would garner his or her share of propaganda. "We've done nothing wrong, Commander Ericson," Colin declared. "All we wish to do is worship with our faithful on your world."

"You *have* no faithful on my world, Fairwood."

The VeilBeast snorted, and Colin gave a tight smile. He could feel the Presence surging, climbing, growing. "You won't *allow* them to be visible, Commander. You close your eyes and pretend that they don't exist because you can't see them. Children do that all the time. No world fails to know MolitorAb. You can't shield yourselves forever. We intend to meet with the MulSendero here and pray with them. That's all. If that constitutes a threat to you, it is only your own perception that makes it so."

"Your religion is outlawed within the Holdings. *You* are wanted on outstanding warrants from Chebar and Medee."

"I am not responsible for stupid *laws*, Commander. I obey a higher authority." The VeilBeast hammered against its walls, making Colin's voice almost strident. Yet there was a compulsion to it as well; FirstBred Pale watched openmouthed from her netting. Ericson seemed quizzical, staring at the distorted mask of Colin's face. The commander's response was slow. He stumbled into it as if suddenly remembering to speak. "I don't intend to let you stall by arguing with me, Fairwood. Turn your ships around. If you don't, I'll be forced to take offensive measures neither of us wants to see."

"You'd be killing innocents, Commander. Your men would be firing on..." Colin paused and the Presence twisted his face into a leering grin. "Well, to resort to cliché, you'd be killing blameless men, women, and children. This isn't a military expedition you're confronting, Commander. It's simply a group of devout worshipers of the true God. Ordinary people. Your threats seem rather beastly and harsh to me. Can you really expect your gunners to obey you, knowing that the hulls they breach will spill out entire families like their own? Picture the faces as they die, Commander Ericson; visualize the torn bodies, the explosive decompression, the maimed crying out with soundless screams—then imagine that happening to your wife, your children, simply because they were of the wrong faith."

Colin's voice throbbed with the VeilBeast's power; he could feel it burning in his throat, the words tumbling unbidden from some well within him. Pale gawked; even Ericson backed away from his screen, puzzled and hesitant.

"You have military craft among this devout, peaceful group of yours, Fairwood," the man said at last. His sarcasm was flat and ineffective against the throbbing energy of Colin's voice.

"And how many of your cruisers would be required to neutralize them, Commander? Three? Four? I didn't ask for them to be here; I'll even send them back. Now, is *that* satisfactory, Commander?" Colin's voice was sweet reason—there seemed to be no logical reason for Ericson to deny his requests. In Ericson's cruiser, the crewmen all waited for the inevitable agreement. Only Pale was with Colin, only she could smell the electric tang of the VeilBeast.

Yet Ericson shook his head slowly, as if against his own feelings. "That's an empty offer, Fairwood. You have already revealed your intentions. I have no guarantee that you haven't loaded some of your farships with weaponry. Turn around, Fairwood. Turn around for the sake of all those innocents you claim to be so concerned about."

Colin shook his head in return, and his voice was sadness, his voice was pity. Ericson seemed so gruff compared with the Sartius Exori, so unbending and unreasonable. "No, Commander. You can't keep the Sartius Exori from his own home. I have come to pray where I first prayed. Do what you must, and may MolitorAb forgive you for it."

Colin cut power to the screen. Ericson's face dissolved into darkness even as he began to speak.

It might have worked.

The bluff might never have been called. The strange assemblage of farships might have descended unmolested. Certainly Ericson seemed shaken by his conversation with Colin Fairwood. He immediately sent an urgent, coded message to Ascendant Culper and the rest of the Conclave, who immediately met via com-link in an extraordinary session. In the intervening hours, the *Anger* and the rest pushed forward toward the swelling curve of Old Earth. Already they were beyond the plane of lunar orbit, and Ericson fretted about the ability of his lumbering cruisers to keep the Fringe ships enclosed. When his orders finally came, after an acrimonious debate among the Ascendants, nothing had changed. "None of the farships shall be permitted to land," was the consensus. Ericson could only shake his head.

The Holdings fleet had never been tested under battle conditions. None of his people had ever been required to fire on more than unmanned drones. The commander wondered, when it came time to stop Fairwood, how many of them would sit before their override switches, unable to act. They'd all heard Fairwood, and Ericson had seen the fear in the eyes of his subordinates.

It might have worked.

The priest SlowBorn Brightness was aboard the *Vigilance*. Most of the thousand or so Stekoni among Colin's followers were there as well. As one of the Sabbai, SlowBorn Brightness was the chief religious leader of the Exori's Stekoni, and the *Vigilance*—unlike the cramped farships—had the capacity to separate its human and Stekoni passengers. None of the Stekoni enjoyed being there, for it certainly put them at risk, but logistics had dictated the arrangements. With all the uncertainty and outright fear this venture had produced among them, none of the Stekoni particularly noted the odd listlessness of their priest.

Her scent was a heavy musk, the odor of troubled contemplation. The robe of her office was mottled across her sloping back and ringed under her frail arms with patches of copious secretions. Had she felt that she could, SlowBorn Brightness would have sought out one of her followers and comforted herself in that way. She felt she could not afford the intimacy, could not afford to let one of them sense what she was feeling.

Nothing had gone as she had been told it would. The Stekoni hierarchy had thought that the Sartius Exori could be controlled. They had thought they could use him to turn human against human. SlowBorn Brightness had never agreed with the strategy, but her superiors had insisted that MolitorAb had given them the Sartius Exori to use for the good of the MulSendero. Since the majority of humanity was not of their religion, since that same majority had cast out the Stekoni ungraciously, since the Zakkaist dislike for the Stekoni was so obvious, it was only rational that the Sartius Exori was a tool to be used against them.

None of the Stekoni would ever have thought to oppose the Zakkaist church directly. The concept had never occurred to them. It was safer to let them weaken themselves.

For a time, that had worked well. The theory had held until Colin Fairwood had shown that he could unify as well as divide. The tool had become too unwieldy to handle, and the Stekoni were suddenly fearful he would come to an agreement with the Zakkaists who hated them.

SlowBorn Brightness had, under the compulsion of the higher-caste priests, done several things she considered shameful since she had joined the Sabbai. Her worst deed was to let the Holdings fleet know where Colin intended to leave the Veils; she'd also thought that would be the last shameful thing she would have to do. The confrontation was to have been the catalyst that would hurl faction against faction.

Now it seemed that the Sartius Exori had slipped the trap.

Melancholia smelled like dill; resignation was an underscent of basil.

The human crew of the *Vigilance* consisted of civilians and several retired naval officers—a slipshod and inexperienced unit. The deck officer of the third shift was James Murray, a gangly and likable elder whose sinus problems made him more tolerant of the Stekoni than most. The captain, anticipating problems on the shifts to come, was sleeping; the bridge crew was, as usual, understaffed and tired. Murray glanced up from his logbook as SlowBorn Brightness approached. "Good evening," he said. His smile was slow; he seemed to recognize the priest more by her robe than by the fur pattern or facial features.

"Good evening, James Murray, and the blessings of MolitorAb to you. Please, go on with your duties. This one was only restless; she would distract herself here for a time if you do not mind."

"Go ahead," Murray answered with a wave of his hand, his attention already back at the log. "Just don't bother any of the others." He bent his head over the book again. It was perhaps fifteen minutes later, hearing a whisper from one of the crew members, that Murray laid down his stylus to see SlowBorn Brightness standing beside the empty console of the *Vigilant*'s offensive banks. Even then he was not immediately concerned until he noticed that the Stekoni's hand was on the contacts and the lights indicated that the board was, somehow, activated. The nearest person on deck was two meters away.

"SlowBorn Brightness," Murray said very softly. *It must have been an accident,* he thought. *She couldn't have done it deliberately; Stekoni don't ever kill.* The priest seemed transfixed, lost in some inner argument with herself. Her fingers trembled above the contacts but did not touch them. "Please back away from the board, SlowBorn Brightness. Back away; it's live." He slid his hand under his own console, touching a silent alarm that would alert the captain to trouble. At the same time, he tried to gauge the distance between himself and the priest. Around the bridge, they all stared at the Stekoni, silent and wondering.

Murray thought he could make it. He crouched, tensing.

SlowBorn Brightness heard the faint rustle of his clothing, and it broke the stasis that held her. Her hand plunged toward the board as Murray leapt, his hands outstretched.

The pulse of stripped high-energy particles slashed out in the general direction of the Holdings fleet. It hit nothing as alarms shrieked wildly. The actual response was over before anyone could react. Sensors locked on the *Vigilance;* the weapons systems of the Holdings' ships searched their programs and found the appropriate orders; if fired upon, retaliate. At the center of a grid of computer-directed weaponry, the *Vigilance* had no chance at all. Even as Murray belatedly dragged SlowBorn Brightness down, the cruiser glowed like a tiny sun and exploded. Debris slammed against the shielding of the nearest ships.

The deadly, doomed dance began. With a hopeless bravado, the Fringe cruisers began a counteroffensive as farships scattered before them. Harsh commands filled the broadcast bands. Invisible, deadly lightning arced from side to side as shields began to glow a dull, hot orange. The Holdings fleet began to move, closing on the Fringes craft.

It was, quite literally, carnage.

The farships, helpless before the onslaught, fled any way they could. To his credit, Commander Ericson immediately gave the order to ignore any Fringe craft that headed outward, and most of the disabled craft were left to drift. Still, the greater portion of the farships streaked into the barrier of the Holdings navy, trying to shield themselves among the larger cruisers and hoping that in the confusion they might have a chance to escape. Toward Old Earth they went—close to the world, the navy cruisers' ability to maneuver would be curtailed, and none of them could enter an atmosphere at all.

A thousand ships made it past the gauntlet of the navy. Few of those were so lucky twice. The orbital defenses decimated them.

The night sky was full of quick, dying meteors.

The *Anger* was not among them. Her drives had been sheared off in a glancing blow from the *Vigilant's* debris. Intact but helpless, she tumbled with the rest until a Holdings patrol ship made contact with her.

CHAPTER TWENTY-NINE

Man no more knows his own time than fish taken in the fatal net, or birds trapped in the snare; like these the children of men are caught when the evil time falls suddenly upon them.
OLD TESTAMENT, Ecclesiastes 9:12

All prophets see with the eyes of God, and as they walk their road, they can see the end of their time approaching like a mountain of stone. Each prophet is a suicide, for he could have turned aside and chose not to do so. The prophet is but a mere man or woman until the mountain is entered.
THE WORDS OF THE SARTIUS EXORI,
Farewell 173:8

They came to him as he lay helpless in the burning heat.

Kiri was first, holding a red-faced child in her arms. She bent down to kiss his sweating face, straightening again with a sad half smile. "Look, Colin," she said. She brushed the blanket away from the baby's face so that he could see the infant. Dark eyes stared at him. "She's a beautiful child, yours and mine," Kiri said. Colin tried to speak, to move—he could not. He could only gaze at Kiri and the child with silent yearning. "I keep her for you, love," Kiri said. "I tell her how much you would have loved her; when she cries at night I hold her to my breast and rock her, telling her of you. Colin, Colin..." Long, dark hair swayed over Kiri's face as she shook her head. "I pray that She releases you, Colin. You never asked for this, never really wanted it. If you'd known, you would have pushed it all away." She covered the baby again, crooning softly to her, and began to walk away. Colin tried to turn his head to follow her, tried to call out and beg her to stay, but his body lay still, disobedient to his commands. Seeing her again tore open the wound in his soul; his love for her was like a searing brand. Tears slid down the side of Colin's face and he couldn't wipe them away.

He couldn't even call her name. He closed his eyes, wanting to scream his frustration.

"Whom do you weep for, Sartius Exori? Are you crying for all those you have killed in your name?" A cool hand traced the path of moisture on his cheek and he opened his eyes to see Anna Crowell. A hand at either side of his head, she smoothed away the tracks of his sorrow with surprising gentleness. "You should weep for those who live as well, Colin. Weep for the daughter who will never see her father; weep for her mother, who could have loved you if you had let her. Weep for the ones whose spirits you slew yet whose bodies live on."

"Do not weep at all, Sartius Exori." The words came with the musk scent of a Stekoni. The ghost of Crowell dissipated like a fog in the morning wind. Quick heat battered Colin again, and through wavering curtains of air he saw SlowBorn Brightness. "This one will cry for you, for she has made the mistake of the Zakkaists, thinking that she could know the intention of MolitorAb."

"There is no guilt in being a prophet, for the prophet is always mad." Roland Naley stood behind the Stekoni priest, leering over her shoulder. Colin could barely see him in the shifting haze. "Hey, you have no more control of yourself than a damn lunatic in an asylum," Naley crowed, his eyes bright and piercing. "The only reason the common folk let you walk in their streets is because they're afraid you have some power to hurt them. Otherwise, they would lock you away with the other fools who wander around spouting nonsense; they would let you sit in your own excrement in a padded cell and gabble to the walls all day. You're no different, Colin, and no better."

Colin tried to shake his head. He managed only a slight movement, but the motion shimmered outward like a tidal wave, fragmenting the scene before him. Naley and SlowBorn Brightness were swept away, howling. When the world had settled again, there was a sweet breeze, and Huan Su's face peered down at Colin, old and wizened, his oriental features curiously sympathetic.

"Ahh, Colin," the old man wheezed. "If only God had wanted me to live, all this could have been avoided."

Colin tried to speak; this time words came out slowly, gaspingly. "I . . . could have saved you. You wouldn't . . . let me."

"I was a proud man, Sartius Exori. I didn't want my comfortable, familiar world broken. It seemed worth risking death to keep that. You should remember that, my friend." The shadow of a smile tugged at the corners of Su's mouth, and the epicanthic folds crinkled around his eyes. "Many would prefer to die than to change. Even you, perhaps. At least in dying, you learn truth."

"What . . . is the truth then?" Colin asked, pleading.

"I see that you are awake. Good." It seemed a strange thing for Su to have said. Colin blinked, trying to clear his vision, and found that Su's face had altered; it had lengthened and was now more Caucasian than oriental, and the sparse hair was thick and black-flecked gray. Everything swam into sudden focus.

The face was Culper's. Colin lay in a small, bare cell, stretched out on a tatami mattress that had been placed on a cold shelf of concrete perhaps a meter above the floor. He was shackled with his hands above his head, his feet locked to the bottom of the shelf. He could smell the odor of urine and wondered if it was his own.

The Ascendant stood beside him, dressed in a long azure robe with the triangle of ben Zakkai at the breast and the sleeves carefully rolled up. The handsome face was smiling with smug satisfaction.

"Where *are* you?" Culper drawled mockingly, anticipating Colin's question. "That's what most ask when they find themselves here. You're in New York, Colin Fairwood. Home at last, like the prodigal son, though I dare say you won't find a forgiving parent anywhere. Certainly not in these cells below the cathedral."

Colin's body ached, as if he'd fallen down a flight of stairs. Turning his head to one side, Colin could see long, mottled bruises on his arms. He moved his limbs as far as his bonds would allow and found them stiff and balky. Panic began to make him shake, and he took a deep, calming breath. Inside, he could feel the brooding mind of the VeilBeast, curled deep as if asleep or wounded itself. He prodded at it: *Beast, I need your power. Wake up.* It could not be aroused. He could sense only that it watched, quiescent.

"Where's Pale?" Colin asked. "Where are the others?"

"More questions? Ahh, well." Culper shrugged, pouting. With a swirling of his robe's hem, he moved to stand near the blank metal door of the cell. "The Stekoni was captured with you; she is here as well. Two other Sabbai—Joshua the Buntaro and Samuel Conner—were taken from the farship linked to yours. We have other of your followers here as well."

"Miriam? SlowBorn Brightness?"

Culper shrugged again. "I have no news of them, though our reports say that one of the Sabbai escaped back into the Veils. Tell me, Fairwood, do you know how the battle went?" When Colin didn't answer, Culper strode over to him with a snarl, curling his fingers into a tight fist. He let Colin regard the whitened knuckles, the tensed muscles, the grin of pleasure that spread across his face. Then, with a shout, the Ascendant plunged his fist down into Colin's face. Colin heard the *crack* of cartilage as his nose shattered under the blow. Blood spattered across skinbase and ran salty into his mouth. Colin screamed with the pain, writhing against the chains. Bright spikes of light slashed at his eyes; the room whirled around him. He thought he was about to lose consciousness. Cold sweat broke out over his body. He gasped for air.

"Let me tell you," Culper said. His deep voice was very near Colin's ear as Colin fought to breathe, openmouthed. "Let me tell you, Sartius Exori. You lost thirty thousand or more, along with most of the ships you came with. In our fleet, your people killed two hundred and damaged three cruisers slightly. If that had been all, I might be inclined to be kind to you. But a few of your Buntaro fanatics managed to get through the orbital stations. It should please you to know that they descended like burning demons from hell, like the spawn of your devil MolitorAb that they are. Tokyo Cathedral is a ruin now, as is the one in Berlin; the Ascendants living there died with them. Two Ascendants and a half million others, Exori. A half million innocents who had nothing to do with this war. Their souls will point accusing fingers at you when you stand before God, Fairwood."

Colin could feel the pain beginning to subside. The blood flow lessened as a heat spread through his face—the VeilBeast's fingers. Culper gazed down at Colin with eager fascination. He nodded.

"So you truly can't be killed," he said quietly. "But you certainly feel pain, don't you, Fairwood. I wonder just how much damage your body can heal."

Culper turned away abruptly and went to the cell door. He rapped on the frame, still watching Colin. When the guard swung the door open, Culper nodded to Colin's blood-streaked face. "Clean up the bastard and get him some clothing. Then get the other three ready as well; I'll gather the Conclave. We'll want them in the chamber within an hour."

The conclave hall was crowded and warm with the heat of bodies. The Ascendants sweated under the impassive eyes of the cameras, though the recording of this session was to be kept entirely private for the moment. A certain paranoia lurked in the minds of the Church hierarchy—they were not about to allow a live broadcast after the unpredictability Colin had demonstrated in the past. For the moment, the Sartius Exori was theirs. He'd shown no disturbing abilities as yet, but the Ascendants were hedging their bets. Prophet, rogue mutant, latent telepath, charlatan: whatever Colin Fairwood was, he would not be allowed to embarrass them.

The elders were arranged in their tiers, the space between the sloping risers filled with those dignitaries and assistants able to wangle permission from their respective superiors. The mood of the assembly hung somewhere between jovial and serious. The events of the past few days had left them all unsettled. All too painfully, they could feel the quiet symbolism of the two empty seats in their ranks; they had all viewed the pictures of the devastation in Tokyo and Berlin. They were well aware that the Sartius Exori had been directly responsible for the loss of Medee to the Fringes. Each of the Ascendants feared what might have resulted had the thousands of ships at the Pretender's back been warships. While the Holdings public cried for retribution, the feeling of the Ascendants was more akin to relief.

Their own navy was now mobilized under Commander Ericson. At need, they would venture into the Fringes themselves to deal with unrest and future threats. The elders had seen that Ascendant Culper's apprehensions were well founded.

All the murmuring speculation died as the ornate doors at the end of the hall swung back. Colin entered, followed by Pale, Samuel, and Joshua. Weapons out and ready, guards paced alongside them. The prisoners' hands were cuffed, their legs hobbled with short chains.

Colin had seen the hall before, when he had lived in New York. He and Hallan Gelt had once stood in this very place, part of a group of awed tourists. The distant wall behind the Ascendants shone with the symbols of the three mingled faiths, circumscribed by the Zakkaist triangle. Reflections shimmered on the tiled floor, and in their own triangle were arranged the plush seats of the Church's leaders. When Colin had last seen this place, long decades before, the seats had been empty and three great wooden chairs had been standing in the center of the tiers—the places for Allah, Yahweh, and the Father, the guide had explained. Now in that arena was a small circle of metallic rods the height of a man. The Ascendants brooded down on them.

Colin felt their eyes turn to him. The massed enmity was a silent assault. The VeilBeast felt it: the thing stirred, rising through the layers of Colin's mind like some dark creature of the depths seeking sunlight. The VeilBeast tensed at the sight of the Conclave, at the empty circle set before them. Colin and the others were herded between the rods to stand at the circle's center, their restraints clanking on the tiles. Then the guards stepped away and a switch was closed.

Sparks leapt between the tips of the posts. There was a harsh crackling and the sharp smell of ozone. "They're certainly afraid of us," Samuel whispered. He tried to laugh, but his amusement sounded hollow and false.

Colin paced the circumference of the circle. The robed Zakkaists peered down at him; he could see them leaning forward in their seats, examining him like some insect pinned under a microscope. The defiance in the VeilBeast touched Colin, and he turned the ravaged landscape of his face up to them, letting them contemplate the sight.

Within the confines of the rods, the deep fear of FirstBred Pale was a rank stench. Colin smiled quickly at the Stekoni. "This one had thought—" Pale began and could say no more. Underlids hazed her eyes, long fingers knotted together at her waist. Colin hugged her to him for a moment, the handcuffs making the gesture awkward, and stroked the smooth, soft fur of her back. "Be calm, FirstBred Pale. I promise you that you won't die here. *None* of you shall die here," he finished, glancing at the other two.

"I'm not afraid to die for you, Exori," Joshua said. "That would be my glory, as it was Aaron's and Kiri's."

"Then you didn't understand their deaths at all," Colin answered. Motion caught his eyes; Culper was rising. The VeilBeast prodded Colin, and he spoke loudly before the curator could straighten up.

"I had hoped to return home to conciliation. I suppose that I should have expected no better than what I've received. The Church of ben Zakkai has become so weak that it fears even the prayers of the MulSendero."

"You'll speak when you've been asked a question, Colin Fairwood," Culper answered coldly. He smoothed the folds of his robes. "Any further outbursts and I'll have you removed from the room. The Ascendants have gathered to pass their sentence on you."

"A sentence? Then I am to have no trial."

"Do you deny your guilt?" The voice came from the right; Colin turned his head to see Dmitri Vesilov glaring down. There was no sympathy in the man's dark eyes, only a dull, steady loathing. "Do you deny that you fled Chebar illegally in company with a wanted Buntaro terrorist? Will you say that you had nothing to do with the Medee coup? I heard the words of the assassins who came for me when I went to Nexus, and I know who led the murderous farships here. Do you deny that you're Colin Fairwood, the Sartius Exori?"

"Some of what you've said, yes, I deny," Colin answered. "Your 'terrorist' was the woman I loved, whom *you* killed along with my unborn child. And *I* sent no assassins, Ascendant Vesilov. As to my identity, look at my face. I could never deny these injuries or forget where and how I came by them. *Here,* Ascendants. Here by this very cathedral."

Vesilov ignored that. He reclined against his cushions. "Then you plead guilty. All that remains is to determine what we shall do with you."

"If you believe that, then none of you have learned any wisdom at all. What a poor God you worship, if He is so powerless to compel you to see."

"Our God has all the power of the Universe, Pretender," Vesilov declared.

The VeilBeast laughed at that, moving in Colin's throat. He spoke the words it fed him. "Then if He is omnipotent, he is also cruel and not benevolent. No God can be both. If omnipotent, He could have created a perfect universe in which pain and evil and strife did not exist; if benevolent, he would not then have made this one. I *know* the pain of existence—you have all shown it to me more than once." Colin's gaze flickered over to Culper, and the curator stared blandly back. "Even MolitorAb isn't so vain as to claim omnipotence. If there was such a final power, there would be no need of poor prophets such as Simon ben Zakkai or me."

"We've heard enough, Fairwood," Culper said. "You defile Prophet Simon when you compare yourself to him."

"No, let me speak," Colin insisted. "I know that there are many paths to God. That is what the MulSendero preach and that is what MolitorAb says to all of you. I tell you: *The path you've chosen is treacherous.* " The VeilBeast touched his words with fire. The potency in his voice left the Ascendants momentarily stunned, and the VeilBeast chuckled. Silence bound them for several seconds until Culper stirred and pointed down at the prisoners.

"We are not here to discuss theology. Our only concern is to mete out your punishment."

"Then kill me," Colin answered. "Kill me—or are you afraid perhaps you can't? Give me the gun; I'll shoot myself. I'll drink your poisons, stab myself in the heart." The VeilBeast roared and Colin shouted with it. "You're *fools!* Haven't you seen what the

Sartius Exori has done? *With the power MolitorAb has given me, I could force any of you to turn his own hand against himself!"*

The gift of the VeilBeast coursed through Colin, burning. The energy in him was as full as it had been on Dridust, on Medee, on Kellia. FirstBred Pale gasped behind Colin, and the Exori felt the sudden hope of Samuel and Joshua. "You, Ascendant Vesilov," Colin cried. "You were so afraid of me that you left Nexus and abandoned the chance of an understanding between us. I tell you that if I had wanted you I would not have had to send others." Colin held out his chained hands in front of him, palms upward as he regarded Vesilov's round, flushed face. "I could have taken you at will."

Colin's visage was strained with effort as the VeilBeast poured itself through him. Taut muscles bunched under the skinbase. He began to close his hands slowly, curling his fingers up and in. "I could have closed off your throat like this, Vesilov," he declared. His voice was mesmerizing, as if he spoke into each Ascendant's ear. Almost a whisper, it reverberated with a sinister warning. The power held Colin in thrall now; everyone in the hall could sense the Presence. Their eyes moved from the Sartius Exori to Vesilov— the Ascendant had raised his hands to his collar, gasping. His face had turned a bright, impossible scarlet, and his eyes were bulging and wide with fright. Vesilov seemed to be trying to speak, but they heard only a desperate grunt.

"Can you feel the terror, Ascendant? Can you feel the slow ending of your life as your body starves for air? That is all I needed to do, Vesilov. I don't need servants for that."

Colin opened his hands again. Vesilov took a great, gulping, loud breath.

"No!" Culper shouted as the Ascendants, their momentary paralysis broken, began to roar their own protests. Culper gestured to one of the guards and the rods around Colin and his disciples flared with brilliance, tossing arcs of blue lightning through the center of the circle. The others cried out and fell; only Colin stood, the electricity snapping about him, the VeilBeast screaming wordlessly with Colin's voice and retreating before the pain.

Colin went to his knees on the tiles.

He toppled.

Culper stared down at the sprawling figures of the Sartius Exori and the Sabbai. Taking a deep breath, he shouted into the tumult. "His own words have convicted him. We can't afford to return this man to the MulSendero. Do we all agree on this?"

They answered him with an acclamation. Culper nodded, seeing in that affirmation the genesis of his own full power.

"Take them to their cells," he said to the guards. "We will consider their fates and deal with them as we must." He bowed his head to the symbols of his church, the holograms twisting on the wall. Culper felt exultation.

"May God guide us," he said.

Colin shuffled along, trying to keep his feet under him as the guards dragged him away. Their fingers dug into his arms; his head lolled. As he struggled to bring himself back to consciousness, the VeilBeast prowled within him. *You see, Colin, there is no other way,* it cried. *The Black Beginning comes. At least this way there is hope. MolitorAb promises that peace will come.*

Despair weakened Colin's will; the VeilBeast threatened to burst out entirely. Colin's own doubts echoed the Presence's arguments. *It is time. You knew that eventually there would be no choice. It is time.*

But I hate it. I don't want it to be this way.

It is the way of all Her prophets from the beginning. Why should you be able to escape it? Choose then—but know that if you choose to be Fairwood now, you'll still die here, and the others will die with you.

Why did you have to wait so long to give me the choice? I can't choose now. It's not fair.

The VeilBeast only laughed. Colin shook his head groggily.

He felt his stomach lurch and knew they were descending. He lifted his head. Pale and the others were with him, crowded into the compartment with nine guards. *Give yourself to me,* the VeilBeast pleaded. *Give your will to me. You have tried the other way and it didn't work. The Ascendants won't listen. No God willingly falls to the next.*

Your hands are bloody enough, Colin Fairwood.

Colin sighed. "All right," he whispered aloud. The VeilBeast surged up, melding with Colin. A new energy pulsed in his body. Colin straightened, swinging about in the confined space of the elevator, his motion slamming the guards against one another.

"Hey!" Struggling to recover their balance, some reached for Colin, others for their weapons.

The VeilBeast roared at them. "BE STILL!" it commanded. "DO NOT MOVE!" They obeyed. *You see, their faith is weak already.* Colin brought his cuffed hands before his eyes; the electronic locks snapped open with a dry double click. He let them drop clattering to the floor and punched at buttons. The room dipped, swayed, and began to rise. As it did so, Colin touched the slumping bodies of his disciples. The guards still held them; the Zakkaists watched unprotesting as the prisoners stirred under Colin's hands. He took the bonds from their limbs, laughing at the inner struggle he could see in the guards' eyes. "Everyone should be obedient to the messenger of MolitorAb," he told them.

FirstBred Pale was the first to come fully awake. Her eyes went wide to see him. "Where is Colin Fairwood?" she asked. "You do not smell of him at all."

"I'm still here, Pale. Why do you doubt me?"

"This one does not sense him," she answered. Samuel and Joshua were up now, staring wonderingly. "Samuel, the VeilBeast..." Pale began, turning to the others.

"I see him, Pale." Samuel nodded to Colin. "Exori, what do we do now?"

Joshua snorted at that. The old man took a stun prod from the lax hand of one of the Zakkaists and then removed the man's pistol, belting it around his own waist. "That's simple enough," he said. "We get the hell out of here." He grinned triumphantly. "Exori, when we get back to Nexus with this tale, you'll be able to do whatever you want to. We'll unite the Fringes entirely under you—come back here with the fleet we should have had in the first place—"

Under the Beast's silent, haughty contemplation, Joshua's voice slowly trailed off. "You enjoy this too much, Joshua," Colin said.

They felt a soft rise and fall; the elevator slid to a halt. The doors parted and they were looking out into a corridor on the level of the Conclave hall. The faint sound of voices could be heard to their right. "Go on," Colin demanded, gesturing left.

"The guards—" Joshua protested, but Colin waved at him to be silent.

"They're harmless. They have no faith," he said. The elevator doors closed. They heard the whine of the motor.

Turning away from the sound of the Ascendants' debate, they moved quickly down the corridor to an intersection, where Colin led them left again. "Where are we going?" Samuel asked.

"Follow me," the Beast snarled in answer. "Either that or go back to the Ascendants."

They followed. The group moved through a maze of branching corridors, past offices and empty rooms. The Exori seemed to know his way, never pausing at the choice of turns. Impossibly, they were never confronted, though some of the offices they passed were occupied, though they often heard voices and footsteps receding from them. Eventually, Colin came to a halt. They could smell a breeze from outside, a fragrant wind laced with a metallic tang. Here the corridor led into a high, expansive room. Several two-person shuttle cars were ranked along the opposite wall. People moved among the shuttles, talking, hurrying on errands, or simply lounging. Steel doors in the center of the wall had been slid back in their tracks, leaving the room open to the air. Beyond, in the evening sky, they could see the huddled towers of ships resting in the pulse slings. Colin whispered to the Sabbai as they stared: "The Ascendants' craft. Most of them are just atmospheric ships. One or two should be fitted with Stekoni drives, though—you'll see the pods on them. Take one of those."

"Sartius Exori, are you not going with us?" Pale pressed against the wall. Beige paint darkened where she touched.

"No, FirstBred Pale. The Ascendants are all gathered. MolitorAb has chosen this time."

"Exori—" Joshua began; then a shrill wail echoed through the room in front of them. They could see startled people lurching to their feet, scrambling to posts. The sirens keened; the doors to the field began to slide closed.

"Move!" Colin grunted. "Ignore all the rest. MolitorAb protects you."

At a lope, they entered the space. No one seemed to notice them immediately in the confusion, but they were far too conspicuous, with FirstBred Pale and Colin's face, to be ignored for long. Some-one standing near a desk shouted: "The Sartius Exori!" Colin broke into a full run. A man wearing a mechanic's uniform stepped in front of him; Colin cuffed him aside. He paused at the doors, waving the others through the narrowing opening. A pencil of light blistered the wall paint above his head and he ducked, sliding through the gap himself and rolling onto the tarmac. "Find a ship!" he shouted. "Go on!"

"You must come with us." Samuel had planted his feet stub-bornly. FirstBred Pale glanced at the array of Zakkaist crafts and stared imploringly back at Colin, but she stayed beside Samuel. Joshua waved from a ramp. "Here! Quickly!" he called.

The doors of the building groaned to a halt, shuddering, then began to open once more. A guard shouldered his way out. Colin raised a hand and he fell back, stunned.

The Beast howled. "Go!" he screamed. "I will take my own ship."

Samuel shook his head and sprinted toward Joshua, who had gone through the hatchway of the farship. "This one will stay with the Sartius Exori," Pale declared. "She will go in his ship."

The Beast would have struck at Pale for her insolence, but Colin forced his hand down. He tried to smile. "You can't do that, Pale. Not this time. Please, for my sake, go on. I need someone to tell the truth about me. I need someone to help Crowell and my daughter. I need you to build MolitorAb's church. Please."

Pale blinked, confused. Her own panic and the sudden harshness in Colin's gaze as the VeilBeast returned decided her. She ran across the field with her quick, loping gait. Samuel pulled her into the ship. The hatch closed and a slow, rising whine came from the ship as it fed power to the pulsers.

A bolt of searing agony lanced Colin's shoulder. The VeilBeast screamed. His left arm hung useless, pouring blood, as his shirt smoldered around the wound. Colin swung about, gesturing, and the one who'd fired at him collapsed to the ground. Others were spreading out from the doorway now. Spotlights flared around the field. Colin hurried toward the nearest farship, the VeilBeast glaring defiantly over his shoulder at his pursuers. They aimed weapons at him; as on Horeb, nothing touched him. Panting, he went up a ramp, slammed his fist against the lock mechanism.

He heard the thunder of another farship being flung into the night sky.

Reaching the control room, he slipped the nervelink cable around him, grimacing as it rested on his injured shoulder. He touched the sticky contacts to his spine. The ship came to life around him. Colin ignored the safety checks and overrode the automatic systems survey. He willed the craft to rise. The force of acceleration, like a gigantic hand, slammed him back into his seat. He gritted his teeth against the pain as the force pressed against him for long seconds, and then he let the ship tumble backward over on its spine. He activated the system drive as the craft canted over and pointed its nose to the ground. Again he was thrown back, fighting the pressure. He put the view from the nose cameras on the screens before him; through the orange glare of heat on the shields he could see the city spread out below him, revealing the scar that was the ruins of the Obdurate shrine. There, to one side and bright against the greenery that masked those relics of Colin's past, was the cathedral. Colin shunted the farship to one side until that edifice was centered on the screens. He kept the drives full open.

He watched, the VeilBeast chortling all the while, until the image swelled before him and exploded.

CHAPTER THIRTY

This one wept to hear the Sartius Exori's words, for she knew he had seen the time when he must return to the Veils. She could see the pain within him, the torment that had wracked his soul since he had been chosen. He lifted his gaze to the stars and prayed: "This one wishes that She would show him another way."

But She was silent, and the VeilBeast rose in him again so that he was dangerous to be near. His was the molten smell of fury. "It is the time of the Black Beginning," the Sartius Exori cried. "Go away from me before it takes you, FirstBred Pale." His voice was heavy with the burden of his guilt and sorrow and he also said to her: "This one prays that you forgive him when the chaos finds you, and that yours is the voice the MulSendero hear. Remember, FirstBred Pale, that this one destroys because he must, but destruction is not this one's legacy. The Black Beginning will pass—hold tightly to what is this one's until that time."

He said no more as this one left him. The Sartius Exori turned to his bitter task, and the Church of Simon ben Zakkai was riven by his blow.

When the ship that carried the Sabbai fled into the Veils, all heard the wail of the VeilBeast as It died. Then the Voice of MolitorAb welcomed the Sartius Exori and bade him to join Her.

THE TESTAMENT OF FIRSTBRED PALE,
183:23–27

With his final act, the Sartius Exori opened a way for the poor of the Fringes to share in the wealth of the corrupt Zakkaist church. On that day, despite the Black Beginning that they knew would descend, the faith of MulSendero was swelled by those who had seen the truth of MolitorAb.

The churches that day were full, and many gave their riches into the hands of the priests.

The Sabbai were glad, for in that sign they foresaw the greatness of the churches they would one day build.

THE TESTAMENT OF MIRIAM, 56:45–46

288

* * *

The Sartius Exori came down upon the cathedral as a vision of the righteous hand of MolitorAb. He shouted to them as the ship fell, saying in words that thundered with the power of God: "This is the justice you have earned, the justice you would have given me! See how MolitorAb deals with Her enemies—She returns their own venom to them a thousandfold! Only by fire can the land be cleansed of the foul creatures that infest it!"

The Sartius Exori destroyed them all and cast the Church of Falseness into great confusion. The vast multitude of heretics were everywhere flung to their knees to pray and beg forgiveness, and the worlds began to turn to MolitorAb.

Thus was the Sartius Exori willing to give his church into the hands of the Sabbai who had served him best, knowing that they would follow the trail he had blazed for them.

THE TESTAMENT OF JOSHUA, 101:34–38

Some of his people mourned his passing. Others said that the Sartius Exori had never died at all, that in the instant before his farship struck the spires of the cathedral and brought death to the Ascendants, a light of a brilliance so intense that those who witnessed it were instantly blinded flashed about his ship. This was the hand of MolitorAb, they said, come to take Colin Fairwood to the peace of the Veils.

Still others claimed that by dying, the Sartius Exori proved he was only a man like any other.

The worlds were left in chaos, leaderless. The Black Beginning that was foretold came to pass.

Who can say what the Sartius Exori might have been? Ask Colin Fairwood himself when you pass through the Veils. Call his name into the colors of the void and listen to the words that enter your dreams. Certainly any answer I might give you would be no more correct than anyone else's, yet I am certain that the man I followed was what MolitorAb molded him to be. If I failed to understand the reasons, the fault is not his but mine.

Sartius Exori, listen to your disciples calling to you in the winds of the Veils.

Come to them. Say to the skeptic: "I am what you saw that I was. I am what you need me to be. You are the creator."

THE TESTAMENT OF SAMUEL, 87:122–129

BIO OF A SPACE TYRANT
Piers Anthony

"Brilliant...a thoroughly original thinker and storyteller with a unique ability to posit really *alien* alien life, humanize it, and make it come out alive on the page." *The Los Angeles Times*

A COLOSSAL NEW FIVE VOLUME SPACE THRILLER—
BIO OF A SPACE TYRANT
The Epic Adventures and Galactic Conquests of Hope Hubris

VOLUME I: REFUGEE   84194-0/$3.50 US/$4.50 Can
Hubris and his family embark upon an ill-fated voyage through space, searching for sanctuary, after pirates blast them from their home on Callisto.

VOLUME II: MERCENARY   87221-8/$3.50 US/$4.50 Can
Hubris joins the Navy of Jupiter and commands a squadron loyal to the death and sworn to war against the pirate warlords of the Jupiter Ecliptic.

VOLUME III: POLITICIAN   89685-0/$3.50 US/$4.50 Can
Fueled by his own fury, Hubris rose to triumph obliterating his enemies and blazing a path of glory across the face of Jupiter. Military legend...people's champion...promising political candidate...he now awoke to find himself the prisoner of a nightmare that knew no past.

THE BEST-SELLING EPIC CONTINUES—
VOLUME IV: EXECUTIVE
89834-9/$3.50 US/$4.50 Can
Destined to become the most hated and feared man of an era, Hope would assume an alternate identify to fulfill his dreams ...and plunge headlong into madness.

AND COMING SOON FROM AVON BOOKS
VOLUME V: STATESMAN
the climactic conclusion of Hubris' epic adventures:

AVON Paperbacks